INSATIABLE/ UNFORGETTABLE

A New Collection
of Erotic Tales
Edited By
JOHN PATRICK

STARbooks Press, Herndon, VA

Books by John Patrick

Non-Fiction
A Charmed Life: Vince Cobretti
Lowe Down: Tim Lowe
The Best of the Superstars 1990
The Best of the Superstars 1991
The Best of the Superstars 1992
The Best of the Superstars 1993
The Best of the Superstars 1994
The Best of the Superstars 1995
The Best of the Superstars 1996
The Best of the Superstars 1997
What Went Wrong?
When Boys Are Bad
& Sex Goes Wrong
Legends: The World's Sexiest
Men, Vols. 1 & 2
Legends (Third Edition)
Tarnished Angels (Ed.)

Fiction
Billy & David: A Deadly Minuet
The Bigger They Are...
The Younger They Are...
The Harder They Are...
Angel: The Complete Trilogy
Angel II: Stacy's Story
Angel: The Complete Quintet
A Natural Beauty (Editor)
The Kid (with Joe Leslie)
HUGE (Editor)
Strip: He Danced Alone
The Boys of Spring
Big Boys/Little Lies (Editor)
Boy Toy
Seduced (Editor)
Insatiable/Unforgettable (Editor)
Heartthrobs
Runaways/Kid Stuff (Editor)
Dangerous Boys/Rent Boys (Editor)
Barely Legal (Editor)
Country Boys/City Boys (Editor)
My Three Boys (Editor)
Mad About the Boys (Editor)
Lover Boys (Editor)
In the BOY ZONE (Editor)
Boys of the Night (Editor)
Secret Passions (Editor)
Beautiful Boys (Editor)
Juniors (Editor)

Contents

Editor's Note

Most of the stories appearing in this book take place prior to the years of The Plague; the editor and each of the authors represented herein advocate the practice of safe sex at all times.

And, because these stories trespass the boundaries of fiction and non-fiction, to respect the privacy of those involved, we've changed all of the names and other identifying details.

INTRODUCTION: GETTING IN TOUCH
John Patrick

In a very real sense, the stories in this combined collection are long thank-you notes to those who helped me, and our other authors, make it through another night.

As you will read, all of us have a lot in common. A love of luxury when it's right for the occasion, for one. And I won't go so far as to say we are all insatiable, that's why we have divided this anthology into two sections, but we all do share a joy in having sex. And although we're willing to wallow in the comfort of downy furniture and enveloping service – actually, that is probably my major talent – none of us hesitates to strike out on our own when a new opportunity, no matter how elusive, knocks. We relish the feeling of being off-balance, even a bit afraid, when plunging headlong into the unknown. Especially when an adorable urchin or a handsome stud is involved.

The enjoyment we get from all this plunging in sometimes very exotic locales is beautifully evoked by Gustave Flaubert in Flaubert in Egypt, translated by Francis Steegmuller:

"This is a great place for contrasts. Splendid things gleam in the dust. I performed on a mat that a family of cats had to be shooed off – a strange coitus, looking at each other without being able to exchange a word, and the exchange of looks is all the deeper for the curiosity and the surprise. My brain was too stimulated for me to enjoy it much otherwise."

And speaking of being stimulated, these sharp, insightful, understatedly eloquent stories are so powerfully imagined (or remembered) that they capture our interest fully, becoming provocative portraits of a wide range of individuals, including muscleboys; street-smart characters; the insatiable Two Kevins, foremost connoisseurs of teenaged dick in Fort Lauderdale in Peter Reardon's remembrance; past lovers such as Jack Nichols' Kevin and Carlos and my own Donny; and boys just coming-of-age such as Ricky, an unforgettable boy from the past of Ken Anderson. Proving the potent power of these sexy lads, Ken recalls: "I don't know if you're familiar with Zamfir, but he plays Panpipes, and the CD was here, and I'm sitting on the upstairs porch, listening to it. One of the numbers is from the soundtrack 'Picnic at Hanging Rock.'

"I'm also trying to figure out why I'm obsessing so. Ricky was hot sex, yes. He was obviously uninhibited, and his sex drive freed up mine. But the hook I swallowed caught deeper than that, I now realize. I have a reputation for being top man, in general as well as in bed, a man in control of his life, but there was something so vulnerable and trusting and intimate about Ricky I can't get him out of my mind. I just sit here, listening to Zamfir, recalling how Ricky cradled my boot, how he looked wearing my cap, that soft, impulsive kiss, the hunger in his starlit eyes.

The part that really baffles me is that I felt so at home with him. Here I am with all these intellectual pretensions, and there he is – forgive me – so sweet and pure. If I called him, what would happen? And if something did, what would my friends say? I can hear the jokes. But maybe we could just live here. I'd write great books, and he'd – well, he could do whatever he wanted. I can imagine him walking through the woods, listening to the birds, just being. And just being happy. I think I could make him happy, and I know somehow that making him happy would make me happy, too.

"Getting involved like this is not very smart, I know. I can't write. I can't sleep. I can't even read. And I'm not quite sure what to do. My gut response is to get in touch. Wouldn't you?"

...The first time I slept with a man, he touched me down there and asked if he could do it. Of course I knew what he meant, despite his reluctance to name the act. The word itself makes it sound like a violation. Which of course it is.

At first I didn't answer. He asked again and I said no. He wanted to know why and I said it would hurt, which of course was true. That satisfied him for a while, and he busied himself with other things, caressing my skin as if molding clay. Gently he asked if I'd ever done it before. I hesitated before saying no, which made it sound like a lie...

Eventually I let him. I don't know why – partly because he seemed to want to so much, partly because on some level I wanted to know what it was like.

I knew right away that I'd made a mistake.

- from "Coming Up For Air," by Martin Stephens

THE ROOM FOR LOVERS
John Patrick

In one way or another, it seems I have written about every boy I've ever encountered – my dark angels, hustlers, lost boys, porn studs – and, of course, some I've only fucked in my dreams. But I've never written about Donny. I've started to write about him many times but always gave up in frustration – there was just so much baggage with a six-year relationship, it kept getting in the way of what I considered the heart of the story: the fuck that precipitated our final break-up. But now I feel enough time has passed that I can approach it objectively, because the tale belongs here, with other tales of guys who just couldn't get enough.

I met Donny in a bar in Pittsburgh on a Tuesday night in June 1972. I was in town on business with a client, Leland, also married and gay-on-the-sly. Somehow, Leland and I had managed to link up, client and gofer, and he'd even blown me once in a tiny booth in an adult movie house back home in Cleveland where we had gone after lunch. A couple of weeks later, in a hotel room in New York, he wanted me to fuck him and I just couldn't get it up. Attempting to keep him happy, and keep the advertising account, I told him my lack of rigidity was due to the fact that when I looked at him all I saw was Kathy and the kids. But, truth be known, he didn't appeal to me in that way. He was a friend and I owed him much – he had shown me the gay world – but fucking him just wasn't in the cards.

Leland said he understood. In fact, he became rather like my pimp. That night in Pittsburgh, for instance, Leland was the first to notice Donny. "He's looking this way," he said.

"Who?"

Your type, that kid over there."

I had early on specified what I was looking for: cute, young and blond. Now, amazingly enough, everywhere we went Leland would find one for me. At the time, I didn't fully appreciate it. Nowadays, I wish I had Leland around.

I moved to the stool next to the cute, young blond. We exchanged introductions. I was in lust. So was he. Opposites attracted. Leland bought us drinks, and then agreed to take us back to the hotel.

Donny, sandwiched between us in the front seat, told us about his life, all the while kneading my crotch. He was starting art school in the fall, which involved moving to a city sixty miles away. At last, he would be away from his mother and father. For my part, about all I said was that Leland and I were traveling together on business and that we were both married. Unlike some of the boys I tried to pick up, my marital status didn't bother him. In fact, it turned him on.

In the elevator, we kissed and tongued each other all the way up to the eleventh floor. By the time we got to my room, our shirts were completely unbuttoned and, as I was closing the door behind me, he was unzipping my pants, pulling out my erection and going down on me.

"Oh, god, what a monster," he gushed, stroking my cock, now dripping with his saliva.

I thought I'd entered heaven, not a hotel room.

Having my cock entering Don's mouth was an easy task. Getting him to let go was the difficult part. All he seemed to want to do was suck on it which, considering his exceptional ability was fine with me. When he paused briefly, I was able to make it to the bed and, with my back against the wall; he soon was lying between my legs, slathering my prick. He attended to my prick as it had never been tended to before. I was enraptured. When I came, it seemed as if nearly thirty years of repression gushed out of me. He was ecstatic and eager to keep at it, to see that explosion again.

But, no. In those days, I was into getting what I could never get at home: a good ass-fucking. He allowed me to undress him and suck a bit on his well-formed, seven-inch cock and then he tended to the fucking of my ass as best he could, although I could tell his heart wasn't in it. Still, when he came, it was glorious; being the era it was, I could savor the incredible feeling of having my insides filled to overflowing by the love juice of a horny teenager.

After he came, we lay happily together, talking, well into the night.

The following morning, I was in the shower when Donny appeared, joining me, and dropping to his knees before me. He was, I decided at that moment, too good to let go.

On the way home to Cleveland, I told Leland that I had to see Donny again. He told me I was crazy. "Married men eat and run," he said.

I wanted to run all right...run after Donny, not away from him. I could think of nothing else. Each night I would take my little son out for walks and stop at the phone booth on the highway near our house and make a call. If Don wasn't there, I'd just leave a message so he knew of my constancy.

Finally it was agreed, I had to come back to Pittsburgh. I concocted another business meeting and left on Monday morning, driving alone this time, and Donny met me at the hotel about noon. He didn't want to have lunch, he wanted to have me. He was insatiable. I was insatiable. It was a match made in heaven. Monday became Tuesday and Tuesday became Wednesday. But I had no more excuses. I couldn't conduct business by phone any longer, I had to go back to work, back to my family.

When home, I returned to the nightly phone ritual. I couldn't stay on the phone long enough. I called him from work. I was going mad with longing. For Donny.

On Friday night, I confronted my wife. I told her I had to go away for the weekend that everything was fine, I just had some thinking to do. This led to a terrible row but I left anyway. In the car, I had plenty of time to think. What was I doing with an 18-year-old anyway? Here I was thirty, married with two children, and had an executive position in advertising. Such an entanglement would ruin me financially, perhaps professionally. I began to regret every mile I traveled. But once I reached Pittsburgh, pulled into the hotel parking lot and saw Donny, his muscles bulging out of his shirt and pants, standing by the front door smiling at me, all my cares left me.

Before I had a chance to say anything, he told me he had made up his mind, he was moving to Cleveland. He could go to art school anywhere. But I was only in Cleveland. And he was willing to accept any time I had to give him.

At first, that was acceptable. But after only a week, when I was not with him, I could only think about him. My wife knew something was terribly wrong. I confessed.

My revelation to my wife that I was moving out to live with another man sent her to the hospital. Her psychiatrist told her that I could not "change" unless I wanted to. My wife was put under heavy sedation, the children were bundled off to my wife's parents, who were properly horrified, and they had my parents call me. "Whatever makes you happy," my father said. I promised to come down for Christmas – with Don.

I sold all my stocks and bought a second-hand Volkswagen; we moved into a tiny apartment convenient to the bus line. Don registered at the University and the next few months were blissful. We fucked and sucked morning and night and all weekend long. We were inseparable.

After a month, my wife came out of the hospital but could not look at me, so I had to make do by talking to the children by phone. My son, five, wanted to know when I would be returning from New York." I had been away so often, that's where he assumed I was. My daughter, nine, lost in her own world of school and pretty clothes, was oblivious to it all. Eventually, I was to begin having them with me every other weekend, if I agreed that Don would not be there. The children met Don and we concocted a plan: Don could be with us provided Mommy didn't know.

Mommy also didn't know there was trouble in paradise. I, apparently, was more insatiable than my young lover. It reached a point where sex would cause arguments. While Don's desire for me had cooled to what he called a "normal" level, I remained insatiable. Don determined the only way I was to be "controlled" was to be placed on a schedule: Three times per week. He said he would prefer it if I could alternate, a suck and a fuck, because his ass was beginning to hurt.

Then I discovered benefits to this ploy. If I had used up all my "chits" for the week, and Don would be horny, that sex would be "on the house." And then I got a promotion at the agency and was back traveling again. This meant that my sex with Don was suddenly rammed, in more ways than one, into a few delirious days, and the other nights I was on my own, able to revert back to my tomcat days in the gay fleshpots of the modern world. I quickly found that less urgency in scoring meant, paradoxically, more scoring. Because I was getting abundant gay sex at home, I really didn't need any more when I went out of town, but not needing it meant I constantly had it, literally, thrust in my face.

Meanwhile, I expected Don to be waiting at home by the phone. The craziness of this notion quickly evidenced itself. I arrived home one day from New York to be told that he was going to spend the summer as a go-go boy. He took me to the club and I watched him stripping before a bevy of women. I even photographed him at a special "show" at the burlesque house. Watching the women go crazy as he stripped off his clothes and wiggled that incomparable ass at them made me desire him again beyond all reason. And, since I was the one driving him home, he had no choice but to succumb to my advances once we were safely at home. Dancing made him horny as well so, again, no one was counting.

As the summer continued, I traveled and Don danced. By August, things were, I found, getting very warm in Cleveland. I returned after four glorious days in New York to the news that Don had been "seeing" another dancer, a guy named Joe.

When I found out "seeing" Joe meant Donny was getting fucked senseless by a hot Italian on our own living room rug, I flew into a rage. "But we don't use our bedroom," Donny blubbered.

"Thanks," I sputtered, trying to keep from slugging him.

Not only was Donny the cutest, sexiest person I'd ever met, he was also one of the most honest. It was impossible for him to keep secrets, lie, steal. He was the antithesis of all the hustlers I'd known and I suppose that's what attracted me to him. But with honesty also comes, in one so young, naiveté, and Donny just couldn't figure why I would be upset over this latest turn-of-events.

"This is the first time I've been with someone else since we got together. Now you're always on the road and I get lonely."

"Poor baby," I said, pouring a stiff drink. I knew that if this ever happened, that Donny would go to bed with another man, it would somehow end up being my fault. I was prepared for this, sort of.

Donny admitted to having disclosed all manner of details about us to Joe. He even showed Joe a picture of me naked. Donny told me what Joe had said: "'He's good looking and he's got a big dick but his body isn't much.-

I kept my temper. I wanted nothing more than to throttle Joe. Finally, when Donny wouldn't let me fuck him – Joe's fuckings had been brutal – I was determined to meet this stud. I stopped at the gay bar downtown for a couple of drinks and, thus fortified, was ready for the confrontation. I called the number I had found in Donny's address book. Joe lived with his parents.

He was surprised to hear from me. His parents were out of town. Yes, I could come over.

It was a large, well-kept home in a predominantly Italian neighborhood of Cleveland.

"I'm glad to talk to you," he said, fixing me a drink at the mirrored bar in the living room.

"Oh?" I sunk into the opulent sofa. Inside, the house looked like a set for one of "The Godfather" movies.

"Donny's been having a lot of pain lately," Joe said, fixing a drink for himself.

"I know. I haven't been able to fuck him for a month. I've had to settle for three blowjobs a week."

"He does give good head, doesn't he?" Joe said, handing me my vodka on-the-rocks.

I winced. Joe was rather plain-looking, short and dressed in a torn gray sweatshirt, ragged Levi cut-offs, and sneakers without socks. Far from my idea of a hot Italian stud. Anyway, I was into pretty blonds in those days, exclusively, and to me, this kid appeared rather shabby, almost pitiful.

"Don wants to move out, get an apartment with me," Joe said, standing before me, sipping his drink.

This was news to me. I held my temper. "Do you think the pain would end if you two were living together?"

Joe stepped away, sat on the matching sofa directly across from me. "Your pain maybe. I just don't think Donny's used to rough sex."

"No. Pretty vanilla I'm afraid."

"I don't mean to hurt him, you understand."

"He tells me your cock curves sharply to the left – "

"No secrets, eh? Of course, and you've got a monster there. I've seen the pictures."

"I know. Donny told me he's told you all the family secrets."

"I think he gets off on telling me all about what you two do."

And he tells me about what you two do."

He finished his drink and got up. He stood at the entrance to the kitchen, leaning against the wall. I noticed a bulge at the crotch of his Levis that hadn't been there before. He was getting turned on by this. "So you know?"

"How rough you can be? Yes. I know. I have no acquaintance with such things and I don't think Donny had either. You'll have to give him some time."

He stroked the bulge. "We're going to Chicago this weekend."

"I know."

The head of his cock peeked out from the edge of the cutoffs. I felt like asking if I could go with them, then thought the better of it.

"Of course," he nodded.

"Yeah, he tells me everything." I stared at the head of his cock, imagining Donny's mouth on it, loving it.

Joe kept on stroking. More of his cock appeared. It was cut. A nice head on it. "But what he doesn't know won't hurt him."

I was lost in the dreamy picture of Donny sucking Joe's cock. Finally, I looked up. "Yeah?"

"I didn't tell him this story. It's kinda funny."

"Oh? What story?"

"See, I remembered you from the Bette Midler concert." "God, that's over two years ago. A lot's happened since then. Donny. My divorce. Now this."

"Yeah, this," he said, revealing it all to me, pressing it against his thigh. "Anyhow, you were with your wife and I thought you were the handsomest man I'd ever seen." He let his cock free, rattled the cubes of ice in his glass, then set the glass on the counter and walked into the living room. Most of his half-hard cock had slipped under the denim.

"I guess when I am wearing a suit you couldn't see that my body was nothing."

"I didn't mean that the way it sounded. I was trying to put you down. I am terribly jealous of your two years with Donny, of how good it has been for him."

"How good?"

"Yeah." He sat down next to me, so close I was sure he could feel my fear.

"Pretty vanilla I'm afraid." I finished my drink.

"Pretty is what it is – " He reached over and stroked my crotch. Tentatively at first, then getting no resistance, firmly.

Now it was my turn to shake the cubes in my glass. "My, you are versatile." You are too, I understand."

"Hardly ever get the chance. Donny doesn't like to fuck." "I know."

"We know everything about each other."

"Thanks to Donny."

"Yeah, thanks to Donny."

We embraced. It was a full, sensual kiss. He ground his crotch into mine. I reached down, squeezed his now stiff penis.

"Why don't we go into the bedroom?" he asked, breaking away, getting up, and offering his hand.

Nodding, I let him pull me up. I wrapped my arm around him.

The phone rang.

"You go on," he said, pointing the way. "Go to the big bedroom at the end of the hall. I always use it when my parents are away. I'll be right along."

The bedroom had a heavy air of sensuality. It was a room for lovers. I thought. Blue and gold brocade curtains. A chaise lounge of red velvet, dark golden mirrors, a pink bathroom, circular, windowless.

Being in this place for lovers, lust and rage engulfed me. I lay on the bed, now in its pristine perfection; it still seemed warm, warm from their bodies. Joe's and Donny's.

No, I thought. Donny doesn't like beds. He likes sex everywhere but in bed. I looked at the chaise. Yes there, I thought. Yes, Joe likes this bedroom because of the chaise. He fucks Donny on the chaise.

I undressed and threw my clothes on the floor. I lay on the velvet chaise and slowly, methodically, began masturbating. With an agonizing pleasure, I began picturing the two of them in the room, standing before the mirror, Joe behind Donny, shoving it in. That crooked penis making Donny cry out.

Suddenly Joe entered the bedroom, stopped, and stared at my erection, now at full mast. "God," he gushed, "it's bigger than I'd even imagined it was."

I said nothing, just cupped my balls and offered it to him.

He stepped over to the chaise, stood over me, stroking the bulge in his cut-offs again. That was Donny on the phone. He was worried that you hadn't come home for dinner. He even asked me if you were here. "What did you say?"

"I said that was the stupidest thing I'd ever heard." "Good for you."

"Good is right," he said, sliding down onto the floor before me, stroking the shaft of my cock. He sucked the balls first, then slowly took my cock into his mouth.

As he slavered over my prick with his warm tongue, I teased his nipples with my big toe.

He withdrew it for a moment. "This'll just be our little secret?" he asked.

"Of course."

"Okay," he said, sliding it back in again.

"Can you take it as well as you can dish it out?" I growled.

"Oh, yeah," Joe said, between sucks, his eyes shut.

I could have been anybody. I was just another big dick to Joe, not Donny's lover. But the fact that I was Donny's lover and Joe was, more recently, Donny's lover, made his scene even more exciting.

"Suck it, shithead," I said. "Get it ready for that tight asshole."

He went on slavering it. Spittle ran down the shaft, onto my balls, onto the blood-red velvet. I leaned back and closed my eyes as he greased me up with his saliva.

"I'm going to have you begging for mercy." My nasty man act caused my cock to ooze precum. He lapped it up greedily. His cock leapt from the cutoffs as I yanked them down his legs. It was a good seven inches and it did careen alarmingly to the left. It would take some getting used to. I ignored it. It was the cock that fucked my lover. I wanted nothing to do with it. What I wanted was Joe's ass, virgin territory as far as Donny's perky pecker was concerned. I ordered Joe to get on all fours on the chaise. Little as he was, he looked perfect there, offering his hairy butt to me. I spit into the crevice, not once but three times. I jammed a finger in. Tight. And I thought Donny was fight. Two fingers drove Joe crazy. Three sent him into orbit.

"Please, take it easy," he said as my cock pierced his asshole.

"Sure," I said, slamming it into him with all the force I could muster after three vodkas.

I grabbed his curly hair and began riding him, slowly at first, then with increasing momentum until my pubic hair was brushing his asscheeks.

"Oh, god," he moaned as I withdrew a few inches of it, then slammed it back into him. "I've wanted this for so long," he moaned.

"So have I, shithead," I said.

I kept fucking him as hard as I could. He writhed with pleasure, his hands gripping the sides of the chaise. I thought of Donny, home alone, wondering what had happened to me, I thought of Donny, here on this chaise, in Joe's position, and I reached under him and took his erection in my hand. I suddenly wanted it. I couldn't explain it, it was just something that overcame me. I pulled out.

"Okay, now it's my turn."

"What?" Joe said, looking over his shoulder.

I slapped his ass, hard. "You heard me, shithead. I want to feel that crazy prick."

Joe had been ready to come, hadn't anticipated this turn-of events. Breathing heavily, he stood up and let me lie on the chaise. Big as I was, I was in danger of sliding off, but I wanted to risk it. I wanted to see Joe as Donny saw him, watch Joe fucking me as Donny watched him. See Joe coming as Donny did. I laid back, spread my legs wide, offering myself to him. He was dazed, confused, disappointed. This wasn't what he had in mind at all.

"Okay," he said. He left the room for a moment. When he returned, he had greased his cock. In his hand he held the lotion. He poured some on his fingers, prepared me. The more I looked at that cock, the alarmingly curvy cock, the less I wanted to do this but I was determined.

He took my ankles in his hands and slowly guided the absurdly bent cock into position. As he sunk it into me, I closed my eyes. I moaned. Then I groaned. 'Ye gods,' I thought, no wonder Donny's sore.' My ass went one way, his cock another. He only had a couple inches of it in me when he began pumping gently. He didn't want to hurt me.

This isn't so bad,' I thought, after watching it straighten out as it entered me fully.

As he again was close and began plunging it in me, beads of sweat appeared on his forehead. He was good. Damn good. The pain was there, of course, but it was not overwhelming. I was suddenly jealous of Donny, having this hot little Italian fucking him. Joe began trembling, quivering all over. He was coming. He couldn't stop himself. I couldn't either. I stroked myself heatedly, threw my head back and spurts of my jism stained the blood-colored cushion. I too had left my mark in the room for lovers.

MY NIGHT CALLER
John Patrick

*"Of my 66 years, 61 of them have found me a member of the
brotherhood; I came out, at least to myself, at the age of five.
In the '30s and '40s, I was lucky enough to have fun with cousins
my age. In the '50s, I had my first romance with a faculty
colleague. In the '60s, I came out to the area and tried the baths.
In the '70s I was lucky enough to be visited by my night caller,
a former student. In the '80s, I had my second romance.
This decade is still forming!"*
– Ralph in Tacoma

Joey came in the night. And came and came and came. He could never get
enough. After awhile, neither could I. I hadn't believed it was possible that two months
after I saw Joey graduate from high school with honors he was earning credits toward a
masters degree on my front porch.

I had closely followed Joey's progress (and the incredible undulating of his
hips) over the two years he was at the Unionville school where I taught mathematics.
Joey had a keen mind and math was his favorite subject; he became my favorite pupil.
But as much as I admired him and the awesome sight of his hunky young body poured
into jeans too small for him, he was off limits to me, being underage and, even worse,
and my student. However, the images of him, naked before me, warmed many a cold
night.

Which brings me to the warm night in July when, unable to sleep, I had gone
out onto the front porch and was sitting quietly in the dark with my feet up trying to
identify the sounds I was hearing from the yard. Suddenly, there was a sound I knew
quite well: "Pssst – Teach." Joey was forever sharing confidences with me, whispering
the latest gossip about his girlfriends. He had so many relationships I had trouble
keeping up. But, Joey, apparently, never had any trouble keeping it up. "I'm always
up," he'd kid me, his eyes falling to his crotch.

"All boys your age are up."

"Not as up as me," he would chuckle and then be off to meet one of the lucky
young ladies who, I was sure, were feeling first-hand how up he really was.

Now I was saying, "What's up?"

This got Joey chuckling. As he ambled up onto the porch he said, "Not much
these days, Teach."

"Oh?"

He dropped down in the chair across from me and spread his legs invitingly
in front of him. I couldn't help it – I just kept staring at the humongous bulge at his
crotch. "Looks like you're up right now."

His eyes fell to his crotch and then back up at me. 'That's the problem. I'm
up all the time but I can't get anything."

"You? You can't get anything?" Dirty blond hair, baby blue eyes, and the
face of an angel. He couldn't get anything?

"That was all a lie, Teach. I let everybody think that. People will believe
anything if you tell them enough times, you know?"

"A lie? You aren't always up?"

"No," he chuckled, "I'm always up all right. The part about putting it in 'em. I've never put it in any of 'em. None!" "I'm relieved to hear that."

"What?" he asked, leaning toward me.

"Oh, the diseases you could get from those pussies – you could die from 'em."

"But what a way to go, eh? Fuckin' die of fuckin'!"

"Why are you telling me this now? Did you decide you needed to confess to someone?"

"Yeah, I guess. I'd go see a priest but I'm not Catholic."

"Well, you've come to the right place. You can confess anything you want to me, you know that. In fact, I might be able to help you out of your predicament."

The word "predicament" (and the way I said it, emphasizing just the right syllables) got Joey laughing again. "Yeah, dic all right." "See, you can laugh about it. If we laugh at our troubles, they tend to disappear."

"Sometimes I wish this would disappear," he said, slamming his fist down on his crotch.

"You're just highly sexed, with no way to vent it. You aren't really attracted to those girls and all the boys you know who are gay are dreadful sissies."

"How did you know?"

"I'm not 'Teach' for nothing."

It was decided. We would do something about Joey's predicament. I asked him to stand up and unzip his pants. "Out here?"

"It's after midnight. Everybody's asleep and besides, that's why I have all those trees in the yard."

He needed no more encouragement. Down went the zipper, out came the cock. It was hard all right, jutting up at a rakish angle and sort of waving to the left.

"The girls don't know what they're missing," I said, sitting up straight. "Now, bring it over here and let me examine it more closely."

He smiled and stepped before me, the stupendous thing in my face. I examined it as closely as I could in the dark and dabbed the pre-cum with the tip of my finger. You are up in more ways than one."

"Yeah, I've been up but what about you?"

"Me?"

"Yeah, you. I've known it from the first day of class." "Known what?"

"That you liked me a little too much."

"I don't think anyone could like you too much. I mean, there's so much to like." With that I finally took the throbbing penis in my hand and began stroking it. "So very much."

"Do you like it?"

"I love it."

"Why don't you kiss it then?"

"I'm afraid if I got started I wouldn't want to stop." "C'mon, kiss it."

I was right. I didn't want to stop with a kiss. Although I did try. I kissed it all over, trying to prolong it, make up my mind. I kissed the ballsac, almost every sweaty inch of it, before going back to the gleaming phallus again. I pulled back and it bobbed before my eyes, tantalizing me.

"What's wrong?"

"I just want to look at it. It is a very nice cock, Joey." "Don't stop kissing it. That felt so good."

When someone pays me a compliment, I feel I must pay them one. "It's easy to be good when you have something good to work with."

You really do like it?"

It was a foolish question that deserved no answer except the one I gave him: totally engulfing the cock in my mouth with one giant gulp. This shocked him and he put his hands on the top of my head, steadying me as I began to suck. I realized this was the first time he had ever touched me. His hands felt warm, firm. After making a few preliminary passes back and forth on the rigid shaft, I could feel he was in the mood to control things. He started thrusting his hips and as he held my head I let him fuck my mouth with it. The orgasm came upon him quite suddenly and at first he was going to withdraw the cock but I held his buttocks. I wanted it all.

It was a scene that was destined to be repeated almost every night that summer, before Joey went away to college. On his return visits home, he would make my porch one of his first stops...but always – and only – at night.

KEVIN, CARLOS & ME
Jack Nichols

From May 1966 to August 1966

Carlos was with Cuban friends when we met on the sidewalk. He stood out prominently because of his dark good looks. Speaking no English, he used his friends to translate so we could negotiate after stopping in our tracks and staring at each other.

His posture, projecting dignity, was nine-tenths a rather proper, conservative bearing. He seemed never off balance so that his smile, unfortunately, was restrained. We couldn't joke with one another because I knew no Spanish. We'd never know the joys of one-on-one conversation. As long as we'd hang close, Carlos's friends would surround us to keep us from moping in utter silence.

Physical rapport was on the horizon, but I had no way of knowing how limiting sex – by itself – might be. Our sexual communication began that first night after I'd enjoyed a classic Cuban meal at Carlos's apartment. His roommate, Ori, did the dishes and went out to the bars, leaving me to grin absently at my catch.

I didn't have to explain anything to him about my present circumstances, about my lover, Kevin, about my obsession with Kevin's return. Carlos had no way of understanding. I didn't tell him that I saw him that first day as one with whom I'd spend time while waiting for Kevin to re-emerge. Though I chose him for his looks, hoping if Kevin saw us, to make Kevin jealous, I had, initially, no idea that Kevin would see us. And, if he did, I failed to anticipate what effect his seeing us might have. I was, as I've said, irrational. A basket case, perhaps.

Carlos was built. Naked, he was a joy to behold. We lay first on the living room sofa and then moved to his bedroom where I climbed atop him and kissed him passionately before greasing my cock and pushing it into him to the hilt. He groaned, clutching my shoulders, while I held his black hair and fucked him without mercy.

It was the first time I'd had sex in three weeks, not long, perhaps, but enough time to make me damned horny. Carlos's ass was beautiful, his chest and arms strong, well-shaped. I was able to fuck and enjoy other parts of his body simultaneously, licking his biceps and his underarms, gently sucking his pees. Then, returning to his face, I looked him squarely in the eyes while he looked back at me, his frame rising and falling with my own.

As I fucked him, I appreciated his silence. The looks he gave me said more than any words could match. He was completely at ease with me, and there was no clumsy fumbling, no premature withdrawal, no hurried clutching. One reason for our immediate liking for each other had to do with the way our bodies fit together, but beyond that, and the question of handsome appearances, we had nothing In common.

I bent and, while still fucking, took the head of his long, thick cock in my mouth. He helped me with this feat, and little by little I was able to take more of him into my mouth.

I could tell he was enjoying my acrobatic ability, his fingers running lightly through my hair, pushing gently so that the simultaneous action took place in rhythm.

The fuck seemed to go on indefinitely. With my mind occupied by my postures, I was in no rush to come. But Carlos, finally, began giving those telltale signs he was ready. His breathing came in fast gasps. Then he moaned. It was a long, high-pitched moan and I kept going until I felt his anus tightening in spasms and hot spurts hitting the back of my throat. I rose up and let go, my body convulsing as I came inside him, gushing. I was truly out of control.

Then we lay for a few minutes, surveying each other's bodies, relieved. There was, of course, nothing to say except bueno, maybe. I knew that much.

We rose and showered, stepping into the stall together, soaping down and kissing lightly under the drizzle.

Barely a month passed. I changed jobs. After nearly three years at the technical college, I was ready for new pastures. I was hired at an upgraded salary by a training school for cashiers and PBX operators to whom, from behind a desk, I sold courses. I rented a luxury efficiency overlooking the rooftops of the capitol.

Perhaps I'm not the first man who has reacted, when put on hold by the one he loves, by calling on somebody else. I was completely preoccupied with Kevin, something Carlos had no way of knowing. Luckily, I thought, he can't ask me any embarrassing questions.

Carlos's friends were a cheerful lot. They encouraged my relationship with him. When he spoke to them in Spanish they gave him respectful attention. Occasionally he told a joke – which I didn't get – and they'd laugh uproariously. Most of the time, though, he maintained a very serious demeanor.

I helped him by giving him five hundred dollars to secure passage out of Cuba for his 14-year-old nephew. The nephew took a plane to America via Spain. Carlos was mucho grateful. He pressed, through his translators, to move in with me. I said okay, perhaps too quickly, because, just as quickly, Kevin found out. The years have obscured for me an exact memory of Kevin's reaction. I do recall tears. And his statement: "It didn't take you very long, did it?"

"How'd you expect me to act?"

"I don't know. Not like this."

"What can I do?"

"Nothing now." Kevin sounded final.

"Nothing? Will there be something sometime?"

"I don't know."

"I love you, not him."

"Does he know that?"

"No.

"Then you're being unfair to him, to me, and to yourself." "And I suppose you're being fair, leaving me hanging?" I was angry again.

"Let's not argue."

"If you'll just say the word, well live together again and really try to get along."

"No."

"Why?"

"I shouldn't have to explain," sighed Kevin. "Just go home to Carlos."

"I'd rather spend the night with you!"

"Would you like Carlos to know that?"

"Not particularly, unless you'd live with me again."

"You're getting nowhere with me," Kevin said pointedly. The more you say the worse things get."

"Because of Carlos?"

"Because of everything."

Understanding? I had none. Empathy? That was lacking in me too. If I'd had even a modicum of romantic strategy, I might have dredged up both understanding and empathy, but instead I pushed and pushed angry, feeling I'd been duped and dumped not knowing how or why. Kevin wouldn't say goodbye, but he wouldn't say come hither either.

I called Kevin at his Job at the University, begging him to meet me for lunch.

"Not today," he replied.

"Tomorrow?"

"No."

"Why not?"

"Just leave me alone."

"Do you have a date?" It was I who waxed jealous. "None of your business."

"Why don't you just dump me?"

"Is that what you want?"

"No. I didn't mean it."

"I don't think you know what you mean," said Kevin. "When will you see me? Just answer that one simple question."

"There's no simple answer," he retorted.

Sometimes I'd meet Kevin outside his office at lunch-hour. Carlos didn't know about these meetings, and Kevin hadn't asked for them. I was obsessive. I was a sneak.

DOUBLE YOUR PLEASURE
Bert McKenzie

I first spotted him on the Washunga trail, a flash of blue and red. I had no idea what he looked like head-on, but as he sprinted swiftly by me, I was certainly attracted to what I saw from behind. The man was trim but with a muscular torso. I could tell from the blue spandex tank he wore, skin-tight and accentuating the curve of his spine.

He also had long black hair hanging over his shoulders. It reminded me of a rock singer's as it bounced with each stride. But what really caught my attention was the tightly muscled ass, the firm buns moving in the lycra shorts as he ran down the jogging trail.

I had been walking slowly, cooling down before driving home, having completed my own run. And yet in an instant I was dashing off again in a vain attempt to catch up to, or at least follow, the attractive runner. But I was no match for him. I was already tired out and he was covering ground like a race horse.

The man must have been a serious athlete. I soon settled back to my own leisurely pace and tried to think about something other than sex. For some reason my body had kicked into high gear when I saw that magnificent ass and I was already sprouting a hard-on, pushing out obscenely at the front of my shorts.

Ten minutes later as I sat beneath a tree, taking a breather before heading across the grassy park to my car, I saw him again. I recognized him by his shoulder-length hair and the red lycra shorts, but the blue tank had been removed. He carried it as he slowly jogged back the way he had come. Now that I saw the front view, my dick grew hard again. His trim body was a thrill to behold, a firm chest covered in dark curly fuzz narrowing down to a line slashing his muscled abdomen. And the prominent basket at the front of his shorts was a sight for thirsty cocksuckers everywhere. He didn't look to be wearing a jock from the way his dick was outlined by the shiny red material.

As he jogged past, he looked down at me with crystal blue eyes. Then he smiled, a wide, sensuous mouth beneath a thin black mustache that gave him a mysterious Latin look, and said, "Hi." I gazed back, giving him my best, "Come, fuck me" smile, but he jogged on. I instantly felt stupid. Why couldn't I have managed to say something more? But then what did I want, a conversation? I knew I'd probably never see him again. Then he turned back to look over his shoulder, tossing his thick mane of hair. He was looking at me!

I didn't want to appear too obvious so I glanced down, and that was when I realized how visible my dick was! It had pushed down the leg of my shorts, the swollen pink head poking out and flashing a sparkling drop of pre-cum. He couldn't help but see it. Maybe that was why he slowed to a stroll and glanced back over his shoulder. Then he winked at me, tucked his tank into the waistband of his shorts, stepped to the high stone wall beside the trail and with a jump, grabbed at the top of it. In a moment he'd boosted himself up, over and out of sight.

The jogging path borders the old Fernwell estate. It was Mrs. Fernwell who'd left the money to the city to establish the trail in the first place. I climbed to my feet and walked over to the spot where he had disappeared and looked up at the wall. The Fernwell estate had been empty since old Mrs. Fernwell died but there were still plenty of "No Trespassing" signs and the area was supposedly watched by a private security company to avoid vandalism to the house and grounds.

I figured my friend might be inviting me to join him for some fun in the woods. But it wouldn't do to get caught fucking on private property by the security company. I thought I had better warn him. But when I climbed down on the inside of the wall, he was nowhere in sight. The grounds were thick with trees, a tiny forest. I quietly walked along hoping to catch sight of my mystery man.

I finally spotted him beside a tiny stream that ran through the property. It was the Washunga Creek along which the trail was built. As soon as the runner reached the creek he stopped, pulled down his shorts, and treated me to the sight of his dick. It appeared long and thick, not overly so, like a beer can, but quite a mouth full, nicely proportioned in a large way. He reached down and lifted it, then let go with a stream of piss, arching out and into the water.

You can join me if you like," he said, glancing back to where I stood. It startled me because I thought he was unaware of my presence. "I just had to take a leak. Man, does this feel good."

This is private property," I said as I walked over to him. "Yeah, I know."

"They patrol this place. You could get in trouble."

He just smiled as he shook the last few drops from his dick. Then he pulled on it, massaging it as it began to grow hard, the mushroom-shaped head peeking out of a sleeve of skin. This feels great. Even better than pissing. You sure you won't join me?" He smiled again, a lecherous grin beneath his mustache.

My dick was already throbbing, and as I stood in a state of indecision, he reached out and cupped the front of my shorts, then slipped his hand down under the elastic waist and gently stroked my shaft. "We could get caught," I said as I suppressed a shudder of delight.

"You worry too much. Suck my dick."

I dropped to my knees before him and in one quick gulped, sucked his hard cock into my mouth and down my throat. I began to bob my head in furious abandon, playing with the foreskin and running my tongue in tight loops around the swelled cockhead.

"Hey, partner, slow down. I want to enjoy this." He pulled back, sliding his dick from my mouth, then kicked off his shoes and dropped down on the grass to pull off his socks and shorts. As I knelt there, my own cock screaming for attention, he stretched out naked on the warm grass. "Now, strip those shorts off and come join me. Let's do it right."

I was extremely nervous, but his calm demeanor spoke to my mind while his lithe, naked body spoke to the lust building in my balls. I obeyed him, stripping naked and dropping down beside him. He instantly rolled on top of me, grinding his slimy dick into my belly as he covered my face with his hair. He pressed his mouth to mine, forcing his tongue between my teeth, drawing my own tongue into his mouth in a wild, passionate kiss.

We rolled about on the grass until he broke the kiss and quickly switched positions to allow me access to his moist prick while he slowly bathed my balls and gently licked down toward my asshole. I gasped in surprised pleasure as his tongue reached its target. It licked and tickled, then pushed hard, forcing its way through my pucker as he began to really eat my ass.

In an instant, he pulled free of my lips, rolled me over onto my stomach and dived in, forcing his big dick into my willing hole. It had been some time since I was last fucked, but it's just like riding a bicycle. You never forget how. And I knew I would never forget the feel of that huge, uncut dick tunneling its way into my guts.

"Oh, God, fuck me!" I begged as I pushed back, meeting his thrusts. "Drive that dick in my ass."

"Yeah, babe. You're one hot fucker. You know how to work that hole." He taunted me as he picked up the tempo. I could feel my own balls drawing tight as he continued to slam home. "Oh, babe, take it deep in your ass," he cried as he unloaded into me. With a groan of animal pleasure [began to shoot my own load, my hot cream squirting out into the grass as my mysterious lover filled my butt with his juice.

He slowly withdrew, sliding his wet, slippery cock out of my cum-filled ass, and pulling me close, our naked bodies entwining as we shared another passionate kiss. Then he stood up, picked up his clothes and walked off through the woods. I turned to watch as he disappeared through the trees still bare ass naked. 'How I'd like to fuck that ass,' I thought as I gathered up my own clothes and quickly dressed.

A week later I was back at the Washunga trail, walking slowly along, cooling down, when he jogged by me. "Hey," I called, and he turned, tossing his hair and glancing over his shoulder. This time he was only wearing the shorts, and I saw he had shaved off his mustache. He waited while I quickly jogged up beside him. "How you doing?" I asked, trying to sound friendly, my dick already beginning to push against my jock in anticipation of repeating our first encounter.

"I'm okay," he replied with a smile, but his eyes were blank, as if he had no idea who I was. I suddenly felt very foolish. Our short fuck in the woods had meant a lot to me, but it was obviously just a quickie he didn't even remember. Then he dealt the crushing blow. "Do I know you?"

I wanted to turn and run the other way, but his crystal blue eyes held me rooted to the spot. We, um, met last week," I replied.

"We did? I'm sorry, I don't remember. You are...?" He held his hand out. I slowly took it. "Bert," I answered softly.

He crushed my fingers in a firm clasp. "Glad to meet you again, Bert. I'm sorry I didn't remember you." His eyes quickly ran down and up my body. I must have been a sight, dressed in stained sweat pants, wearing a short cropped tank top, and dripping with sweat. "Real sorry," he added, smiling again.

I felt foolish, but my cock had ideas of its own, so I spoke up. "You going to climb over the wall?" I nodded toward the Fernwell estate.

He had a surprised look on his face, then said, "I guess it is a short cut."

"Want some company?" I asked.

"Well..." He seemed nervous and indecisive. "Okay, I guess so." He stepped over to the wall and gripped the top, then struggled to climb up and over it. I was surprised that he didn't seem as agile as he had been the previous week. I quickly followed him, joining him on the other side, then we began walking through the woods, my friend leading the way.

"So, Bert, where did we meet?" he asked, obviously uncomfortable at not remembering our encounter.

I couldn't believe it. "Here," I said, as we passed the Washunga creek and kept on walking up the hill.

"Here? We met here? Are you sure?"

Now I really felt stupid. He didn't remember it at all. "Yeah, I'm sure." We walked on in silence and I began to feel that I had made a mistake. Where were we going, and why was I following the man who didn't remember fucking me just the previous week? The silence grew unbearable and I felt that I had to say something, so I said the first thing that popped into my head. "By the way, I like you without your mustache."

The man stopped in his tracks and began to laugh, a deep warm sound from the pit of his stomach. "No wonder," he said as his chuckles began to subside. "I'm Lane," he said. "I'll say one thing; he sure has good taste."

"What?" I didn't understand him at all. The guy had obviously flipped.

"Come on. I'll show you." He grabbed me by the hand and pulled, stepping up the pace as he climbed the hill. I followed along feeling more and more disoriented. As we crested the hill, I saw we were approaching the back side of the Fernwell house. It was a huge, stone structure surrounded by the wooded grounds.

"Hey, this place is supposed to be patrolled by a security company," I said as I slowed down.

"It used to be until they sold it."

'They sold it?"

'To me and my brother," he replied. "Come on." He continued on toward the house and up to a patio beside a cool blue swimming pool. As we stepped onto the patio, he called out. "Hey, Linc, I just met a friend of yours." A man sat up from a reclining chair by the pool, and I stopped short. It was an exact double of my friend, only this one wore the thin mustache, and he was entirely nude. Lane turned back to me with a grin, his left hand reaching up to brush his nipple. "In case you can't tell, we're twins."

Linc slowly climbed to his feet and stepped over beside his brother, running his hand down his chest, brushing his nipple and striking the same pose. "Identical twins," he added. As I stared in open mouthed amazement, I saw Linc's dick begin to stir. "Come join me by the pool. Lane, why don't you get our guest something to drink."

"Sure," the brother without the mustache said and disappeared into the mansion.

I followed Linc to the side of the pool where he'd been lounging and I started to sit down beside the patio table. "I guess I made a fool of myself, coming on to your brother like that," I said.

"Lane's a little slower than I am. You probably surprised him, but we are identical twins. We have almost the same tastes." He then grabbed me, pulling me up out of the chair and pressing his hard body against me, his rising cock poking me in the stomach. Linc's tongue again forced its way between my lips as he reached lower and slid my sweats down over my ass. Then he dropped to his knees before me, tugging at my jock and releasing my dick.

"That's more like it," he said, easing me down beside him at the edge of the pool. We found an air mattress and climbed onto it, quickly slipping into a 69 position.

"Your brother won't mind?" I gasped as Linc began to bathe my balls.

He paused long enough to answer my question as I went down on his hard shaft. "Why should he? He's got to find you as hot as I do." We both went back to work on each other's body, sucking and slurping.

I managed to catch a glimpse of the other twin coming back out of the house. He was still dressed in the lycra shorts and carrying a tray with a pitcher of ice tea and some glasses. He took one look at us and set the tray on the table. "I might have known that if I left you alone with him for a minute, you'd make a pig of yourself," he admonished his brother who was distracting me with his nimble tongue action on my sensitive asshole.

Linc paused long enough to reply. "You could join in," he offered and rolled onto his back, pulling me up on top of him. Lane lost little time, stripping off his shorts and tossing them aside, then demanded my attention by stepping over and putting his long dick in my face. I opened my mouth and allowed him to slide it between my lips, the smooth feel of his cock pushing against the roof of my mouth while my tongue enjoyed the tangy taste of his foreskin.

After a few minutes, Lane pulled free and Linc stretched out on his side, pulling me down next to him and sliding his cock between my ass cheeks. Lane dropped down on the other side of me, shoving his ass against my own prick. It was obvious that this hunky man pressing up against me wanted to be fucked. Just as I found my dick nudging against his moist, hot pucker, Linc's rod lurched forward, punching into my sphincter. He thrust hard and really speared my ass. The shock and surprise caused me to jump forward as Lane sank back, burying my own dick in his ass.

We all three lay still for a minute, adjusting to the fit. I had never been in the center of a three-way before. This was a new thrill, having a hard dick up my ass at the same time as I was stuffing another hot man's butt with my own meat. Linc pressed forward, raking his dick across my prostate and sending waves of pleasure shooting through my guts. Then he slowly pulled back. As he did so, I drilled into his brother's hole. Lane responded by hunching back, his hungry ass swallowing my dick to the root.

He then pulled away as I pushed back, impaling myself on Linc's hard tool. We began to work together, building a smooth steady rhythm. I felt like a piece of a well-oiled machine as I humped back and forth, a shaft of pleasure skewering into me, then my own shaft plugging the hole before me. I was the filling in a human sandwich, getting my thrills from both directions.

I hugged Lane to my chest, wrapping my arms around his muscular torso and running my fingers through the black curls on his pumped pecs. At the same time, Linc slipped his hands around me and down between my chest and his brother's back so he could play with my nipples, teasing them into tiny erections. We began to pick up speed. From the moans and gasps of pleasure coming from my twin sex partners, I knew they were both quickly approaching the point of no return. I closed my eyes and concentrated on the sensations flowing through me, rivers of excitement shooting in my guts and coming out the other side. I realized I was about to blast as well.

The orgasm hit us all at the same time. With a cry of animal lust, Linc punched into me, flooding my guts with hot sperm. Lane pushed back at the same moment and I began to unload into his sucking hole, shooting my own cream in long spurts into him. He began to shudder as his cock exploded, squirting geysers of cum out onto the air mattress. I felt as though I was going to lose consciousness but I kept on bucking.

In a few minutes, we all relaxed, Linc rolling onto his back, his cock pulling out of my ass with a wet plop. Lane likewise eased himself off my wilting dick. "Intense," Lane gasped as he caught his breath.

"I told you we have almost the same tastes," Linc said with a grin. "I like a hot ass to fuck, and he likes a hot fuck in his ass." I had a feeling I would be working out less on the Washunga trail and more at the old Fernwell estate. As they say, "Double your pleasure, double your fun."

GETTING BUTCH
Peter Reardon

In 1980, the two Kevins were the foremost connoisseurs of teenage dick at Broward Community College. As the most prominent members of an elite clique of gay youth from the surrounding Fort Lauderdale area, they ruled over their little "club" from one particular table in the college lunchroom. Every school day the club members would gather at the table to eat lunch and gossip about who's fucking and sucking who or who just came out to their parents and other topics relevant to gay teens. Getting into the club was simple: you had to be young, cute, gay (sorry, no queens allowed) and willing to have sex with at least one of the Kevins – if not both. This last requirement was easy because both Kevins were barely 19 years old and very attractive.

Kevin One was the spoiled son of a bank president. Thanks to Daddy he had an expensive sports car, a fabulous wardrobe and a generous allowance. With his blond hair, blue eyes and perpetual surfer-boy tan he made quite an impression whenever he zipped into the campus parking lot in his cherry-red Corvette. The whispers among the other students that Kevin One was queer seemed only to add to his mysterious allure. Considering his family's wealth and influence, he could have entered any university he wanted but chose instead to attend BCC because it offered the best local facilities for the only area of study he was truly interested in – the pursuit of beautiful boys.

Kevin Two also came from a well-to-do family but his parents were more strict and old-fashioned. They did not approve of their Kevin's association with the other Kevin. ("Showering children with money and expensive toys does not build character and that boy proves it!" said Kevin Two's father on more than one occasion.) Denied the luxuries lavished upon Kevin One, Kevin Two had only his looks, wit and personality to attract friends and lovers. Although smaller and more slightly built, he was the better-looking of the two. Like a Norman Rockwell wet dream of all-American youth, he was boyishly handsome with a beautifully smooth face and freckled cheeks that made him appear to be years younger than 19. He used his deceptively youthful appearance to great advantage when he indulged in his favorite vice – the seduction of younger males.

The two Kevins were more than best friends; their shared passion for youth and beauty made them soul brothers and sometimes partners in crime. No attractive boys were safe from their enormous sexual appetites. Seduction was the ultimate game for them and working together they had amassed an impressive track record of unlikely conquests ranging from supposedly straight college jocks to underage street trash. Their many successes had caused them to become unbearably cocky about their ability to corrupt the morals of any desirable young person they chose.

One day during lunchtime, with most of the club members gathered around the usual table, Kevin One began explaining his theory of homosexual behavior: "There's not a guy anywhere that can't be persuaded to do something queer with another guy if the circumstances are just right."

While this notion was the cornerstone of the two Kevins' sexual philosophy, it was not an opinion shared by all members of the club. Brian, the oldest and wisest member, slammed his milk carton down on the table in disagreement: "Oh, shit, Kevin! There's always going to be some guys that will never have a homosexual experience no matter what the circumstances are, whether they're on Fire Island, in prison or in your bedroom."

"No way."

"Hey," Brian said, point a finger towards a figure in a far corner of the lunch room. "How about Cochran over there? He could be the poster boy for incurable heterosexuality!"

Butch Cochran was easily the most beautiful person on campus, male or female. He had the face of an angel and, a champion swimmer, his torso was magnificently sculpted by vigorous workouts in the pool. Whenever he wore jeans he displayed a bulge in the crotch that promised much more than a mouthful of prime teen stud meat. The bubble-like contours of his butt inspired sighs of frustrated desire whenever he sauntered past the club's table.

"Oh, man, I would do anything – anything – for just a taste of that," said Kevin One hungrily.

Even Kevin Two had to admit that Butch was an object of lust beyond even his formidable seductive powers.

Brian, his voice twinging with disappointment, he said, "I was on the swim team with him in 12th grade and I managed to give every cute guy on the team at least one blow job except him. The closest I got was seeing him in the showers with a raging hard-on. God, what a beaut he's got between his legs! But when he saw me starin' at him, he blushed and ran out of the shower. I can tell you for sure that there's not a queer bone in that beautiful body."

"Oh, yeah, but there will be after I put this queer bone inside him," said Kevin One lewdly grabbing his bulging crotch.

The gathered club members laughed at this monumental display of hubris. Kevin One had clearly gone too far this time.

"Look, Mr. Irresistible," Brian said, "the only way you're even gonna get close enough to find out what brand of underwear Studboy over there wears is if you suddenly grow tits and..." He paused, smirked, and then went on, "I was gonna say 'pussy' too but all of us here know you already have one."

The club members all shrieked with laughter at this last remark but Kevin One was not amused. He had just been dared to seduce Butch and once presented with such a challenge his brain clicked into overdrive. As he began devising ways to accomplish this queer Mission: Impossible, he realized that maybe Brian was right, "tits and pussy" might very well be the way to get into Butch's pants. Suddenly Kevin had an idea, a thunderbolt of inspiration so ingenious that it could lead to the two Kevin's most thrilling erotic adventure yet. "Okay, smartass. What would you say if told you that I'll get into Butch's britches before the month is over?"

The club greeted this announcement with a chorus of disbelief.

"I'll bet a hundred dollars that it will never happen," said Brian confidently.

"Then we have a bet, my friend. I'll have that boy's cock in my mouth before the month is through and I'll prove it."

They shook hands on the wager and, since lunch was over, one by one the club members left the table leaving the two Kevins by themselves.

"Are you crazy?" moaned Kevin Two. "You, of all people, should know you're never going to get anywhere with Butch Cochran."

"Yeah, I know I won't, but my sister might...and she owes me a big favor."

"What's she going to do, suck him for you?" asked Kevin Two. 'That'll be really fulfilling. Just what are you thinking anyway? "

Kevin One leaned over and whispered his plan in the other Kevin's ear. It was a plan so daring that it just might work and all he needed was his sister's help. Kevin's younger sister, Kristen, was an unusual girl. She was both a brilliant honors student and a sex-crazed party animal. With her fashionably short punk haircut, she resembled a willowy feminine version of Kevin. Like her brother, she had a weakness for big cocks and cocaine.

Kristen had achieved a certain dubious notoriety for her part in what became known as The Skip Johnson Affair. This incident happened at a wild teen orgy the year before at Skip's house while his parents were out of town. A couple of party-goers searching for a vacant bathroom caught Kristen and Skip in flagrant delicto in an upstairs bedroom. Skip was on his back completely naked, tied to the bed with luridly colored scarves. Kristen, naked too, straddled him in a 69 position as she leaned over a line of cocaine that trailed down from his navel ending in an extravagant mound on the tip of his massive erection.

Upon being discovered, Kristen casually took a sniff from Skip's snow-capped cock and invited the intruding couple to join her. The female half of the couple fled at the sight of this sordid tableaux but the boy, Troy, accepted Kristen's invitation and soon they were both polishing the powder off Skip's sugar-coated schlong. In a frenzy of drug-fueled bisexual abandon, Kristen and Troy began licking the last traces of cocaine from the shaft of Skip's plump cock. This unexpected oral teamwork brought Skip, securely tied to the bed and in no position to object anyway, to a tremendous, messy climax that sent jets of hot jism flying onto his smooth muscular chest. After his orgasm, a satisfied but anxious Skip begged Kristen and Troy not to tell anyone about the kinky three-way lest his fame as a ladies man be tainted by any hint of bisexuality.

Of course, youth knows nothing of discretion when sex is involved and soon scandalous tales of bondage and blowjobs occurring at the party began burning through the grapevine. Accounts of the incident differed depending on who told the story: Skip's version left out the bisexual element, Kristen's version included every sleazy detail, and Troy, in a moment of homosexual panic, claimed that Kristen gave him a blow job.

All this gossip and innuendo simply enhanced Skip and Kristen's reputations as erotic thrill seekers. But Troy, tired of dodging persistent rumors that he was gay, soon retracted his story and, in one liberating rush, came zooming out of the closet. The two Kevins, always on the lookout for fresh talent, took a sudden interest in him and under their expert instruction he soon blossomed into the most accomplished cocksucker in the club.

Ever since the Skip Johnson Affair, Kevin One thought his sister might one day play some useful part in his obsessive campaign to suck or fuck every available boy in the world. With a hundred dollars and his reputation hanging in the balance, now was the time to enlist Kristen's special talents to help lure Butch into his web of teenage lust. Being an observant and cunning brother, he had compiled quite an extensive file of dirt on Kristen, and was prepared to blackmail her if necessary into participating in his plan to reach his ultimate goal : cramming every delicious inch of Butch's big, succulent dick into his hungry mouth.

Happily, Kevin One found he didn't have to extort his sister. Once she learned sex and money were involved, she was eager to help. Kristen dated the jock a couple of times last year and told her brother Butch was really "sweet and sexy ...and dumb." She listened to Kevin's scheme and upon learning how crucial she was to its success promptly demanded half of the $100 prize. Kevin readily agreed; he was hardly playing this game for the big money, he was in it for the big meat.

Kevin's plan was to have Kristen get real friendly again with Butch, then invite him home one night when their parents were away on of their regular yachting weekends. Once there, after plying him with drugs and alcohol, she'd suggest getting naked and naughty – thus setting the stage for the plan's masterstroke.

Since Kevin and Kristen's parents next scheduled getaway was just two weeks away, they needed to set the wheels of seduction in motion as soon as possible. Like a teenage Mata Hari, Kristen began using her feminine wiles on Butch right away. She knew from her previous experience with him that he, like all horny youths, was ruled by his libido. To Kristen, boys were just simple playthings, as easily programmable as robots. All she had to do was push the right buttons and Butch would easily become an enthusiastic sex slave. After all, considering Kristen's new kinky reputation, what red-blooded heterosexual male could resist a chance to experience erotic meltdown with the town's hottest sex bomb?

Luckily, Butch was in between steady girlfriends at the time and eager to have some dirty fun. Kristen proved to be a first-rate temptress and within a week he was buying her lunch, following her around school like an eager puppy, and carrying her books.

At night, he'd have long phone conversations with her that usually ended with him pleading they "get together and do something real soon." "Something" meant sex, of course, and Kristen played coy whenever Butch broached the subject. She knew how to stoke the fire in his loins and she planned to keep him hot and bothered until her parents went away for the weekend. The two Kevins watched with delight as the plot progressed right on schedule.

Kristen arranged for Butch to drop by the house the next Friday night around ten o'clock. Kevin One had stocked the refrigerator with Butch's favorite beer and acquired a bag of high-grade marijuana for additional mood enhancement. As the big night approached, Kevin One could almost feel Butch's hot cock sliding down his throat.

The fateful night finally arrived and the two Kevins met at Kevin One's house after dark. Kristen was already dressed in her sexiest outfit when she answered Kevin Two's knock at the door. He was carrying his Polaroid camera to document whatever might happen later that evening.

"Wow!" he said to Kristen, "you look really great. Butch is gonna cum in his pants when he sees you! Mind if I take a picture?"

"Save your film, you might need it later. Who knows what's going to happen tonight?"

Kevin found his friend in the living room sitting on a loveseat in a corner of the living room rolling a marijuana cigarette. He looked up and smiled wickedly at Kevin Two as he entered the room swinging his camera. "Hey, just preparing a little something for Studboy in case he needs to catch a little buzz to loosen up." He waved the cigar-sized joint in the air. "Good, you brought the camera – "

"Yeah, now we'll have photographic proof to show that skeptical bitch Brian."

"Okay, sit down and let's go over everything one last time."

The two Kevins huddled together on the loveseat and went over every detail of the plan: "You and I will be hiding in Kristen's closet when she brings Butch into the bedroom . Knowing how much Butch likes to drink, he'll already be a little tipsy from the beer I've so thoughtfully provided. She'll then smoke this big joint with him to make sure he's completely zonked into submission. Once he's agreeably intoxicated she'll suggest they get into bed and fool around. Of course, before he gets a chance to actually fuck her she'll insist that he be tied to the bed. She'll explain that ever since the Skip Johnson Affair she's been hot to try bondage again and if he'll let her tie him up she'll give him the best blowjob he's ever had. Once he's helplessly tied to the bed she'll blindfold him explaining that it'll heighten the sensual pleasure. Then I'll sneak out of hiding and give poor defenseless Butch the oral workout of his life."

"What if Butch senses that you're not Kristen? Don't you think he might freak out if he thinks someone else is sucking his cock?" asked Kevin Two in a moment of last-minute anxiety.

"Hey, he'll be stoned and securely tied to the bed and in no position to resist. But just in case, I'll be wearing Kristen's perfume so he'll think I'm her and I've shaved extra close too. Don't worry, I've thought of everything," explained Kevin One massaging the boner he had grown just thinking about his coming masquerade.

Butch arrived at the house precisely at ten. The two Kevins had taken their positions in Kristen's closet and were quietly waiting for his appearance. They could hear the sounds of beer bottles clinking and laughter drifting in from another room.

After about a half hour Kristen and Butch entered the room and fell recklessly onto the bed. They wrestled playfully for a few minutes until Kristen broke free and bounced off the bed to fetch the fat marijuana cigarette Kevin had conveniently left on the top of her bureau.

"Hey, Butch, wanna get stoned?" said Kristen as she placed the gigantic joint between her lips.

"Goddam! That's the biggest joint I've ever seen!" the jock said.

"I like 'em big. Of course, after we get high I may need something a lot bigger in my mouth," purred Kristen.

Butch smiled and groped his growing erection. "I've got another big joint for you right here."

She chuckled, then lit the joint and a blue cloud of pot smoke began to fill the dimly lit bedroom The louvered doors of the closet made it difficult for the two Kevins to see exactly what was happening but they could hear the sound of a zipper being unzipped and the soft rustle of pants falling to the floor. The Kevins could just barely make out the silhouette of Butch standing naked by the bed.

Kevin One, holding his breath, very carefully opened the closet door just enough to get a fleeting glimpse of Butch's bare butt as Kristen pulled him onto the bed. The other Kevin wanted to see as well, so they were both pressed up against the narrow opening to see Butch's tight muscular buns bathed in the warm glow from Kristen's bedside lamp. Like a couple of religious fanatics in the grip of a ecstatic vision, the two Kevins clutched each other in a rapturous embrace. After years of searching, they had found the Perfect Ass and it was so close they could almost touch it.

"Wow...I'm so stoned, I feel kinda dizzy," said Butch, sprawling across Kristen's bed. Sensing that he was now at his most vulnerable, Kristen, wearing only panties, jumped gently on top of him and began wiggling her butt suggestively over his crotch. Butch sighed heavily and began to gyrate his hips in response.

"I'm gonna give you the best sex of your life ... but only if you let me do it my way. "said Kristen exactly as she had been coached by her brother. She grabbed his cock and kissed the tip of it teasingly. Butch moaned in approval. Kristen literally had him in the palm of her hand.

"First, I have to tie you up..." Kristen said.

"You never wanted to tie me up before."

"That was last year. I've learned a lot of new things since then. Either I tie you up and give you the best orgasm of your life right now or you can jerk off in your car on the way home – your choice."

Butch, weakened by a lethal combination of dope, beer and lust, was as submissive as a whipped puppy. Before he knew it, Kristen had him securely bound to the bedposts and spread-eagled, naked except for the scarves tied at each wrist and ankle. Now it was time for the finishing touch: the blindfold.

"Oh, no!" Butch protested.

"Oh, yes!" Kristen said. "It's a well-known fact that blind people have the best orgasms."

Butch had never heard that before but he wasn't about to argue with a beautiful naked girl who wanted nothing more than to give him the best orgasm of his life.

Blindfold in place, Kristen flicked the light off and on. This was the moment the two Kevins had been waiting for. They had been watching as best they could from the closet. Kristen's expert handling of Butch had gotten them both so horny that they probably would have fucked each other right there in the closet (something they hadn't done since they first met in 9th grade) if Butch wasn't tied up just a few feet away waiting to be ravished.

Kevin One had already removed most of his clothes. He stripped off his underwear and his hard-on sprung out like a big rude finger. He quietly opened the closet door and crept quietly toward the bed. When he finally saw Butch stretched out and tied up like some captive slave boy with his enormous stiff cock standing straight up, he almost passed out with joy.

Butch au natural was even more beautiful than he imagined. Smooth, flawless skin covered a sleekly muscular body that looked remarkably tan in the faint lamplight of the bedroom. Every part of Butch was wonderfully designed and exquisitely proportioned, a true work of art. And his cock was its centerpiece: Rising out of a thick bush of dark pubic hair, it towered at least a full ten inches over his washboard stomach. A size queen's dream come true; his thick, veiny slab of man meat with its nicely rounded head, looked like a baby's arm holding a plum. Brian had not been exaggerating what he had witnessed in the shower room. It was the biggest dick Kevin One had ever seen and he wanted to immediately leap on the bed and lavish it with sloppy, cock-hungry kisses, but he managed to restrain himself and fell gently onto the foot of the bed. He wondered if Butch would suspect that it wasn't Kristen who was about to go down on him; he hoped he had used enough of her perfume.

Kristen moved away from the bed and receded into a dark corner of the room to watch the action. Her brother was now just inches away from Butch's crotch. He nestled his head between Butch's satiny inner thighs and began to work his mouth around his balls. He juggled each nut playfully with his tongue as if weighing them. They were big plump balls, heavy with hot creamy cum, and he was going to milk them of every last, luscious drop.

Butch moaned softly with delight as Kevin moved farther south towards the sensitive spot beneath his balls. Kevin knew this would be as close to Butch's butt hole as he was going to get. He stretched his tongue as far down as he could, but just couldn't reach the crack. With long, deep strokes, Kevin moistened the tiny hairs sprouting from this intimate region so maddeningly near Butch's cherry-hole. He reckoned he must have been doing a good job because Butch's contented moans grew louder with each successive sweep of his tongue.

"O0000hhhhhh.... aaaaaahhhhhh," he gurgled ecstatically, his spread legs trembling as Kevin's oral exploration inched gradually towards his cock. Working one long wet kiss up the shaft of the towering erection he finally reached the tip of Mt. Butch. He could tell that it would be impossible to get the whole thing in his mouth but Kevin was determined to get into the Cocksuckers' Hall of Fame even if he had to choke on it.

He began teasing Butch's prick with playful flicks of the tongue. Out of the corner of his eye he saw Kevin Two approaching. He was stark naked except for the Polaroid camera hanging around his neck. He glided silently up to the bed massaging his hard-on with one hand and holding the camera in the other. Kevin One kept polishing Butch's cock helmet till it glistened with pre-cum. He opened his mouth and engulfed the entire head in one hungry gulp. He worked that jumbo cock over in virtuoso style, opening wide to get nearly two-thirds of it down his throat. Butch responded with a slow rocking motion that grew faster until he was fucking Kevin's face with animal ferocity.

Click! Kevin Two moved around the bed taking Polaroids for proof that Kevin One had accomplished his impossible mission. Kevin Two was delighted: It was show time and Kevin One was giving the performance of his life. Kevin Two kept snapping away, stopping only occasionally to stroke his erection. Butch, securely bound and blindfolded, oblivious to the flashbulbs, kept pumping his cock into Kevin's mouth with powerful piston-like thrusts. Butch began to tremble wildly and knock his head against the back bed panel. Suddenly, a warm blast of thick salty fluid exploded into Kevin's aching mouth; he almost choked on the hot milky globs that the jock was shooting down his throat but he somehow managed to swallow every squirt.

Kevin Two continued jacking off even as he was taking pictures and Kristen, watching from her dark corner, massaged her clit to orgasm after orgasm.

To Kevin One, it all seemed like some delirious, depraved dream. Here he was sucking the cock of the hottest young stud in the world while his little sister was looking on and his best friend was jerking off as he recorded it all for prosperity! His plan had worked brilliantly; this was his greatest sexual triumph and, unable to contain himself any longer, he masturbated to a climax so intense it sent semen flying onto Kevin Two a few feet away. Wiping it off his leg, Kevin Two grimaced as he crept back into the closet with a handful of incriminating photographs.

As Kevin licked the last drops of cock-nectar from Butch's draining dick he thought victory had never tasted sweeter.

Finally slipping Butch's cock out of his mouth, he motioned to Kristen. He slid off the bed and she swiftly took his place between Butch's legs. Butch just laid there without moving, his spent cock resting to one side against his thigh, still majestic even in repose. He seemed very relaxed: he must have passed out during his climax either from banging his head on the headboard or from total orgasmic overload thanks to Kevin's superb blowjob. Either way, it made the two Kevins' getaway easier. They grabbed up their clothes and snuck out of Kristen's room just as Butch was waking up. They could hear Butch weakly begging, "Please untie me."

The Kevins stopped to listen. They could hear Kristen struggling to untie the scarves, then Butch say, But you can tie me up anytime, baby. That was the best blowjob I've ever had."

The two Kevins smiled and winked at each other, then snuck silently to Kevin One's room where they undressed and fell into bed. As they hugged each other, Kevin One noticed his friend still had a hard-on that needed tending to. Inspired by his victorious taste of Butch, Kevin One worked over his best friend's cock with lusty abandon and in moments he brought Kevin Two to glorious orgasm. Kevin One swallowed every drop and, as his best friend's cum oozed down his exhausted throat, he had another climax himself.

Snuggling together before drifting off to sleep, they agreed it had been an unforgettable evening.

The following Monday the two Kevins presented the Polaroids as evidence to the club during lunchtime. Speechless with awe and disbelief the members carefully passed the pictures around the table as if they were holy relics. Especially popular was the photo that showed Kevin One giving the camera his best cock-eating grin, a pearl-like drop of semen resting on his lower lip as the bound naked body of Butch receded blurrily into the background. Brian was a sore loser at first, complaining that the Kevins had not actually seduced Butch but had unfairly used the bait-and-switch method to win the bet. Still, Brian admitted Kevin One had indeed sucked the jock off and reluctantly forked over $50.

"That's all the money I have right now, I'll pay the rest later," said Brian sheepishly.

Since Brian was the only member of the club whose cock Kevin One had never sampled, he looked upon this as a window of opportunity. "Hmmmm...maybe we can work out some easy payment plan, if you know what I mean," said the insatiable Kevin, his mouth widening into the same sleazy grin Kevin Two had captured in the photographs.

But that, of course, is another story.

THE ACCIDENT
Kyle Stone

I saw him on the corner, waiting for the light to change. My heart began to pound. Anger churned in my gut. He turned his head and I saw it wasn't Tom, though there was a strong resemblance. This one, too, was young, intense. The bulge at his crotch strained against the worn denim, his jet black hair curled over the collar of his denim jacket. And a wedding band glinted on his left hand.

Fury exploded inside me like hot lava. My foot pulled off the brakes. The car leapt forward.

Thump!

The boy's hand slapped the hood as he jumped back. He stumbled against the rough tangle of fence protecting some construction and his jacket caught on some wire. A rust mark cut across his shirt above his ribs.

"What the fuck are you trying to do? Kill me?" His voice surprised me, deep and throbbing with outrage.

"God! I'm sorry!" Shocked, I jumped out of the car. What had possessed me? When I reached out to steady him, his arm was firm, all muscle under my hand. A swimmer, like Tom? For a moment, he leaned against me, and I felt the warmth of his body through his clothes. Abruptly, he shook me off.

"I've got an interview at 1:30!" he said. 'There's no time to go home and change!"

"We're about the same size," I said, grasping at the practical. "I could lend you a shirt and jacket."

"You wear denim?"

I nodded. "My place is just around the corner."

"Let's do it." He got into the car, one hand held close to his ribs. In spite of his slim build, his physical presence seemed to fill the car, calling up memories I was trying to forget.

"My name's Eric Anderson," I said, easing into the flow of traffic.

"Nick Bonato." He stared ahead, his jaw tense.

I felt I owed him some sort of apology, but my tongue refused to co-operate. One part of me was still in shock that I had reacted with such savagery to a shadow. Guilt kicked in. My hands began to sweat against the wheel. My mouth went dry. What can you say to a guy you almost killed? A guy who turns you on so much you're practically having an orgasm? A guy who wears a wedding ring? Like Tom. I had a brief vision of my passenger in a jock strap and nothing else. I shook my head quickly. History was not going to repeat itself.

"This is it." I turned into my parking spot and shut off the engine. "My place is on the 16th floor. There's a great view." Shut up, I told myself. You'd think I was a rental agent, for fuck's sake. I fumbled my keys but finally I got my front door open and ushered him inside.

I led the way to the bedroom and slid back the mirrored closet door. Nick emptied his pockets, took off the jacket, stripped off the shirt, all very business-like. I felt I should leave, but I couldn't tear myself away, anchored by that powerful physical magnetism and the ghost of Tom in the mirror. I just stood there staring at his well-developed shoulders, admiring the play of muscles across his back, the tender curve of his spine as it disappeared into his jeans, the dusting of dark hair on his arms. I wanted him. I could almost taste the hot salt tang of his flesh.

"I need a shirt," he said. He turned and I saw a streak of red along his rib cage.

Without thinking I reached out and touched him gently, as if I hoped to heal the pain with my hand.

He flinched. "Look, let's get something straight, okay? I don't need a nurse. I need clothes. Then I need a drive to the Parks Department building."

"Fine," I said. "Just fine."

I stalked out of the bedroom while he finished dressing. I wondered if almost killing someone is like saving his life. Would I have to be his slave? Forever? In spite of the fantasy possibilities, it was not a pleasant prospect. I kept seeing that wedding ring as I hunted for my keys.

That night, I dreamed about Nick Bonato. And the next night. And the night after that. Friday night it was one of those vivid Technicolor productions and I woke up with a raging hard-on and a pounding in my head. Only it wasn't in my head, it was at the door.

I pulled the sheet around myself and padded to the door. On the other side, a blond giant in bicycle pants stood grinning at me.

"Package for Eric Anderson," he said. He winked.

I let my sheet slip down further, showing off the definition I had worked at so hard.

"Nice outfit," he said, handing me the clip board.

As I scribbled my name, I wondered if this was the jacket and shirt I had loaned Nick. A quick look told me there was no return address. "Fine," I muttered to myself. "Just fine."

"I'll say," said the courier. He licked his lips.

My cock responded even before I noticed the growing bulge in his tight pants. "Get in here," I growled.

The sheet slid to the floor.

I had often wondered how they get out of those poured-on spandex shorts. My blond friend had no trouble peeling them down over his bulging thighs, releasing a thick springy cock. I pulled the blond man down on the floor and devoured his mouth, his tongue, my hands sliding through the thick fur on his chest. He was sweaty and smelled like sunlight and the hot street sixteen floors below.

When I came up for air, he wrapped his legs around my waist and flipped over on his back, taking me with him. He began squeezing me closer in the vice-like grip of his thighs, releasing, squeezing, and making our cocks throb with the pressure. I stared into his grey-green eyes. My breath came in shorter and shorter gasps. I could feel his body gather itself under me, the muscles tightening, beginning to thrum like a well tuned engine. My own nuts tightened. There was no sound in the room but the slap of bare flesh and the sharp harsh panting of our lust.

Suddenly he grabbed my head and clutched it to his hot chest. "I'm coming!" he shouted in my ear.

Our bodies vibrated together, bucking against each other with the force of our release. I closed my eyes.

"God! Look at the time!" My sex partner pushed me off him abruptly.

My bare ass hit the cold floor hard. "Hey!"

"Sorry. Got a tight schedule." He grinned as he reached over for my sheet and wiped himself off. He grabbed his pants and eased himself into them. "Hand my the t-shirt, will you?"

I don't like it when things move this fast. I threw it at him. Hard. He only laughed.

"You're cute when you're mad," he said. He bent down and kissed me, before loping out of my life.

I sat on the floor, smelling the sex and the sweat and feeling curiously unsatisfied, sort of the way you feel after pizza when what you really wanted was barbecue chicken. I pulled the package over and ripped it open, checking through the pockets in case Nick had left me a message.

I was still looking, when I heard someone at the door. I paid no attention, thinking the courier had come back for something. He hadn't.

It was Nick.

We stared at each other, Nick dressed in jeans and a white shirt open halfway to his waist, me sitting naked on the floor with the denim jacket in my arms like a security blanket. Hours passed. My mind screamed no, not again. Not another married man. My body shouted yes. I was glad I had the jacket to hide my growing erection.

"Hi," I said at last, trying to sound neutral.

"I've been waiting in the hall. It sounded like you were busy."

I felt my face go hot. Nick had no right to just appear like this. Unannounced. Unexpected. "You should have called."

He smiled for the first time and I felt my heart knock in my chest. "I wanted to surprise you. Guess I did, right?"

I nodded, once again at a loss for words. A little voice whispered, what's wrong with a little casual sex? I shivered.

He stood in front of me, hands thrust into pockets, dark eyes burning into mine. Suddenly he dropped to a squat, never breaking the look between us. He reached out and picked up the jacket, tugging it gently from my hands. "Oh my," he breathed. His eyes dropped to my swollen cock that said everything I seemed incapable of saying about how much I wanted him. "What a way to celebrate."

I cleared my throat. You got the job?"

"Yeah." He rubbed his crotch absently, watching my cock lift towards him.

Then he stood up and began to get out of his clothes. I lay back and watched, stroking my already hard cock. Nick tore off his shirt, kicked off his shoes. The zipper of his fly purred open and his jeans slid to the floor. His legs were long with muscular calves. Dark hair swirled over his flat belly. He peeled off his bikinis and sank to his knees beside me.

"Looks like you've been celebrating already," he said, drawing one finger down across my damp stomach. I caught my breath as his nails snagged through my moist pubic hair.

"I was just getting warmed up. How come you sent a courier with the jacket if you were coming anyway?"

"If I'd known what he looked like, I wouldn't have."

I pressed my lips to the fading bruise around the scratch on his ribs. It was my mark on him, the one thing not perfect about his body. I opened my mouth and blew against his warm skin, making a noise that set off his deep rumbling laugh.

He pulled me close. When I left here, you looked like you wanted to run me over for real."

"I did."

"Yeah?"

"You reminded me of someone. It doesn't matter now." I traced the outline of his lips with my tongue.

"Good." He wrestled me to the floor and sat on my chest while he scooped up his jeans, felt in the pockets and produced a rainbow variety of condoms. He was obviously planning to stay a while. He handed one to me, ripped one open with his strong white teeth and slid down onto the floor between my legs. Then his large hands went to work on my cock, his fingers teasing, caressing, and nipping at my balls, even as he unrolled the bright red latex along the length of my penis. My own hands were shaking with excitement as I reached for him and began to fit him with a neon green sheath.

You have a great sense of color," I remarked, and then caught my breath as he slid his hands under my ass and pulled me closer. His mouth covered mine, his tongue exploring, tasting of mint and a hint of tobacco. I opened my legs wider, leaning back into the cradle of his arms as I felt the nudge of his insistent cock demanding attention. We rolled back onto the rug and my legs reached high, my heels digging into his muscular shoulders. As he entered me, I held my breath and looked down, watching the bright green sheath slowly disappear inside me.

"Ahhh," he said. He paused and looked into my eyes.

At that moment, I felt a shivering sense of rightness, completeness, as if I had been waiting for this for a long time. Not just his cock inside me, but the smell of him, the feel of his arms, the tickle of his breath on my face, the way the hair on his chest swirled around his flat brown nipples. It was right. All right.

I stopped thinking then because he started to move, to undulate and thrust and sweat. I hung on to him, feeling his passion swell and finally explode. Then, while he was still catching his breath, I reversed our positions and slid inside him, letting his anus grip the head of my bright red cock for a moment, before I slowly slid deeper, deeper, feeling his body react, guided by his own desire deep into his bowels.

"Oh yes," he breathed. His hands reached to grab my shoulders and pull me down so our bodies were pressed together, glued by our mingled sweat as my hips ground into him. "Oh yes!" He moved under me, responding to every driving thrust, staying with me almost as if afraid to lose an inch of contact between us.

I felt my whole being quiver and tighten and suddenly explode in wave after wave of release, and beneath me, Nick's body answered with a shivering caress of those unseen silken muscles against my shaft, driving me on to bliss. Finally, the bright red latex slid back into view.

"Red and green." He grinned at me. "Like traffic lights, right? Like when we met?"

I grimaced, not wanting to think about that.

"Let's do it again."

"Wait. First I have a question." I thought I felt him stiffen and my heart sank. "I made the mistake of having an affair with a married man once. I'm not doing that again. Your wedding ring. You're not wearing it today."

"That's my secret."

"No." I hoped my voice sounded firm, in control. "I'm involved, now." Are you?"

I nodded.

He smiled. "It's the only thing about me that's fake. I wear it job hunting – to make me look older. You know, stable." "Stable shit!" I pushed him away roughly.

"You little shit! Come here!"

We struggled briefly, falling to the floor in the process. I kissed him.

"It was almost worth getting run over," he said after a moment.

"You're never going to let me forget, are you?"

"Never." He grinned, and reached for a canary yellow condom.

WHITE NIGHT
Edmund Miller

Rick stepped out of the shower and shook his hair. As he toweled himself dry, he paused to look at himself in the full-length mirror. "Nice front," he said, eyeing his definition critically. "Still very good from the side for thirty-three," he continued, turning and giving his tummy a few sharp raps. "And not bad from behind either," he finished up, throwing a glance over his shoulder. "If only someone would come along and make it all worthwhile," he thought, "a man of principle, someone who knows what he wants and knows how to get it, a man on a quest. Yes, that's it; a knight in white armor." Rick pulled on his jockstrap and smiled; perhaps he would find the White Knight that very evening.

Climbing the stairs to the Mineshaft, Rick reviewed his wardrobe: boots (dirty), jeans (torn), T-shirt (torn), denim jacket (well worn) – yes, he should pass. The bouncer took his money after shining a flashlight on his feet to make sure he was wearing boots or lace-up shoes and not loafers and after it seemed to Rick – sniffing the air to make sure he wasn't wearing cologne. Only natural male smells are allowed in the Mineshaft.

Rick fingered his golden fringe of a beard and wondered whether he should resent the bouncer's suspicions. Was he too pretty for real men to trust? Is it even possible to be too pretty? And could the White Knight put such questions to rest for him? He tried to put them out of his mind for the moment, turned in a ticket at the bar for a rye and ginger, and, in the accepted way, swung around on his barstool to face the room.

This outer room at the Mineshaft is pretty much like any raunchy cruise bar. Standing around staring through one another were forty or so guys in various degrees of leather drag. The older ones, Rick noticed, seemed to be wearing more of the stuff. Were the younger ones counting on youth and looks to take the place of chaps and chains? Or was it that they couldn't afford the stuff?

Having downed a few rounds of rye and poppers, Rick was ready for love. He stripped off his jeans and left them in the check room. As he headed for the game rooms, he saw an old trick coming out and quickly averted his eyes. Not the White Knight. The trick was wearing leather chaps over skin and sporting a massive arch of erection. Rick looked back nostalgically and saw the trick head for the bar.

Rick sighed but went on into the game rooms. He found a secluded corner with a place to lean and set himself up. He leaned his head down and into the wall, crossed his legs at the ankles, and let his buns do their stuff. They got their fair share of feeling up in the passing crowd, but for ten minutes or so no one stopped. He figured the young, good-looking guys wanted to be pursued. And the shy ones must have wanted more immediate response than he was about to give to a casual caress.

The men Rick wanted to interest were different. He waited the ten minutes knowing some real top men must have passed him by. But he was content to wait because he knew it's hard to know what to put your hands on first at the Mineshaft.

While thus meditating on the art of cruising, Rick felt a familiar, pleasant sensation. Someone had slipped two fingers up his ass and was giving him a hot finger wave. He didn't look back, preferring to fantasize about the White Knight. The fingers hit the spot repeatedly, and Rick's cock responded in the predictable way. A hand reached around and freed the cock from his jockstrap. While stroking Rick's member with an affectionate nonchalance, the someone behind him stepped up to the open invitation and laid a long piece of meat into Rick's hole. The strokes were slow and sure at first. Rick could feel a hairy midsection periodically snuggle up to his hips. And big loose balls slapped against his thighs. Rick took another hit of poppers and saw black and yellow spots in front of his eyes. Was this the White Knight at last? The guy speeded up his strokes and slapped at Rick's thighs and scratched his back. At last the stroking stopped, and Rick felt the thumping cock shoot into his guts as he shot off himself into the helping hand.

'This had to be the White Knight," he thought, as the long cock slid slowly out of his ass and swung against his legs. The guy was still leaning against him, was running a hand over Rick's body and sending shivers of excitement through him. In fact, through he could hardly believe it, Rick was sending up a new erection before his old one had even gone all the way down. His erection was waving in the air. This number was for kissing. Rick began to turn around – slowly, drawing out the experience, keeping his eyes shut at first, throwing his head back.

And suddenly his eyes were open. Something new was happening. It was quite pleasant. But it wasn't quite right; it wasn't next. He was twisted half around by this time. He looked down and behind him. Rick's someone was on his knees down there eating ass. Rick spread his cheeks, arched his back, and pushed the head further in with his left hand. "Ah, this is hot!" he thought, as the tongue searched deep into his asshole, reaming each separate pucker.

And yet his erection had gone down. Though he whipped at his cock with his right hand until it was sore, he couldn't get it engorged enough to keep the head from slipping back behind the foreskin. Why couldn't he get himself up again? Was this someone back there doing something that the White Knight shouldn't do? Would the White Knight rim? Well, why not? Yes, he might – but not here, not this way, not now. When you have just come at the same time, a little kissing and cuddling ought to be the order of the day. The White Knight has got to present arms and allow you to return his salute before he sticks his tongue up your ass.

Rick abruptly pushed the head away from his ass and, disappearing into the crowd, left a startled someone sitting on his heels. Some time later, fortified by another rye and ginger and calm once again, Rick returned to the game rooms, idly wandering through, feeling up a pretty boy's ass here, and yanking a chain between nipple clips there.

But you don't see much action when you're on the move, so eventually he settled in one spot – the stairwell down to the piss room: there's always a lot of traffic passing through there. And sure enough, in a few minutes he was being pawed in several places. A black leather cap got a lip lock on his cock that was too good to pass up. The guy really knew how to give the tender loving care an uncut love muscle needs. And he went all the way down on each stroke – a difficult job with Rick's eight inches and exceptional width.

Then just as Rick was arching back to come all over black leather, a stranger's firmness probed into him from behind. The movement was swift and sure. And the cock ring and harness he felt on the man behind him were an interesting sensation. But then he started thinking about the White Knight again. This leather cap with come all over it was certainly not a man of authority and principle. But what of the man behind? Rick looked back. He was gray-haired and weather-beaten, but that was O.K. if he had ideals. But did he? What was he doing now? Why he was wiping his mouth on his arm – he was drooling! This was not at all the sort of thing we expect from the White Knight, who is always in complete control. And come to think of it, this guy behind was cutting corners, wasn't he? "Why, he waited till I was engaged with Leather Cap and then as much as took advantage of me!" Rick decided.

He put his hand behind him and with two firm fingers disengaged Gray Hair from his ass – much to the fellow's surprise. The guy raised a number of importunate questions, but his nasty tone only convinced Rick he was right. The White Knight might take you unawares, but he was certainly above recrimination.

Slipping away into another room, Rick found a sling vacant. He hopped into it, putting his left foot into one of the footholds but dangling his right idly while he settled down to wait once again for the White Knight. Many men looked, and some touched, but again, no one did anything serious for some time. He had made himself available. That was as far as he went. Winking and wooing, buying a guy a drink, even making small talk in a bar – all these things were fine in their way. Yet somehow they destroyed the true quality of sexual experience – the spiritual quality of sex. And at this point in his musings Rick had to laugh. "Yeah, that's it. I'm looking for something spiritual in a fuck."

And then as he was still laughing, a firm hand grabbed his swinging right foot and placed it securely in the foothold. The top before him was rather unassuming to look at. He was slim and serious and clean: not one of your gut-heavy leather queens with a five o'clock shadow. He had serious, thin lips. And his eyes were sharp and green. He was in a plaid lumberman's shirt and was wearing glasses. Rick was pleased. Femme wouldn't do. But there is something more masculine about a guy who doesn't have to say it all with clothes.

For the second time that night, two fingers made an easy entry into Rick's ass. They made a few firm parries, but the Man with the Glasses did not try to stimulate Rick's prostate or tickle his thighs. Rick knew that the thing to say next was "Take it easy!" but he scorned such prissy cautions. If a guy doesn't have sense enough to take it easy, you are in trouble even if you can pull yourself off his arm and cut the scene short. But the test of course is pain with pleasure. You wait for the man who can give you just the right balance, and you don't have to talk about the partial successes.

"Oops." This was the thumb slipping in. The Man with the Glasses was not a fast worker, but he was a methodical one. He twisted the fist around in Rick's tight hole, and Rick arched his back in exquisite pain.

"Eehah." This was the full fist slipping all the way in. The man was greasing the wrist of his right hand and continuing to turn his fist around in Rick's insides. He still had said nothing, and Rick liked that. Then the Man with the Glasses spread Rick's ass apart with the fingers of his left hand and started easing his right arm all the way home. He never once pulled back. Rick saw stars without even taking another hit from his inhaler, but he liked it that this guy went straight after what he wanted. The White Knight would do that.

Finally, Rick felt the elbow snug up against his ass. Quickly the man pulled his arm all the way back to his fist, and Rick let out another gasp of pleasure. But he had little time to enjoy this new pleasure because almost immediately the man thrust his arm all the way back up to the elbow. When Rick was again conscious of what was going on, he realized the man was pumping his arm in and out at a more reasonable pace. Rick was in love.

Then the man stopped his pumping and, with his arm halfway home, opened his fist. Rick went into new ecstasies. The man dragged his fingers down along Rick's insides and pulled his hand part way out, hitting the prostate at last. Rick's cock leaped to attention. Surely here was the White Knight.

Rick's mind was at peace. His search was over.

Then he woke from his reverie to feel a new sensation. Could it be? Yes, another hand was caressing the first. Eight fingers – nine – were in him. Circular motions were harder for the Man with the Glasses now, but his rhythm was steady. In went the second thumb. And suddenly Rick had a double fist in his hole, and the forward thrust was beginning again.

Rick's mind was no longer at peace. One had room, of course, for the White Knight's lance. But did one have this much room? The Man with the Glasses seemed to be saying, "Yes." At least, he thrust on, twisting his arms around one another and turning Rick on to new highs. Poppers were mandatory now, and Rick took some needed hits. And suddenly it was working. Rick drifted off. "Yeah, this is good. Very good." The White Knight had carried him off to a castle in the air. The world was beneath him. There were musk roses in the Mineshaft.

Then, suddenly, it was over. Rick blinked, dropped one leg, and pulled himself up in the sling. Where was the White Knight? He jumped up, stumbled a bit, and rubbed his sore ass. He thought it best to get to the bathroom without delay. As he went, he thought: 'Would the White Knight leave you in the lurch this way? Surely the Man with the Glasses could not have been the White Knight after all. But he's out there. Perhaps I'll find him tomorrow.' And now Rick smiled; his quest for the White Knight was going well.

MUSCLES
Leo Cardini

It was a sunny, Saturday afternoon during that extraordinary spring of '77 when I had just turned nineteen and my life was a merry-go-round of workouts, disco dancing and bedtime partners. I was in my room, resting on my unmade double bed, wearing nothing but an old, loose-fitting pair of Jockey shorts that made it easy for me to reach in and play with myself. Through the two partially-opened windows, over the tinny sound of the black and white TV I wasn't really watching, I could hear the kids playing out back in the courtyard. It reminded me of when Kevin – that's my best friend – and I were young, because even then all the neighborhood kids used to gather there. Boy, I never realized what a racket we made.

Anyhow, hearing the kids outside made me think of how when I was their age, only the rich could actually afford to live in this turn-of-the-century rectangle of brownstones that surrounded the courtyard, taking up one entire block of Jamaica Plain. Kevin and I never dreamed back then that someday we'd be sharing an apartment here. But then, there were a lot of things we did these days we never dreamed we'd be doing!

Oh, in case you've never heard of it, Jamaica Plain is actually part of Boston. Very working-class. Mainly Italians (like me), Irish (like Kevin) and Poles. Everyone knows everyone else's business, no one ever seems to move out of the neighborhood, or, for that matter, even leave it to go into Back Bay or the South End, which of course Kevin and I do all the time because that's where all the gay bars and discos are, and where most guys like us live.

So there I was listening to the kids outside, thinking about my life, and, of course, playing with my cock.

Yeah, I know; I just can't seem to keep my hands off it. Eventually, I slid my jockey shorts down to my ankles. I was just lazily fooling around with myself, propping up my half-hard cock and watching as my cockshaft tilted to one side, and then, with a little help from my hands, to the other, when suddenly, I heard the front door to our apartment open and then slam shut, setting all the picture frames on the wall rattling.

It was Kevin, of course.

I counted to ten and bingo! There went the refrigerator door also slamming shut.

So I yelled out to him, "Bring me in a beer too, will ya, Red?"

He hates it when I call him "Red," which is of course why I do it. You see, he's still sensitive about being a redhead, because when we were young, the other kids were always making jokes about it. And when we were in junior high and our pubic hair was coming in, that flaming bush of his was all the reason the other guys needed to point it out in the communal shower we all had to share and make wisecracks. Well, guys are still eyeing his crotch in the showers, but now it's because they're envying him for that incredibly big piece of meat that hangs down between his legs.

Kevin stepped into the bedroom, took one look at me playing with myself, and made an exaggerated show of rolling his eyes. He handed me the beer, saying, "Here, wrap your hands around this!" and then began stripping off his clothes.

But I just stuck out my tongue, set the beer on the night table, and with both hands aimed my cock at him.

"What's a matter? Jealous I've got a playmate I like better than you?"

He grabbed his cock through his jeans and said, "You kidding? So you've got eight inches. That's still one inch less than me, and always will be, smartass."

"It's not the meat, it's the motion."

"Yeah, sure...but anyhow, I gotta tell you; after you left the Twelve-Seventy last night..." (That's our favorite Boston gay bar.) "...to go sucking cock in the Fens like the cheap slut you are, guess who spent the night with a Broadway star!"

"Huh?"

"Well, not exactly a star yet. This dancer who's in town with that new musical on its way to Broadway...uh, what's it called?"

"Dancin'?"

"Yeah, that's the one, I think. Anyhow, this morning we went out to brunch – not breakfast, but brunch, like they do in New York City – with some of his friends in the show. And they said that with a body like mine..."

"So that's why you weren't around earlier, when Norm dropped by."

By now Kevin had his jeans off and was sitting on the bed, bending over and pulling off his socks.

"Norm dropped by?" he asked sitting up again, forgetting all about what he was saying.

"Yeah. So what did they say you could do with a body like yours?"

"So why'd he drop by?"

Now, I've got to explain about Norm – Norm Pulaski, that is. He's one of the guys we grew up with. Lives just down the street from here, right around the corner from where me and Kevin's families still live.

Well, Norm is one heart-throb of a guy. Not very bright, but handsome as hell; broad forehead, full, sensual lips, unbelievably white teeth, brown, puppy-dog eyes, and a thick mane of wavy, dark brown hair that he parts in the middle.

And what a body! He's a little over six feet tall, and broad-chested, with muscles everywhere you look. And the fairest, smoothest skin the world. Not a single blemish on him anywhere. Believe me – I know.

Oh, and his butt! I used to watch him stripping down after gym class, wondering what it would be like to be the backstraps of his athletic supporter, stretching across those two firm asscheeks that pressed so tightly together like two evenly-matched opponents locked in battle.

So are you surprised when I tell you he was one of our high school's football stars? But now that we've graduated he's a mechanic at his father's garage, and he spends his spare time hanging out with all the same dumb jocks he went around with in high school.

Except he's not exactly like the rest of them – not as loud-mouthed or narrow-minded. I mean, we've even got him smoking grass with us, which is how I got to suck his cock.

Yeah, I really did! You see, three Saturdays ago...but, that's another story. *

Anyhow, when I told Kevin about it, the situation was almost the same as it was now. Kevin had just come in and was stripping off his clothes, assuming he'd jump into bed next to me and we'd end up fooling around with each other, when I surprised him with what had just happened.

And then we had sex.

That's one thing we've never stopped doing with each other – having sex. In fact, some of our Boston friends say we're not just best friends, but actually lovers, except we don't realize it yet.

Anyhow, Kevin's always had the hots for Norm, too. Like he's got this fantasy about walking into the high school locker room when he thinks there's no one else there. Then he spots Norm, bending over untying his sneakers, one foot on the floor and one on the bench, wearing nothing but a pair of white gym socks and a jockstrap. So Kevin tiptoes over to him, gets down on his knees behind him, struggles to pull his hard-as-rock, creamy white asscheeks apart and sticks his tongue right in there, all the way up...

"C'mon asshole. Why'd he drop by?"

"Oh, I don't know. Maybe he likes my company."

"So what happened?"

"Suck my cock first, and then I'll tell you."

Kevin leaned over, took my cock out of my hands, and started sucking on it. Like it was instinct, his free hand went into his briefs, pulling out his own fat, floppy dick and stroking it.

I'll tell you something; no one, but no one, sucks cock like Kevin. I mean, I might be only nineteen, but I've been around. And I don't mean to brag, but hey, I've got a pretty good body. You see, until I was fifteen I was a real chicken wing. Then I started going to the Back Bay Health Club. To be honest, I started going there because I'd heard it was really gay. But then, when I saw what went on in the whirlpool and in the shower stalls, and the type of guys who got the most action, I really got into developing my body. By the time I was eighteen, I was one of those guys getting all the attention.

Anyway, the point is I'm pretty successful when it comes to attracting guys, so I'm not totally inexperienced when I tell you that no one gives a blow job like Kevin. But when you consider how much he likes cock, I guess it makes sense.

But no sooner did he start sucking me off then he suddenly stopped in mid-blow with his teeth digging into my cockshaft. Not hard or anything, but just enough for me to know it's his twisted way of saying, "So tell me about Norm first, or I'll bite the fucking thing off."

"Okay, okay! Here's what happened...'

It's just about noontime and I'm getting off the trolley from my workout at the Back Bay Health Club. There's Norm standing outside Mae's Grocery Store. One look at him and I get that tingly feeling in my cock that draws my attention to the way it rubs against my briefs with every step I take.

Norm's dressed as usual, looking kinda like L'il Abner. You know, worn out, beltless jeans that cling to him like they're a size too small, and a tight white T-shirt threatening to burst into shreds every time he flexes his muscles.

Well, as soon as he sees me, he comes right over. "How's it going, Tony?"

"Not bad. You?"

"Really great, man."

Then he picks up my stride and starts walking with me as I head for the apartment.

"You been working out?"

"Yeah."

"Thought so, from your gym bag. jeez, you're getting to look just like that statue they got in the window down at Continental Coiffures."

"Michelangelo's David"

"Huh?"

"That's the name of the statue."

"Oh. Yeah. Anyhow, you're getting to look just like him." Though I don't let on, I'm really flattered.

"So listen," he continues after a pause. "I just scored some real primo grass. From Benny. Said it was sens....sens..." "Sensimilla."

"Yeah. That's it. Sounds kinda Italian, doesn't it."

" Yeah."

Now, Norm and his friends aren't grass smokers. To them, that's something only hippies and faggots do. But Norm's always been curious about getting stoned, which just goes to show how different he is from the rest of the jocks, and Kevin and I kept turning him on until finally three weeks ago I succeeded in getting him stoned, which is when I got to suck his cock.

"The only thing is," he continues, "I can't find any place to roll some joints."

"Your bedroom?"

"Fuckin' Stan's in there studying." (Stan's his brainy kid brother.)

"Your father's garage?"

"You kiddin'?"

"The restroom there?

"Uh...no lock. And besides, it's filthy."

It just so happens I was in there last week sucking off Carlos, the grease monkey with the ten-inch dick, and so I know the lock does work and that it's pretty damn clean. So I figure either he doesn't know how to roll joints – it does take practice – and he's hoping I'll do it for him, or he hasn't forgotten that blowjob I gave him and he's hankering for a repeat performance.

"You can roll some at my place if you want."

"Yeah?"

"But you'll have to get me stoned, too."

"Sure!"

Once we're inside the apartment, I pull a package of rolling papers out of my gym bag (you never know when you'll need them) and toss them onto the second-hand coffee table in front of our second-hand sofa that goes with our second-hand everything else and say, "Here. I'll be right back."

I go into the bedroom, toss my gym bag into the closet, and shove the dildo, Vaseline and male mags that are sprawled around the floor under the bed, just in case we might end up in there.

Then I go out to the kitchen and yell into Norm, "You want a beer?"

"Yeah, sure!"

I come back into the living room with two beers. Norm's got the grass and papers scattered all over the coffee table and it's clear he doesn't know the first thing about cleaning grass or rolling joints.

He looks up at me with a sheepish grin. He's so cute – all muscles and embarrassment – that I want to reach over and tousle his hair.

But instead I just let out a little laugh.

"Here," I say, handing him a beer, "let me show you how it's done."

I sit down next to him on the sofa. As I lean forward over the coffee table, I hoist my butt a few inches closer to him. Our thighs press against each other. I pretend I'm so pre-occupied with the grass that I don't notice.

"Hmmm. Well, first of all you have to separate the grass from the seeds and the twigs."

"Yeah?"

"Yeah. Like this."

So I show him how to do it, expertly cleaning enough of the dime bag to roll into a joint.

Then, as I take a matchbook cover and corral the cleaned grass into a small pile, I feel his upper arm press against mine.

My heart leaps up, my cock stirs, and it's a miracle I'm actually able to concentrate on rolling a joint.

When I'm done, I turn to Norm and hold the finished product up for his inspection.

"Wow," he whispers in admiration, "You did that like there's nothing to it."

His face is so close to mine. His lips so ripe... tempting...accessible.

I hesitate to consider if I dare press my lips against his.

Unfortunately, this creates a noticeable awkward pause, which Norm retreats from with an unnecessary clearing of his throat, dispersing all the possibilities the moment held.

"So let's get stoned!" I say, with an exaggerated show of enthusiasm to pretend like nothing's happened.

"Okay!"

Well, I light up and we pass the joint back and forth between us. It turns out to be really good grass, which I wouldn't expect from Benny, who usually has crap, though I don't have the heart to tell Norm.

After about a half-dozen tokes, I happen to glance down at my crotch. The bulge in my jeans makes it as plain as can be that I'm getting a hard-on. And it keeps growing, exceeding my usual eight-inch piece of Italian sausage, like some science fiction movie monster that nothing can stop, mutating out of control. Soon it'll be taller than the Prudential Tower, drowning hundreds of panic-stricken citizens running through the streets in a flood of hot, steamy cum!

Oh God, am I ever getting stoned!

"Wow!" Norm says, pulling me out of my fantasy. I swear he's staring at my crotch, but all he says is, "Good grass!" as he passes me the joint once again.

He slowly runs his right hand across his chest, which of course drives my crazy.

But I understand why he's doing it and say, "and it's a real physical high, too, isn't it?"

"Yeah."

I hand him the joint and he takes another toke.

"Kinda makes you horny, huh, Norm?"

"Umm," he says over the grass he's just inhaled, passing me the joint again.

But I wave it away and he puts the small roach that remains in the ash tray.

Then, after he exhales and quickly refills his lungs with fresh air, he says, "Christ, horny's not the word for it! When I get like this, I can't even think about anything else until...uh...you know."

"Well, we could jack off."

"Yeah," he says, sounding like he'd settle for a jack-off session but actually had something else in mine.

Well, by now I'm stoned enough to get a little ballsy. "Or I could give your another blowjob."

"Yeah, you could...but...umm..."

"But what, for Christ's sakes?"

"Well, when I was over here before you said maybe some time you'd let me...uh...fuck you?"

"Well, why the hell didn't you say so in the first place!"

"I don't know! It's not like I'm used to asking guys if I could fuck them! Besides, supposing you changed your mind?"

"Does it look like I've changed my mind?" I ask, standing up in front of him. My cock's pressing out against my Levi's barely inches from his face.

He looks at it and goes, "Wow!"

I rub my hand along my lengthening cockshaft and say, "C'mon, let's go into the bedroom."

You should've seen the eager smile that lights up his face as he gets up, revealing that he's got the healthy beginnings of a hard-on of his own snaking down his left pants leg.

Once were in the bedroom, I go to help him off with his T-shirt.

"That's okay," he says, jumping back at my touch.

Then, with an embarrassed smile, he says, "I guess I'm just not used to these things."

As he begins to remove his T-shirt himself, I wonder what's going on in his mind that it's too personal for me to pull off his T-shirt, while it's okay for him to stick his cock up my ass.

Anyhow, I slowly remove my own while captivated by the splendid performance of his torso as he lifts off his T-shirt. He's got such a massive, well-defined chest – white as alabaster, which the spread of brown hair between his pecs serves to emphasize – and such powerful, bulging arms that it looks almost ridiculous. I mean, all that equipment just to pull off a thin, frail, cotton T-shirt. Though not so ridiculous, I realize, that I don't practically drool over his every little flex-muscle movement.

We drop our T-shirts onto the floor. Norm stands there, looking at me like he doesn't know what to do next. I undo my Levi's, prompting him with an eager nod to do the same. We bend over at about the same time to lower our jeans. I notice that, while I slide my briefs off with my Levis, Norm keeps his on.

As he straightens up, I exaggerate the trouble I'm having getting my big feet through the pants legs, just so I can remain bent over, savoring the view of Norm's big fat cock pressing up towards eleven o'clock against his white, low-rise briefs.

"You're gonna suffocate that poor thing," I say, getting down on my knees in front of him as soon as I get my jeans off.

I slowly lower his briefs, relishing every inch of their descent. His heavy cock plops out right in front of my face. I pause to admire this huge, pale monster with the intricate network of delicate blue veins running along it. It's so fat that his purple-pink cockhead – substantial in its own right – looks several sizes too small for it.

He's half hard and rising. The wonder of his cock stiffening and stretching towards complete erection holds me spellbound.

By now I have his briefs down just below his knees. I leave them there and wrap my hands around his bulging calves to balance myself as I lean forward to take his cock into my mouth.

Actually, I expected Norm would be kind of skittish about us having sex again together. I see out of the corners of my eyes that his two large hands, hanging down at his sides, are twitching, like they're absorbing all his nervousness and uncertainty.

43

But the irresistible magnificence of his cock, the lush forest of brown pubic hair above, and his big, low hanging balls in that smooth skin, pinkish ballsac, hold me so entranced I'm willing to risk how he might react. I wrap my lips around his cockhead and slowly suck the first few inches of his dick into my mouth, amazed all over again at its remarkable thickness and fleshy feeling.

Then I take in more of it. And more. And still more.

As I hear Norm let out a low, prolonged moan, I feel his cock growing inside my mouth.

Then I dismount him. His heavy cock bounces around, struggling against gravity, as it searches for my mouth.

In order to fight off the temptation to go ahead and suck the cum out of him right then and there, I have to remind myself that he wants to fuck me.

I stand up. Norm has this odd, strained expression on his face, like pain and pleasure are clashing around inside of him. His mouth is open like he wants to say something, but nothing comes out.

I lean forward to stick in my tongue.

Shit! This breaks the spell. He quickly jerks his head to one side and tightly shuts his eyes and mouth like he'd just been forced to swallow some bad-tasting medicine.

So I quickly close my own mouth and give him a swift peck on the cheek. He silently winces, takes a few clumsy briefs-around-the-ankles steps away from me, and sits down on the edge of the bed, his alluring, softening cock hanging heavily down between his legs.

"Sorry," he says. "It's just that...I don't know."

I stand in front of him, my cock softening. My left hand automatically wraps itself around my cockhead, tugging it over to one side.

"Sure, Norm. You don't mind me taking your cock in my mouth and sucking on it, but I try to slip you my tongue and you act like...well, I don't know what. I mean, it's not like I'm trying to get you to suck on my cock, or something."

I release my cock and it bounces up half hard again in front of Norm. His eyes go right to it.

He stares at it and then says slowly, "I could try to suck on it, I guess, if you really want me to."

I can see the way he studies my cock he's truly thinking about what it would be like to take it into his mouth. I get so turned on by his intense gaze it's like I can actually feel his eyes scanning my shaft. It responds by stiffening, steadily rising up in front of his face.

Then, after a pause, he reaches out with his right hand and makes a tentative fist around my cock, as if he's trying to steady it in order to contemplate my cockhead, which can't stop throbbing, now that it's got his attention.

"Go ahead," I urge.

It's like he's hypnotized by it.

But it's wet," he weakly protests.

"That's just pre-cum. See."

I reach down and grab his own cock, holding it straight up. "Just like you."

Then I bend over, arcing my head around his cock-holding hand, stick out my tongue and delicately scoop the bead of pre-cum off his piss slit and into my mouth.

As I straighten up again, I say "Ummmm," to show him what a tasty treat it is.

"Yeah?" he says doubtfully.

"Yeah."

Woodenly, he leans forward, like any sudden movement would break a bone. I can feel the tension in his body by the way he's gripping my cock. His hand's practically shaking.

He slowly pushes his tongue out and then quickly lifts the pre-cum off my cock, shutting his mouth quickly when he's done.

Now, was that so bad?"

"No," he answers.

But I notice he doesn't go back for more.

Well, I figure I've put him through enough for one day. Although – shit! – he was that close to sucking on my cock.

Anyhow, I just laugh and shake my dick out of his grasp to let him know it's alright; he can let go of my cock and I won't be offended. And just to confirm it, I punch him in the arm, real buddy-buddy, the way he and his friends always do to each other.

"Maybe some other time," I say. "I didn't mean to make you uptight, or force you to do something you didn't want to do. Besides, we came in here for you to fuck me. I'm sure you'll like that."

He laughs nervously. I can see something's going through his mind.

"There was something I wanted to ask you, Tony." "Yeah?"

"What's it like?"

"What do you mean what's it like? You're about to find out, aren't you?"

"No. I mean, what's it like to have someone's cock up your ass. Especially one like yours."

He grasps it again and inspects it from several angles. "I mean," he continues, "it's so big."

Actually, his cock is bigger than mine, but I decide not to steer the conversation in that direction.

Instead, I say, "I could show you what it's like to get fucked."

He let's go of my cock like it had suddenly turned red hot. "Oh I don't think so," he says nervously.

But you can tell that behind the words there's a lot of debating going on.

"You've never stuck your fingers up there, or anything?"

I can't resist the urge to grab hold of his cock again, ever so slowly stroking it.

"No!"

But I can tell he's lying.

"I could rim you. That would give you some idea what it's like."

"What's that?"

"I stick my tongue up your ass."

"Gross!"

"Gross? It's heavenly!"

"Really?"

"Especially when you're stoned."

"Hmm."

I can tell he's weakening.

"And if you don't like it, all you'd have to do is say so. I mean, it's not like you're some ninety-pound weakling I can bend to my will."

I take this opportunity to run my free hand across his pees. Reflexively, he pulls his shoulders back to present his chest at full advantage.

"And then I'll let you fuck me," I offer.

His cock twitches in anticipation, a warm, fat monster trying to squirm out of my hand.

"Well...okay."

What a swell guy!

"What do I do?" he asks.

I let go of his cock and take my hand off his chest. "First, get up on the bed on your hands and knees."

He kicks off his Jockey shorts and mounts the bed, his two feet dangling over the side as he moves into position.

"I feel kinda of silly like this," he says, craning his neck around to see me.

"Believe me, you don't look it! A butt like that...but move up to the headboard so I can get on behind you."

"How's this?" he asks twisting his head around again after he's crawled into place.

"That's just fine, Norm."

I situate myself behind him on my knees and say, "Now you just relax and leave everything to me."

Supporting himself with his forearms, he rests the right side of his head on the pillow and mumbles, "Okay."

I place my hands on his firm, creamy-white asscheeks, surprisingly warm to the touch. Then I pause to fully appreciate my good fortune. Who'd ever have thought that one day I'd have Norm in my bedroom just waiting for me to stick my tongue up his ass?

I look into the narrow ravine of his asscrack, savoring the sight of his pink, puckered butt hole. And as if this close-up inspection by itself isn't enough to drive me crazy with desire, he keeps clenching it, as if to lure me in.

I slowly spread his asscheeks apart, watching how it pulls his butt hole slightly open, creating a tiny dark hole leading into this beefy hunk, untouched by human tongue.

And then, ever so slowly, I move my face in, nearing this rear entry to this high-school football hero, opening my mouth, sticking out my tongue, until finally – contact!

With the tip of my tongue I delicately travel around the wrinkled ridge of his asshole, surprised – as I always am on such occasions – at the silky softness of a part of the body which has such a base function and crude reputation.

"Oh!" from Norm, in the tone of "So that's what it feels like!"

I withdraw my tongue to ask, "You like that?"

"Yeah," in the tone of "Who'd ever have imagined it?"

I touch his butt hole with my tongue once again, reliving the thrill of that first contact. But this time I get a little bolder in my exploration, snaking it in a fraction of an inch.

I feel his body shift as he presses his head harder against the pillow and lowers his chest in an attempt to make his rear regions even more accessible to my probings.

By now, all my apprehensions that he might freak out on me are gone and I slip my tongue further into his hole. "Oh!"

And a little further.

"Ohhhh!"

I push his asscheeks as far apart as I can get them and probe still further.

"Oh, my God!"

And now I begin slipping my tongue in and out, listening to his moans – long drawn out ones and short staccato ones, rising and falling like a roller coaster ride – encouraging me to work my tongue inside him with complete abandon.

Then his body shifts, alerting me that he's now balancing himself to free his right hand so he can stroke his cock. At what better moment – when I've totally seduced him into the pleasure of a good rim job – to withdraw my tongue, and pull my face away.

"Huh? What's the matter?"

"Nothing. I just thought I'd get us some poppers."

I sit up, stretch over to my night table and pull out a small brown bottle.

"You ever had any, Norm?"

"Uh...I don't remember."

In other words "no." But Norm's always afraid the guys will think he's inexperienced when it comes to anything having to do with sex – which he pretty well is.

"Here. Now watch."

Norm sits up, resting his ass on the back of his heels to observe.

I shake the bottle, unscrew the cap and hold it up to my left nostril, blocking off the right one and inhaling, then repeating the process with the opposite nostril.

"Like that," I say, holding out the bottle for him.

Norm takes the bottle from me and inhales eagerly, perhaps taking in more than he should for a first time. As soon as he hands the bottle back to me, a worried look of "Maybe I shouldn't have done this!" crosses his face as I'm screwing the cap onto the bottle again.

I know I have to act quickly.

"Put your head on the pillow again, and stroke your cock," I hastily order him.

As he does, I move back into position behind him, quickly repositioning myself. Not wasting a second, I pull his asscheeks apart and stick my tongue in, probing his hole just in time to feel the effects of the poppers wash over me.

Then the poppers hit Norm full force also. His body shakes with his vigorous jacking off as he pushes his asshole out to welcome more of my tongue inside.

Well, the two of us go popper-high crazy. Norm stretches and strains his muscular body in all sorts of ways I can't keep track of, since I'm busy plowing my tongue up his ass and pushing my face forward like I'm trying to eat right through him. We become two wild, rutting animals, ferocious and helplessly uncontrollable in our need to satisfy our lustful instincts.

Somehow, Norm manages to twist around and flop onto his back, forcing my tongue to slip out of his asshole. I find myself lapping him under his balls with the flat of my tongue so fully extended out of my wide-opened mouth, my jaw's actually aching. After several slurps, I move up to his balls, pushing myself forward until the next thing you know my body shoots up between his bent legs until I find myself above him, supporting myself in push-up position.

I lower my face to kiss him. And again he turns his head aside!

Ah, the poppers are now wearing off, and he still can't abandon himself to a simple, direct kiss. So I kiss him on the throat instead, fighting off the desire to bite into his goddamn Adam's apple.

Then I move down to his chest and bite into the nub of his left nipple.

"Ouch!"

I let go and pull away. Surprisingly, he pushes my head forward again against his out-thrust chest. I bite into his nipple again. He lets go of my head, freeing me up so I can give it a good tug. He responds with a low, drawn-out moan.

"More poppers!" he says like his life depends on it.

I reach out to where I'd left the poppers on the bed. Not there. Shit, they must've rolled somewhere else!

I sit up and widen the area of my search, padding the palms of my hands around the disheveled bed.

"What's the matter?" Norm asks straining his head to see what's going on.

The poppers had somehow ended up at the foot of the bed. "The poppers. Here they are."

"Let me have some more, huh?"

"And then you'll fuck me?"

"Don't you want to rim me anymore?"

"You like that, huh?"

With an eager smile he says, "Yeah!"

Aha! Now to turn situation to my advantage!

"Well, that'll give you some idea why I want you to fuck me. Remember, that's what you wanted to do in the first place." "Okay. But, maybe you'll rim me again some other time?

And play with my nipples?"

Success! And this from the guy who up to three weeks ago was a complete virgin!

"Sure, Norm, but for now...

I stretch over the side of the bed and blindly search under it with my left hand until I locate the jar of Vaseline.

"Whatcha doing?"

"Vaseline," I say, pulling it out from under the bed and holding it up to him.

"See? It's just a lubricant. Now, lie on your back. Yeah, make yourself nice and comfortable."

Norm obediently complies. He folds the pillow over in half and shoves it behind his head, all propped up so he can watch me.

With my left hand, I scoop some Vaseline out of the container.

"First I'm going to get your cock all greased up. Something that big's gonna need some help getting inside me."

Flattered, he beams as he watches me prepare him.

I wrap the fingers of my right hand around his ballsac and tug at it, forcing his cock off his abdomen until I get it standing straight up.

I rub the Vaseline off along the underside of his cockshaft. Then I make a fist around his organ. My fingers can barely encircle it. I rotate my hand around his cock while gradually moving it up and down to spread the lubricant all over him. His dick surges with a sudden infusion of blood and he lets out a low groan.

I move my fist up around his cockhead and twist it like it was an uncooperative cap I was trying to screw loose from a bottle.

48

"Ah!" sharp and emphatic, as his mouth shoots open and he tosses his head from side to side to absorb the overflow of stimulation from his sensitive cockhead.

Once I have his dick all slick and shiny, I release his cock and balls, and dip my greasy fingers into the Vaseline again. Lifting myself off my heels and shoving my ass outwards, I reach around to lubricate my butt hole. My fingers inside my ass send waves of oozy pleasure along my cock that always make me feel like it's dripping honey.

"Okay," I finally say, "Do you want to mount me from the rear, doggie style, or do you want me to lie on my back? "Hmm...whichever you like, I guess."

After all, this isn't the type of decision Norm has to make every day of the week.

"I'll get on my back. That way I can watch you."

So we switch positions. I rest my head on the pillow and pull up my legs as Norm repositions himself between them. "Now, press your cockhead against my asshole."

He very carefully, very deliberately follows my instruction.

"Now put your hands behind my knees and push my legs back. Yeah, that's it. But further. Don't worry, I'm very limber. Okay, now shove it in."

Well, he gets me into position, and then moves himself back and forth on his knees until it's easy for him to apply a little pressure against my butt hole. Then he pushes.

Bingo! His cockhead slips in with no trouble at all.

"Now just keep pushing until you're all the way inside me." Slowly, inch by precious inch, he shoves his big fat cock into my asshole, filling me up and driving me crazy.

Eventually it can't go any farther. What a sight! His cock's lost to view, and all I can see down there is the overgrowth of his pubic hair spilling over the fork in my legs.

I grip my cock and slowly stroke it up and down while admiring the magnificence of his muscular torso rising above me as he strains to keep my legs pushed back and his cock planted all the way up my ass.

"Am I doing it right?"

Are you ever! Now, just push it in and out, like this," I say, indicating he should imitate my jack off strokes.

Well, the first several times he seems to have a lot of difficulty. But with a little more pressure against the back of my legs, pushing my knees up almost over my shoulders, and with readjusting his own until he finds just the right position, he finally manages to establish the easy in-out rhythm he needs.

It isn't long before sweat appears on his forehead, highlighting the strained, intense look on his face. His mouth hangs open and his eyes looked glazed over with heavy concentration. I reach over for the poppers, shake them up, unscrew the cap. "Here."

Resting his cock half in, half out of me, he leans his head forward. I place the bottle under one nostril while blocking up the other. He inhales deeply like someone underwater for too long. Then we take care of his other nostril.

I press the poppers to my own nose and take two efficient inhalations, quickly screwing the cap back on the bottle and tossing it to my side.

I look up at Norm towering above me – massive chest, powerful arms and hard, flat abdomen – holding me spread apart as his cock fills my ass. I savor this perfect moment as I feel the tidal-wave effect of the poppers surge through me.

Norm groans and slowly works his cock in and out of my butt hole, clearly spurred onwards by the powerful inducement of the poppers.

To think, this guy plowing me up the ass is someone I've known all my life; not just some number I'd met in a bar or behind the bushes in the Fens. I mean, we were kids down the street from each other, we were in the same first grade class, and we graduated together.

The popper high passes. Were so settled into each other, its like we could fuck and cock stroke our way through eternity.

Oddly, I suddenly become aware of the noise that's been floating through the window from the kids playing outside, just like we used to when we were their age.

"I see London, I see France, I see Bobby's underpants!" someone chants in a singsong voice, followed by a chorus of high-pitched squeals.

As the noise dies down, I hear the insistent creak of the bed swaying under the force of our activity, rocking back and forth like we were two kids in a playground testing the limits of some new amusement.

We're going at it like two animals. The headboard starts slamming against the wall. Sweat begins to trickle down from Norm's armpits, our breathing becomes fast and heavy, and the air in the room seems to become thicker and more humid.

Through the window comes another wave of shrieking laughter.

Norm stares me right in the eyes. It's clear we're connecting on some level that runs deeper than the raw frenzy of the moment in which we're rapidly approaching orgasm.

His fuck strokes quicken, turning brutally insistent. With each thrust the headboard bangs loudly against the wall behind it. "Ah! Ah! Ah!" the two of us chant, blocking out the noise of the kids outside.

And then, with one loud, prolonged "Aaaaah!" Norm thrusts his cock all the way into me and holds it there, letting his cum gush out, warm and abundant. At the same time, my own cock releases spurt after spurt of jism that lands all over my chest, my face, and (which I didn't discover until afterwards) the headboard.

After a pause, Norm quickly withdraws his cock and violently rams it into me a second time. Then a third, fourth, and fifth time, forcing all the cum out of his cock, the loud knocking of the headboard against the wall recording each new gusher. Soon he comes to a stop, resting his cock inside me. By now I've worked all the cum out of my own dick. Still holding it in my fist I rest my hand on my abdomen and watch as he very carefully, very slowly pulls his cock out of me. It's already softening and hangs fat and shiny between his legs.

Norm lowers my legs until my feet rest on the bed and sits between them with his ass on his heels.

I reach under the bed, feel around, and grab the trick towel I always keep there just in case. Then I move to a sitting position and go to wipe off his cock.

"Whattaya doing!"

"Cleaning you off, stupid. What's the problem?"

"Oh. Yeah," he says, laughing with embarrassment. But as I begin to clean his cock it's clear he doesn't feel comfortable about it.

So I say, "You're a big enough boy to do it yourself. Here." "Thanks."

As Norm takes the towel from me and wipes the Vaseline off his cock, there's an uncomfortable silence between us. Just like three weeks ago – when I gave him that blow job – neither one of us knows what to say now that we've shot out loads. And we can't just pass it off this time as one of those things that occasionally happens between two guys.

Norm's finished cleaning off his dick. He looks at the towel like he doesn't know what to do with it.

"Just throw it under the bed. I'll deal with it later."

He does, and moves to a sitting position, feet on the floor, looking down between his legs with his hands on the edge of the bed. He's deep in thought.

Finally, still looking down, Norm says softly, "Does this mean I'm gay?"

"I dunno. Does it?"

He looks me right in the eyes. I have never seen him look so sad in his life. I could swear he's on the verge of tears. But all he says is "Hmh."

He places his right hand on my right ankle and slowly moves it up my leg, following with his eyes. He stops at my kneecap. "Whatcha doin', Norm?"

He doesn't respond. Instead he leans forward between my legs. Is he going to try to blow me? But then he stops himself and sits up again.

After a pause he says, 'That health club you go to?' 'The Back Bay Health Club?"

"Yeah. Is everyone there like you?"

"You mean gay?"

"I guess so."

"No. It's pretty fifty-fifty. Wanna come with me some time? We can work out together."

"You'd let me do that?"

"Sure. Sundays I usually go around noon. Wanna meet me here tomorrow?"

"You bet. It's a date."

A date! A date with Norm!

And then, getting up, he asks "Mind if I take a shower?' " Go right ahead."

While Norm takes his shower, I lounge around on the bed, playing with my cock and thinking about how he's such a nice, sweet guy that I'd do anything for him.

The kids outside start screaming again. This time it's a battle of did so's and did not's.

To think, once upon a time we were the kids playing around out there.

Maybe you can say we're still playing around. But now we've taken our games inside. And have they ever changed!

"So then what happened?" Kevin asked, as he continued stroking his cock, which had been hard for quite some time now.

"I joined him in the shower, actually. We got horny all over again and then he let me fuck him!"

"Wait a minute," he said skeptically, though I could tell he was leaving room for the possibility.

"What do you think happened? When he was done with his shower, he put his clothes back on and left."

If I know Kevin, he was feeling just a little bit jealous right then. After all, he's always had the hots for Norm, too. Maybe even more than me. But I'm the one who got to suck his cock and then get him to fuck me. And now I've got a "date" with him to go to the Back Bay Health Club.

"So do you think he's gay?" Kevin asked after a pause.

"I don't know!" I heard myself snap at him in a voice full of annoyance, like I was trying to whack him in the face with my words.

Funny, but I kind of resented the question. It's like I was getting to feel a little protective about Norm.

"Aw c'mon, Tony!"

"No. I really don't know. Fuck, he doesn't know, himself. Hey! What the hell you doing?"

What happened was Kevin had pushed me over onto my side and had shoved his dick up between my asscheeks.

"I just want to feel where Norm's cock has been. Maybe slosh around in his cum."

"Speak about vicarious thrills."

"Yeah. You don't mind, do you?"

"Not if you don't mind sloppy seconds."

"Fuck you!"

"But you are, my dear, twisted friend, you are."

And as I felt Kevin's cock enter my ass I started to giggle, which Kevin didn't know what to make of.

It's just that it struck me funny that right then I should hear one single kid outside yell, "Ready or not, here I come!"

LIVING DANGEROUSLY
James Medley

Luke Summers was the most brazen, cock-hungry guy I ever knew. Farm boy-pretty is the only way I can describe him; you could almost visualize a stalk of oats hanging out of his sweet lips. I use that word advisedly, his lips are sweet, moist and full, incredibly kissable. He had short blond hair with a cowlick that hung seductively down over one of his robin's-egg blue eyes.

But Luke was butch as hell, even if he was pretty. And he would do absolutely anything to get his rocks off – as many times as possible. The boy was insatiable. The dirtier the sex, the better he liked it; I never heard Luke call anything kinky. He was into getting it on with straight guys, gay guys, butches, ferns, didn't matter, anything so long as it was male. One day he was an exhibitionist, the next a voyeur. He loved to be pissed on, with a little SM thrown in. And Luke had a mania for public toilets; I think the riskiness turned him on. Anything dangerous was right up Luke's alley. Any kind of fantasy got his juices flowing. And, lucky for me, one of his favorite fantasies was to have sex with a man in uniform.

When I first met Luke, I was on the road a lot, with the eastern half of Tennessee as my territory. Wearing my company's neatly starched blues, I drove a delivery route for a potato chip and snack company, calling on the little independent grocery stores in the isolated mountains, and the smaller ones around here in Cedar Flats, one of which was the neighborhood market Luke's parents owned. I remember when I first laid eyes on him filling orders for his father, I thought he was the cutest kid I'd ever seen. I soon got the impression Luke didn't think I was too bad either, because he'd always make it a point to stop what he was doing and come over and chat while I carefully restocked my display. Then one day when his parents were gone visiting relatives and Luke was minding the store alone, I made one of my routine stops. There were no customers in the store and Luke was crouched down behind the counter, propping his head up with his elbows gazing at me with those striking blue eyes. Although it took much effort to concentrate, I managed to restocked my display and total the bill. When I presented it to him, he bent down behind the counter then came back up.

"I can't get this door unstuck," he said in his reedy voice. Can you give me a hand, Ben?"

I stepped around the counter and didn't see the door he was talking about. What I did see was his cock. Hard. He had hauled his monstrous meat out of his tight Levis and was holding it tight at the base, his pee-hole open and round, a clear bead of dick-drool, oozing from the hole, staring at my face, which must have turned twenty shades of red.

"I've got a little problem with this too, Ben," he said, wagging it at me like a club.

"Ain't nothin' little about it," I managed to say. But it is obvious you have a problem."

"Wanna suck it off for me?" he asked, grinning.

I threw a boner like a baseball bat, no slow swelling thing, but an immediate and intense, turgid erection.

"Hadn't you better lock the front door?" I asked by way of assent.

"Nah, I don't mind. I keep it out half the time I'm back here anyway. I always do when you come in, Ben."

No power on earth could have prevented me from dropping to my knees and going down on him. His meat was cut but had a big fleshy patch of cock-skin lumped up below the swollen glans. It was darker than the rest of his gleaming red cock. I swirled my tongue all over the cock-head and lapped at his lube-juice drooling out. That hunk of dick-skin was fleshy and rubbery and I licked on it like an ice cream cone, all upward slurps to the head. I sheathed his knob between my lips and he bent over and started feeling my prod. I thought I was going to shoot off in my uniform pants. All this time I'd been admiring this hot little kid and, all of a sudden, he comes on to me. I was in heaven as I slurped on his dick.

And then, just as quickly, I was in hell because the screen door opened and two women walked in. They were engaged in an animated conversation about the high cost of living. I pulled off Luke's cock in a flash, jerking my head away. Luke placed his hand on the back of my head and pushed it back on. "Keep sucking man," he hissed under his breath, leaning down and tonguing the words in. Then he moved my shoulders, indicating I should get under the counter. There was enough space under there and I did. I went back to sucking on his juicy root, trying not to make any noise. "Good mornin' ladies," Luke said, as cool as you please. "Let me know if I can help you with anything."

I slowed my sucking, savoring the taste of the kid's tender meat. I got it down my throat till my neck bulged out. But there was no way I could take it all. I unzipped my pants and dragged out my own leaking rod. Just as slowly, I masturbated. Luke stood there watching the women making their selections. I sucked. They finished and brought their purchases to the counter.

"That'll be all today?" Luke asked brightly.

"Oh yes," one of them answered. "It's so hot outside, we don't feel like lugging too much home."

"It's hot inside too," Luke said, ringing their order. "Real hot." "Are you coming to the church social Friday night, Luke?" the other woman asked.

"Oh, yes ma'am, I'm sure gonna come."

And he did. Breathing normally and talking to the ladies about their church, he flushed a gusher of sweet jizz down my gullet, just muscle-jerking his juice out in heavy spits. I swallowed and swallowed; I loved his mellow boy-seed.

When Luke finished bagging the women's groceries, counting out their change and they had left, he went down on me. He'd barely gotten his smallish lips around my root before I unloaded what seemed like a bucket of cream down his throat. He sucked it hungrily and wanted more. As he was licking me off, he jacked himself off, then ate his own spunk when it came in his hand.

I was twenty-five then but don't look any different now; sandy hair, thin, a dark complexion and wiry, and "kinda sexy," I've been told.

Though I was fascinated with Luke's virile nature, raw uninhibited sexuality, and reveled in the excitement of sharing sex with him, there was more than a little jealousy in my feelings for the boy. I would like to have had Luke all to myself and not share him with anyone. Unfortunately, that was not the case. But those very qualities which attracted me to him, were the same ones which prevented that sort of monogamous relationship. On those occasions when he would visit my house, I delighted in our spirited, animal-like sex. And I loved being with him by myself. After the first year, I was in love with Luke in the worst possible way. I had told him so.

"You've gotta realize Ben," he'd said. "I'm a whore. I don't want to settle down with anyone. I like sex and I like men and I like a lot of them. It wouldn't work. I just want to be best friends and fuck-buddies. Understand?"

Over the next several months my love had evolved, becoming an almost paternal kind of love, as if he was my gay son. When I was fourteen, I admitted to myself I was gay and after that never bothered going through the pretense of dating for the rest of my high school years. I had no regrets except that I did like children and often wished I had a son. Luke became my son. He was also became an obsession with me. I kept telling myself I should stay away from him, but I couldn't, so I accepted being only a small part of his life; it was my only way to be near him,

One afternoon, Luke and I were lounging around my apartment after a particularly athletic romp between the sheets, and he confided some of his secrets to me.

"I know old Miss Tenpenny that works in the dime store shaves her crotch. Ugly old thing."

"How would you know that, Luke?'

"I peeped in her bedroom window one night and saw'er lying there naked."

"Going for old ladies now, huh, Luke?"

"No, Ben. Her boss, Grover was in there with her. He's got a big prod and he was fucking the living bejesus out of her. From the window, I could see that old fucker ramming into her naked gash."

I knew this was another of Luke's bizarre sexual practices, sneaking around at night and peeping into bedrooms, masturbating if he caught any action. I had warned him of the serious consequences should he be caught doing this. Luke knew more about the affairs and sexual preferences than anybody in town as a result. He could tell you who was cheating on his wife, with whom and how often, what they did to each other in bed and so forth. Certainly was more aware of people's private lives than any of the residents of our small town would suspect. He said I was the only person he told this to. Through Luke, my knowledge of our quaint little town's inhabitants was vast.

"I really like you Ben," Luke said.

"I like you too, Luke," I said. "Perhaps too damn much." "But we're having fun, ain't we? Isn't that what's life is all about?"

"Some people think there are other things, Luke, things more important than sex."

Luke was silent for several minutes, staring off into space. Then he smiled and said, "Hey, Ben, sex makes the world go around. You know, people makin' babies and havin' fun doin' it."

But there is a dichotomy, Luke, between our animal and spiritual natures."

"A what?"

"A dichotomy. Two sides. It's like it takes both to make us complete, humans. What do you do during those hours when you're not fucking?"

He chuckled. "Think about fuckin'."

"Be serious, Luke. You have a fine mind, you should develop it. Would you like to go to college?

"Nah. I ain't too much for books. Unless they're fuck books." Exasperated, I threw up my hands. "What am I gonna do with you, boy?"

Luke smiled. "You could fuck me again."

"Get serious. Is this a reputation you feel like you have to work at or something?"

He shook his head sadly, as if I was missing the point." I know I'm not like everybody else. I don't want to be like everybody else. It's not that I don't want to grow up. I have. More like – I still want to feel like a kid. Y'understand?"

I nodded.

He went on, "See, the way I look at it, people grow up and he went on, "You see, the way I look at it, people grow up and they stop seem' things in the way a kid sees 'em, in magical ways. Our little old town was magic for me when I was younger. The river was magic, flowing like it did past me, going to somewhere I'd never been. I could sit on the bank and look at it and it was like the river talked to me and told me about its travels, where it had been, where it was going, how it wound through the countryside and past strange cities, making me feel like I'd been there along with it.

"Places like Oz in that movie were real in my mind. I don't ever want to stop seem' faces and animals in the clouds, or hearing the birds sing in the morning. There's a mockingbird outside my window and if I didn't hear it every morning, I'd feel like something died inside of me. Shucks, I can't explain it very well."

"You're doin' well. Go on."

"Well, I know I've got to have responsibility and all, worryin' about the bills like my folks do, but I still want to keep from growin' old like them. That's all they think about, makin' more money. But it just doesn't seem that important to me. As long as I've got a roof over my head and food in my belly and a friend like you and enough cock, what else do I need?"

"I guess we're a lot alike, Luke," I said dreamily. As he was talking, I had gone into a near reverie of reflecting upon my own youth. "You see, that's exactly why I'm driving a potato chip truck. I didn't go to college. My parents offered to pay my tuition but I was more interested in dick. And then I met you and I understand a little of the way they feel about their kids."

You mean breeders?"

"Yes, if you want to call them that. It's a nasty word and I don't much care for it. But I can see why they would like to have the best they can get for their children. Like you. I'd like to pay for you to go to college. I make enough, I can swing it. What do you say Luke?"

"I don't think so, Ben. I ain't cut out for it."

"Did you ever read Huckleberry Finn?"

"No."

"Then I'm going to give you my copy. I think you're still young enough to appreciate it, seeing things the way you do." Luke shrugged. "Okay."

I sought to expand the dimension of our relationship beyond the sexual. I wanted to possess Luke's mind if I couldn't have his body all to myself. And I resolved to make that my goal, my purpose for the rest of my life.

I started to sing. "Oh Susannah, don't you cry for me. I'll be coming from Alabama with a banjo on my knee."

Luke took up the second line. "Rained so hard the day I left, the weather it was dry. Sun's so hot, near froze to death, ah, ah – can't seem to remember the next line."

"Susannah don't you cry," I finished for him.

I was as happy as I'd ever been in my life. He slept with me that night.

The following week, the entire town was buzzing with the news about Miss Tenpenny and Grover's disappearance. Grover's wife was bemoaning the loss of her husband at Summer's Market.

"Of course I didn't say anything to her about it," Luke told me that night. "I didn't let on like I knew anything."

I was savoring the feel of Luke's magnificent young body which I'd just been inside of. He was idly toying with my limp penis.

"You're going to get caught some day Luke. The laws are pretty strict about peeping toms," I admonished him again.

"I ain't hurting anybody. If folks don't want to be looked at, they should keep their blinds closed and their lights turned off." "I suppose you know the ones who don't keep their lights turned off pretty well by now, huh? Have a regular little route probably."

"Somethin' like that. I know the mayor's old lady likes to get choked when she comes."

"I've read about that. It sounds kind of dangerous." "Yeah, I don't think I'd like it."

"Thank God! Finally, something you don't want to experiment with."

"You still ain't shaved me like Miss Tenpenny."

"We'll get around to that. Who else is getting poked these days?"

"Well, you know the twin brothers, Johnny and Cleatus Budreaux, work in the mill?"

"Yes. What about them?"

"They swap their wives all the time. And they watch each other fuck them. One night, after they'd gotten the broad off and she had gone back to her house, Cleatus went down on Johnny. The way he did it, you could tell they'd been doing it for years."

"Don't tell me. That's going to be your spring and summer project, to make it with them?"

"Well – "

You already did?"

"Just one. Cleatus."

I knew Cleatus and Johnny Budreaux from the local tavern. They were Cajuns who had moved here from the bayou country of Louisiana and, I'd always thought, were as mean as cat shit. Rednecks, they fought incessantly in the bar, carrying a chip on their shoulders you could make two-by-fours out of, daring anyone to knock it off. You could hardly tell them apart since they were both dark and swarthy, rough looking customers. Their faces looked like two miles of bad road.

"How did you do that?" I asked, not really wanting to know. "Same as you. Under the counter."

I shivered visibly at the picture, jealous. I had cherished that memory as something special between us.

Luke could read it in my eyes. He was so damn perceptive towards sentiments and he could sense men's attraction to him in an uncanny way. The kid should have been a psychologist, he had such a natural ability.

"But he was nowhere near as good as you, Ben, can't suck cock for shit," Luke said earnestly.

"You have such a delicate way of putting things, Luke. I don't want to hear about it."

"Well, you were out of town. What's a guy supposed to do?"

"Certainly not keep your dick in your pants. That would be asking too much."

"Aw, Ben, don't be like that man. Shit, you're the only person I have to talk to, tell about what I see and feel and all. Don't get jealous man, it's just seven ccs of body fluid."

"What?"

"Seven cc's. I measured 'em. I jacked off in this little prescription bottle last week. After I came, I set the bottle behind my bed. When the juice was all drained down to the bottom, that's how much it was, seven cc's."

"You really believe that, don't you Luke, that that's all there is to it? Squirt a little juice and there's nothing else?"

"It seems pretty clear to me. I don't know why folks make such a fuss about it. It's not like anybody was going to get pregnant or anything. What's the big deal?"

"Maybe someday you'll find out."

"And maybe not. Did I tell you about Susie the Slut comin' onto me?"

"No."

"Yeah. I was sitting in my place down on the river last week. I'd finished all my chores early and took the afternoon off. Old Susie comes up to me, starts in about how she never made it with me, telling me how cute I was, how much she'd like to. I didn't want to hurt her feelings so I told her if she had a brother as good looking as she was, I'd grab him in a New York second. Course that pissed her off and she threatened to tell everybody in town that I was queer. 'Go ahead,' I tell her. 'I'll have more customers than you.' She lit off like a house afire."

"That doesn't bother you, people knowing you're gay?"

"Like having blonde hair and blue eyes?" He chuckled. "Hell, I was born this way and wouldn't have it any different. I love it. I love bein' gay, and can't imagine anything but."

I just shook my head.

"Hey, would you come with me one night, Ben, out peeping?"

"Are you out of your gourd boy?"

"Aw, Ben, why don't you live a little dangerously, take a chance now and again? Besides, I get lonely out there all by myself. I see people inside their warm little houses, making each other feel good. And here I am outside, whacking off alone. C'mon, man."

Luke wheedled and cajoled like that for twenty minutes, finally telling me about two guys who lived about four miles outside of town.

"I'd go out there more often except it's so far. And I made the trip a couple of times and didn't see them. We could use your van. They really get it on. And you know something else?"

"What?" I asked, growing impatient with Luke's insistence. "I think they know I'm watching."

"What makes you think that?"

"They put on a special show, making sure I see everything. They're both farmers and pretty young and real good looking. C'mon, Ben, go with me."

Feeling as weak as a drained dish towel, I reluctantly assented to his request. I suppose I was half mad with jealousy and desire to be with him, was honored that he would want me, wanted to share his secret vice. That little bit about being alone had done it. I threw all caution to the wind and said, "Yeah, sure."

"Good. Now shave me."

I went to the bathroom and got my razor and shaving cream. I snagged a towel from the rack. When I returned, Luke was hard again, lying on his back with his fat poker in one hand, cupping and fondling his balls with the other. Just insatiable, as I've said.

As I crawled onto the bed and kneeled beside him, Luke put his hands behind his head and watched me. His chest was as hairless as a baby's butt anyway so I smeared up his groin with the thick white cream and worked it over his genitals. He got a satisfied look in his eyes as I held his cock aloft and started shaving his thick blond pubic hair. I didn't expect this would be any great turn-on for me, but as I pulled the razor through the foam and saw Luke's smooth young crotch revealed without any hair, my dick jerked to attention. I carefully skinned off all the luxuriant pubic hair at his groin and wiped it on the towel.

Luke could muscle-jerk his big cock so that it slapped his belly like a drum. He began doing that, keeping one hand behind his head and stroking my hard meat with the other. His cock thumped his belly. Now my balls and ass," he said.

He splayed his legs as wide apart as they would go and I shaved his balls till they were bare and glistening. Then he turned onto his belly and I pulled his ass-ditch apart and took the can of shaving cream and foamed it off in there. Then I smeared him up good, up his crack and covering his butt-globes till he looked like he was wearing underwear.

His hand on my cock and mine up his butt-trench, was about to bring me off again. Meticulously and cautiously, I shaved him till his rosy little pucker was winking from his bare butt like a star at center stage.

The way Luke kept hunching his buttocks up and down, pushing back onto my hand, let me know what he wanted then. I spit on my hand and glided my middle finger between his slickened up crack.

"Put it in me," he whispered huskily. I teased his bare hole then gradually eased my finger in. Inside of Luke, his flesh was tender and soft, like a dark, rich pudding. I worked another finger in and juicily fucked him with them. "More," he groaned. Three fingers and he squirmed and wriggled. Four fingers tightly together, I eased up his asshole. He moaned sharply. Five and he started humping the sheets. Past the knuckles and up to the flat of my hand, I got my gooey fist inside him, inside his clean, sweet hole. I swabbed his ass-walls with my fist, around and around, gyrating my hand. I twisted my fist up to my wrist. Luke grunted and panted. W e ha d never done this before, something in the outer reaches of my experience. I wasn't certain I was ready for it then. I held my fist still, feeling his muscles slowly relaxing. I rotated my wrist in soft gentle motions, letting him get used to my arm filling him. He was ready for more.

I eased my forearm up his chute, funneling my way to his depths. His bunghole stretched to accommodate me. The wrinkles of his pucker smoothed and gripped my arm, his bunghole stretching to accommodate me. The hair on my arm was soon soaked with his juices. It trailed over his naked skin like the soft tendrils of a grapevine.

I was in him all the way. The bulge of my muscle before the elbow wedged him apart.

"Fist-fuck me, Ben," he sighed. "Fist-fuck me till I cum. Make me come."

Now this is going to sound strange, but it was like a solemn ceremony, just Luke's soft sighs and repressed breathing, no loud grunting and groaning, no frenzied rutting, no dirty talk, a silent communion with Luke's most secret insides, the middle of him, his essence, core.

Luke pulled my body down till my groin was at his head. He turned his face sideways and tenderly sucked on my cock as I explored his most sensuous pit. I reached a hand under his moving inside him, kneading and working on the inside wall of his belly. His hard cock was hot against the back of my pressed hand.

This boy was what I lived for and I possessed him that way. He was totally at my mercy, allowing me, trusting me, letting me penetrate his young body to the very center of his being, a union so complete that I dominated him totally, was one with him, joined, united as he sacrificed himself to me. For those few minutes, I owned him. He offered a total consecration to my needs and his. I dedicated myself to pleasing him. It is difficult to describe; as though our carnal act was a mental fuck of searing proportions, a near religious ritual, if you will.

Inside of Luke's tender young body, I felt his thoughts and desires. I understood him and knew him in a way I had never done before. He consecrated himself to me and I felt sanctified. Impaled on my arm, Luke seemed to experience all his most intense sensations, now shivering and trembling, now taut and relaxing, sucking my cock slowly then harder, biting occasionally. I didn't care. I would have done anything for this boy. He was mine.

And then I came. He swallowed my milk and I thought of it as a kind of communion. Then he came on my hand; that, I decided, was a baptism. All in all, it was a glorious celebration of the flesh. My reward for living dangerously.

- This story has been adapted from material appearing in the author's forthcoming collection, "Country Boys, City Boys."

A NIGHT AT THE NOTCH
T. B. Davis

August 14

A roadside picnic area by day, a rollicking sex haunt by night, Girty's Notch is bounded on one side by the highway and on the other by the forested islands dotting the mile-wide Susquehanna River. Folklore has it named for its rock cliffs as an Indian trail mark; the government has the Notch registered as a natural site possessing unusually scenic beauty. For once, they got something right, because some truly unusual scenic beauties can be found among the many who linger in the fanciful shadows cast by a full moon.

These are the men who prefer a sexual alternative: night cruising for group action. There is the usual eye-balling in the parking area, a mind-game to reassure even the best sexperts that no one present for the night party is a basher, vice cop, or worst of all, a sexual psychopath. Once knowing smiles are exchanged, the men who love men, like myself, undo their tight jeans for an orgasmic feast meant to thrill the best aficionados of sweaty hot mansex.

When I go to the Notch, I know what I want, yes, what I need: to drown my rock-hard body amidst a group scene with totally naked, hard-driving, muscular jocks.] am driven by primitive urges to share in the chase and capture with like-minded, sexually uninhibited cock-and-ball worshipers. All public, promiscuous, and perverted.

Wearing a tight pair of black 501's, a red body shirt, and a starched jock, I spread-eagled my tanned body upon a shellacked picnic table. Casually smoking a Marlboro, I gazed at the Milky Way, fantasizing that each star was a man, that every stellar pulse was that man's throbbing, shiny cockhead. I felt my groin swell, undid the five snaps, and began to ease myself into that manly art of slow, prolonged, repeatable masturbation. Every masculine dude knows his cock was meant to be jacked-off by his own sure hand. Here's the routine: Very lightly stroke. Increase then decrease the rhythm. Rub the bloated flesh with stiff fingers. Squeeze the purplish glans head. Jerk it hard to erectile perfection. Hold it straight up. Let flaccidity soften the alerted dick. Repeat the process. Feel the heat of your exploding cum spray the upper torso, full face, and beyond.

In my peripheral vision I noticed voyeurs, three of them, all of them good-looking studs. I raised my back and shed the body-hugging red shirt, hoping the sight of my hairy chest, squeezable nips, and muscle-rippled stomach would stall thought and jump-start some action.

A lean, twenty-something stud grabbed my freestanding pecker with a tight grip. I leaned over to see his own cock was jutting forward. The other two stood nearby, stroking their dangling cocks and balls: still waiting, forever willing. My mouth began to water. Gazing a last moment at the stars twinkling in the sky, I shut my eyes. I silently begged all three of them to lightly rub then wildly whack their stiff pricks on my roughly whiskered face. The image of sucking all three god-like cockheads at once sent my body into a sweaty shake.

I doubled the top man's grip on my cock, now streaming precum. After lifting my jock-strapped, bubble-butted ass, my unknown master stripped me clean. My outstretched, now fully nude, prostrate body was his. A light summer's wind aired my best gifts for all their lips, mouths, and tongues: a seven-inch bulbous cock, swollen low-hanging nuts, and a pre-stretched sweet-tasting manpussy.

The acknowledged leader, his knowing face all smiles and his uncut dick all action, expertly balanced his protruding privates over my face. The sight of his mushroom-headed cock, immense downy balls, and self-lubed rosebud was a night wanderer's dream made real.

Having fully exposed their spongy, triangular crotches, the other two playmates now stood on both sides of the picnic table, their moistened horse-dicks straining for a spontaneous foursome.

Very slowly I tongue-twirled my partner's cockhead, carefully nibbled at its heart-shaped underside, then mouth-locked his bloated knob. A final dart into his flanged pisshole drove him to whack his donkey dick across my face. 'Take my big dick, man. Take and suck it whole!"

"Yeah," I groaned, "give me that dick bone. I want to deep throat it all night long!"

"Take it... Be my slut... Swallow my load!"

I anticipated my throat muscles contracting upon his reddened cock meat and, just before the oral plunge, I yearned for all four of us to get head rushed by the irresistible scent of heavy poppers and musky underarms. I thought about a frisky four-way with group oil massage, mouth-watering cock sucking, voyeuristic piss action, and finger-mouth anal probes. As his cock engulfed me, burying as it did to where his whispy crotch hairs smothered my face, I felt we were both on fire: our lock unbroken, uninterrupted, un-endable.

"Suck on my nuts," he said softly.

First I caressed and stretched his ballsac to gauge its miraculous diameter. I tried in vain to snare orally his two heavy balls at once, but due to their mass, I had to alternate between each. I bit for even heavier ball play. We were both almost oblivious to either time or place. I twisted his nutsack and mouth-gripped them as hard as possible. Sensing he felt pleasure, not pain, I stuck my middle finger into his scrotum to massage his own asshole.

"Eat my ass, man...Come on, bury your face in my hole!"

"No," I replied, my gaze now fixed on the two onlookers.

He stood up, ignoring his stark nakedness, and my eyes were fixed on the manly grandeur of his rotating underside. "Be my man. What do you say we rim these two guys"?

At his question, the other two hunky men backed off slightly to regroup under the canopy of a stately oak tree.

A force beyond impulse overwhelmed me. I was compelled to be the night tryst's bottom man, par excellence. As if to prove it, I crawled butt-naked on all fours toward the over branching tree. A good-looking, bare-chested trucker parked his rig just off the adjacent highway and the streaming lights semi-floodlit my arched, snow-white backside. I imagined him as a state trooper spotlighting my public park nakedness, warning me of lewdness, then joining in the lucky fun.

Reaching the old oak, I stood up, relieving my hot man piss at the base of its trunk. The other three men did likewise, enjoying the backsplash of the golden gift upon our strong, widespread legs. We had marked our spot with the most unmistakable of male urges. Without speaking, we began the moonlit rite of homosexual thanksgiving.

The lanky, well-hung, uncut man with soft, shoulder-length blond hair amongst us four leaned against the bark. He had the face of an Adonis, the sex organ of an Eros. His partner, who never spoke a word, was cruise-wise to uncircumcised penile pleasures. With a tin of jellied lubricant he gently massaged the soft, smooth foreskin until the leg-straddled man's wet, glistening cockhead emerged oozing with clear, sticky precum. Belly flat on the thick green grass, I raised my face to receive its wavering strand. Flexing three well-greased fingers, the unspoken man then massaged his blond, hairy manhole as my picnic table buddy sucked wildly on his meaty, retracted cock.

The distance driver killed his truck lights. Only the close sound of the easy flowing river and surprise glow of airborne fireflies enveloped our masculine rendezvous.

Sweating profusely from the sheer exhilaration of receiving a synchronized finger-fuck and blowjob, the tree-leaning stud shouted out.

"Oh guys! Don't fuckin' stop! It feels so good. Make it last, make it hotter!"

The three of us turned him around to oil and massage his broad, tanned shoulders and ivory butt. We all repeated the same adjectives: "Fucking hot...Yeah...Fucking hot. Oh yeah, oh yeah! Man!"

My top man began to eat his golden-haired ass. His tongue darted in and out, overshooting the pink rosebud, his mouth finally echoing loud suck sounds from within the tastiest recesses of the fully bent, heavily moistened, receiver's ass.

As the lube man swallowed the blonde's pulsating prick, I repositioned myself in a tuft of grass to watch the hormonally-charged movements and I felt as if I was being mesmerized by a triple-X-rated homemade video. Close to a blood-blistered dick, I jacked-off so intensely my cock felt like it was on the verge of its best distance shot. I got up and slimed the blonde's balls with my own spit, then, this time, swallowed both of his shaven nuts whole. Only half-satisfied, I directed rapid kisses to every inch of inter-male sex contact. Then, in my drooling finale, I lovingly tongue-lashed the lube man's dancing prick, sucked the top man's ass-eating mouth, and shot a load of cum upon the blonde's curvaceous ass.

Retrieving my clothes, I wished them triple luck, Notch-style.

ONE OF JIMMY'S FRIENDS
H.G. Mann

It's another day when nothing's happening; some days are just that way. The promise of adventure usually doesn't call ahead and say here I come, get ready.

The weather has turned sour, like the second day after you burn your tongue on some hot instant because you didn't want to fix the good stuff. There's too much wind to open the windows and it's too damn muggy with the sea air to feel cool. I flip on the AC and try to entertain myself with the latest issue of PC magazine. Just as I am getting to the really good parts, I hear footsteps on the front stairs. I know most of the regulars by now and these are loud, unfamiliar footsteps. A shadow across the window reeled me into the action. I rise to answer the knock on the door.

It's one of Jimmy's friends: A tall, dirty-blond, green-eyed youth who has stopped by a couple times in the past month. He rides his bike out from town. It's a long ride and today it's very warm: his red T-shirt is damp and there is a thin sheen of sweat on his forehead.

I've been wary of this one from the beginning. He likes to talk about getting arrested and going to jail, not my favorite topics. I watch him, in a casual way, and listen with one ear.

He never sparked my fuse before but times are slow and... maybe it's time to take this one for a test ride. You know, check out the gears, try the seats, maybe get a look under the hood, check out the size of the trunk.

I get him a beer from the kitchen while he uses the remote control to find a kick-boxing event on TV. He drains the can as the chat nicely turns to being in shape. Mostly his, and how many pushups he's pumping these days. I offer him a new event, Marine-style. You know, raise your feet eighteen inches or so off the floor by resting them on something and then proceeding to pump, from the fingertips.

He tries a few from this new angle and is impressed by the extra force. He offers how he often does regular pushups with a friend, who weighs 205, sitting on top of him.

"Really?"

"Yeah."

"How 'bout doing some with me leaning on you?" "Sure," he says as he reaches for the floor again.

My hands resting on his back, he easily runs through a series of ten of these.

"How about sit ups?" I offer as he turns over to sit. "Okay."

I sit on top of his now outstretched legs and he begins a rapid session of quick far aways and real close toe's as I count in my head. Thirty, fifty, seventy five, ninety one, two, three, seevveenn, eeiigghhtt, nniinneee, a hundred.

He has reached his limit; now he's hot, sweaty and tired. He is also showing a bit of a hard-on through his dirty denim cut-offs. I lift up the bottom of his T-shirt and draw it up to his chin, then off. Now I get my first look at his chest: smooth, hairless, not a scar or blemish to be seen. His nipples are dark and broad. At the waist, not a trace of dark hair, only the light blond tiny hairs of youth. This is better than I could have imagined. He lets me massage that firm stomach and chest and I pause to feel the soft orbs with their now projecting points. I move up off his legs and rest in a sitting position over his crotch. A few wiggles and the now hardened member snuggles comfortably into position between my cheeks. My hands begin to play across his chest like a harpist with new strings, each sensation tingling my fingertips. He is smooth and warm everywhere: deltoids, biceps, triceps, pectoralis majors, and, I am sure, rectus abdominis. I slide down and bring my fingers to the button on his shorts, open it, then pull the zipper down. He lets me pull the shorts off him and now I am determined. The lowering of his shorts dragged on his underwear. Now the slight ridge at the base of his manhood shows revealing the small patch of fuzz that shadows the skin for a couple of inches around the base of the mast. The staff is large. A whopping eight inches, cut and very round.

But as fun as this was, I very much want to check out the other side. I raise myself and tug at his elbow letting him roll over onto his stomach. I lower the briefs further to reveal firm, tight buns. I slide back up again and wiggle into position. Nice. Jimmy said I'd like this one. I told him whenever he found a kid that needed some help, you know, a twenty for a blowjob, send 'em over. And I'm beginning to like this boy more and more. His back is every bit as delightful as his front. Smooth tan everywhere but the area below the waist. I begin to wonder what it would feel like to have him on top, thrusting into me. I would lie beneath him with that strong cock pushing between my legs. My hands would run the field of his backside, helping his motion with a grasp of those two halves. I imagine his breath on my neck and the weight of his torso pressing down on me, our chests rubbing, his nipples squashing down on me, when he rolls over, exposing fully now the erection. It throbs mightily and, for now, I am content to give him the relief he wants. It's worth a twenty and then some.

He holds my head down on it, forcing me to choke on it. He puts both hands on my head now, tugs at my ears, setting his own rhythm. It won't be long now...

WAITING FOR JOE
James Wallen

"Hi. This is Joe. Thanks for calling. I'm not able to come to the phone right now but if you'll leave your name and number, I'll get back to you just as soon as I can."

Chris hesitated, then put down the receiver. Should he go to the next name on his list? He reached for the classified and re-read Joe's entry: "Erotic massage – plus. Friendly nude jock 20, 5'9, 155, 29w, smooth, super defined. Call Joe anytime." An image of muscled youth fired his crotch. He re-dialed and left his message.

Stretching out on the hotel bed, Chris tried to relax but the waiting unnerved him. He rose and peered out the 15th story window into the thick night fog. A shiver of anxiety coursed through his body. Restlessly, he began switching TV channels. Finally the phone rang.

"Hello."

"Hi. Is this Chris?"

"Yes, it is."

"Chris, this is Joe."

"Hi Joe. Thanks for calling."

"Sure. So, what can I do for you?"

"Well ... I called in response to your ad."

"Yeah?"

"So maybe I could ask ... ask a few questions?"

"Shoot."

"Well ... do you make out calls?"

"Sure."

"Okay, and so, uh, could you tell me more about yourself."

"Sure. I'm clean-cut, brown hair, green eyes, big pets, narrow waist, tight bubble butt, well-hung and, yeah, I really like showing it off."

"How much does all that cost?"

"Eighty in, a hundred out."

"Okay."

"You're in Room 1537?"

"Right."

"You think I can pass through the lobby in my old 501's and a ski jacket?"

"Shouldn't be a problem. The elevator's on the left as you enter the lobby. If anyone stops you, just tell them you're a student coming for a tutorial and have them call me."

"Got it. Oh, one more thing: should this student wear Calvin's, a bikini, jockstrap, or zilch under his 501's?"

"Oh, briefs, so he can pose, tease, strip. But make those thin, white briefs, okay?"

"You got it. See you in fifteen minutes."

Chris busied himself with a fresh shave, shampoo and blow dry, put on a pair of boxer shorts. He fiddled some more with the TV, then switched on the FM, finding an easy rock station. Joe's relaxed telephone style had eased his nerves but anxiety mounted again as he waited. Could Joe have sensed it was his first time? Ten minutes. Twelve. Fifteen...he kept glancing expectantly at the door, then fine-tuned the radio, pulled the drapes over the window, tore up and sprinkled his penciled phone list into the waste basket beside the bed.

Seventeen. Twenty, twenty-five. Joe must have underestimated how long it would take. Chris studied his reflection in the closet mirror. Nautilus workouts at the gym were helping him ward off a mid-thirties decline. He dropped to the floor and whipped through a dozen push-ups, relishing the feel of pumped arm and chest muscles.

Thirty five minutes. He picked up the classifieds again. The sculpted pecs and ripped abs of a headless torso labeled "Scott" offered themselves for $150. Below, a photo of a slight Swede silhouetting a muskmelon ass and cactus spike nipples carried the caption: "Will rub you the right way." Most of the ads were without a photo. Chris had circled "Asian BB, 25, 28w, 5'6, 130. Hard as steel, smooth as silk, have a feel, spill your milk." And "Superhot athlete, bl, bl, 20, 5'10, 155, gymnast strips for you. See Cal come."

Chris looked at his watch. Forty-five minutes. He dialed Joe's number. "Hi. This is Joe...."

Nothing to do but wait. Maybe Joe got a call from someone more promising. After all, Chris hadn't told him anything about himself. Chris stretched out again, turned to a second page of circled classifieds. "Buffed black student, 6'2, 195, 20, muscle perfection, sensuous, safe, versatile. 24h, in/out, $75." Circled just below was: "Handsome, Hot, Horny. Jerry. 24h." Farther down the page: "GQ looks, smth, hard, tan, 5'11",160 lbs, fabulous chest, beaut. buns, pwrful thighs, endowed, mutual rub and JO. Call Tom, 5:30-10 eves, wkds anytime." Next column: "Student swimmer likes massage men 35-50. Will close books, shed bikini, concentrate on you. 23, 5'8, 140 dimpled butt ..." Chris dozed off.

The phone rang three times before he reached it. "Hello." The receiver slipped from his hand. "Sorry..."

"Chris? This is Joe. I took a spill on my motorbike on the way to your hotel. Got sideswiped. The street was wet and ... well, I had to get checked over at a clinic so I'd be covered by insurance. That's where I am now. Didn't mean to stand you up."

"Oh, no problem. Are you okay?"

"Yeah, they're about to release me."

"Good "

"So, Chris, it's about 10:30 ... are you still interested?"

"Well sure, if you are. If you're not feeling up to it that's okay. But, sure, it's fine with me. Depends on you."

"Okay, tell you what. How 'bout I come over, you give me a stiff drink, scotch if you've got it, and we'll see how it goes? No obligations either way. Suit you?"

"Yes. But take it easy, no rush. See you when you get here."

"Thanks, Chris, thanks a lot."

Chris didn't have any liquor in the room. He hardly ever drank. He dressed and went out, found a liquor store nearby, got some scotch. He filled the ice bucket with cubes from the machine down the hall, carefully positioned a couple of glasses on the bureau. He stripped back down to his boxers, brushed his teeth, did a new batch of push-ups, smoothed the bed, followed the slow advance of his watch.

There was a soft knock on the door. He froze. The knock was repeated but louder, more demanding. Fumbling with the chain lock, Chris opened the door.

There stood Joe in a dark blue ski jacket and well-worn 501s. He had a radiant smile despite a small bandage high on the left side of his forehead. He was, Chris decided, more incredible than he had fantasized. Sharp green eyes, wavy short-cropped, dark brown hair, ruddy cheeks, thick lips, strong chin.

As Joe stepped in, they shook hands briefly. "Where's the bar?" Joe asking, stepping deeper into the room. He removed his jacket and dropped it in a chair. He stood over the improvised bar and glanced back at Chris. You bought a bottle just for me?"

Chris stood by the door staring at his paid stud. "Yes."

Joe wore a dark green shirt that was secured by only one button at the waist, revealing thick nipples on a smooth, thickly mounded chest.

Turning his back to Chris, Joe asked, "You want one?" "No, no thanks."

Joe dropped two cubes in a glass and poured the scotch over them.

"So you hit your head and what else?" Chris said, walking up behind him.

"Scraped my leg." Joe pointed to a tear baring a white bandage beneath his Levi's. "But nothing's broken." He gulped his drink.

"Oh, dear."

"Hey, I'm fine. My Honda wasn't even scratched. Just me." "Have another..."

"Thanks," Joe said, turning back to the bar, pouring another strong one. "You must be some kind of a health nut. No drinking, helluva good body."

"Thanks," Chris said, dropping down onto the bed. "I work out, watch my diet. If you don't take care of yourself you go to pot. I want to still look good when I'm forty..." Chris suddenly felt self-conscious and he let his words trail off.

Joe finished his second drink. "Man, this is good scotch."

"Your nerves calm yet?"

Joe laughed. "I'm gettin' there. I hope you don't think I'm a drunk or somethin'. I just need to relax a bit."

"Why don't you have another one and then sit down, over here, next to me?" He patted the mattress.

Joe poured another, then fell to the bed. "Hey, Chris, you know something? I'm new at this. Totally. No shit! I got laid off and somebody told me I should do this, staked me for the ads, but I don't know if I'm cut out for it. Maybe I had the accident because I was nervous. All the way over here, I was thinking, 'What am I doing? What will he be like, what will he look like?' But I sure never expected -

"Expected what?"

"Well, that you'd be – " Joe finished his drink, set the glass on the floor.

"Be what, Joe?"

"Well, you're a handsome guy. Don't ever let anybody tell you you aren't."

"I won't."

"You don't need to call a service, Chris."

"I'm a stranger in town and I have only tonight. I didn't want to take any chances."

Fingers trembling, Chris undid the one fastened button of Joe's shirt, exposing and caressing the sharp contours and taut nipples of the boy's sculpted chest. Moaning softly, Joe reached over and brushed a throbbing mound of cotton-covered cock. Chris tugged at the open shirt tucked into his 501's and pulled it out and off. He gasped, shook his head, took a deep breath then began fondling the nipples that jutted impudently above Joe's abdominal ladder. "Christ, you're unbelievable!"

69

"So are you ... unbelievable," Joe murmured, gently groping the cock that pulsed under Chris' briefs.

"So, Joe, did you remember to wear thin white ones?" Chris asking, pinching Joe's left nipple.

"Why don't you find out?" He squeezed back on Chris' cock.

Slowly, Chris unfastened the 501's, unveiling a white bikini which, detached by a raging hard-on, gaped forward from his corrugated midriff. Reaching behind, Chris eased Joe's jeans over the asscheeks, thick thighs and tapered calves. He removed Joe's boots and then tugged the jeans completely off.

"Okay!" Joe shouted. "Step back. Show time! Turn up the music!" Joe moved rhythmically with a pelvic thrust that sent his cock jutting out of the bikini. Turning about, he flexed his ass, tugged and snapped the white elastic, slid his right hand over the smoothness of his body and down to his bulging briefs, which he took to hoisting and dipping in time to the slow rock tune on the radio. He repeatedly whispered: "Dig it Chris?"

Chris stared, mesmerized as Joe's stiff cock and wiry underbrush appeared and disappeared.

Smiling, Joe swigged another shot of J & B, climbed unsteadily onto the bed and began a wobbly prance. Suddenly, he toppled backwards, grazing his head on the oak headstand.

"Christ" he grimaced, looking up into Chris' worried face.

"Take it easy. That body's too beautiful to mess up any more tonight. Too beautiful – " He rubbed Joe's inner thighs.

"Yeah, okay. You're right." Joe looked at his bandages, then back at Chris. "So how about some help from a friend, Chris? You are a friend, right? How could a guy like you be just a john? If you were just a john, though, you'd be only the second. Yeah, my first was this mousy little toy salesman. Scared shitless. He couldn't get it up. No matter what I did, he couldn't get it up. Practically threw his money at me and shoved me out the door before I could get my pants on. He was a john. But you – " Joe seized Chris' arms. "You're a friend, Chris. A hunk of a friend."

He jumped off the bed and went back to the scotch again. "God, Chris, I'm still shakin'." He turned to face Chris. "But look at that fucker reaching up for you. Too big for thin white briefs to hold, huh? Think they'll split from the pressure? Shit, maybe I'll split, split in two for you. How about that, Chris? You want to split me open tonight?"

Chris could scarcely believe his ears. "I'd like that."

"You'd like it! I'd like it!" He motioned for Chris to stand up. "Now, pull those stupid things off and let me see what's gonna split me open."

Chris stood up and slowly lowered his boxers.

Joe watched intently over the rim of the glass as he finished another scotch. "Christ! It's huge! Oh, man, it's jerkin', no hands! Do it in time to the music ... that's it, wow! What a weapon. You could shoot me dead. And Chris, yeah, yeah... your balls? You must have balls! That's it, push that teaser all the way down. God, you are gonna split me open! Look at that fucker!"

Joe set his glass down on the bureau and collapsed on the bed on his belly.

Chris mounted the bed and poised over Joe's tanned body. His cock arched out and rubbed against the white bikini that still clung to Joe's rear. He took a bottle of oil from the nightstand and began to slowly, sensuously massage Joe's hard muscles.

"How does that feel, Joe?"

"You're more 'n a friend, Chris. You're fuckin' fantastic. Now I think I'm the john. Oh, shit, I'm floating. You know how to...to send a guy into the clouds. I'll do the same for you, and more, Chris. Promise. Hey, man, pull off my bikini. Please, pull it off."

Chris leaned forward, muzzled the white cotton, edged it over the butt and legs, breathed deeply of its damp aroma.

Joe reached behind him, found and fondled Chris' bobbing sex. "Oh, c'mon, Chris, split me open." Chris' cock slipped snugly into the crack of Joe's ass. As he shoved it all the way in, he eased his hands under Joe's chest to seek and squeeze his nipples.

"Oh, Chris! Oh yeah, yeah...Fuck me, fuck me." The scarcely audible whispers trailed off. The monologue ceased. Joe's breathing shifted to a slow, steady rhythm, matching the rhythm of Chris' thrusts deep into Joe's ass. Chris came quietly, almost triumphantly. Slowly he eased his spent cock from Joe's asshole and ran his hands up and down the slick skin before kissing first one asscheek and then the other.

He slid from the bed, fastened the chain lock on the door, turned off the lights and the radio. He stood over the bed for a moment, fingering his tingling, cum-coated cock that grew hard again, still yearning for Joe's attention. He smiled as he slipped back into bed next to the smoothly muscled body that would eventually awaken in his arms. As he pulled the sheet over their bodies, he decided some things were worth waiting for – and some more than once.

ANGEL: THE FUCK-BOY
John Patrick

"Angels, they say, are messengers,
and while an angel may die, the message
the angel was sent to impart never does.
It lingers in your heart like a favorite piece of music
and brings you comfort when you can't find your way."
– Holly Palance

"Where is he?" I ask. Someone different is pushing the library cart today.

For weeks now, I have looked forward to Friday afternoon. To Angel. That's what I call him. Just the sight of him is heavenly, a slender, blue-eyed angel with a halo of blond curls.

When he first delivered books to me, I caught his eyes wishfully turning, forming a link, a bridge, a bond. Then came the notes tucked into my books. Little notes. I would return with long notes, making my desire clear. Last week, he pressed up tight against the bars and allowed me to feel his crotch. He wears no underwear under his jailhouse blues. I wanted to kneel down, take it out, suck it, but it was the middle of the day, after all. "Later," he promised.

Now the trusty answers, "Kid's in the hospital. He tried it again."

"Tried it?"

To end it."

"Oh, God."

"Yeah, but he's gonna make it. Youngsters like that bounce back. Anyhow, when he recovers, they're gonna put him in there with all you other crazies."

"Here?"

After six months in solitary waiting for trial, the doc told me

I was eligible to be put in the cellblock with "all the other child molesters." I keep telling him I never even touched the kid and, besides, he was 16 going on 17 and had more experience than me – he was hardly a child. A goddam stud is what he was. And just because I wouldn't buy what he was selling, he said I had. But he had the photos I took of him and that was enough for the sheriff to get an arrest warrant.

"Yeah, you're gettin' in there just in time for Christmas," the jailer said as he lead me down the corridor to "Delta" cellblock. "You'll love it in there. They even get a fuckin' tree to decorate." Two-man cells, a large day room with a TV. Twelve lost souls, each on potent medication. Some have tried to take their own lives. Some are religious fanatics. Others are child molesters or abusers. One guy even carved up his mother. I guess the feeling is no matter how despicable the crime, life must be preserved, at least until trial and conviction, then the boys at the joint can deal with them.

"...What I have been working toward all my life," my old pal Jimmy, visiting me, says genially, "is quality and character. Quality of things, of life. Making life sublimely simple. In a way, I am beginning to envy you in there."

"You might envy me more if you got a load of the Christmas cheer I might get."

"Oh?" Jimmy is my age, overweight, balding, and loves youth as much as I do. He doesn't want to spend his money on hustlers that would be too demeaning, so he's spending a bit on my defense, such as it is.

"Yeah, an angel is coming. On gossamer wings."

"A what?"

"A kid. Just eighteen. He could pass for sixteen I swear. Beautiful. Truly, an angel. A little Christmas cheer from on high." I wink. "A bit tardy I'm afraid."

"Well, it's about time you got something to cheer you up," Jimmy says with a benign smile. "Better late than never."

"...You're everything I ever wanted in a man," Angel says, leaning his head against the pale green concrete wall of our cell.

"You're mellow, intelligent and..." He hesitates, then, grinning broadly, continues: "Great sex." He playfully rolls his tongue across his lips and adds, thoughtfully, "But, you know, I still wanna respect Ron. I don't wanna do anything on the day I call him...you know, on Fridays."

As he says this, the song playing on the radio is: "If You Say My Eyes Are Beautiful, It's Because They're Looking at You."

"Never on Friday," I mumble. Yes, I can forego Fridays. "Doing it" on Fridays has caused trouble between us...the only thing we fight about and it's silly. After all, we have the other six days...and nights.

When Angel first arrived at the cellblock, just before Christmas, he slept most of the day alone in a vacant cell down the hall. But it wasn't long before he felt strong enough to take his meals with the rest of us and visit me in my cell. We were familiar at once. I put my hand on his thigh. "Later," he said. He agreed to share the cell with me.

That first night, our faces touching except for the pale, thin ray of moonlight between us, we whispered to each other how much we had longed for the moment when we could have sex. And he kissed me full on the mouth...and I kissed him back. At lights out, I went to his bunk, to the cock he had already made hard for me. It matched the rest of him, beautiful in every way. He let me suck those seven inches of perfectly cut teenaged meat for just a few minutes; he wanted to be fucked.

I stood and he seized my erection. "God I want to feel that in me now," he whispered. "But we have to be very quiet."

I nodded. Soon, his head crushed to the pillow, he moaned in mock protest as I battered his buttocks, my sex filling him.

By the shaking of his head, he demanded me to stop. He demanded I go deeper. All the panting, the pain, the thrusting and the twisting ended in thunderous orgasms for each of us. After I had come inside him, he jerked off and it seemed as if all of our pent up emotions spewed forth, soaking the mattress with sweat and come.

Other times, outside our cell, we talk about the past. I know he's making up much of what he tells me, but it entrances nonetheless. He said he tried to kill himself twice, just before his court appearances, in a vain attempt to get the court's sympathy. We got along so well, I went so far as to suggest that when we were both free, maybe we'd try to make it together as lovers on the outside.

Last night he said, "I want to see you again, but I've been let down so many times, I'm not counting on it."

"I know," I said. "And Ron's waiting."

"Please," he said, eyes downcast. "Let's not talk about him."

I have become a jealous lover. Ron was there before me. Angel was the product of a broken home and when he was fifteen Ron took him in. Although they fought a lot, they stayed together two years. Eventually, Ron took a job in Michigan and Angel elected to stay in Florida. He began hanging out with his brother, who had been in and out of foster homes and detention centers most of his young life, and soon the two of them were heavy into breaking and entering, robbery, drugs, and hustling. Angel quickly learned how to roll over for a man who had money...or at least something worth stealing after the sex was over and the man had fallen asleep. It was a scenario I had heard, with seemingly endless variations, hundreds of times. And now I think of those young men...the ones whose subtle hints and glances I had ignored. What of them? Could I have loved them too?

"...There's a different set of rules in jail," Reverend Michael Foley says. "Homosexuality is accepted as a fact of life." He is a kindly, affable Baptist preacher who has come to my cellblock every Thursday afternoon. We talk and read the Bible.

"How you accept it," he goes on, "deal with it, recognize it for what it is, determines if it is evil. To me, it's neither good nor bad. It just is."

All I know is the reality of Angel's perfect pecker poking out of his jailhouse blues every afternoon at four. It's become our routine, if I suck him off during the afternoon lockdown, I can fuck him at lockdown at night. I don't come during the suck because I want to save it for the evening. Angel comes, of course, and I swallow it all. It's the most delicious sperm I have ever tasted. I told Jimmy it was the nectar of the Gods. He's stopped coming to visit me. I think his envy of me has finally gotten the better of him. It's silly; I'm in here, he's free. Some people are prisoners of their own making.

...If you say my eyes are beautiful," Angel murmurs, looking up from his Stephen King paperback.

"They're playin' our song," I say with a grin.

As he continues to hum along with the tune as it plays on the radio, I whisper some more of the lyric: "If you're wondering why I'm smiling, it's because I'm happy with you. I could hold you close forever and never let you go."

When the tune is over, I step over to his bunk and stare lovingly into his eyes. "I'm putting you and those baby blue eyes of yours in my book," I tell him. "Who knows, maybe it'll be the last chapter." I run my hand up his thigh.

"Later," he says, playfully pulling away.

The lights go out. The guards make their last bed check. At the sound of the steel door slamming shut, I make my move to Angel's bunk. By the time I reach him, he is already standing on the bunk, facing the wall, his legs spread apart. As I climb behind him, he bends slightly at the waist, then lowers himself onto me. I kiss his neck and shoulders and revel in the tightness of his splendid ass. We can't take long doing this. He jerks himself as I slide it in and out, come. As he comes, I hug him tightly.

Back in my bunk, I switch to the earphones and watch Angel fall into a deep, post-orgasmic slumber. The tune they're playing now on the radio: 'The angel in your arms this morning is gonna be the devil in someone else's arms tonight." I smile.

"...They've come for me. Gotta run...I'll write!" Angel says, kissing me lightly on the cheek. Hurriedly, he steps from the cell, his roll of dirty linen tucked under his arm.

Tears well in my eyes as I watch him vanish down the corridor. He doesn't look back. He has a 15-year sentence hanging over him. That translates into 7 1/2 years with good behavior. Surely he could have taken a minute to properly say goodbye.

"Hi," the note says in a childish scribble, instantly recognizable. Remembering how Angel fretted over every sentence of every letter he would write, asking my help, giving up, trying again the next day, what I hold in my hand is as precious as gold.

"I miss the days in #7," he writes. "I miss you, miss your big dick, miss everything. Your cards really make my day. My brother Danny got sentenced yesterday...get ready for this...two 100-year sentences and one life sentence, all running consecutive!

Now let me tell you about this flea and nigger infested camp. It diffently (sic) has its ups and downs. I'm constantly getting tried by the niggers. Three reasons why: I'm white, pretty and young. A few weeks ago, a nigger grabbed my ass. So I did what any respectable man would do. I punched him in the mouth. My mistake was to do it with about 20 other niggers around. So I got jumped and kicked a few times. After they had their little fun with my body, I carried myself over to the clinic and got three stitches in my bottom lip. I also got a few bruises but the important thing is that I punched out the nigger that grabbed my ass. I'm sure in the future they'll think twice about grabbing for me.

"Other than that, I get the usual verbal comments from blacks. I can handle that, but if they touch me, that's a different story altogether. I'm not about to be a fuck-boy or let on that I'm g--y (sic)! My father and his wife Sarah come to visit me once a month. I try to get them to come just that often figuring that's not asking too much. I love seeing them. I don't think they realize how much it means to me to see them. And guess what, my father made the Police Officer of the Year for the whole state of Florida!

"...Ron's doing fine. He's getting by and is keeping in touch with me. Next month he'll be sending me a radio. I miss you, John...

"Who loves ya baby? Love, Angel."

I return to the words again, searching, straining to find more than is there, any secret messages that would give a clue as to how he really felt. All I know for sure is that it was a labor of love to write it and it is always a labor of love to read it.

My reverie is suddenly disturbed by raucous laughter. I curse them, the jackasses down the row.

"Grow up, asshole," the burly, tattoo-laden one yells from his cell. He's the head of the local KKK. At least he was, now he's going to have to serve two years for trying to blow somebody away. I will probably get four years for not blowing somebody's cock. Justice.

As a protective measure, the Klansman has been put in here. The guards don't think there will be trouble because we have only one black currently in residence and he's a transvestite, heavily medicated. "If you don't shut your face, I'll come down there and shut it for you," the Klansman shouts. "This is a jail, asshole, not a fuckin' Holiday Inn! If we can sleep all day with all the noise, you ought be able to sleep with the talkin' we're doin'."

I get back into my bunk, plug my radio speakers into my ears and try chilling out. Yes, I should be able to deal with what they dish out. And the fact I can't is testimony to my growing impatience. My nerves are raw. There seems to be no end to the waiting. The prosecutor has been granted one postponement after another. Even my attorney needed a postponement. "Slow walking" is what he said they are doing with me. Little did I realize just how slow. And now Angel's letter makes me long for those lovely days with him even more. I begin a reply, telling him about how unbearable the days have become without him. And how all the loosely connected scenes seem to have congealed, imparting one clear, inescapable message: I must be losing my mind.

And as I continue to write my letter to him, "If You Say My Eyes Are Beautiful" is playing again on the radio and I drop my pen. I lean back against the cold concrete wall and my hand goes to my erection. I close my eyes and I begin to dream of the day Angel and I will both be free to love again – and pray that Ron's not still around.

- Especially adapted by the author for this collection from material originally appearing in "Angel: The Complete Quintet."

THE SMACKING OF HIS LIPS
John Patrick

I was always being detained by his lips. Tracy's lips. They were such lovely lips: rich, full, pink. He used them to arouse me as no other boy ever did, before or since. And then his lips would part and take me in, all of me. Far, far down his throat. For Tracy, sucking cock was as natural as breathing. He inhaled my cock, all nine inches of it, as he seemed to do his food. My cock, I suppose, was food to him. And he took all of my cum. It never failed to astonish me how he could take it all, swallow it, never spit it out. We were lovers in the early '80s, when we didn't worry if someone did that.

In the terrible days after we parted, I barely moved from my bed. I kept insisting it was always Sunday and I didn't have to. It was the only place in the house where I could feel his presence. The crisp, clean scent of him clung to the sheets, to the pillowcases. Dirty thoughts filled my mind. Memories of the nimbus of his fingers caressing me. When he touched my flesh, I grew crazy with desire. I had never had so many orgasms.

It was warm and humid that summer, excessively so, and we would loll in the sun, then make a dash for the gulf. The gulf was over eighty degrees yet it still felt cool. He was a powerful swimmer and I would lie on the inflated raft and watch with great admiration as he did his laps.

Tracy. There was never a prettier name than that. Could be a girl, could be a boy. In my case, it was a boy. Not yet a man, really. A man-child. So helpless, so eager, so beautiful.

In my lust for him, sometimes I went into a passionate rage, not knowing where I wanted to put my cock, up his ass or down his throat. Any way was fine with him, so I would alternate. I would alternate our positions, first with him on his back, then on his stomach, then side by side. The suck, too, could be had in any number of positions, with me on my knees, over him, with me standing up, him sitting, me lying back, watching. Or in the car at sixty miles an hour. He was flexible. I realized I had found my perfect lover.

Then he realized he was the one. He could never get enough.

It all began one night when claustrophobia set in. Florida is not at its best in the summer, with each day a carbon copy of the last, with temperatures hovering in the 90's and it is too uncomfortable to leave the house during the day. Claustrophobia always sets in. I lived for the nights, for a pleasant dinner with friends, then a trip to the parks, the baths or the bars. Fearful of the parks and bored by the baths, I made a circuit of the bars, usually ending up at my favorite in the late '70s, the KiKi in downtown Tampa. It had the lack of pretension, the sleazy ambiance that always makes me feel at home. When it was finally condemned in the name of urban renewal, the bartender Floyd and his following moved to the Karousel Klub on West Platt, where amid chaos and ugliness, there always seemed to be a modicum of beauty.

The night I met Tracy, I was following my usual practice of taking in the entirety of it and, within that, disregarding the things that disgusted me and concentrating on the things that seemed to grow more lovely with every drink. Suddenly, at the opposite end of the bar, I saw a new face, a fine face, one that inspired me to rise and take a closer look. I stood behind him and drank in the sight of the young lean, beautifully tanned torso and, when he turned to see who was staring at him, the sly smile. He wore no shirt and I admired the highly developed pectorals. The jeans were filthy and he showed no basket but his face was divine, his dishwater-blond hair falling over it because of an unflattering cut. Considering the totality of it, I knew with a bit of scrubbing, a bit of polish, this could be a diamond.

At first, he was paying unusual attention to the balding, 50-ish man sitting at the bar to his left. I observed the interplay for a while until finally the man got up to go to the john. My desire for the boy was so great that I threw caution completely to the wind and approached him. "Whatever he's paying, I'll double it."

The boy blinked, shook his head incredulously, then smiled.

"Okay." Saying nothing more, he reached up and yanked his T-shirt from a rafter above the bar and began moving towards the exit.

As we approached my Mercedes roadster, he chuckled, "Oh, yeah."

"I like it," I said, unlocking my door and hitting the button to open his.

As he slid into the leather bucket seat, he asked, "Where do you live?"

"At the beach," I replied.

"All right," he said emphatically, then introduced himself as simply 'Tracy.' It would be several days before I knew his last name.

During the 45 minute ride to the beach, he laid his history on me: he was from Texas, had only been in town a short time, had a job at Intertel fixing phone lines and his car had broken down so he had no way to get there. I vowed if I had anything to do with it, he wouldn't have to return to that job.

After a drink at my bar, we retreated to the bedroom and I went to relieve myself. When I returned to the bedroom, he was sitting on the edge of the bed nude. He wrapped his arms around my torso and hugged me, then proceeded to devour my cock. In my heightened state of sexual hunger, I came very quickly, but not without appreciating the quality of his efforts. He seemed to have no desire for me to reciprocate so I joined him under the covers and he fell asleep in my arms. The next morning, he repeated the process, this time jacking off to climax as he blew me. At the height of our passion, I asked him to stay a few days. This involved picking up his things, which were, to use his phrase, "stored" at a man's apartment in Tampa. He told me he lied about the car, he didn't own one, and had lost his job at Intertel. He reminded me of Jean Genet's line, "For a time I lived by theft, but prostitution was better suited to my indolence."

We went to the man's apartment and I witnessed my new lover's ability to open a door by sliding a credit card between the lock and the jam. I knew then I would never be safe from him. Still, he was quite methodical about taking only those things that he said were his and left a note for the man. On the way home, we stopped at a department store and I bought him a few new items of wardrobe, then got his hair cut and highlighted. That night, dressed for dinner, he was absolutely stunning. We celebrated our good fortune with a bottle of champagne. When we returned home, he hurriedly undressed me and began blowing me. When I was hard, he undressed himself, lay face down on the bed and moved his hips seductively, offering up the prize he had not shared with me to that point. I kissed the ass cheeks, then invaded the space between them, first with my tongue, then with fingers coated with lube. Before long, I was charging my swollen flesh deep into his anus and he was bucking to meet every stroke. I wanted it to continue long into the evening but I came quickly, so excited was I at finding such a perfect sexual match. I crushed him with my spent body and we kissed.

The next night, after a late supper, we lay beside each other on the chaise lounge on the deck, a salty gulf breeze blowing. I entered him gently and soon his cum was gleaming in the moonlight, splattered against his thigh. Palm tree shadows skittering across my tanned skin, I went crazy finishing inside of him. After I pulled out and lay back, he said he wanted to watch a movie on TV so I went to bed. Upstairs, I switched off the light and the moon was like a lamp outside, illuminating the ripples of the Gulf. I closed my eyes and fell asleep at once, like the falling of a shutter in a camera which ends a time exposure. I dreamt and it was a nightmare of images. When Tracy opened the door, I woke with a start. "I'm sorry," he said, cuddling next to me.

"I'm not," I said, rolling over on top of him. He held me as I moved into position between his legs and rubbed my cock against his. I kissed him violently on the mouth and he squirmed under the pressure. In a few moments, he reached for the grease from the nightstand. I got on my knees as he applied it to himself, lifting his legs to the ceiling. I entered him slowly and he wrapped his legs around me. Kissing him as I ground into him, I came quickly, then we lay in each others' arms and I fell asleep again. I slept peacefully and, if I dreamt, I didn't remember it the next morning.

Around noon, Tracy got up and, as he was coming down the stairs, still nude, I sat at the table eating a Swiss cheese sandwich on pale crusty bread, slathered with mayo. I felt like Isak Dinesen, who only ate white food. The beautiful blond boy dropped to the cushion of one of the bar stools, just staring at me, a look in his eyes that was at once hopeful and desperate. I smiled, almost as if saying to myself: Take it easy. Enjoy this beauty for it too soon shall pass. But somehow I sensed it wouldn't pass quickly, not this time. It had been two days of bliss. The monotony of the summer had been erased in a single, decisive stroke. I knew what I was doing.

As he approached me, I held out my arms. He kissed me as he lowered himself into my lap. In a matter of moments, he was on his knees between my legs, fellating me with an eagerness that shocked me. I closed my eyes, sighed deeply and prayed that this one not pass quickly.

In order to keep Tracy, I knew I had to invent something for him to do. He was enamored of my computer so I took over the fulfillment operations of the real estate magazine I owned. Like everything else he took up, Tracy became immediately proficient at coding the subscriptions and processing the labels. A routine developed. In the morning, he would work at the computer, then take my second car, a Corvette, to the bank and post office. Our lunch consisted of wine, sandwiches and sex, usually him simply blowing me but sometimes a full-blown fuck, depending on his whim. Then he would run on the beach and go swimming in the Gulf while I worked. Dinner was a fancy affair at a fine restaurant. I loved to watch him eat, his appetite was enormous. Afterward, we'd bar hop, see a movie, go shopping or just go home. The affection seemed to flow out of him: He could never ride with me without holding my hand; I could never stop spending money on him. Evening always ended with his tribute to me, namely the fuck, usually with him on his stomach, moaning in ecstasy with my every stroke.

As the summer turned into fall, we flew off to Key West for Fantasy Fest, California for Thanksgiving, and New York for Christmas shopping. It seemed I had found the tonic for my boredom in the person of a loving 20-year-old. But having Tracy with me presented a problem because several months before I met him, two of my regular fuck buddies had taken permanent lovers and, to fill the void, I established a business relationship with Ronnie, a boy I had met through a service and photographed. After our initial photo session, which ended with a glorious fuck, Ronnie would occasionally call seeking funds. It seemed he was forever broke. I agreed to sex for $50 but questioned what would happen if his young lover Brett found out. "What he doesn't know don't hurt him," was always Ronnie's comeback. Eventually the two called it quits as a couple and Ronnie moved back to Sarasota. Now it wasn't just $50 he needed, it was a car. I bought him one, telling him he could work off the payments. He understood completely. Since my parents lived in Sarasota, most often, I'd drive down to see them, and work Ronnie into my busy schedule.

Once a week, I would leave early and, late in the afternoon, stop at the Tropical Palms Motel, renting room Number 7-A for my assignation with Ronnie. The woman who owned the place gave me a "day" rate, $20 cash, knowing I'd only use it for an hour or so. Once in the room, I'd have a drink, snort some coke and wait for Ronnie to come and make his car payment.

After Ronnie and I talked, we did a few lines of coke, then I would make the first move, stroking his thigh, which was usually naked since he invariably wore clingy nylon running shorts. I would work my fingers up under the fabric and into his crotch. When he became aroused, we would lift ourselves from the bed and strip naked. Then he would lie down on his back and I would shove a pillow under his ass. Sliding between his legs, I would suck his cock, usually for about five minutes. While Brett had a stubby, ordinary cock, Ronnie's was a true sucking dick and I would have been happy to worship it for hours, but when I felt Ronnie could stand it no more, I scrambled onto my knees, applied lube to my fingers and prepared his anus for my assault. I hoisted his legs over my shoulders and took his firm, lightly hairy buns into my hands. As I slowly entered him, he began to masturbate. It usually took less than two minutes for him to come and then I lowered myself onto his chest and, holding him in my arms, I finished. I enjoyed this part the most because I kissed him full on the mouth, sometimes three or four times, then lay in his arms briefly. I felt a oneness with him that I liked to think went beyond sex-for-hire. It was the only time Ronnie actually touched me physically.

I stoically accepted the fact that I was merely a convenience to him, a pleasant but strictly hands-off, second hand user of what he had so abundantly to offer: sex. But, occasionally, there would be a glimmer of something more. "I love you but I'm not in love with you," he told me once. "I appreciate everything you've done for me."

On those rare occasions when Ronnie would drive up to see me rather than the other way around, he would mention that he'd either seen Brett at the bar or was going to stop and see him while he was in town. Afterward, Brett would call me and recount every breathless detail of their encounter. He may've just been with you, but he had plenty left."

I told him I was glad to hear that. "Nothing worse than a limp Ronnie."

"Ha-ha! That'll be the day!"

In a way, it excited me to think that I had prepared Ronnie for his assignation with Brett, confident that while I had been the active one in our encounter, Ronnie would have had to play the aggressor with Brett. "It wasn't like that in the beginning," Ronnie told me once, but that's what it became. Yeah, it was really boring."

It seemed the worst thing in the world for Ronnie was to be bored. I sometimes fantasized what it would be like to have him around all the time but the reality of it was I would have been a basket case just trying to deal with his boredom as well as my own. No, I reasoned, it was better this way, once a week, "slam bang, thank you, sir." And, as it turned out, I outlasted all of Ronnie's lovers, with the exception of Brett, of course, who was, after all, his first and only true love.

After Tracy moved in, my needs were fulfilled and I begged off the weekly ritual with Ronnie, but only for a couple of months. I began to miss his beautiful cock. I justified duplicity by telling myself that I had made a deal with Ronnie long before I met Tracy and a deal was a deal. During the first few weeks of our relationship, Tracy understood my need to go to my parents alone but in order to see Ronnie, I switched the occasion to a late lunch instead of dinner. I would return to the beach in the late afternoon, still fresh from the sex with Ronnie and Tracy would be all over me, missing me, wanting me. For the first time, I had to refuse him, postpone the event until after dinner. He agreed, but, even though he never said anything, I knew if it had been me I would have been curious about it.

One day I was on my way to Sarasota to meet Ronnie when the car phone rang.

"Please come," he cried. He had been to the bank and on the way home he had run a light.

When I arrived at the intersection where the accident occurred, I found the Corvette was totaled but he was not harmed. "It's a miracle," I said when we were in my car following the tow-truck.

He was numb. "I'm so sorry," he kept saying over and over. "But you're all right, that's what matters."

"But the car."

"Really, you've done me a favor. I couldn't afford it anyway. Now the lease is paid off."

But our routine was broken. Tracy lost his license for six months. My young lover was deeply depressed. He moped around the condo for days. One day, I returned from the bank to find him gone. Minutes dragged into hours. Finally, he showed, stoned out of his mind. He sat at the bar while I fixed drinks. Before I had a chance to vent my frustration with him, he fell backward, narrowly missing a glass topped table. I put him to bed.

The next morning, he was still passed out when there was a knock on the door. It was young, insatiable Brett. I had begged off every call he had made to me since Tracy moved in but now he couldn't be denied. My anger with Tracy was such that I wanted to attack someone, something, and Brett provided the perfect outlet. Although he had many young lovers, he would, on occasion, drop by just get a fuck. I was ready for him, but before I let things go to far, I wanted to show off my prize. We went quietly to the bedroom and I opened the door. Seeing Tracy was still out cold, I let Brett have a peek. When we returned to the living room, he said, "God, he's gorgeous. You've gotta have me over sometime for a three-way."

"Tracy's not that kind. Funny as it may sound, he's very jealous of me."

Brett groped me. "Yeah, I know why."

We went to the garage and I locked the door behind me. As I leaned back on the hood of the Mercedes and began massaging my hard-on, Brett dropped his shorts and backed over me. His hand steadying my erection, he lowered himself onto it, then pushed. He jacked off as he bounced up and down in my lap. We came simultaneously, but I was still in the mood to harm. I turned him around and made him lie across the hood while I continued to blast my flesh into him.

Later that afternoon, Tracy finally awakened. Part of me wanted to listen, the other part couldn't afford the hassle. He had become a hassle.

Eager to make amends, he wanted sex. He caressed my arm, my thigh. As always, I bloomed under his magic touch and, as he eagerly took my cock in his mouth, I knew I was beginning to think too much.

He lay face down across my knees and I played for a time with his bubble butt. I stroke it, pinched it all over, rubbed my hands up and down the division, then pulled the cheeks apart. I put my lips there and slathered the area with my saliva. He was always clean. I never feared touching any part of him. I reached under him and played with his erection as I worked my tongue into his anus. When he was close to coming, I worked my fingers in and rolled him over. I mounted him and slid my erection into him. Holding his cock tightly, I began to fuck him in earnest; heaving his bottom up to meet my plunges, he came more intensely than I had ever remembered. I followed suit, and, after a final wriggle of my cock in his ass, we lay in each other's arms, breathing heavily. I decided to try to work things out.

But, as the days went by, his afternoon disappearances grew more frequent and prolonged. Occasionally he would return home after running on the beach and mention he'd met a girl and they had talked, but I reacted so negatively to such information that he stopped providing it. When he didn't show until after dinner, I would be furious with him and we would fight, only to make up and have sex, but I realized he had begun to feel trapped. I could sense he was psyching himself into enjoying the sex, pretending that it mattered. Early on, he had maintained he was basically straight, showing a peculiar lack of interest in passive sucking or active fucking. Those things, he led me to believe, he did with girls. I began to sense just having a place to stay became a sorry excuse for his sticking around. It had become a difficult, complex relationship of dependence and attachment, one that often arises between victim and victimizer, abuser and abused. We each had our own idiosyncratic moral vision and it became a thing of knots and complications, often sending me into despair but without somehow ever becoming truly hopeless. With each argument, it seemed it was an appalling revisiting of the past upon the present. Finally, I suggested we both seek psychiatric help. Tracy agreed but went only once, to take the test and to have a short chat with the doctor. A week later, the doctor confronted me.

"If you stay in this relationship, eventually one of you will be harmed. Terribly harmed, perhaps physically, indeed mentally." In a few moments, he told me everything I knew about my lover. I was amazed that a test and a simple chat could reveal so much about someone. "Oh, there's no mystery to it," the doctor said. "We study sociopaths like him all the time."

I wanted an answer to the question that might give focus to my dilemma: why? But this was the very answer the experts couldn't provide.

"We have few definitive answers," he said. "These people have had troubles from their earliest days. We have studied heredity, looking for a genetic explanation and there has been some evidence that it plays a role."

"Yet Tracy's parents aren't criminals. His father works for the phone company in Texas."

The doctor shrugged, as if the answer was beyond reason. "He may be lying to you. These people learn to become good liars, effective manipulators, as you've seen by his taking you on sexually, effectively learning to assert control over his world. But no matter how much in control they think they are, these people are completely unable to sustain meaningful relationships with anyone. If you know what's good for you, you'll end this."

Tracy was strangely silent when I returned from my visit to the doctor. He had told me he would not return. To him, it was so much "idiosyncratic bullshit." He seemed to sense from my quiet demeanor that I was deeply troubled. He did what he always did in these moments, cajole me into sex, knowing that at the height of orgasm, all is forgiven. I fucked him and he was happy. We went to Tampa to dinner. I had too much wine and, mixed with the coke I had done earlier, I became unreasonable. We argued about the psychiatrist. I wanted him to see him again. He refused. He left the table and called a cab. I followed him. I knew he would go to the Karousel, to return to the place where we had met, to remind me of what a treasure I had found there amid the sleaze. As he was paying the cab driver, I parked the Mercedes and ran to him. Under the influence of drugs or booze or both, my wayward intelligence gutters like a candle. I grabbed at him, tearing his shirt. He swung and connected with my eye. I saw black and fell to the ground on the street in front of the bar, blood spurting from my eye.

The bouncer witnessed the scene and came to my rescue, whisking me to the hospital where an eye surgeon happened to be on duty. After stitching my eye, the officials asked me to stay overnight. When I refused, they ordered me a cab and I had the driver take me to where I had parked the Mercedes. The bar had closed; the lot was empty. I paid the driver $40 to lead me to the beach. On the way home, I recalled the trauma connected with my father's beatings. Fear. Pain. Hurt. Embarrassment. Degradation. Humiliation. Anger. Resentment. Powerlessness. Helplessness. Revenge. When he'd been drinking, I knew to keep my distance. The worst time was Friday nights, when he would watch boxing. The slugfests would put him in such a state that once they were over, he would seek me out, berate me for being such a sissy and throttle me as I lay helpless in my bed. If Mother had not intervened, I'm sure I would have been killed.

One of the consequences of corporal punishment is that it sets the stage for the child to try out the behavior he has experienced. In my case, I nearly killed several of my pets. When I tried this, I was scolded and often spanked. Very confusing. So I learned that I needed to grow bigger before I had the right to be violent. I learned that Dad's rules don't have to be consistent. I learned to mistrust dad. Dad's love was painful. I looked forward to growing up so I could be just like Dad. Mean. Tough. Big. And, maybe, just maybe, I would be big enough to kill him.

As I grew older, I sought out people I could dominate so if they disobeyed, I could discipline them. Power coursed through my body as I would lash out at the girl I dated in college and who eventually became my wife. My violence worked on her. I had earned my privilege of power. The cycle of violence was complete except for one thing, I didn't need to kill my father. I saw he was slowly killing himself with drink. And my wife couldn't take it. Most of the time she spent locked in our bedroom.

But Tracy was not so easily disposed of. My violence did not work on him. He fought back and his rage was greater than mine.

When I arrived at the beach, Tracy had packed his things and the two suitcases were sitting by the front door. He sat on one of the bar stools.

"I'm sorry," he said.

"So am I." It could have been much worse, I realized. It was as much my fault as his. More really. If I hadn't been drinking, hadn't been doing coke...but, still, it had been boiling up for weeks.

"I'll call a cab," he said, reaching for the phone.

I let him make the call. He could always tell the cab he'd called in error.

"I wish you wouldn't go – " I muttered, finally, as I lay down on the couch in the living room with a sigh.

"Does it hurt?" he asked, standing over me nervously.

"No, it's numb. But I'm sure it'll hurt tomorrow and then when they take the stitches out in a week or so. But what hurts more than anything is what I've done. What I've done to us."

"It was me. I haven't been right since the accident. I thought you'd take me back to Tampa right then but you didn't."

"No. I couldn't. I love you. I love you but we can't live together."

"I know. I've been all messed up. I really want to date girls."

"Perhaps this was just something you had to try out. Now you have to put it behind you. And it won't worry you anymore."

I rented a car for him for two weeks and gave him enough money to rent a room and keep himself together until he found work. He called every day and finally I agreed to see him. For lunch.

He didn't bother to knock, just walked in. I was opening a bottle of wine and when I looked up my anger with him, with myself returned. He was so beautiful I wanted to smother him with kisses but I stood where I was, waiting for him.

"Hi," he said sheepishly, sliding onto one of the bar stools.

"Hi." As I poured the wine, a chill descended upon me. I handed him his glass and he sipped it.

"Tastes good," he said, smacking his lips.

I came around the bar and sat next to him. He took my hand and squeezed it. I shook my hand free, like a young boy confronted with an over ardent admirer.

He shrugged his shoulders and brought both hands to his glass of wine.

He said he'd gotten a job at a gas station in Tampa and he was dating the owner's daughter, who was only 17. "Nice pussy?"

"Shit, I haven't got that far yet."

"That's right. Take it easy. When they're that young they need to be broken in slowly."

My denial of his power was coming at a cost of sentimentality. I remembered what my psychiatrist said, that such repression is unhealthy. Sooner or later the hate turns up. In my case, it was the fine line between love and hate. I could only hate something I loved so much. I wanted to cry but instead I smiled and kept listening as he chattered on.

We sat at the bar and ate chicken salad sandwiches and then I cleared the dishes away. When I returned to the dining room, he was still sitting on the bar stool but now he was nude. "I've missed you," he said, stretching his arms wide, "s0000 much!" He had an erection. He must have missed me. Then, looking down at my crotch, he smacked his lips. That did it.

I stepped close to him, letting his arms envelop me, press me tightly against his smooth, hard body. We kissed. It was a harder, more urgent kiss than any I had remembered with him.

His hand groped me. Feeling my swelling erection, he whispered, "Yeah, you missed me, too."

The removal of my shirt and shorts was swift and he was on his knees, sliding my prick between his lips, down his throat. Before long, he was on his back on the carpet, his legs spread wide, and I was between them, entering him. As I lowered myself on top of him fully, his arms held me again and we kissed. It was as if nothing had changed. Yet everything had changed. As I climaxed, I thought about offering him a hundred a week just to visit me on Fridays for lunch, but by the time I had withdrawn my prick and was lifting myself from the floor, I came to my senses. He seemed to sense I was remorseful. As he pulled on his shorts, he said, "It's not right, is it?"

No, I'm sorry. This will have to be the end. I can't go through this. Neither can you. I love you more than you'll ever know but it's just no good."

"No, it's me. I'm no good," he muttered and raced out the door.

I slipped into my shorts and ran after him but by the time I reached the driveway, he had driven away.

Three days later, I found the little rental car in the drive, the keys in an envelope on the front seat. There was no note of explanation.

Now, in my mind, I often write little notes to him, notes that always end with: "Tracy, my dear Tracy. Just once more I would like to hear the smacking of your lips after you've made me come. Just one more time."

TEACHER'S PET
Bert McKenzie

I admit that I had a few experiences with other guys. They were mainly confined to circle jerks and some mutual masturbation. And at the time I wondered if I might not be queer. But fortunately, my freshman psych class taught me that this was a typical phase through which all young men pass. I was as "normal" as all the other guys.

I majored in theater arts and education, got a teaching certificate, graduated, got married and moved to Dunwater, Kansas. It was a little railroad town, population 4,000. My spouse decided to stay home and be a housewife while I taught English and drama for the high school, directing their plays. And for several years we were happy. Well, perhaps happy is an overstatement. Let's just say we here contented with our lives.

That was before I met Kelly. He was an athlete, one of our school's track stars. His senior year he had several electives to fill, so he took Stagecraft as well as Acting. No sooner did he appear in my classes than I knew I was in trouble. It began with the dreams.

Kelly came into my classroom dressed in his track outfit, the loose-fitting shorts and tank top. As I sat behind my desk he would walk up and take a seat in the front of the room while the other students filed in and took desks around and behind him. I glanced up to see him slumped in his desk, his legs spread apart, and I noticed that I could see up the loose fitting leg of his shorts. To my shock and surprise, Kelly was not wearing anything underneath. I could just make out the shape of his dick as it rested over his balls. While I watched he smiled at me, reached down and scratched himself, further revealing his equipment.

I decided to begin class and was about to stand up when I realized that I wasn't wearing any pants. My own cock climbing into an erection beneath my large wooden desk. I couldn't move, lest the class see that I was naked from the waist down. Then Kelly stood and walked over to the side of my desk. He hoisted one leg up and sat down, his dick sliding out of his loose shorts, only inches from where my right hand rested on the desk blotter.

Suddenly I was lost in the intensity of the moment and my orgasm began. I awoke to the realization that I was having a wet dream, something that had not happened in years. It was hard to explain to Karla when she woke up because the bed was shaking. I simply had to tell her I was dreaming about her. But I knew I had a problem.

Deciding to do something radically different for the spring play, I chose the ancient Greek comedy The Frogs" by Aristophenes. It would stretch the talents of my students as well as showing these small town locals that classical theater can be as entertaining and funny as Neil Simon.

The students from my acting class were all required to audition, and to my surprise, Kelly did remarkably well. Since he had the best physique, I cast him as Heracles. We went right into rehearsals and in six short weeks the show was almost ready for performance. Then my dreams came back and I again had trouble explaining my nocturnal emissions to Karla.

Mrs. Sanders and her home economics class helped with costumes. Being a frustrated designer, she had a marvelous flair for the theatrical and managed to come up with Greek costumes that looked like something other strategically draped bed sheets.

When I saw the remarkable amount of skin showing on the guys, I began to suspect her of being a bit of a lech herself.

At our dress rehearsal Kelly walked onto the stage in only the tiniest of loincloths. His shaggy blond hair was pulled back with a headband and he had fur covered boots climbing to mid-calf. He was stunning, his athletic body showing all the promise of youth, and his costume stirring up images of the quintessential caveman. The only problem was his pale complexion under the harsh stage lights.

After the rehearsal, I called him aside and gave him a jar of Texas Dirt. It was a red powder that was used as body paint.

When applied with a damp sponge, it colored the skin a nice ruddy bronze that looked natural under the colored theater lights. I explained that he needed to apply the paint to every part of his body that showed including his legs, arms, neck, and chest. Kelly smiled a crooked grin and asked, "How can I get the makeup on my back?"

"Get another cast member to help you," I replied.

"Oh, I thought maybe you could do that," he suggested.

That night I dreamed I was gently painting Kelly's body. As I applied the sponge to his bare chest he moaned softly. The damp sponge was cold and as it passed over his pecs, his nipples poked out into tiny erections. "Don't forget my legs," he said.

I dropped to my knees before him. I began to run the sponge up his right leg, over the calf, past the knee, up the inside of his thigh. My hand didn't stop. It slipped beneath his loincloth and I felt the contact of flesh against flesh. He wasn't wearing the jock strap Mrs. Sanders had dyed to match his costume. I felt his warm balls against the back of my hand. Kelly reached down and pulled his loincloth aside revealing his dick which was half erect and pointing at my face. Again I awoke to an incredible orgasm. Now Karla was really worried and she insisted that I make an appointment to see a doctor. It bothered her that I wasn't interested in sex when awake, yet had been routinely having wet dreams.

Opening night was upon us and I went backstage to offer some last-minute words of encouragement. Then I saw Kelly. He was a mess. His makeup was splotchy and streaked. "I asked Ben to help me with it," he whined, "but it looks like I've got leprosy."

"You didn't use enough water," I said. "Come on." We only had a couple of minutes to fix the body paint. I pulled Kelly into the dressing room and grabbed the sponge and the Texas Dirt. Wetting the sponge in the sink, I began to smooth out the splotchy makeup job. It didn't take much work, just a little attention to detail. "You see," I said as I gently brushed the damp sponge across his chest. "Long, even strokes."

The damp sponge was cold and as it passed over his pecs, his nipples poked out into tiny erections. "Don't forget my legs," he said and I suddenly experienced deja vu. Dropping to my knees before him, I began to run the sponge up his right leg, over the calf, past the knee, up the inside of his thigh. My hand was shaking as I reached just under his loincloth. "Are you okay, Mr. McKenzie?" he asked.

I managed to nod as I turned away to put the sponge back on the counter. "Break a leg," I said, trying to regain my composure. He smiled and headed back toward the stage. I continued to kneel on the floor, trying to will away the erection that was forcing a tent in my suit pants.

The play went well, getting laughs in all the right spots. I'm not sure if the audience really understood it, but at least they thought it was funny. Afterwards I had to smile as parents came up to congratulate me and tell me how fond their children were of me. Then the audience was gone and I turned to lock up the building. There were only a few straggling actors just leaving.

"Are you the last?" I asked Jake as he headed out the stage door while I killed the lights.

"Kelly's still in the shower washing off his body makeup," he said and slipped out, the door closing with a metallic clunk. I was alone in the building with the young man who had stirred up such strange desires in me. I took a deep breath, shook my head to clear it and headed downstairs toward the locker rooms in the basement. Kelly was just a normal student and this odd desire was something I could certainly control. I only wanted to hurry him along so we could both get out of there.

I heard the water stop as I stepped into the boys' locker room. "Kelly," I called. "Are you about finished?"

He stepped out of the shower room. "Sorry, I had to wash all that goop off me," he apologized. "I really like to take long showers." He stood there for a moment, as if intentionally giving me a chance to see him in all his naked glory.

His body was just as gorgeous as ever, perhaps more so with the sparkling drops of water glistening on his bare skin. But now, I could see all of him. My eyes were instinctively drawn to the area that had been hidden by the loincloth. His dick was now revealed to me, long, thick and cut, hanging over his ample balls. It was surrounded by a dense patch of curly blond hair. I was struck by the thought that it looked more like a man's dick than a boy's. Then I remembered that Kelly was probably eighteen years old. He may have been young, but physically he was a man.

That short pause seemed like a lifetime, then he turned and grabbed a towel and began drying his hair. His head was covered with the cloth so I took my time gazing at his body. I watched him without his knowledge. I watched his cock, admiring its shape and form. Then I turned and hurried up the stairs, frightened by the reaction of my own body.

I waited just outside the stage door, gulping in the fresh air and hoping this was all just another dream. In a few minutes Kelly came out, dressed in his street clothes. He started to walk away, then paused as if he had forgotten something. Turning, he came back and walked up to me, standing quite close. "I just wanted to say thanks for casting me and giving me this opportunity. I've really enjoyed working with you. This acting shit isn't much different from sports, but I think it might be a lot more fun."

He held out his hand and I took it. We shook, and he held my hand in a firm clasp, holding it a bit longer than I felt was necessary. Then he turned and disappeared into the shadows.

The next night was closing night. In a small high school like Dunwater, plays only run for two nights. After that you don't have an audience. We met at the auditorium as usual and the actors went off to the dressing rooms to get into costumes and makeup. This time Kelly managed to get into his body paint without my help. The play ran its course and the final curtain dropped.

The cast and crew were out of there in record time, everyone heading to the pizza parlor for the cast party. I was about to kill the lights when Jake slipped by saying Kelly was still downstairs. I locked the door, turned off the mains, leaving on just the dim glow of the work lights, and headed for the basement. Kelly was slowing down my appearance at the cast party. This time I was determined to simply step in and hurry him on his way.

As I entered the boys' locker room the water was running. "Kelly, let's get a move on," I called. There was no response. I waited a moment and called again. "Kelly, let's go." There was still no response. I took a deep breath and stepped over to the shower room.

He was standing under the stream of water. It splashed and sprayed off his head, streaming down his bare back and ass. I noticed how smooth his ass cheeks were, firm and round, like a dancer's. Instantly my body began to respond and I tried to leave, but I couldn't move. Then he turned and looked at me. His dick was already half way erect, standing out from his body.

"Why don't you come join me, Mr. McKenzie? The water really feels so good."

"What?"

"Hey, you know you want to. I know you want to!'

I managed to take one step back. "I don't know what you're talking about."

He grinned. "Ever since you saw me in that loincloth you've had a boner." He stepped out of the water and started toward me. "You've got one now." Kelly pointed to the tent in my slacks. "It's not fair. You get to see me with my clothes off. I want to see what the hard dick looks like."

I shook my head. "Kelly, you don't know what you're saying. You're a student ..."

"I'm 18. I know what I want. I want you to touch me. I want to feel your hands on my body, like last night when you were putting on my makeup. I want to feel your hands on my tits, on my legs, on my ass, on my balls."

By now he was only a step away from me. He reached out and slowly unfastened my tie, then slipped off my sport coat and began to unbutton my shirt. "I . . . I shouldn't do this," I protested.

"But I want you to." He ran his hand down my bare chest, playing with the curly black hair, teasing my nipples. Then Kelly started to work on my pants, unfastening my belt, unzipping my fly. "I want to feel it in my mouth and I want to feel it up my ass."

He dropped to his knees on the wet tile and yanked my pants and briefs down in one jerk. Then, just as quickly, he swallowed my dick, burying his face in my pubic hair.

All was lost. As he sucked, I realized this was even better than the experiences I had in my younger days, even better than with Karla. She never sucked my dick like this. And when I came in his mouth, it seemed like I couldn't stop. But eventually I did. Then I slowly sank back onto the wet tile floor.

"I really wanted to do that," Kelly said as he slowly pulled off me and stood up. "But there's something else I want to do." I looked up at him standing over me, and I saw his own dick pushing out hard and firm. I understood his desire, and simply nodded my head. He stepped close to me and took careful aim, pressing his beautiful eight-incher against my lips. At last I knew what it was like to suck his dick, to have him press forward into my throat. This was no wet dream; it was really happening.

By the time Kelly and I made it to the cast party it was almost over. We both spent too much time in the shower.

That night I realized my life was about to change. The spring play was over and all that was left of the year were final exams and graduation. That spring Kelly graduated. That spring I got a divorce. Kelly went on to K-State as a freshman; I returned to K-State as a grad student.

We both have learned a lot over the years. I'm still directing plays. And Kelly still likes to take very long showers, but then so do I.

ARIA
Ken Anderson

We pardon in the degree that we love."
– Francois, Duc de la Rochefoucauld

Billy

Butch and Billy were buddies.

Butch had picked up the nickname because of his haircut. It made him feel butch. But he had to admit the idea was Billy's. Billy also had suggested the tattoo on his groin, a small blue flame just above the hair. Billy had a tattoo in the same place – a little devil.

Butch had recently broken up with his girlfriend. Or rather, she'd broken up with him because, she said, he'd rather spend time with Billy, which was true. Something inside him had never caught fire with girls the way it had just being around Billy.

When Billy found a girl, Butch would sleep alone, but on certain nights, when a girl wasn't available, Butch would get so conspicuously drunk that the next morning, nauseated, with a splitting headache, he simply couldn't remember exactly what had happened between them. Or so he told himself.

Butch did know that when Billy needed cash, he hustled, roughing up older, more defenseless johns. If he wanted sex, he took it, then robbed them. If he didn't, he just robbed them, then beat them up. Assault, robbery – such gross bravura was macho to him.

Sharing and tenderness, of course, were queer, and so it was as if, despite their closeness, there could be only so much human warmth between Butch and Billy, and most of that on Butch's part. If Butch tried to show any real affection in public or private, Billy turned ice-cold, and the more Butch tried to thaw him out, the harder he froze, and the more consumed with him Butch became, until, at last, Butch would do just about anything for him, even robbing the old man.

The idea had first occurred to Billy one night at the Dynamo, a hustler bar-- a dark, smelly dungeon of a basement with brick walls, stone floors, and a tangle of pipes curving in and out of the cloud of cigarette smoke overhead. Men of various ages and dress leaned on the bar or propped themselves against pitch-black tiers along the walls, drinking beer, talking, and listening to the Rolling Stones.

Outside one night, Billy watched a drunk drop his keys as he stepped from a cab. In the bar, he kept an eye on him, then, at the appropriate moment, introduced himself. He went home with him, to a house in the suburbs, a large stucco place all pediments and Palladian windows, and outside the door, in the morning twilight, he leaned on a pilaster, jingling the keys in his pocket, waiting to see how the man would react. When the man discovered that his keys were missing, he was disturbed, of course, but took a second key from the midst of a boxwood in a planter on the stoop. Apparently, he had lost keys before.

The night of the robbery, Billy checked the shrub, and sure enough, another key, like a forgotten Christmas ornament, dangled in the boxwood, just catching the light. He and Butch moved to a set of lit windows at the side of the house, then, each outside one, crouched in the dark, watching the man put on a record, then settle into one of two, facing, sunset-yellow, Chippendale armchairs. Through the sheers, Butch could see that the room was a well-furnished, well-decorated den. To either side of the chairs stood little antique tables, and the bookcase was filled with, besides books, an assortment of objects: a small globe, a model ship, porcelain bowls and vases. All he could see of the man was that he was wearing a plaid robe and that his hair and eyebrows were a fleecy white. Peering through the window, listening to the muffled music rising to its climax, Butch finally realized that the man must've been staring at something on the bottom shelf of the bookcase.

When the music was over, the man rose to move toward the stereo, and Billy took the move as cue to slip on their gloves. Billy crept toward the front of the house, Butch the back. The man was playing the music too loud to hear Billy unlock the front door, but strangely enough, as Butch quietly stepped onto the patio, he found a set of French doors wide open.

The original plan was to tie up the man, then rob him, but the plan, as whole lives do, went awry. The man had put on the same music, an operatic piece, and as it swelled once again, Butch and Billy stepped into the room through opposite doors, Billy behind the man and Butch in full view. But as Butch slowly approached him – stepping onto the polished hardwood floors, then onto the Oriental carpet, then around a side table – a couple of odd events took place, throwing Butch off for a second. First, there were mirrors to either side of the opposite door, and as Butch stepped around the table, he saw not only Billy but also himself entering the room. In a black-leather jacket, Billy looked out of place. Then the old man did not respond as Butch had expected. For a moment, the man sat with downcast eyes, then, somehow in sync with the music, lifted his gaze and smiled as if he knew Butch, as if he were not surprised at all that Butch had dropped in.

Butch did what he'd rehearsed in his mind. He drew his switchblade, then flicked it open, and the man rose with difficulty, but unalarmed. He could've been rising to lower the volume. He stepped forward, and his hand went up as if to welcome him, to touch him on the shoulder, guiding him to a chair.

Butch had moved to his left around the table, and Billy had made a similar move behind the man, completing a sort of inverted S. To Butch's horror, Billy stabbed the man in the back, practically lifting him off the floor.

"Take that, you old fag," he snarled, jabbing the knife deeper and deeper.

Billy stepped back, the knife at his side, and the man, gulping air, collapsed near a footstool.

"Why'd you do that?" Butch gasped. You didn't have to do that!"

And at that moment, he was found guilty and locked in jail, even if it were only the jail of himself. Guilty against his will. "Didn't think we'd leave a witness, did you?" Billy snapped, kicking the stereo in one spry, karate-like move.

The stereo leapt as if hurt, then froze, quietly obedient. "Didja?" he shouted.

A strange silence settled on the room.

In disbelief, Butch slipped off a knapsack and set about rummaging downstairs while Billy first cleaned the knife in the bathroom, then lurched upstairs. Butch rifled the living room, the dining room, a bedroom, an office, collecting a sizable cache of silverware, various trays and candelabra, and a wallet.

When he returned to the den, he refused, at first, to look at the body, scanning the landscape paintings, the Queen Anne secretary, the various decorative objects sitting around the room – chinoiserie, lacquered boxes, small, bronze statues of Ephebes. He smelled furniture oil, and he could hear Billy up-stairs, tromping around, dropping items into his duffel bag.

The old man groaned, startling Butch so much that he jumped back, knocking over a brass floor lamp. The man moved with the languor of a snail, his arm outstretched, bubbles of blood forming at his lips, then popping. It was as if he had forgotten, or had been momentarily unable, to perform one last task. Then he struggled, in a final effort, to point toward the shelf. He looked at Butch, then gradually turning his head, died, his eyes wide open, fixed on the silver frame.

Butch let the knapsack slump to the floor with a rattle. Then he cautiously inched across the room, following the line of sight up the man's arm – his gaze finally coming to rest on a black and white photograph of the man with his arm around a much younger man who, to Butch's bafflement, looked just like him. He picked up the picture, incredulously studying its happy moment. The shot was apparently taken at a beach house, and the resemblance was so striking that the younger man, in a swimsuit, could've been Butch's brother. Lifelessly, Butch dropped the picture, and it bounced on the carpet near one of the footstool's claw-and-ball feet. The old man's finger, even in death, still pointed to it.

"I don't want any of this," he muttered as Billy entered. "What's with you?" Billy asked, peering at him.

Butch gawked at the picture, then at the man's bright, pellucid eyes, the sublime expression.

"Come on, " Butch said, disgusted, lunging for the door.

"Check everything?"

Billy grabbed the knapsack, glancing around the room. "Drawers, closets?"

Butch stormed from the house, up the tree-lined drive, and Billy labored after him, complaining in a loud whisper, "Hey, wait up. We could've cleaned out the place. No tellin' what an old queen like that's got in there. You know how they like art."

He said the word with the utmost contempt.

Then: "I wanted to pump him once before we –"

Butch struck him down with such a deft, abrupt blow that he knocked him out, the bundles of goods spilling open in a jumble of clangs and clanks.

For months, Butch dreamed about that night over and over, but in the logic of the dream, he and Billy were playing the same role. Dripping wet, they were wearing swimsuits, and when Butch flicked open the knife, Billy stabbed the man. But the reverse was true as well, and when Butch stepped back, he could see that it was Billy, not himself, who turned pale, paralyzed with fear. Holding his loins, the old man floated off the floor, suspended like a saint on what seemed to be, from his ecstatic expression, exquisite joy, a joy which he – or was it Billy? – simply could not tolerate, frantically jabbing him like some large balloon that could pop and let them wake.

Tony

Ten years later, Butch found himself standing in a gay bar, cruising an older man named Tony, Antonio Riscatto, whom he had noticed there occasionally. After the murder, he'd gone from women to men, then, never quite satisfied, from younger to older men, at first hustling, like Billy, then from time to time becoming involved.

He'd donned his usual outfit that night – cowboy boots, faded jeans, and a checked, short-sleeved shirt – then entered the bar around midnight. He moved around, listlessly watching the go-go boy and drinking beer for about an hour, and had been standing at the bar quite some time before he noticed Tony sitting nearby at a small table.

Tony had dark, Italian features, the looks of someone who twenty years ago, because of his fine lines, could've been a distinguished-looking model. The same face now on an angry man would've been intimidating, but on Tony it was simply that of someone serious, not severe, just serious, a quality softened by the seductive hint of a smile.

Butch also noticed that Tony was dressed differently from most men in the bar. Most of the younger men were in denim; the older, in frumpy suits. He, however, was wearing slacks and a narrow belt, a long-sleeved shirt with the sleeves turned up, tasseled loafers and argyle socks. The slacks and shirt were about the same color, a light beige, and made him stand out, though the effect was casual, perhaps even unintended. Overall, the outfit looked comfortable, cool, and relaxed, as was his manner.

Tony lifted his gaze and smiled as if he knew him, then rose and stepped forward, signaling a waiter.

"Hi, " Tony said. "How are you?"

"Fine."

"I'm Tony."

"Glad to meet you," Butch responded, shaking his hand. "I'm Butch."

Tony smiled, then offered a chair, "Have a seat."

He had high cheekbones, a large, gruff nose, and a strong mouth. When seen face-on, Tony's jaw, like Butch's, stuck out on the sides.

"What are you drinking?"

"Scotch, " Butch said. "Scotch on the rocks."

"Two Scotches," Tony said to the waiter.

A couple of drinks smoothed out the conversation, easing the chemistry between them, but Tony didn't size up his tricks so much by what they said as by their faces when they said it – the eyes, of course, the set of the jaw, but also the very draw or give of skin in smiles. In short, he was studying Butch perhaps more than he thought.

Butch's close-cropped hair, his thin eyebrows and lashes made his features look even firmer, more chiseled than they were. But Tony decided that his was a tough face to read, a real riddle. The overall effect, however, was definitely one of strength. Even in the dim, illusory light of the bar, he could tell that Butch had a strong, well-sculpted face. The nose was rounded just enough to give the youth a blunt, sensual air.

Tony followed the line of the jaw, the curve of the chin. He'd snagged himself a real stud, he thought, and he had.

After enough time, Tony asked, "What do you do?"

Butch looked him straight in the eye and asked, "What'd you have in mind?"

Tony liked his freshness, but Butch slacked off, biting his lip. "Just about anything," Butch confessed, meaning work. "Right now I'm a day-jobber. Know what that is?"

You just show up on the site."

Butch seemed to have an easygoing attitude, a certain animal obliviousness about himself, Tony felt, that would make him easy to please and, whether or not he admitted it, quick to please others.

"Construction," Tony mused. Looking up, he said, "I can see you're in shape."

"I've worked hard all my life," Butch said. "'Bout all I have to show for it is

_ "

"A hard body," Tony overlapped. He noted his broad shoulders, the snug shirt, then asked, sitting back in the chair, "But have you had a hard life?"

Toying with his glass, Butch looked from under his eyebrows in such a way that his forehead creased, one of the few wrinkles Tony could detect in his otherwise smooth skin. It was the same look he'd seen on body-builders when they posed, a vain look, of course, but one that always made him smile inwardly and sadly.

"What do you do? " Butch asked.

"I manage a bank."

"Must be money in it," Butch joked.

Tony hesitated, then said deliberately, "Yes."

He touched his glass to his lips as if smelling it, and Butch noticed his ring, a flat, square topaz, as well as the deeply etched lines around his mouth. Tony had good, but dull skin, not glowing like Butch's, and his beard was the kind that he had to shave twice a day.

"Yes," he repeated, "there's money in it."

The dancer took a break, and the lights went down. The general focus of the bar seemed to dissolve into a momentary confusion.

"What time is it?" Butch asked, suddenly restless. "My watch is broke."

Absently, Butch gripped the edge of the table as if, charged up, he needed to flex his arms.

One thirty," Tony said. "Meeting someone?"

"Maybe," Butch snapped, flashing moody.

Tony felt the full force of the youth's green eyes, sad, uncertain, vulnerable eyes set in solid cheekbones. But Tony had some powerful eyes of his own, cool-blue, like his mood, and so deep-set that, in bar light, it was hard to sort the dark eyebrows from the dark eyes themselves. Such honest, piercing eyes, Butch knew, could see through nonsense.

"Maybe not," Butch said, relenting. "Maybe I'll just go home. Been a long day."

Butch could tell from Tony's soft smile that he was the type who could forget wrongs easily. He might be good for him. 'Too much to drink?' Tony asked.

"Not anymore than you, I bet."

"I have an uncanny ability to remain sober. Cold sober." "I try to practice moderation myself."

"Moderation," Tony said, turning the phrase over. "Above the door of the Temple of Apollo at Delphi were carved two slogans: 'Moderation' and 'Know yourself.'"

"Oh, yeah?" Butch smiled.

Near the man, Butch felt pointless and hesitant. He admired Tony's Buddha-like composure. He sensed that he could be someone important in his life and resolved to seize the opportunity, to play out the line for a bite. And Tony bit.

"Why are we here?" Tony asked slowly, carefully. "Why are we here?"

And so Butch let Tony pick him up that night and take him to a two-story, Georgian house in one of the few remaining in-close neighborhoods in the city. Butch had never seen anything like it. The whole place was decorated in Art Deco.

A couple of months later, he let him take him to "Turandot." Butch had also never seen anything like an opera, but Tony said that he had his own box and they could leave whenever he wanted. Butch didn't leave, however, and Tony was so impressed by the tears he shed over the aria, Calaf's "Nessun dorma," that a great love took root in his heart.

To Butch, Tony's bedroom was like a less detailed, yet just as fabulous, scene from the opera. The bed was situated on a dais, and above it loomed a mural of a cherry tree swept by wind and trailing, against a smoke-grey background, hundreds of small, pinkish-white blossoms.

On the drive home, Butch had kept to himself, but when they entered the room, he dropped to Tony's feet and began to cry.

"I'm sorry. Forgive me, please. I never meant to – " "Shh!" Tony said, squatting, mussing his hair.

When they'd met, Butch's hair was so short that Tony couldn't tell much about it, but now that he was letting it grow, Tony could see that it was a crisp, light-brown with highlights, the kind of hair that stood up on its own. It glimmered at his touch, and he savored the thick feel of it, the clean smell of it, the presence of the young man's thoughts near his hand.

"Shh," he said. Then holding Butch's chin, he smiled, "Look at me."

Butch searched his face with ashamed eyes.

"I forgive you," Tony said. "Whatever's troubling you so much, I forgive you. Yes, sure," he stressed, taking his arms, lifting him to his feet.

He held him, rocking him like a child. Then Tony realized that there really was something more than a beautiful melody that had moved Butch to tears. Some cancerous guilt was gnawing at his soul, the knowledge of which at first disturbed Tony. Then out of sheer love, out of the need to console someone as he himself – or, for that matter, anyone – would wish to be consoled, he granted him a full pardon, he gave him another chance. All Tony knew was that Butch had been very kind to him. Surely, whatever Butch had done and felt so badly about could not outweigh the quiet voice of his kindness.

"He who is forgiven little, loves little," Tony said in a strangely rehearsed tone of voice.

"You forgive me completely," Butch asked, gulping air, "no matter what I've done, no matter how bad?"

Tony spoke directly into his face.

"There's nothing you could've done which I wouldn't forgive. You're a good man, Butch. So stop all this nonsense." Smiling, he joked, "Te absolvo. Set your mind at rest."

"Thanks, thanks," Butch gasped, flushed, hugging him tightly – the pang of his joy only as sharp as the painful memory of the murder.

The clear, bright eyes, the hand still pointing the way to him-self, the photograph of the man with his arm around him – the whole terrible scene flashed before him with perfect clarity, then sank into obscurity. For the first time since that night, he felt as if some heavy chain had been struck from his heart. The paralytic walked. The prisoner was set free.

Tony led him to bed, where he collapsed, in his tux, and fell into such a deep slumber that Tony had to undress him, a task which he found not entirely without its rewards. Though he was by now thoroughly familiar with the intimacies of his body, including the small tattoo, the moment was, in fact, his first chance to study him at length in the full glare of the lights. The various facets of his face, he knew, like those of an intricate gem, were little windows through which, if he were not blinded by them, he could glimpse the fiery hub of the stone. Or was what he saw there not revelations, but reflections of himself, of what he wanted to see?

Butch's skin had the smooth luster of a polished surface, except for a couple of creases Tony discovered under the eyes and around the mouth. His tan made the firm skin look even smoother – the color of his cheeks, like cast bronze. Even his beard looked smooth. His cheeks and chin didn't have the coarse, dull finish of the skin of someone more mature. Then he realized that Butch was the type who would never have a rough beard. He noticed the peach fuzz just above his shave line. Such fine, pale hair.

As the dating progressed, and Tony was more sure of himself with Butch, he broached a certain subject.

"What's your real name?" he asked, driving to a mountain cabin he'd rented. "I mean your given name."

Butch leaned over as if to kiss him, but instead said, "Vic. For Victor."

"Victor," Tony said. "I like that. I think you've got a little Italian in you."

"I think I've got in a little Italian."

Tony smiled sheepishly.

"Mind if I call you Vic."

"All right with me," he beamed, his eyes steady, observant, probing Tony's motive.

He figured Tony thought Butch was a boy's name, but could use Vic when he introduced him to friends.

In his own restrained way, Tony also begged him to move in with him.

"You don't have to dote on me," he stated very business-like. If you could just be there for me from time to time."

And he was, against his better judgment – immediately after an embarrassing, yet outwardly insignificant, incident in a bar.

Vic had moved through the preliminaries with a pretty Latin number and was just on the verge of bringing their conversation to a successful close when speaking of Tony, he said, boasting, "A rich banker. A golden opportunity, you might say."

Since Vic and Tony frequented mostly the same bars, it was not uncommon for them to run into each other occasionally, and at that moment Vic's blood ran cold, dead cold. Somehow he sensed Tony's presence.

He faced Tony, then said, setting down his beer, "Sorry. Just bullshit, you know."

Tony knew only too well that there were other men, for himself as well as Vic, but at the thought of losing him, his love metastasized, as if through the bloodstream, the roots growing deeper and choking his heart. Despite himself, his mouth sagged. His eyes raked the floor. He drooped like a puppet on a string. Then he reached inside and found the courage to straighten himself up, forcing a smile.

"OK," he agreed, studying Vic's face, accepting his explanation.

Vic draped an arm over Tony's shoulder, furtively glancing at the number as they left.

"Said he had an eagle on 'is ass," Vic smirked, stepping into the streetlight.

"And you thought you'd like to see it fly," Tony conjectured, his voice indulgent, calm.

His patience with men like Vic had long since become a solemn ritual.

Vic pressed his left hand against the wall, bracing against the building, effectively blocking Tony's way.

"'Bout your offer," he said. "If it still stands -"

"What offer?" Tony asked, his hands in his pockets.

Vic stroked Tony's head: hair like thick, black smoke laced with smoky strands of grey swept back from the widow's peak on his high forehead – every hair in place, unlike Butch's kink.

"You know, 'bout moving in.' Then, referring to a noisy neighbor, he joked nervously, That guy upstairs's driving me nuts."

At first, they continued the open relationship, as Tony expected, but the older Vic got, the less he needed to satisfy his sensual appetite, the more he needed to satisfy some strange, dark need in his soul. It was as if the only purpose he could find in life anymore was to spoil Tony.

When Tony finally believed that Vic really cared for him – at least, was bound to him somehow – he decided to go ahead and set him up financially.

"You don't have to work, if you don't want to," Tony promised. "You can do whatever you want. Whatever you want is fine with me."

Vic didn't want just to sit idle. So, unofficially, he became one of Tony's assistants, a courier of sorts, taking care of matters within his means, trying to make himself as useful as possible.

Tony also decided to take him to Italy both to visit relatives and to enjoy what Tony had never dreamed of: a real honey-moon.

The first morning, when Vic woke, the high, cracked ceiling looked unfamiliar. He was nude, wrapped in sheets, his head sunk in a giant, fluffy pillow, but he couldn't recall where he was. All he knew was that it was early and that he felt wonderful – pleasantly numb, yet sensually keen at the same time – the most well-rested he'd ever felt. For a while, he simply lay still, letting the world materialize around him. Then he remembered the night before.

A party in their honor was already in full swing when they arrived. Tony's Aunt Octavia introduced them to an excited troop of family and neighbors, then immediately set about organizing a lavish picnic on the lawn. Yet when the guests lingered and the family failed to turn in, drinking and singing late into the night, she waited for an opportunity, then sneaked them off toward their room, and since there was no electricity in that wing, stopped to light a couple of candles on the way. "I'll show you the way," she said furtively.

Octavia was almost seventy, and age had eroded what was obviously her youthful prettiness down to thick, mannish features. She wore plain clothes, no makeup, and her hair pinned in a bun. Her one concession to vanity was a pair of simple gold earrings, and yet she showed a rare flamboyancy of spirit which belied her reserved appearance.

Opening the door, she handed Tony a candle, then asked, You have a good time?"

"Ci stiamo divertendo moltissimo," Tony answered.

"Di prima classe," Vic said, showing off the phrase. "Oh, grazie," she smiled, patting his hand.

Her eyes sparkled. Her face softened to a sweet, thoughtful expression.

"Tony's a wonderful man," she confided, "and I know that a friend of his must be wonderful, too. Enjoy yourselves," she winked. "Il sole non brilla nella tomba." She kissed them on the cheek, then urged them through the door, whispering, "Buona notte."

"What?" Vic asked when she'd closed the door.

"'The sun doesn't shine in the grave,' an old saying of hers," Tony mused, noticing a splotch of missing stucco.

He touched the stone underneath, then began undressing, hanging his clothes neatly in the wardrobe.

"I'd forgotten how content she is," he explained.

Vic tore out of his clothes, dropping them over a chair.

"To her, life's simple," Tony said. "People know what they like, as long as they don't impose it on someone else."

Vic climbed among the luxuriant linen, his body, except for his buttocks, a raw brown against the twilight clouds of the sheets.

"When I first broached the subject with her," Tony said, "I told her a boy in the village had made a pass. Really, it was the other way around, and she may have known that. But know what she said? 'Taste everything. Then you'll know what you like.'"

When Octavia had heard they were coming to visit, she set up a spare room, and it was, in fact, spare in the sense of sparsely appointed. The room was spacious, cool, and resonant; it was furnished with a big double bed with a night stand to either side, a large mahogany wardrobe, and a desk with an oil lamp and chair. A large Oriental carpet covered most of the stone floor, and two faint, threadbare tapestries faced each other across the room: the one over the bed, of Hercules with a sword and Iolaus with a flaming brand; the one on the opposite wall, of Hebe with a wine cup.

Tired and tipsy, Vic had only a vague impression of the shadowy room, a stored stage set from some grand opera.

"Smells damp in here," he whispered, excited. "Like bedding down in some ancient ruin."

Tony blew out the candle....

Vic heard a rooster crowing somewhere far off, then a closer sound – the brittle clink of china – and turned to peer through the long, breezy sheers leaning into the room. Beyond them sat Tony in his plaid robe and leather slippers, sipping tea and reading a paper, and beyond him spread a deep-blue sky fading to haze. The screams of children playing erupted from somewhere outside, somewhere far below, and Vic leisurely rolled over and reached for his robe.

When he stepped barefoot onto the cool tiles of the terrace, he could also hear the twitter of birds and, from a great distance, the faint bass of a dog barking. The table was set with yi tsing ware, a bowl of oranges, and a small vase with ferns and yellow lilies.

Tony sensed his presence and, smiling over his shoulder, said, "Octavia sent the kids off to play so as not to disturb us."

Vic strolled to Tony, then standing near him, eyed both the pot of tea and pot of coffee Octavia had laid out, the sugar bowl with the spoon in it, the cream, the bread, the butter, the marmalade. The aroma of the coffee curled to his nose.

"Need anything?" Tony asked, turning the page. "The oranges are from the orchard."

"No, I'm fine," Vic said, slipping a hand from a pocket, touching Tony on the shoulder. "I'll get some coffee in a minute."

Tony smiled at him, patted his hand, then resumed reading. Vic gazed at him awhile – the silver woven into his hair at the temples, the white smear of talcum on his chest where the robe lay open, the tan glow of his legs as they slipped from the robe.

Then he moved to the balustrade and, leaning on it, took in the orchard, the gardens, the dewy grounds. The house was situated on a height and afforded quite a view. Among the trees floated Chinese lanterns, leftovers from the party. He heard a trickle of laughter and caught the last, colorful glimpse of the children disappearing into the orchard. Down the hill, to the right, glimmered the liquid sapphire of a small, smooth lake. Tiny suns danced on the surface, then burst with glare.

He turned to watch Tony, and a hush fell over the terrace. He wanted to say something. Perhaps just thanks. He wasn't sure.

And so it was near Firenze, on the terrace of Tony's Aunt Octavia's house, that the picture was taken that would become, for Vic, the keepsake more treasured than even Tony's house and the rest of a substantial legacy. Only the odd alabaster flask which Tony had bought at a street market seemed to hold as much mysterious significance. Tony had objected to the conspicuous bottle of baby oil they used, and so they had kept their lubricant in the flask, set like bric-a-brac beside the bed.

Tony had developed angina, a condition he'd managed, through his great poise, to hide from Vic, and after the fatal heart attack, Vic grieved unbearably. It was as if he had seen himself and the rest of his life reflected in the iridescent sheen of a bubble, which popped. At least, he knew that for a few years he'd made Tony unquestionably happy. Their life together was the best he could do, or so he thought, to make up for the one great error of his youth, the unspeakable secret he'd locked in his soul not only to protect himself, but, after Tony had chosen him, him as well.

How strange, he thought. They'd both kept secrets from each other.

Kit

Then – out of loneliness, he assumed – he was drawn to the bars again. Enough time had passed, he felt, so that he could desire someone again without diminishing Tony's memory, and it was actually the good influence of his lover's memory that, at first, compelled him to turn, instead of to the Dynamo, the hustler bar, to the Library, a more conjugal, middle-class disco.

The Library was appropriately dark and smoky, too, but at times flashing lights penetrated even the most quiet corner and there was less smoke, smoke intertwined with the scent of aftershave and cologne. There were bookshelves with real books, a thick carpet, and, around the parquet dance-floor, comfortable sofas and armchairs, but the feature Vic liked best was a wide terrace overlooking one of the major streets in the area.

Young professionals on the way up and the older, more established businessmen who could help them gathered there – especially on Friday afternoons after work – and, from time to time, he'd meet a young man.

"Hi, I'm Vic," he'd say, introducing himself, squinting in the glare.

"Hi," the blond, brunet, or red-haired young man would respond. "I'm Peter." Paul or John...

In time, he'd formed a coterie of young friends, including Allen, one he was particularly fond of, and thus the pain of Tony's death eased, transformed, in fact, to a sort of vague, triste concern for the young men, who now seemed, if brash, also confused and vulnerable. His motive, as far as he could understand it, was, in a certain sense, pure – a rock they could grab, a lit window in a distant house.

For a while, Vic considered pursuing Allen. Allen was a neatly groomed, well-dressed brunet with the sort of solid good looks noticed only when he dressed up or someone realized what a gentleman he was. His body was not very well defined, but he was lanky and hairy in a callow, yet virile way, and what he may have lacked in physique he made up for in geniality. Allen was better than the rest, Vic decided. Allen was more interested in what a person looked like inside. But it was for just that reason that he was not Vic's type. Allen was not especially driven to seek out older men.

Then came the nights when, after a few drinks, Vic would fail to score, when he felt he needed to, and was just too lonely to go home alone, returning to the Dynamo, as he told himself, for old times' sake. One swing by the bar, and it was as if the alcoholic had picked up a drink, the addict lapsed into his poisonous addiction. This time, however, he frequented the place in a different guise, not as the worshiped idol, but the suppliant john. He'd met Tony there, he reasoned. Perhaps he could do something for someone like himself. Besides, to the initiated, there was nothing like the base kick only paid sex could give.

"Hi, I'm Butch," he said, slipping back into his nickname. "Hi," the Rocco, Lou, or Joe would laugh and sometimes respond, "I'm butch, too."

Thus, he played the ostensibly cheerful Vic at the Library until around one, then the lonely, compromised Butch at the Dynamo.

The hustlers performed, then took his money, sometimes threatening him for more, goading him with names like faggot or fruit. The names meant nothing to him, but one night he made the mistake of picking up a particularly hot, hyped-up punk. He stole a watch, which Butch ignored, but when he tried to rough him up, repeatedly jumping against him, like a dog, Butch surprised him with his strength and savvy.

"I ought to smash your face, you little – " He stopped just short of becoming his adversary, then added, "Don't you know it's you you hate!"

"Sorry, man. I'm sorry," the boy cowered, covering his head with his hands. "Thought we'd play around."

They exchanged a strange look, one of panic and desire. Then the boy fled.

Some nights, however, the bother and risk, the stupid, swaggering abuse, hardly seemed worthwhile, and the liquor and late hours seemed to be taking their toll. When he felt like that, he'd simply sit home alone, watching television or playing over and over again "Nessun donna," the aria which Tony had chosen, over his strong objections, to be their song.

Once more, he would put on the record. Once more, the somber night would cast its eerie spell, transforming the silent, moonlit garden. Once more, Prince Calaf would be waiting for him, gazing at the stars. The broad, slow, magically flowing melody unwound from Calaf s heart, repeated, like an echo, by the strings, repeated, like an even more distant echo, by the faint, tremulous chorus, building finally toward the full orchestra's passionate statement of the conquering power of love. His pulse throbbed, and all at once one night he thought he'd solved the music's riddle. The exquisite strings, the dark pavilion, were, in fact, an echo of his feelings, and the more he listened to the aria, the more he understood the mysterious link between the clusters of notes and his deep longing – the more he understood that he simply had to love just one more person before he could peacefully live alone.

And so it was with a pleasant surprise that he finally met Kit, a young motorcycle mechanic who seemed very comfortable with him, who seemed to respond to him immediately, as he had with Tony years ago. One day, Kit had roared up in a park, wearing torn jeans, a knit pullover, and unbuckled biker's boots, in short, clothes he could slip out of quickly. When Butch noticed that the top button of the jeans was unbuttoned, adrenaline flared through his chest.

"Your bottom lip's 'bout the sexiest thing I've ever seen," Kit said, high, running his thumb across it.

Kit was a warm, masculine, sun-bleached blond. His oval face had softer lines than those of the men Butch had known, lines that, in reflex, curved to a sunny laugh. But there was also a vague trace of some coarse anger in his eyes, a warning easily missed, just as someone could miss, though the eyes were grey, the brown motes ringing his iris. Since he was fair, he turned pink in the sun, not tan, and his cheeks broke out with a sprig of acne, as well as roses. His hair was straight, about medium length, combed back in a shock as if he'd pushed it back with his hand or the wind had flattened it as he sped off on his Harley.

They dated. Then Butch entered upon his second long-term relationship.

Early on, Kit had confessed that his father had died in a fight at a labor union and that he had a twin, Kirk, serving time for burglary.

But giving him a strange smile, Butch replied tenderly, as he well might, "Well, I'd better run you outta here then. It's clear you've got bad blood."

Afterward, the two hardly ever discussed the brother except the few times a year when Kit would visit him, bringing him cash and cigarettes.

Butch told Kit about Tony and partly about the aria and how Tony had died at breakfast one morning, clawing his shirt, but Kit did not respond to the aria, Puccini, or the arts in general the way Butch had. Still, Butch sensed a sensibility in the youth, something thinking, feeling, perhaps even helplessly responsive to Butch's needs. They went to ball games, movies, and concerts, to Italy, Spain, and Greece. They climbed a flight of steps outside, yet parallel to their trips as well, and it was only a matter of time till Kit would suddenly break down one night and tell Butch – quietly listening, yet inwardly overjoyed – how much he cared for him. Butch said that he cared for him, too, but because he did, he still wanted him to see other men, men more nearly his own age.

At first, what Kit took to be Butch's rejection cut him deeply. Kit thought that he was lying to him, that he was simply tired of him and wanted him to leave.

"Cockroaches, all of you!" Kit glared, stung. "Filthy, little cockroaches, crawlin' around in the night."

Grabbing his shirt, Kit slammed him against the wall. Then yielding, he sighed, "I just want – I just want – " A hurt spark arced from Kit's eyes.

"Big fakes!" he scowled, releasing him. "Big goddamn fakes!"

"No," Butch replied. "I'm not."

And in time Kit did see that Butch was not like the others, that he was truly a godsend.

A photo of the two replaced the one on the shelf, but not in Butch's thoughts. In fact, he arranged situations in which Kit could meet other men, and the one Butch thought might take did, like a fire – Allen, the enlightened trick who'd grown into a friend. Few would see what they had in common, he knew, but he also knew that inwardly they fit together well. Their sense of fairness matched. Their differences would stoke the marriage.

As Allen would say, "Blue collar, white collar – the same red blood in our veins."

In short, Butch short-circuited his own affair, fostering theirs, not only setting Kit up in a steady job but also setting them both up in a large flat on the top floor of a handsome co-op. He visited often just as they dropped in on him, and the more all three went out together, whether to a movie, nightclub, or game, the more Kit and Allen began to think of Butch as a sort of wonderful father-in-law or, in the pejorative nomenclature of the time, an auntie. Strangely enough, when everyone had settled into the new arrangement, Butch reverted to his real name again.

Besides the bedroom, Vic began to spend more and more time in the den, a somber, yet elegant room with black, lacquered bookcases, ebony armchairs, and a dozen or so silver picture frames with mirrors instead of photos. Depending on which fixture he turned on, the mirrors reflected oblong spangles around the room – on the walls, the draperies, the ceiling.

One night late, just as he was adjusting a mirror, directing its reflection through one of the grey, ghostlike sheers, someone knocked. He turned down the aria, then tied his robe and moved toward the door.

When he opened it, Kit stepped inside, his eyes red and puffy.

As they entered the den, he asked, "Forgive me, please."

He looked so troubled that Vic embraced him, patting him on the back. In a flash, Vic remembered kneeling at Tony's feet, feeling the blessing of his hand on his head, being lifted and rocked like a child, and all at once, the affection Vic had felt for Kit was like an eclipse compared to the bright revelation he felt then. Tony, he believed, must have loved him the same way.

But he could not imagine the source of Kit's grief, and a swarm of reasons swirled through his mind. Were the tears tears of joy? Had he, not Kirk, committed the burglary – or some other awful crime? Had he been unfaithful to Allen?

Vic knew that for most people attachments burned themselves out. Even real love dimmed over time to a small, yet steady flame. Was the small, dim flame simply not enough against the great, dark loneliness of life, the weight of which, for some reason, Vic himself had felt bearing down upon him more and more of late, despite Kit's husky voice on the phone, despite Tony's handsome smile in his dreams. Tony had accepted the mystery of Vic's own humbling breakdown, accepted it or read into it. Perhaps he should simply accept the mystery of Kit's.

You okay?" Kit asked, stepping back, gazing at him.

And Vic realized that Kit had been crying not over any of the reasons he'd thought of, not even a statue, book, or aria, or even an old man's brutal death, as he had years ago, but out of his deep concern for him, out of devotion.

"Living here alone," Kit said. "In this big house."

Kit glanced around the room – at the roll-top desk, the Chinese panels, the African rug where they'd cuddled and slept.

"I'm not alone," Vic countered. "I have you – and Allen." "Maybe we should've moved in here," he said, stepping past Vic.

"I don't think so," Vic smiled, turning. "Look," he began again, placing his hand on his shoulder. "I love you, more than anything else in the world. And I know you love me."

Kit grabbed the back of an armchair.

"But I also know you love Allen."

"Not like you," Kit insisted. "I should be with you, not him. I'll change," he blurted, facing him.

Vic knew that he meant he would be even more loyal, even more emotionally committed.

"Let me move in with you," Kit pleaded, touching Vic's arms. "No," Vic replied, adamant.

He hesitated.

"I'm not that different from a father to you. You and Allen go for each other the way gay men should."

Their happiness was his happiness. He wouldn't have it any other way.

"I know you two. I see you every week." Then with an amused look, he joked, "It's time I sang the melody alone." "What?"

"I want to spend some time to myself," he explained, moving off, deliberately lying to him.

Then he knew that, basically, what he'd said was true.

"I made you happy," Kit claimed, following him. "I know I did."

"You did," Vic agreed, turning. "You do. But what about Allen? You're just going to rip out his heart and throw it away?"

Once smoking pot with Vic, Tony had told him how certain Mediterranean tribes drugged victims before sacrificing them, and it was with much the same ineffable euphoria that he was willing to sacrifice himself as well.

"Making you happy g-gave me – " Kit stammered. He leaned on the bookcase, the words stuck in his throat. "A purpose in life," he said. "Nothing ever made sense. It didn't make sense till you."

Vic turned Kit around, then held him, rocking him as they stood in place.

Head bowed, Kit clinched the shoulders of Vic's robe, then groaned, "No."

He was not only disagreeing with Vic. He was rejecting one of the basic conditions of life – its awful loneliness, what had kept him awake at night, like a fever, then hid in his heart by day.

'Tell me you forgive me, please," Kit insisted, hugging him tightly.

Vic looked him straight in the eyes and said, with the utmost seriousness, "Yes, I forgive you." He cupped his face, then added, 'There's nothing you could do I wouldn't forgive."

"Completely."

"You're a good man, Kit. You are a good man," he stressed. You know that, don't you? Don't you?"

Kit nodded. His joy at being forgiven was only the mirror of Vic's at forgiving him, at forgiving himself.

"Now stop worrying," Vic said, "and sit down."

Yet they remained standing near the bookcase, staring at each other.

"And you're OK?" Kit asked again, finally releasing him. "I'm fine," he grinned. "Believe me. Just call me now and then."

Kit stared at him, then collapsed into a chair. Standing there, Vic took in the graceful mouth, the cute nose, the rash brushstroke of his eyebrows. All of a sudden, he realized just what he was giving up.

"What?" Kit asked, glancing up, his lips open, firm, wet.

Vic thought for a moment, then smiled, "Nothing. Forgot I turned on the stereo. Couldn't figure out where the music was coming from."

Kirk

The years blew by like leaves, and Vic was transformed into the grey moth of the aged: still slim and handsome, but his features less defined. He'd always had youthful skin, and it was not as rough and wrinkled as it could have been. Overnight, it seemed, his hair had turned to fleece, and he combed it in a sort of ducktail to cover a thin spot. His eyebrows, as well, looked like wisps of snow – his eyes downcast in thought more often now.

He liked to wear an old, brown cardigan to keep warm, even in summer, and he was just slipping out of it to go to bed one night when Allen called, as he and Kit did often, whether to make plans for dinner or just to check on him. Recently, he'd grown moody, they thought.

"Kit's down with a cold," Allen said. "How are you?"

After the call, Vic turned in, and fell into a light sleep in which he dreamed that as he opened the patio doors, he discovered someone sitting in one of the wrought-iron chairs. Tony lifted his gaze and smiled as if he'd been waiting for him. He rose and stepped forward, his hand up as if to welcome him. Or was it a benediction? But something about the dream disturbed Vic, and he woke to avoid it. His curiosity got the better of him, though, and he rose to check the patio, fumbling for the old sweater.

There was no one there, of course, but he decided to take a seat and kill a few minutes till he felt sleepy again. Lately, he'd had trouble sleeping and wished that the night, pleasant as it was, would be over. Despite the fact that he'd deliberately given up Kit, life solo, even at what he considered his advanced age – he felt much older than he was – did not sit well with him. He wished that someone were, in fact, sitting with him and imagined Tony idling in the other chair, saying nothing, just gazing at the stars as he had on Octavia's terrace in Italy, just being there – for him.

Waking from the dream, he gazed at the stars. They made him think of the trembling dew in Italy. They made him think of the glimmering lake and, across town, Kit asleep in Allen's arms, and finally a great peace, like the hush in the yard, fell over him.

"My secret lies hidden within me," he murmured, paraphrasing the aria. "No one shall discover my name."

He peered deep into the dark bushes, like shadowy figures, at the end of the lawn, then rose slowly. He wanted to hear "Nessun donna" just once more before turning in.

Once the music began – the tenor blooming into song – he gently picked up the picture of Kit and himself arm in arm at a sidewalk table in Mykonos. They were making a toast to the camera, and the glasses of Campari looked like huge rubies.

Perfect, Vic thought, lingering over their expressions. Well worth the price.

Then he thought of the merciful picture in the drawer, the one of Tony and himself, then remembered the one in the old man's den, this time serenely. Love, like music, swelled in his heart – love for himself, for everyone – and he realized, to his great surprise, that he was not only the boy in the frame, but also, now that he'd aged, the old man.

The knife, he knew, would not really hurt.

ENOCH
Keith Banner

The first time I heard a KISS song was with Terry in the attic of his stepmother's house. It was a hot July afternoon, a Saturday. Terry's little cream-colored transistor radio vibrated with "I Wanna Rock 'n' Roll All Night and Party Everyday" as we tried to find an old Frisbee. We were bored as hell. The attic smelled musty and raw. Old sweaty furniture sat in shadows, and little holes in the roof let in dusty sunshine. Terry had on shorts and was shirtless, his feet in ragged sweat socks. He was muscular, and his face was lean, with small brown eyes and a pushed-in nose. He'd gotten a perm last week, a loose afro like a nest. Terry's step mom, a beautician named Lulu, had given him the perm because he said he didn't want to have to wash and comb his hair all the time.

He was busy with his summer job, painting little natural-gas pipe sheds for the gas-company. I didn't have a job, but sometimes I hung out with Terry on the job, watching him paint the little buildings that were usually beside abandoned railroad tracks. Terry was seventeen, and I was fourteen.

"Look under that couch over there man," Terry said. His skin was red and peeling, and still had little flecks of white paint on it from yesterday. He lifted a bird cage up off an ornate, broken-down bureau.

"Sure."

I got down on the floor on my stomach. Under the couch were four mousetraps. One had a dry carcass of a mouse in it, and I avoided looking at it. The KISS song on the radio made me feel weird, because I'd seen pictures of KISS in a People magazine at the grocery store, and since then I'd always thought they were devil-worshippers. My dad made me listen to gospel music, because he was the music director at our church. Dad hated Terry. Terry wasn't a churchgoer. His dad was dead, from a bad liver.

I got up. "Nope," I said.

The tinny rock song continued. Terry went back deep into the attic, into the speckled darkness. Sweat snaked down my face. I was fat and wore a sweatshirt with cut-off sleeves. The sweatshirt helped me hide my flab. I wore shorts and a pair of sneakers. My hair was cut to my skull, Dad's work. Dad had big black shears, and every other Saturday night he would set up a barbershop in the kitchen. As I pulled back a big painting of a dark ocean to look behind it, I thought about how I'd watched Terry's step mom give him the perm last week. Lulu was thin with dyed blonde hair, and she wore heavy mascara. The perm fluid smelled sickly sweet, like hot candy. Terry's tall body had been suspended near a yellow tub of water on the dinette-table. Lulu's hands massaged the perm fluid in. Terry had talked all the time through about how much time this perm would give him in the mornings.

The KISS song went off. I felt relieved. I saw the KISS faces from People again: one guy had a long tongue, with a white demonic clown face, vomiting blood in concert. Next was a song by Led Zeppelin, the DJ said. Then the radio went off.

"Fuck," Terry said.

He ran out of the back of the attic to his little square radio, picked it up off the floor and slammed his hand against one side, but nothing happened.

"I need batteries," he said.

"Yeah," I said.

Terry took the back off the transistor radio, then threw the batteries under the drab sofa, pivoting his arm as if he were throwing dice. He replaced the cover.

We ain't going to find a Frisbee up here," Terry said, defeated.

"Yeah," I said.

Terry went over to the couch and sat down on it. He wiped sweat off his forehead. The silence in the attic had bird-chirps in it. Terry just sat there, and I felt queasy, wondering why Terry was even my friend. He was older and had a job, and yet he hung out with me all the time. Once Mom said that she'd heard Terry was retarded. I thought about Terry's bedroom. He had little Mead notebooks filled with pictures of movie and rock stars, cellophane-taped to notebook paper. Raquel Welch, Burt Reynolds, Elton John, The Bee-Gees. On some of them, Terry had written in careful printing the date and what magazine he had cut them out of.

Terry took off his sweat socks and rubbed his toes. "It's hot up here," he said.

"Yeah," I said.

I moved near the bird cage, near the wall, and started fingering the rusty spokes of the cage. An old bird smell came out of there, raw ammonia, the dustiness of feathers. Terry pulled back his curly hair, slouching on the sofa. I looked at Terry's radio beside his thigh. Again I could hear the echo of KISS. I saw them: black-leather costumes and painted-up faces, long hair, spiked heels and electric guitars. My dad played George Beverly Shea and Tennessee Ernie Ford singing "Amazing Grace," "I've Found the Light," "Just As I Am," and other tunes at night. I remembered last summer, when I hadn't known Terry – how I'd won a contest for memorizing the most Bible verses at Vacation Bible School: 37. Dad, who'd run VBS, had crowned me with a construction paper crown with glitter on it at a night-convocation in church. I'd also won a huge Hershey Bar, which I ate that night in my bedroom. One Bible verse came into my head then: "And Enoch walked with God: and he was not, for God took him. Genesis 5, verse 24."

Terry slipped off his shorts and sat there. "No Frisbee today," he said.

He was hard, and he just started doing it. I watched, and my cheeks got hot until they felt hard like baked potatoes. I was smiling, but it was a mask. To me, he looked scary and beautiful with his face opening up with the pleasure. To the slight sucking sound from what he was doing, I pulled down my jeans. Terry started moaning.

I stood near the bird cage, my underwear still on, watching him, and suddenly I wanted to cry. I thought I could smell Terry's loneliness as I watched him jack off: it was the smell of old furniture and rotten wood and dusty feathers. But the sadness only mingled with my own heat and desire. I hated Terry for a second, but only for a second. Mostly, I was impressed. His cock was very beautiful, I began to think. The heat got intense, like radiation. I pulled down my underwear, keeping my shirt on.

Terry rose off the couch, making an arch with his body, his head pressed against the back of the sofa. His head went back and forth as he started to come. It was like, for a second, I couldn't breathe any more. But soon I was caught up in a breathless fury as I took my cock in my hand.

Then the bird cage fell off onto the floor, making a sound like someone pounding on a piano, but neither of us could stop.

PRINCE CHARMING
William Barber

"So this is Prince Charming!" Rinaldo fluttered with enthusiasm. Buddy blushed. I made the introductions, and within moments Buddy was seated in the salon chair, the three of us reflected in a large, antique, oval mirror. Rinaldo ran his hands through Buddy's thick black hair.

And just what did we have in mind?" Rinaldo asked, giving me the fish eye, and waiting to see who would reply to his question.

Naturally, I spoke first: "We would like something trendy but distinguished, something that would wear well on an open yacht."

Rinaldo's unflinching eye was on me, and it seemed to look through me to observe my adoration for Buddy. He poked and pulled at Buddy's hair, turning his head this way and that. I stood nervously, hoping that what he decided on would create the desired effect.

"Perhaps," Rinaldo said, "we should just go Disco Grease Helmet."

The thought of associating such an unflattering name for a haircut with Buddy upset me.

"Nothing too drastic, Rinaldo. He's doing the Hamptons, not Xenon."

Rinaldo did not care to be challenged on his knowledge of the proper haircut, and he shot me an angry look. "You want a French twist, perhaps?"

"No, I want something...perfect."

Throughout this exchange, Buddy sat wide-eyed in the chair, looking back and forth between us, as if he were watching a tennis match. He would not be consulted in the matter of his own haircut.

"How about something absolutely Tomorrow!" Rinaldo grew excited.

"Tomorrow?" I asked worriedly.

Rinaldo's hands got busy again in Buddy's hair. "I'll perm the snot out of the top, leave the back long and straight, and then shear it right to his temples in the front."

Buddy's eyes lit up in anticipation of a cut so totally avant-garde. I put the kibosh on that one right away.

"Darling, we're not filming Star Wars," I insisted. "We can't have him walking around looking like Woody Woodpecker."

"I'm not talking Gladiator's Revenge, for Chrissake!" Rinaldo grew testy.

The decision seemed to grow more impossible. To do anything to alter Buddy's natural good looks would be ridiculous, and yet the right haircut would be the crowning glory. It would be worth the trouble, if we could only decide what was right.

Outside Mr. Rinaldo's salon, the summer of 1980 was becoming much like any other summer in New York. The breeze off the Hudson River, which usually lingers into May, had subsided and the air conditioner in the storefront whirred.

For me, Buddy was the essence of that summer. At 20, he came to New York University to study film and acting. He had transferred in mid-January from Kings College, in some lost and forgotten coal-mining town in Pennsylvania, where he starred in one or two student productions. Shakespeare had aroused a passion for literature. It became my lucky pleasure to have him in a class I was teaching that semester on the literature of the Renaissance. I still recall the shock of Buddy's unique beauty, the morning I first laid eyes on him while calling roll. I remember the clothes he wore: Levis and Pendleton, with work boots crusted on the edge of the sole with dry cement.

A cowlick in his pitch-black hair stood up like a small hand waving, as it would through the next few years that I knew him.

His skin was a shade of white one seldom sees, the fairest of the fair. It contrasted starkly with his thick black hair which, until this very moment under Rinaldo's fingers, in a pageboy. His jaw was strong, and even though he must have shaved an hour before, his beard was visible under the whiteness. His face was Anglo-Saxon, a throwback through the centuries to a ploughman tilling the field beside his master's castle. His expression seemed always on the edge of being startled. His laugh was easy and deep, and a part of almost everything he said. And his teeth were perfectly straight and white, as though his father must also have been his dentist.

One grew hungry just to look at him, buried in disheveled clothing. But his most amazing feature: his wide and expressive lavender eyes, muted by a pair of odd, wire-rimmed glasses. The glasses were the touch that brought him back to earth, the accessory that humanized rather than enhanced.

If I were a sculptor assembling objects to recreate his skin, hair and eyes, I would use bone china, mink, and lapis lazuli. Like these fragile materials, Buddy's kind of beauty could not survive unmutilated by life. And did I, by taking him to the best men's hair stylist in New York, begin his degradation?

Rinaldo stepped back and tilted his head to get a different perspective. "How about something that whispers 'Money'?' "Like what?" I demanded.

Rinaldo began to describe what would become Buddy's quintessential haircut, created then and there for him by the hands of the artiste. It would become known as the Buddy Cut. Reluctantly, I gave in to Rinaldo's plea that I trust him, and took a seat near the front. From there, I watched anxiously as Buddy was shampooed, towel-dried, and returned to the chair looking like a wet kitten. With infinite care and loving attention to detail, Rinaldo set to work.

I pretended to read a magazine as long, solid tresses of Buddy's hair fell over the turquoise-colored cape covering his shoulders and onto tile floor. As though chiseling stone, the snipping shears began to reveal a perfect style from the rough diamond of Buddy's Pennsylvania pageboy. As he worked, Rinaldo described his "vision" of a 1930s German aristocrat: sides and back very close-cropped, with the top long. The line between the short and long hair was strongly defined, yet there was something casual about it, comfortable, and most important to the assignment, sexually available.

I had been living in New York for over 10 years. The people of my era had seen what we supposed was all that life could offer. We enjoyed the revolution, from the stage of the Living Theater, to the street in front of the Stonewall. We experienced the St. Mark's Baths, the Saint, and all-night parties at the Paradise Garage. We collected Warhol lithographs, and memorized the score to "A Chorus Line." We trudged the endless dunes between the Pines and Cherry Grove. In revolutionary fashion, we discarded our Izod shirts for sequined tank tops. But by the end of the decade, we bought new alligator shirts in the latest colors. We democratized our sexuality, we kissed in public, and for whatever political or dietary reasons, we reinvented brunch. We also gorged at the Ramrod and at the Mineshaft. We did EST, and then we did the Advocate Experience. Most of all, we understood that each and every one of us would live forever. It was into this New York that Buddy Benson entered, unaware and eager and disarmingly naive.

As the spring semester unfolded, my ability to keep the ephemeral promise of love under control began to melt along with the snow. Buddy's curious, whimsical expression haunted me. He sought out my office and asked my advice. In flight from the raucous dormitory, he stayed at my apartment one weekend, and then through spring break. We did not have sex but, by then it was obvious, even to me, that I was smitten.

One afternoon, at Caffe Reggio, as Buddy and I discussed his paper on Othello's passion for Desdemona, I placed my hand on his and confessed my own infatuation. We were drinking cappuccino, and the steamed milk had formed a white mustache on Buddy's upper lip. He admitted that he did not feel "that way" about me.

As my heart shattered, Buddy went on to confide a secret of his own: he was being wooed by the head of the philosophy department. Dr. Richard Soccer was a scholar of international renown, socially prominent, and a man of wealth. In spite of Buddy's fear and confusion over homosexuality, he found himself drawn to the good doctor, especially for his conversation and wit. Buddy was apparently poised on the brink of a liaison with my celebrated rival.

Love can subsist on very little. To love someone fully is to embrace him as he is, which may include him loving someone else. That is a kick in the teeth, but in time, and with a knack for luxurious martyrdom, it can be accepted. Most choose not to put themselves through this sort of torture – the instinct for survival forbids it. But for some, no sacrifice is too great compared to the sacrifice of never seeing the beloved again.

I knew that I could not put Buddy out of my mind, so I chose to accept a situation that was unchangeable but just bearable. In truth, it would take years for me to come to grips with it. I put my life on hold, and made myself available to Buddy, as...as what, a father? I know now what it is to love a child, and to love that child more than life itself.

When Buddy told me that he was invited to a dinner party in the Hamptons as Dr. Soccer's guest, I resolved to help him put his best foot forward, hence the haircut. When Buddy returned from his weekend nearly destroyed, with a wild tale that came out in pieces over several weeks, I tried to repair him. I memorized every detail as he told it, as if in my parental role I could decipher what happened, and somehow make Buddy whole again.

Rinaldo finished, and shut off the blow dryer. The three of us gathered again in the oval mirror to admire his handiwork. Rinaldo held a hand mirror such that Buddy could see the back of his head, and the dovetail that Rinaldo had expertly layered.

"Do you like it?" Buddy asked with some trepidation.

Buddy studied himself in the mirror, a glimmer of conceit running through his eyes. He dusted the new cut with his fingertips.

"Well, do you, Edgar?"

From gazing at his reflection, I turned to look straight at Buddy.

"Yes," I said quietly. "It suits you."

The change could not have been more radical, but it was obviously correct. Buddy now looked refined, revealed. Yet it was also as if the first layer of innocence had been peeled from him. Over the years, I would watch more layers peel, one after another.

"Do you really like it?" Buddy asked when we were outside. You look...perfect," I assured him. And he did.

We walked from the salon up to Seventh Avenue, and then down to Christopher Street. Just for a hoot, I took Buddy into Boots and Saddle for a drink. Not until we were inside did I realize that this was Buddy's first experience of a gay bar.

The afternoon crowd had gathered. Men occupied every stool at the bar, the rear wall, and the wooden railing like a faux corral fence. One could almost hear the craning of necks as Buddy passed. He wouldn't have stood a chance in there alone. I bought us each a beer, and steered Buddy to the one vacant spot remaining, beside the juke box.

He was nervous. He stood facing me as if for protection, afraid to turn around. He was to behold for the first time what would become so natural to him in the near future-- the adoration bestowed on beauty. Buddy had not yet seen it, and the glare of spotlight eyes that followed his every move made him uneasy. His back was turned to them, but the heat of their predatory stare beamed through.

You look gorgeous," I said. Even in his rough clothes and awkward position, he was the most exciting person in the room. The moment was at hand: it was time to make his bow.

"Everyone is looking at me," he hissed.

"Exactly." I made a motion with my hand for Buddy to turn around. He blushed, his cheeks turning red. Behind the round lenses, his eyes begged for mercy. But I had brought him this far, to the wings of the stage on which he chose to perform, the gay scene, and now he had to face his audience.

Buddy turned around slowly. Several men who had been watching him averted their eyes, but the braver ones continued to stare. The bravest shot Buddy that meaningful, insincere smile of palpable lust, a smile as fatuous as the things we say to one another when we trick. I knew the emptiness that lay beyond. But for Buddy, it was as if a whole new world of acceptance awaited him. Growing up straight in Pennsylvania, he did not understand his own desirability. Girls were to be pursued, though they might reject him. Men had no power to attract: they were deer hunters out to bag a doe.

What a shock it must have been to see for the first time men hunting men, hunting him. I do not think he understood his own value, how he could barter with his beauty, in a society that weighs precise amounts of physical attraction. One of Buddy's most endearing qualities was that he treated his suitors equally, the old and the young, the handsome and the plain. They were all one to his democratic largesse – all but me. It would be his undoing, yet it was the center of his charm. As I watched, men came up to Buddy, smiled at him and spoke to him, told him their names, and asked what he was doing later. He listened politely, seemed willing to comply, and yet was utterly unattainable.

I noticed at one point that Buddy had an erection while being whispered to by one of his less attractive admirers. The paradox filled me with lust and jealousy. I wanted Buddy all for myself, but I also relished the idea of throwing him to the wolves. Perhaps, in doing so, he might come home to me. It was then that I began to study him in that light, torn between desire and disdain. This study continued for years under a pretense of scientific detachment, as one might study a butterfly by piercing it through the heart. I once saw a film on 42nd Street, a trashy documentary assembled from real footage shot at various places around the world. It was intended to shock the audience with elements of a snuff movie – pygmy head hunters devouring the body of an enemy, a tribal fertility rite in Africa, with men performing sexual acts in the soil, that sort of thing. A segment appeared that was purportedly filmed by German tourists at a game preserve. Two families have stopped to take home movies of a pride of lions. We see one of the German tourists, a handsome blond man in shorts, advancing toward the pride. Suddenly, the lions spring on him. The camera filming this shakes, pans to the car in which his wife and daughters scream hysterically, and then back to the lions. The camera advances on the scene until we see quite clearly that the man is being devoured. A male lion has torn open the man's groin, and is chewing on his intestines. The man is still alive: he grasps the lion's ears with both hands. What is so astonishing, though, is the expression on the man's face. It is ecstasy, as if he had known no greater lust and satisfaction. The German tourist slaps the lion's head gently, as if to tease it on. The camera is still rolling, and we see death in live action. But the man is smiling now, rolling his head back and forth on the dusty grass, as if in the throes of orgasm.

I sat bolt upright in my seat to witness this horror joined to beauty. I kept the image in my mind for years, and came to associate it with Buddy. How often have I replaced the ecstatic mask of that poor German tourist with Buddy's face?

To avoid causing a riot, I guided Buddy out of the bar and home to my apartment for supper. Silent in public, he was now in a mood to talk, and I listened indulgently. He decided to stay the night. I made up his bed on the sofa, as he rambled on about his hopes and fears in regard to Dr. Soccer.

Buddy had not yet gone "all the way" with the philosophy professor, but one occasion had led to what he picturesquely called "heavy petting." He glimpsed a vague prospect of ease and comfort, as a kept boy, and the possibility of connections in show business. But he was terrified of submitting to a sexuality for which he had no experience, almost no words. What would be expected of him? What would his lover do? Would it hurt?

I fetched the cognac, poured a shot each into two snifters , and sat Buddy down to a chat about the gay birds and bees. We touched on lubricants, the prostate gland, and how to avoid the gag reflex. Buddy giggled from embarrassment, as I warmed to the task.

Nestled among his natural misgivings lay a more serious problem. It became clear to me, if not to Buddy, that he had already fallen in love with Richard Soccer. Love had crept up from behind and overtaken him. At first, of course, he was the beloved and the philosopher was the lover. But in the past week, Buddy had sensed a shifting of roles – a telephone call unreturned, a puzzling remark. He found himself writing the name "Richard" on slips of paper. Was he preparing to be seduced, or embarking on a seduction?

I had no answer for this, of course. Relieved to see him become drowsy, I tucked him in, still dressed, and planted a chaste kiss on his forehead. He smiled up at me with his eyes closed, a cherub half-asleep.

The next morning, we were up at six. As he showered, I laid out some clothes borrowed for the occasion from a friend whose size was approximate, and whose taste was impeccable. Buddy would need an outfit for the train ride, a change for tennis, a bathing costume, and perhaps another outfit for dinner.

He surprised me by emerging from the bathroom completely naked. This was my first full view – from the rear, as it happened – of Buddy's body. It was perfection. Like his face, it was white all over, his skin the color of milk. His muscles were developed naturally, in smooth curves, without the sharp lines and bulges produced by lifting weights. He had wide shoulders and a massive back, tapering to narrow hips. A V-shaped knot at the base of his spine flared out to form a big, boxy ass, like that of an Australian lifeguard. Each cheek looked to be as firm as a melon. Where flesh folded back to a pair of solid thighs, the crease was straight. There was no superfluous hair.

As Buddy turned to face me, I bit my lip. His pectoral muscles were wide and square, dotted by rosette nipples. His arms were folded beneath them, relaxed and natural. His stomach was flat, and from the button of his navel, a racing stripe of black hair ran down to his groin. There, under a patch of sable ringlets, hung a thick, brown banana of a penis, oversized, but beautifully shaped. It was the only dark skin on his body, and the contrast to the general whiteness was startling.

"You have the Gift!" I exclaimed.

"Do you think he'll like it?"

"Honey, he'll have you driving the Cadillac with that thing. Here, damn it – put this on before you give me a heart attack!" At arm's length, I extended a slinky Jansen swimsuit.

Buddy squirmed into the swimsuit, tugging it up his big legs and over his ass. He tucked his penis sideways into the front, then threw his arms up in the air.

"How do I look?" he asked, turning slowly for me to see from every angle.

"Mere words cannot describe. Now, here, slip into these." I held out a pair of black mohair slacks.

Buddy stepped into the slacks and zipped the fly. The fit was snug, but under the circumstances, all that could be wished. "Turn around," I said.

As Buddy swiveled, he glanced back at me over his shoulder, and placed his hands on his hips. Had he seen Betty Grable do this in a movie? The black fabric stretched tightly over his globular buttocks, with rear seam deeply indented, calling attention to the crack of his ass. I gazed for a long moment, lost in reverie, and sighed.

From the shirts laid out, I selected one of white silk, with long sleeves, and with mother-of-pearl buttons that echoed his pale skin. Black silk socks, a fantastically elegant pair of Italian leather shoes, and a belt to match, woven of tiny leather strips. Buddy would have to wear his own watch, however gauche. I forbade all other jewelry. As a finishing touch, I insisted on a loose, hand-knit Missoni sweater, mostly black, with a searing design across the front in white, red, and a bit of lavender to match his eyes.

"What if I get too hot?" Buddy asked. "Can I take off the sweater?"

"Of course, my sweet. Draped over the shoulders will do nicely, with the sleeves knotted on your chest. Like so."

I stepped back a few paces to take in the ensemble, chewing absent-mindedly on a finger. No bride had ever been so carefully dressed. Automatically, Buddy reached for his glasses.

"No!" I commanded. "Absolutely not!"

"But I can't see without them," he protested.

"That hardly matters. You don't need to see anything – you will be seen. All you need to do is walk around and smile. Now stand up straight, but not too straight. Good, very good."

Without that little distraction on his face, Buddy was unbearably beautiful – god-like, too beautiful for humans to behold and remain alive. Would they allow this trespass, a man so like themselves on earth? Would I? I decided not to tempt fate.

"Put the glasses on," I said.

Buddy smiled, teasing me with his loveliness as dimples formed in his cheeks. In his borrowed plumage, he assumed an air of confidence. Silk rippled over his arms and torso, and his thighs flexed under the fine black cloth. His hair, still damp from the shower, rose from his marble forehead, and swept back as though windblown. He slipped the wire-rimmed glasses over his ears, and again became mortal.

"Yes," I sighed, "That's better."

We took the subway to Penn Station, to catch the Long Island Railroad. As the ancient car rattled through the tunnel, I went through a checklist of dos and don'ts.

"If all else fails, smile," I told him. "It's your lethal weapon."

At 28th Street, a scruffy Negro with one arm got on the train. As the doors closed, he shouted for everyone's attention. "I am a homeless veteran, trying to support myself and keep from crime. Any contribution you care to make will be gratefully received."

The man's voice was harsh, and his manner intimidating. Buddy looked away nervously as the man began at the other end of the car, shaking a paper cup full of coins. Most of the passengers ignored him, but a few dug into their pockets. More coins rattled into the paper cup. As he passed us the man stopped, looked Buddy in the eye, and then moved on.

As the train pulled into Penn Station, and the black man lurched into the next car, Buddy turned to me and stated matter-of-factly: "Fucking nigger."

I was shocked. There was no denying that in one sense, Buddy was an unsophisticated hick.

"Never use that word, Buddy, never. That sort of prejudice might do in rural Pennsylvania, but this is New York City."

Buddy shrugged. Evidently, to him, I was a prissy old thing who did not know the real world.

I walked him to the ticket line, then withdrew to sit on a bench, where I felt a low rumble from the engines below. A gaggle of young men in tank tops and cut-offs passed, bound for Fire Island, dragging canvas bags across the floor, bags stuffed to bursting with essential items. Apart from them, all the travelers seemed gray and worn, caught up in some personal tragedy toward which the train would only take them closer.

I let my focus rest on Buddy, waiting in line. From that distance, his glasses almost disappeared, and I imagined that I could see a thoughtful expression. He had dropped his shoulder bag to the floor and held it by the strap, stooping slightly, so that he took on the appearance of a classical statue of an athlete. He stood out from the crowd.

What is it about the beautiful that makes their lives more interesting? Even the purchase of a train ticket is invested with glamour. Buddy was on his way to a weekend, in the Hamptons, an event not far from the ordinary. But I saw it as his introduction to a world of wealth and power, perhaps a surrender to that world, and certainly a surrender of his male virginity. He saw it in much the same light. He even thought of it as the gay equivalent of a marriage ceremony.

I walked him to the train. We embraced, muttered a few parting clichés, and then Buddy leaped inside. Through tinted glass, I watched him pass through the car and find a seat. When he was seated, he looked for me and smiled through my own reflection, that of worried, middle-aged queen.

The windows could not be opened, and it seemed to me that the boy was now sealed inside the train. He was about to travel farther than either of us knew, to a place from which he could never return, and where I could not reach him.

SUGAR IN THE MORNING
A Memoir of First Love
Jack Nichols

Thirty-five years after we'd met, Tom put things into perspective for me as we talked about how we'd been each other's first lovers. "We were only children," he said warmly.

Yes, we were only children. I was nineteen, still living with family. Tom was a handsome twenty-three, a Navy corpsman. I seldom saw him in uniform, but his body was a sculptor's dream, a farm boy's physique turned out on the rural flatlands of the South. Somewhat shy and self-effacing, he must have wondered at me, a tall city boy, finding my way through a multitude of philosophic enigmas in the Summer of '57. The quaint bar where we met was only three blocks from the White House. There, late in the evenings, Howard, the pianist, chose entry songs for regular customers. For me he chose Marlene Dietrich's theme, "Falling in Love Again."

. Summer passed quickly. Tom adjusted to meeting my family, knowing that they knew we were both gay, a situation which to him seemed incomprehensible. The shapely sailor had never really felt well connected to his homosexuality, being the son of an Assembly of God preacher. He had no way of knowing in advance that I was an infidel, a shameless skeptic much given to expressions of non-belief. Later, when this became clear, he'd scratch his head when I blasphemed and warn me about lightning.

In spite of the differences we've had, I've loved Tom dearly. And, I have no doubt, he's loved me. Those many years ago when I held him in my arms I saw an honest country boy, kind, patient, and perceptive. His was a steadying hand, one that gave me sanctuary when, in the midst of youth's turbulence, I needed it most. Tom was practical, whereas I lived solely for philosophy, considered by some to be the most impractical pursuit of all. He didn't much relish the fact that whenever we moved, my library of a thousand books had to go with us. Though I was on the edge of worldliness, I was not yet philosophical enough to see through the fictions of '50s style romanticism. I hoped we could be the Ozzie and Harriett of homosexuality.

The dates we enjoyed were particularly proper. Tom would park in my family's driveway and ring the bell. My grandmother would answer the door and sit chatting with him in the living room while I put finishing touches on my appearance. Then it was off to the movies, and afterwards to the Hot Shoppe and a vanilla milkshake. When he returned me to my house, he'd park again in the driveway and we'd "neck."

My grandmother knew what we were doing. "Now listen boys," she'd warn good-naturedly, "you mustn't stay out in that car more than five minutes. When I switch on the porch light that means, Jack, that you're to come in." Usually I ignored the porch light signal. She'd up the ante: "If you don't come in I'll have to call the FBI on you."

"Do you think she'd do it?" asked Tom worriedly.

"Hell no," I laughed. "When I was little and wouldn't eat my asparagus, she used to threaten me with phone calls to Herbert Hoover."

I still remember the first time I got into Tom's pants. We'd been necking after one of our dates. I led him from the car into my backyard. "Down here by the flowerbeds," I whispered. "It's so dark nobody can see us." I wrestled him out of his clothes, making entrance to a perfect dimension while he held precariously to the soft, lush grasses.

In early October Tom was honorably discharged after four years of Navy service. We moved into an apartment and set up housekeeping, buying '50s Danish modern and eating wholesome country meals, including cornbread and pinto beans. In mid-October we experienced a bona-fide honeymoon in the Blue Ridge Mountains. On the majestic Skyline Drive among the colored leaves we had our first spat. Ever the dramatic one, I jumped from Tom's moving car. He turned and came back for me. We fell thankfully into each other's arms and all was well again.

Before the year's end, Ken, Tom's Navy buddy, was also discharged and moved across the street. He and Tom found good jobs at American Airlines, while I worked as an auditor at the Staler-Hilton. I didn't care much for Ken, feeling discomfort about his influence. He felt no pride about being gay, but this had no effect on his heavy cruising schedule, one with which he regaled Tom, explaining in titillating detail the measurements of his "tricks." Ken sensed I was unhappy about such chatter, but seemed not to care. After all he'd known Tom for years. Perhaps he was a bit jealous of our relationship, seeing it as an intrusion on his comradeship with Tom.

I suppose Ken must have taken these photos of Tom with me staring today out of my aging album. We're standing proudly by our first Christmas tree. Others show us bundled in overcoats, in the vicinity of the White House, a row of Christmas trees behind us, each tree representing a different nation. Eisenhower was still president in those days. Ricky Nelson was a nationally acclaimed pin-up boy. Sam Cook sang "For Sentimental Reasons" on every juke box. I carried three snapshots of Tom in my wallet to impress friends and co-workers with my ability to land a masculine hunk.

In spite of Ken's intrusions, we were a happy couple, both taking domestic responsibilities seriously. Tom seemed to appreciate my penchant for Marlene Dietrich's "singing." His own tastes were closer to Eddy Arnold, though I remember how he would often troll these melodious lines:

> Sugar in the morning
> Sugar in the evening
> Sugar at suppertime
> Be my little sugar
> And love me all the time.

And, of course, when we went driving in Tom's '54 Chevy,
we sang together from his repertoire of country hymns: Heavenly sunlight
> Heavenly sunlight
> Flooding my soul with glory divine
> Hallelujah, I am rejoicing. . .

It was me who first interrupted our happy routine by insisting we move to Miami. My reasoning was twofold. First, I'd been frightened by bogus government propaganda convincing the citizenry of the day that a Soviet nuclear strike was imminent. Washington, I knew, would be Target Number One. I watched our tiny black and white TV screen as schoolchildren were herded under stairwells, supposedly safe from atomic destruction. My second reason for moving I kept to myself. Ken would be left behind to tell his cruising stories to somebody else. In the summer of '58, I arrived in Miami Beach where I landed a job selling sheet music to stores from a company-owned van. Tom followed as soon as I gave him word that I was employed.

But Tom wasn't happy about the move. Had I been more perceptive, I would have realized he was the sort who, once settled, was unlikely to go elsewhere. He struggled with our furniture, placing it in a U-Haul and, on his way South, stopping in Alabama to visit his folks. Then, while summer heat sizzled, he drove through Florida's Everglades, arriving in Miami after dark. "How could you bring me to this awful jungle?" were his first words upon arrival.

While I worked, Tom took a short vacation. He went daily to a notorious cruising ground, the 21st Street Beach. Sometimes I went with him. We both noticed the most handsome man there, a spectacularly shaped Latino. But it never occurred to me that Tom might be what we called (in the '50s) "unfaithful."

Nevertheless Tom's unhappiness at being uprooted persisted. He begged to return North, and, reluctantly I agreed. Re-packing the U-Haul we began the long drive back to the nation's capital. Somewhere in the Carolinas he unexpectedly confessed he'd "tricked with the Latino. He cried. I cried. He promised it wouldn't happen again. I wanted to believe what the 50's had celebrated for the hoi polloi, that couples could invariably be lovers forever.

I kept a stiff upper lip as we pulled once again into my family's driveway, this time to stay until we could find lodging, and to unload our furniture in their garage. My grandmother complained at the sight of a Florida roach we'd transported, but otherwise treated us well, allowing me to sleep in my old bedroom with Tom at my side, and fixing breakfasts, lunches and dinners with nary a frown.

Within the month we both found jobs and a new apartment. The future looked bright. There was only one hitch: Ken. He moved in to an apartment directly above us. I told Tom of my displeasure. With Ken ever demonstrating the skills of an indefatigable cruiser, and, unfortunately, being an even more loquacious braggart, it was only a short time before Tom was "unfaithful" again. Still, he assured me, he wanted to remain at my side.

Early in 1959, with a small down-payment, we escaped Ken once again, buying an attractive brick house in suburban Silver Spring. Tom was happy at having a garden and lawns to tend. We woke early each morning, breakfasted, and drove downtown to our jobs.

We vacationed in Alabama where Tom's family lived. I met his younger brother, his sisters, nephews, and nieces as well as his sweet, aging mom and dad, salt of the earth people like Tom himself. They never, it seemed, suspected we were gay. As I walked about the little farm with Tom he told me he planned one day to turn it into a much richer enterprise. He kept that promise, using the money he made through the years to buy hundreds of surrounding acres, to rebuild the little house, bringing new comforts to every one of his relatives. Later they came to visit him in Washington and we gave them a tour of the capital city. I remember being with them in an exotic mosque where rules called for us to go barefoot on luxurious Persian rugs. Tom's father, standing under the dome, spoke like the Assembly of God preacher he was: "I believe this here temple is built on the order of Solomon's temple," he said. Marvels taken for granted by city sophisticates seemed awesome to him. Tom was glad to be playing host. He was particularly proud of our new brick house.

What I remember of these days was the cheerful stability we knew. Tom was content puttering around the yard. He took genuine interest in his job, returning home each night full of stories about office politics. As for me, it was difficult for me to take my nose out of my books. I spent much of this period studying the complete works of Robert G. Ingersoll, the silver-tongued agnostic, not to mention the heresies of Bertrand Russell, the speeches of Clarence Darrow, the satire of Voltaire, the revolutionary fervor of Thomas Paine, the utilitarianism of John Stuart Mill, the skepticism of David Hume, the short stories of Saki, the poetry of Walt Whitman, the wit of H.L.Mencken, and the humanism of Corliss Lamont. In an essay I wrote during my twenty-first year I celebrated my contentment:

At present I am quite optimistic about life. Perhaps it is because I am still youthful. In spite of the fact that there are many things that I do not like about the way this world is made, I still find it a very interesting place to live. I have been living for two years with a good friend, and we have now bought a house. Here I can invite my friends and no one objects. Here I can say what I think and no one is shocked. Here, surrounded by shelves of books, I can continue to learn about the world and about all of the things it offers to a mind thirsty for knowledge. I feel comfortably secure, and in spite of international tensions and the threat of atomic extinction, I am content and happy just being alive.

Even so, Tom's erotic curiosity persisted, and, after honest discussions, we agreed we'd be best served by an open relationship, one in which each of us was free to explore our sexualities independently. Tom's sexual viewpoint was quite different from mine, inasmuch as he didn't find openly gay men attractive. He was capable of picking up assorted macho males who didn't self-identify as gay but who, nevertheless, were quite willing to enjoy gay sex as long as nobody else knew..

Many of these males were in the military. He was particularly drawn to Marines, though he complained that they were often too eager to be sodomized, a trait he said could be traced to boot camp training. Even so, he found their macho grandstanding attractive and he possessed an uncanny knowledge of how to step carefully around it in order to hurry them into every conceivable sexual position. He held tightly to two simple rules: don't try to kiss, and don't talk about it in the morning. Later, when he gave me lessons on how to behave in such situations, I too became something of a virtuoso. Since both of us were suitably masculine, these macho men saw us as physical equals and gave us no trouble. But soon I was bored by their antics, hoping for more than physical stimulation.

Whenever I looked at a man with passionate appreciation it seemed only right that I should receive the same sort of attention. Otherwise, I feared, we'd be unequal, a situation for which my ego had no tolerance. Thus I soon lost interest in men who were willing to do everything but kiss. Tom, on the other hand, seemed satisfied by such liaisons and made no attempt to turn any of his brawny one-night stands into romances.

While Tom went to mixed bars where sailors, soldiers and Marines were numerous, I went to the gay bars. I understood his reluctance to join me because Washington's gay bar life was, in the early '60s, staid, and the patrons seemed somehow oddly socialized. There was rampant a stilted bourgeois mentality. Those who ignored "proper" behavior were, if not openly scorned, at least privately criticized. In the bedroom oral sex predominated and anal sex was a subject for gossip. Those who played the passive role in anal sex were labeled "Brownie Queens." Few admitted to such an act. Not until April '61 did I meet a hillbilly who was seemingly free of such urban quirks, and he became, briefly, an idol who got too much of my attention. Though the hillbilly disappeared into nowhere, I told Tom of my infatuation. He seemed unperturbed. Tom loved me like a brother but our sexual relationship was fading. This was, I think, natural. Tom had his own preferences. I was now twenty-three, ready once more to be hitched to the chariot of romance.

In the spring of '62, I went on a spree of self-discovery, hitchhiking with a second hot-bodied hillbilly who'd gone AWOL from the Army. We traveled from Washington to Pittsburgh, to Cleveland, to Detroit and Chicago, returning through Indiana, Ohio, and West Virginia. I went with him to Manhattan and, within months, to Miami. While I was away Tom remained faithfully at his job and worried about my restlessness. I relinquished my financial claim to our house but returning a year and a half later I settled in that house with him, not as a lover, but as a roommate and a friend. From this vantage point Tom watched unconcernedly while I fell flat on my face in a series of attempts to land a new lover.

In '64 I met the lover with whom I'd spend the following decade, and Tom got along well with him since both were "southern boys who understood each other," as my new companion explained. During the first year of this romance I continued to live happily with Tom, while my lover, a soldier stationed at the Pentagon, slept with me at night. In April, 1965 news came that Fidel Castro was imprisoning homosexuals in concentration camps and in the living room of that house were lettered nine of the ten signs used in the first gay march on Washington, a march to condemn the anti-gay policies of both the United States and Cuba.

The signs were spread all over the floor. I sat on the sofa, while Tom worriedly tip-toed among them oohing and ahhing, telling us we were absolutely crazy. One sign read, "Russia, Cuba, and the United States United to Persecute Homosexuals."

"People are going to persecute you!" warned Tom ominously. "They aren't going to like seeing a bunch of queers marching. What are you going to do if some nuts attack you?"

"Everybody will be too stunned to attack us," I laughed. 'They'll just OOOh and ahhh like you're doing."

"Mae," drawled Tom in Alabamese (he'd long before assigned me a drag name, a Southern specialty) "sometimes I just don't know what to think of you."

Just as I'd predicted, there was no violence. Since I'd organized the picket, under the auspices of The Mattachine Society of Washington, it was agreed I should be first in line. Franklin Kameny marched behind me and Lilli Vincenz behind him. A photograph of us marching thus has become an historical relic. It was taken the following month, however, during our second White House demonstration.

Later in that year, Lige, my new lover, rented an apartment near the Pentagon and I moved in with him. I'll always remember Tom's expression as we packed and hugged him goodbye. He burst into tears. Seeing this, I did too. As I stepped into the car and drove toward my new home I reflected on how, though we were no longer lovers, we still loved each other.

In '68, I moved to Manhattan and when I visited Washington through, the years I'd stay with Tom. He watched me mature from afar. In the intervening time he'd never taken a new lover, but seemed happy enough, as he always had, piddling around in his garden. He was devoted to his job where he stepped high on the corporate ladder. Once when I spent the night with him in '88 I got another glimmer of Tom's feelings. Early in the morning as he prepared to leave for work he stuck a thousand dollars in my hand. "I make a lot of money now," he said, "and I don't want this back. I feel I owe it to you on the house which is worth ten times what we paid for it in '59."

119

I knew that it was Tom's way of showing his affection. I took the money. But what meant more was Tom's love.

In '93, during the March on Washington, I stayed with Tom again. It was twenty years since Lige had been murdered at a mysterious roadblock. Logan, with whom I'd shared half a decade thereafter, had died of AIDS. Tom was the only man I'd loved who was still alive, and even he had suffered a heart attack while I, a few months before, had lived through a bone marrow transplant.

It was April again, twenty-eight years after the first march. We were both older, yes, but time had dealt us a good hand. Tom talked about his early retirement. He was well set financially, and the gardens surrounding his house were awaiting his attention. We enjoyed laughter, nostalgia, and honest talk. "What ever happened to Ken?" I asked. Tom hadn't heard from him in many years. In the mid-'70s Ken had married the sister of his departed male lover and had moved to Texas. I chuckled over that one. So much that seemed awry when I was younger seemed so no longer. Sitting in the very room where the historic picket signs had been lettered helped cast an aura of completion over my visit. I gave Tom an album I'd discovered of World War II favorites, sung by a Scottish soprano. His eyes and mine too filled with tears as she sang:

> When I grow too old to dream,
> I'll have you to remember
> When I grow too old to dream,
> your love will live in my heart.

In past years, while he was still a corporate climber, Tom had been fearful of being associated with my gay liberation work. Even so, he'd borne my radicalism with kindly tolerance. Now that he was retired, he was glad at the chance to go with me to the march. We rode the Metro downtown. Each Metro car was filled with jolly gay youths.

Cherry blossoms, dogwoods, and the fresh green of springtime foliage glittered under the warming touch of the sun as hundreds of thousands of lesbians and gay men streamed past City Hall. A small group of Bible Nazis sang hymns to oppose this latter-day show of sodomite strength. Tom laughed at them. They were drowned out by the booming voice of the Reverend Jesse Jackson sounding welcomes over the loudspeakers as we made our way to an area where hundreds of groups had assembled for an orderly procession. After we reached the White House we found seats on phallic posts erected by Ronald Reagan who'd been much worried about terrorist attacks. Hoisting ourselves high enough to peer over shoulders got us a first-rate view of the passing show.

First came vehicles carrying people with AIDS as well as others too infirm to walk the whole route. Then, to swelling choruses of approval, walked seniors and elders, lesbian and gay male parents, the disabled in wheelchairs, and contingents of gay deaf-mutes. Next were assemblies of gay youths, including high school kids holding school colors aloft. The march then began to show a heavy emphasis in favor of dropping the ban on gays who serve in the military. Knowing what I did of Tom's faithful service and others too it seemed appropriate, though, as Tom knew, I'd long opposed the military-industrial complex.

With stirring melodies came the Lesbian and Gay Bands of America, followed by regional groups representing parents of gays, people of color, Asian

Pacific gays, and, for the first time in my memory, there was a strong showing by bi-sexuals.

Tom and I chatted with two lesbians and with a Chinese youth who'd commandeered the posts next to ours. I took a break and got us all Pepsis. When I returned a vast and boisterous contingent from San Francisco was passing. Tom pointed to the police guards standing at the White House gates. They looked alarmed as the roaring crowd surged forward, a crowd which could have overpowered them in seconds. But there were no untoward incidents, only proud and fervent passion flowed outward.

The marchers, because they'd come from Middle America, and because many were stalwart, everyday American youths, reminded me more of Tom than they did of myself. The years had turned me into a philosophical anarchist. Many of these youths still believed, as Tom always had, in their religions, and, probably, were not much given to questioning the Established Rule. Many had lived their lives in small town closets, much as Tom had done. Now both he and a new generation were experiencing a particular kind of joy, one that was old hat to me. They were walking, laughing, and feeling, perhaps for the first time, like free people. Patches of sunlight bathed them in tender glory.

Among those things I'd learned through my early experiences with Tom is that there are no strict divisions between gay and straight men. Men are men, of many varieties, perhaps, but trained to uphold old fashioned macho traditions nevertheless. They wander through bizarre mazes in a malfunctioning culture too long paralyzed because of its inability to celebrate a more intense form of male bonding. When I think back to how Tom and I drifted apart sexually I know now that we were then truly the children he'd said we were. Both of us had, in our own ways, scorned taboos. Both of us had, for a long while, divided our world into us and them. Later, both Tom and I discovered (as the anarchist Paul Goodman had put it) that there is no them, there is only us.

After the great march I prepared to leave for my home a thousand miles distant. I sat with Tom on the sofa and held him again in my arms. Tears streamed down his cheeks, just as they had three decades before. We'd shared much. There had always been real mutual respect, the one factor that bypasses all differences and creates true brotherhood. Life's springtime with Tom had been good, as sweet as the April breezes. No matter how far away he lives, in my reveries I feel him at my side, as gentle as ever and as kind.

RICKY
Ken Anderson

I needed to get away from Atlanta to finish my dissertation, so I borrowed a friend's lake house – you know, one of those classy, rustic places with a huge fireplace and deer antlers over the mantel. My subject was rather abstruse, I admit, the Crusades as the source of modern intolerance, but all I had to do was make some minor changes in the last chapter and type it up. Then two years' work was up for final approval.

Since I really didn't have a deadline as such, I had set up a rather easy schedule. I was to work in the morning – I usually got up at dawn, anyway – nap around noon, and go canoeing or work out with the weights on the upstairs porch in the after-noon. Nights were reserved for reading for pleasure. I had brought along a lot of Christopher Isherwood, Lanford Wilson, and Edmund White.

I hadn't lived there long, however, when, canoeing one day, I noticed the tallest pine on the horizon, a giant of a tree on a high hill directly overlooking the lake. Below the hill, the shore-line was rocky, except that as I rounded a point, a soft stretch of reeds swung into view, and though leery of snakes, I slid the bow in there.

I climbed to a small clearing with a big slab of granite right at the foot of the towering pine. The slab looked like a natural altar to some guardian spirit. The pine was the tallest I had ever seen, more like a sequoia, with branches so high they looked like clouds. The rock seemed a great place to sun, so I stripped – my plaid shirt, my hiking boots, my favorite pair of jeans, everything but my Jockey shorts – and, spreading the clothes, lay on my back. When I had arrived at the lake, I'm ashamed to admit, I was pretty pale and so far had managed more of a hot pink than a decent tan.

But as I lay there, stretched on the rock, all of a sudden I had a vague feeling that someone was watching me. I'm not sure what tipped me off, maybe a stick snapping, maybe the silence itself, but whoever he was, I hoped he got an eyeful.

I had a canvas belt with a brass buckle, and so I rolled over to see if I could catch anyone in the reflections, but made out only, in a flash of sun, perhaps a slight movement just within the woods. It also may have been a slight dent in the buckle. I rolled onto my back again and cupped my hands under my head, pretending to doze, but when I sneaked a peek, could see no one. After a while, I did doze off for a few minutes, then woke, warm and sweaty, with an urge for a swim.

A shelf of smooth rock made a nice platform for diving, and crouching there, I searched the water not for my own image like Narcissus, but for a sign of someone behind me up the hill. I glanced over my shoulder through the trees, but seeing no one, stood and made a shallow dive, almost losing my briefs. I pulled them up, then turned and floated on my back, all loose from the snooze.

Returning to the clearing, however, I discovered my intuition had been right. Someone had been watching me, for as I mounted the crest and the granite slab rose into view, I saw a young man poring over my clothes – timidly, almost reverently touching them, examining them curiously like ancient artifacts. At first glance, he looked in his late teens, a cute brunet with his hair mussed and hanging in his face. But after watching him awhile, I realized he must have been at least in his twenties ...something about his body-build, the play of the muscles in his arms, the fervent way he was picking through my clothes.

He put on my cap, then glanced up at the bill – a red Husqvarna cap from a rack in the house. He put his hand on the shirt, then the jeans, then sat on the edge of the rock, doing what could only be described as caressing my boots. Then he did something even more curious. He hugged one of them, pressing the ridged sole to his T-shirt, gently rocking the boot like a child. He seemed to drift into a trance, then came to and set it down, only to pick up one of my socks, a grey, rag sock, which, when he sniffed it, seemed to send him into raptures. A hit of poppers couldn't have produced more of a heady response.

Smelling the sock, he got up and, looking dazed, lumbered toward what could have been a path or just a narrow gap between the rocks and the woods. I followed him through a shady cleft in some big, round boulders which dead-ended in a cave-like space. The ground was covered with soft, brown pine needles, and a grayish-green moss splotched the stone.

He paused to sniff the sock again, then breathing out a deep, animal grunt, reached to unsnap and unzip his fly, but since his back was to me, all I could see was a thin band of milk-white skin and the notch in his buttocks. When he turned to sit, I backed away, but saw how I could scale the rock to a vantage on top. I'm not sure why I just didn't step forward and confront him. I guess I thought it was only fair to spy on the guy who'd spied on me, and I did.

The next day, I left my Jockey shorts on the rock as well, making a big show of swaggering down the hill. But this time, instead of diving off the ledge, I stepped to the side, out of sight, and heaved a large, flat stone into the water with a big splash. Then I sneaked up the hill and watched him go through my clothes again, but this time, as I figured, making off not with a sock, but my shorts.

I followed him among the boulders, and when I stepped for-ward, he panicked and fell down. By the time he was up again, I had marched over and, grabbing his T-shirt, shoved him against a boulder. Instead of struggling, though, he hugged me as hard as he could, pressing his head to my shoulder – a cross between wanting me to protect him, I guess, but also take him outright. I stepped back and took his face in my hands – the square jaw, those almond eyes, those beautiful lips of his – then directed him to his knees.

Though he had obviously dabbled in fetishes, he was clearly an amateur when it came to real sex. What he lacked in technique, though, he made up for in spontaneity, and the intensity of the experience made me wonder what I'd thought I'd been enjoying all those years. What about this experience was so different from the others – me, him, the woods, the lake, the secret room in the rocks?

I opened my eyes, then stepped back, and we just stayed there awhile, me standing, him in front of me, both of us gulping and gasping. When I thought I'd found my legs again, I stepped over to my shorts and picked them up.

"Meet me here tonight," I said.

Since he'd already mastered French, I thought we'd try Greek.

"Ever been fucked?"

I stepped into the shorts. He was still on his knees, looking around as if searching for something.

"Fucked?" was all he said in a sort of phlegmy-husky, re-strained tone of voice.

He looked as if he'd never heard the word.

Then he said, smiling nervously, "Okay."

When he stood, I slapped him on the shoulder, and he hulked through the passage, zipping his fly. I followed him out of the boulders, but at the edge of the woods, he paused by a tree, picking a pine needle from his shirt, then backed away slowly, casting one last timid, yet wistful glance at me.

When we met that night, I was wearing a garland of, if not ivy, at least pine needles in my hair, and he, as it happened, the red cap and a mismatched pair of socks. When we began to undress, I told him to leave on the cap and sock. All I knew was that I wanted to play out some deep-rooted, pagan fantasy. I just wasn't sure which.

I spread some blankets on the slab, then, without a word, as we sat there naked, showed him how to smoke pot. We could see sheet lightning to the south, and occasionally a quiet breeze stirred the pines. But just barely. From the reeds far below rose a rhythmic chorus of frogs.

When I woke, I was still on top of him, but rolled onto my back. I had no idea how long I'd been asleep, but was sure, however long, my weight and the uneven stone must have been uncomfortable for him, despite the blankets. He turned to face me, and I drew him even closer, turning up the bill to the cap. Then we just lay there, cuddling and gazing into the pine. The steady light of a distant plane, like a tiny beetle, was crawling across the dark blue dome of the sky.

He faced me again, breathing in contentedly through his nose.

"What?"

"Co-logne," he enunciated.

"Yeah, musk," I said. "Sweet colognes give me a headache. What about you?"

He didn't say anything, just stared at me.

Your cologne," I explained.

He shook his head a little. For some reason, he made me think of the small azalea bushes on the north side of the house. They were stunted from the lack of sun, as I could tell he was from another kind of shade. Under the right conditions, though – the cap, the sock, and me – he'd bloomed.

"What's your name?" I asked.

"Ricky," he said shyly. "Ricky Vann. Two n's."

I was sure he'd given me his real name.

"Yours?" he asked.

He had a slight rural accent.

"Buddy," I whispered. "Buddy Chelm."

"Buddy," he repeated, brightening as if remembering some-thing. "You're my buddy," he said.

At first, I thought he was making a sheepish joke, but when I saw his serious smile, knew he wasn't. And then, since my physical desire for him had been slaked, I guess, a tender feeling swelled in my chest. We kissed – one soft, spontaneous kiss, and then I could feel some mysterious chemistry taking over. The look he'd given me was the look of love, I realized – simple, earnest, passionate love, and I felt, all at once, at one not only with him, but myself as well, with the world.

The next day, Ricky didn't show, and I surprised myself with how deeply disappointed I was. There was nothing I desired more than seeing him again, yet now that he was gone – and right away I knew he was – I didn't have even a scrap of his clothes to touch and smell, as he had of mine. No cap, no sock, nothing.

I was restless that evening, but couldn't face fixing myself anything to eat. I couldn't read, so I had to get out, at least until time – though I knew it was pointless – to wait for Ricky. There was a lodge with a restaurant a few miles away, so I decided to try there, donning slacks and a white shirt. At least, going out would get my mind off him for a while.

But halfway through dinner, I just happened to look up when Ricky, amid all the bustle, was leaving with an older couple, presumably his parents. My hand went up, and he saw me, but, strangely listless, looked away. His mother was leading him by the hand as I had down the path to the lake, but then he made a subtle, but apparently anguished gesture. With his free hand, he grabbed the hair at the back of his head. With a jolt, I knew – from the gesture, from his reticence, from his butch shyness – just as I honestly had never known, that something was different about him mentally. He was good-natured, of course, but what's known as slow.

Near the cash register, I stood behind him in line, stunned, just as he stood behind his parents, holding on to his hair – four in a row, like a family, a father and a mother and two sons.

"Thought y'all were leaving this morning?" the cashier smiled, a young woman in a checked uniform.

"Well, we were supposed to," the woman explained amiably, "but Ricky had a spell and refused to leave."

"Ricky, you givin' your mother a hard time?" the cashier asked.

"He's okay now," the man claimed.

Ricky let go of his hair, then stared at the floor.

"Well, Ricky," the cashier chirped, "you can always come back next year. I'll still be here."

"We've already made the reservations," the woman announced.

When the man had paid and the three were leaving, I followed them about halfway to the entrance. His parents strolled into the lobby, but Ricky paused as he had by the pine, casting one last friendless glance at me, then disappeared.

They come here every summer?" I asked, turning to the checked gingham.

I flashed her what I could of my best bedroom eyes.

'The same week," she confirmed. "Very nice people. Some of the nicest guests. The staff just loves 'em."

"Ricky seems shy," I said almost to myself.

"Yes," she said as I looked up. "He's sweet as pie. So – " "Nice, yeah."

I went to the table to get the bill and, when I had paid, checked the lobby for Ricky. The front desk was unattended for a moment, so I spun the register around, then flipped it back a week to get his address. According to the register, he lived in Harrisville, a little town northwest of Atlanta.

I knew he wouldn't show up at the rock, knew he couldn't, but I waited till midnight, anyway. Back at the house, I called information and got his number in Harrisville, and the next morning, I staked out the lobby and restaurant, but somehow missed him. They must have already paid. Since then, I haven't been able to do anything but wait here or wait at the rock, and here it is after midnight again, and I can't go to sleep.

BE MY GUEST
Tom Smith

Dear Child,
Having come to the edge of the woods, I find I am a timid fawn indeed. I feel
an obligation to try again to live up to my calling. I think you will prefer my silent
departing. I am always available to you if you find yourself in any need.
— Nicholas.

That little note was the way my unforgettable affair with Father Nicholas ended. But what did I expect, given its beginnings...

I had no sooner taken a stool at Maw's Craw when Maw's paw fell on my shoulder. "Have a beer on the house," she offered. She stared past me down the bar. There, at the farthest corner, tottered a priest between two seated ruffians or, at any rate, a tall man dressed in a priest's collar and black suit, a purple pluvial, trimmed in blue and gold, draped over his shoulders. "Do me a favor," said Maw. "Get him out of here." Slurred scripture is not attractive and, as I could see even at a distance, he was very drunk.

I took my glass and was amused to see the stools vacated on either side of him as I approached. "What are you doing here?" I exclaimed as if to an old friend or a wayward daughter. The locals in their booth beside us slapped their thighs in hooting admiration. "Let me help you get home."

He allowed me to lead him by the elbow. Maw hurried to get the door. We were able to find his car, parked under one of the elegantly carved lampposts that still adorn that degraded neighborhood. As I arranged him in the driver's seat, I told him that I can not drive. Then I ran around to the passenger's side. He fell all over me at once. I took the opportunity to find his keys, which I handed to him, pushing him off. "This is scarcely the place for gratitude. Can you find the way?"

We drove a long while into the country and through several villages with not a light to be seen. I chattered, watched the speedometer and, twice, handled the wheel. He kept silent. I watched his face to be sure he didn't fall asleep. Apart from the blurring of intoxication, it was a fine face: Flemish eyes, large brow and jaw, mouth like a hovering gull. The most handsome feature was the nose, narrow, long, and prominently arched and hollowed.

His concentration on the road was trance-like. Finally, as we descended a long slope into still another tiny congregation of homes, post office and general store, he swung right onto a side lane and immediately left into a drive between a spired church, square brick with columns, and a tall white rectory. The car stopped abruptly, his big foot breaking, and he slumped-sprawled forward, passed out on the horn. I killed the motor, managed to silence that wail, and pocketed the keys. Reaching across his lap through the folds of his cape, I engaged the safety. The darkness was absolute, except for one light left burning upstairs in the house. Or perhaps he had a roommate, but a roommate would certainly have investigated that blast. The silence was complete. I lighted a cigarette and sat.

I tumbled into the pitch, crossed to the front porch, and attempted the door. Locked, of course. But, here, I have his keys, a jingle of sad and scary stumps. I found the correct one. I found the switch inside. An elegant hallway pulled itself together, wide-paneled, sliding doors on either side, a generous stairwell, white with polished banisters, woodwork, crystal, mirrors, plants.

Leaving the door flung open, I returned to the car to cope with the body. I decided to pull him out from the passenger's side since it was closer to the house. After lifting his feet onto the upholstery, I tugged the legs into the drive until he lay prone on the seat, face up. I straddled his pelvis undoing the pluvial. That voluminous drapery could only complicate our progress. It was no use trying to rouse him. I pulled him to a sitting position, his feet planted on gravel and, my arms under his, my hands locked behind him, lifted. He stood, his whole weight distributed along the length of my body. In this embrace, backing, I dragged him to the porch.

I lowered him to the stone of the fourth step. By a process (now feet, now seat) as tedious to describe as it was to perform (at no moment did he regain a jot of consciousness), I lugged him into the house and upstairs to a bedroom, already lighted and no roommate. Undressing him, spread-eagled on the bed, was no trouble. I was frightfully awake after my exertions, so took my time hanging or folding each garment carefully, caressingly, until he lay naked, a robust figure, breathing deeply now and naturally.

Downstairs, I retrieved the cape with tripping flourishes and locked the car. I locked myself into the stately dwelling and sought the kitchen. By the glow of the opened refrigerator, I scrambled four eggs which I gobbled while wandering through the plan of richly appointed, excellently proportioned rooms, moving through a kind of tic-tac-toe of lights (on/off). So many mirrors! each surprised reflection reminding me, Richard, is alone – alone conscious – in this dreaming house, the priest's purple hanging round me from my shoulders: Snow White's step mom. I settled awhile behind empty John Jameson and a shot glass at the desk in his library: Joyce and Wilde and Crashaw mixed with exegesis and theology. And Swift. I looked for Lewis Carroll unsuccessfully.

A warm and simple intimacy pervaded the dim den. After cleaning up in the kitchen, I returned to the bedroom where he lay beneath a quilted comforter exactly as I'd left him and, having pulled back the silken patchwork, I watched him sleeping while I stripped.

I took him, generous in my cupped hands, and kissed him, but he did not stir. On my back beside him, I welcomed the sun rising beyond lace curtains. Angels rose with it; or they were discovered floating outside the window in formal quartets and trios filling the sky. Geishas and Pans and Yellow-Book Dandies rode the backs of grave and ancient turtles and steam engines.

When he awoke, I asked, "Do you remember me?" His sick eyes did not mean to be insulting. "Nothing happened. Nothing like that," I affirmed.

"I don't remember," he murmured.

"I found you in a low bar in New Pinkerton. You were surrounded by very irreligious ruffians. I helped you drive home. I put you to bed." I could see he was on the verge of confessionals and lacerations, a table I did not wish to have turned on me. "Shower and shave," I recommended. "I'll fix breakfast."

"Thank you."

"Then you can take me home."

"I was very drunk."

"That was obvious."

He drove me home. Sober in the sunlight, he is handsomer than I thought. His name is Nicholas. "Well, I'm sorry I can't have you," I explained as he idled at my curb. "But love is love, as your church teaches." I slammed the door behind me, then

127

turned back. "I have an idea about a present for you. It's important. So you must promise to call me. "

"I'm not sure my church teaches that."

"No. But it should."

"I'm afraid I gave you a lot of trouble."

'That's what priests are for. You owe me at least a dinner." I skipped into the house.

Two days later, he called: "Will you have dinner with me Friday?"

I thought twice before insisting on my previous engagement. He agreed to Saturday. Then he called on Thursday to say we must not see each other, but finally invited me to dinner.

He drove to my door resolving to dismiss me, gently, but brought me home with him. Then faced me from his armchair with the same intention, but confirmed a friendship.

"Yes," I said. "Good friends."

He wanted me to talk about myself and, to please him, I recounted my life and ate his steak and watercress. The wine was likewise excellent. He neither ate nor drank. I spun a long story and agreed to spend the night, in a separate bedroom where, the following morning, I appeased myself, using voluptuous, slow strokes. Next door, Nicky celebrated mysteries and powers. I supposed I was being prayed for and I liked it. I decided to buy him The Collected Works of Lewis Carroll.

Two weeks later, I awoke to find my bedroom swollen with the morning sunlight and an unshaven stranger hanging above me like a heaving buoy. "Gee, you got some pretty hair."

I laughed in his face.

The evening before, Father Nick had taken me to a movie and shared scotch with me after. We chatted about the film.

"We live alone – you and I," he sighed after awhile.

"But not without interruptions," I added. We listened to strange wings whisper against my ceiling.

"You have a mouse I think."

"I have a mouse. I have a cat. I – Drink?"

"No. Thank you."

I took the glasses to the kitchen and mixed myself another. When I returned I found him staring out or, rather, at the dark window. I waited. "Father Nicholas," I said.

He turned to me and smiled. "It's time I started back." "It's a long drive."

He followed me downstairs and, while he wrung my hands in his, Cat slipped between his legs. "We're all mad here."

After Nicky departed, I downed a twelve-ounce tumbler of warm scotch.

Later I blew two sailors in the train station john: Buddy and Popeye. Buddy, a salt sea breeze on that filthy air, had the pinkest glans I've ever seen, a salt-water taffy I gulped in a hurry, while Popeye tried to violate my ear with his impatient pecker.

Then, on my way back, I attracted a shadow that followed me home. He hesitated as I climbed the steps to my porch. Then he walked on. When he looked back, I was holding the big door open.

He followed me up all those stairs and into my bed and, all the while, not a word was spoken. The last thing I remember is a strong tongue up my ass. I must have blacked out, me and my pretty hair.

There you have it: three perfectly good pricks could not fill the void of me, the abyss that is my yearning now for Father Nicholas.

A week later, I sat him with ceremony and compassion at my kitchen table and discoursed across our golden bourbons on the habits and habitats of phthirus pubis, the common crab louse.

I reminded him that, nude, we'd shared a bed. I warned him he was not competent to search himself: you have to know what you're looking for.

Nicholas undressed and delivered himself into my hands maintaining righteous silence. He was clean as, of course, I knew he would be, but – "Here," I said finally, thrusting the oily little bottle at him. He stood, stark still, for half an hour in the middle of my bathroom while I leaned in the doorway, drink and cigarette in hand.

By the time he emerged from the shower, I had stuffed all his clothing into a pillowcase. I led him to the bedroom where I had assembled across my bed clean underwear, slacks, an old white shirt. He hesitated, then dressed quickly, awkwardly. It made no matter to him that the things were fresh and soft and warm and mine. At the sight of his robustness filling my old clothes, I smiled.

Then he started. Filth and fiend and fondue are some terms I managed to interpret on the torrent. I paced my rooms and he pursued me pounding out proprieties and prophecies. I whistled a happy tune, turned on the radio, the phonograph, and wound the clock. I found my glass. He loomed behind me to the kitchen.

I stood hanging on the icebox door. "What am I doing?" "What are you doing!" he thundered.

"Ice!" I said. But my hand closed on a dear little egg that shone in its cardboard scallop.

My palm and the egg landed smack in the middle of his forehead. He was stunned. Then, as he realized the mess spreading from his brow, his expression hardened against the ludicrous anti-crisis I had wrought. "For all you know," I said, "I'm the devil. And god is my pet cat." He stood there wiping yellow and albumen from his eyes.

"Well," I added. "Are you going to stand there?"

He left: forty-five descending footfalls; then I lost count. The next night, I came home and compared translations. At 11:00 PM, I turned on the radio and went to bed. I lay awake until 1:00.

Then I rose furious and scrawled the following consideration:

Old Nick,

In my third undergraduate semester, I studied psychology, sociology, economics, and political science. My suspicions were confirmed. The greedy disorganization the world has somehow arrived at provides no place for me or any other playful, well-meaning human bean (Phaseolus, Dolichos, or Vigna). Conditioned man is not likely to become reasonable in the course of the present millennium. I had pretty damned well live my own life, my own way, and hope no one will notice. As for your blessed Church, remembering its history, I wonder why it doesn't share with Hitler's Nazis Inc and the International Eunuch Trade a shocked and shuddering repute wherever good will and nature rule men's hearts.

– Richard.

I scrambled into jeans and a sweater. Then I folded my message into an envelope and walked it around town, dispatching it at last in the resounding box on the library lawn across the street which I guarded from my bedroom window, the cat in my lap, until dawn.

On Labor Day, scrubbed down and rested after a day's sun dozing out the window, I enjoyed a simple and leisurely dinner of olives and cottage cheese. Vermouth and ice was all that remained to drink and I had just put a record on the phonograph and whirled, in a big-boy shirt and bare feet, into the foyer and, there, halfway up the stairs, he stood, looking sheepish and quite high in my dear old clothes.

"Hello, Nicholas," I said and tugged at flannel shirttails.

He explained he was sorry and taking a vacation: should he take off for the mountains, sorry and alone, or would I come along or could he -

"Be my guest," I said.

He ran to get his luggage.

I slipped into those little white jockeys with the birthmark and skipped downstairs to meet him at the door.

He handed me a wicker basket that rattled charmingly and puffed behind me over an enormous and expensive bag which proved, in a few minutes, to be mostly filled with books and periodicals and packages of note cards. "I prepared for a week of lonely scholarship beside a lake." I spread a cloth on the carpet. We partied on the contents of his wicker: French bread, French cheese, French wine, and Irish whiskey. And French kisses – eventually.

I am not coy. To speak true, I'm usually in bold haste to get on to the next one: living for numbers hardly leaves time for timid. Nevertheless, despite my long-postponed desire, I felt fawn-shy in Nick's new unexpected, willing presence. Anyway, I did not want to hurry. I knelt before him and he lifted food and drink to my lips, dropped tidbits on my budded tongue.

Eventually he brought his lips to mine, his tongue to my tongue, and we shared a long, slow taste of Pick-'n-nick-'n-rick...

My fingers trembled at the buttons of my old shirt, taut across his swelling chest, as he inhaled so deeply the smell of me, licking my temples, my armpits, my nape. Slipping the warm flannel tails aside, he swept the dimpled hollow of my back with his forelock. His fingers drifting the length of my spine to the band of my briefs, he planted kisses at the delta.

"O," I said. "Oh – " And arched away from him. "Let me undress you."

He stood, more than ready to be sprung from my tight garments. I rose before him like a fountain. I had the shirt unbuttoned. I lifted it over the shoulders and pulled it down his back and arms. I dropped again to my knees to unbutton the cuffs. The shirt fell from his wrists drifting down the backs of his legs to the carpet. Simply I stripped him of trousers and briefs. He stepped out of the heap, naked in the moonlight that flooded the uncurtained room. Still on my knees, I removed my own shirt. I sniffed the perfumed hourglass of hair from his chest to his pubes. Cat-like, I brushed against his legs. He was erect now: monstrance, aspergilla. I took it in my hair, across my forehead, down my cheeks. I pushed my face between his thighs, my nose behind his scrotum, then my tongue. I heard his slow moan and I thought it has been years perhaps since anyone has done this for him. If anyone has ever... I knew nothing of my Nick's experience, his past.

I pulled back, sat on my haunches looking up at his enshadowed face and body. The agony of his desire showed through the moonlight: bared teeth, bunched muscle. He looked a very wolf.

I took his length of cock in both my hands, hand over hand, and brought my lips to its head. I kissed it. I opened to it, very slowly soothing down the bated shaft until my lips were anchored round the root. How he howled there in the moon glow as he came, instantly, fiercely. I came too – spontaneous, melting overflow. We'd come again, I reassured myself.

An awful silence followed. Echoes of his passion seemed to recede through timeless caverns of old night. At last, I felt his arms enfold and lift me. He carried me to my bed. He stripped me of my soaked jockeys. He licked me clean. He gave me everything I ever wanted. Again and again and again.

After breakfast, we scrambled back to bed and debated the relative merits of Grand Union and Eatrite because, as I said, "My cupboards are bare." He advised, stretching and snuggling the bedclothes, that I make a long list while he, pushing Petronius aside, fetched from my bed table and browsed an illustrated plant and seed catalog: Belcher's American Nurseries. Are you interested in gardens?"

"I picked that up in a day coach on Long Island. It's colorful." I reached for a pad and ballpoint. "Now then, what do we need? What would you like?"

"Strawberries," he said and slipped his arm around my waist as he showed me the page. "Fragaria," I read and added by rote, "An achene receptacle and not a true berry, they say." I flipped a few pages to lilacs. "Syringa. A nymph!"

He squinted over the italics. "Vulgaris."

"That's you and me. And, look, here's Catnip!" I pushed his hand off the picture. "I didn't know it flowered."

When I returned from the shower, he was weaving brief garlands again. "I've found some goodies for you." He had discovered an orchid from Japan called Angel Flower. "Isn't it manly," I said, zipping my long stem jeans.

Later, Nicholas stood, lathered and dripping naked, at the sink. "I've decided to buy you a garden," he announced. I brought him a generous towel.

He wrapped us up in candy-striped cotton. "Would you like that, a garden?" he whispered, nibbling.

"Oh, Nicholas, it's the loveliest idea I've ever heard of." The man was a whirlwind shopping. We drove out to Farmer's Road for the purpose. At Eatrite he heaped two carriages with steaks and wines and sour cream, and every good thing for a salad, and everything basic or eye-catching, everything. "We'll never eat it all," I protested, knowing we would. I hissed, as he put three salesmen through fast paces at the garden shop.

"That's too expensive."

"Nonsense, I'm rich!" he sighed, "Entre nous, I'm richer than the Pope."

We took all we could stuff into the car. Then there were all those trips on the stairs and running out for hardware and screwing hooks into window frames and ceilings and then the little brown delivery truck arrived. Soon ferns shivered on the windowsills. Small trees, an airy little trio in the foyer, promised me oranges, lemons, and figs. Pink, red, and purple coleus climbed the screens and hung from bookshelves and ceilings. The kitchen brimmed with parsley, chives, sage, mint, tarragon, lavender, basil, and thyme. An umbrella tree performed its mikado in the parlor. Geraniums bloomed everywhere.

After spending the next day reading, sprawled on the fire escape, fully dressed Nicholas decided that we should do the bar scene.

"But we'll have to get you something to wear." The Military Surplus Outlet accepted over his objections my check: it stretched the point of my balance only a little bit and Nicholas looked rangy in blue denim sneakers, jeans, and jacket.

"What's the biblical significance of Levi?" I asked.

Later, at Curly-Q's, Mama went cross-eyed as we passed her by. So did all the family and clients. "I warned you," I whistled down his nape as he strolled ahead of me to a vacant table. Jesse ran to the upright and rolled out a wedding march.

Herself approached to take our order. "What's the matter, Richard? You don't speak?"

We sent Our Lady after drinks. "They're all a little more than kin – and sometimes less than kind," I warned. "So, please, remember it's not my fault."

He chuckled so I'd know he was all right in spite of the pink ears. My nerves, however, surprised me and I really needed that first tonic. Mama said, "Where you been all these weeks?"

"In heaven."

"Ah so – " She lingered. And where's my Kenny boy?"

"Nursing a seaside wake and wallow last I saw him."

She sat down to change the subject. Jesse joined us. "Hi!" he yodeled and Mama neglected to hush him. Hank alone seemed oblivious of our happening. We should have sat at the bar, I thought. "Watch Papa at work," I said. "He's a masterpiece." Jesse and his mama nodded and turned toward the bar.

Later, when we had been left to ourselves, I asked, "How are you liking it?"

"I wish they weren't all so fussy and affected."

"But, my dear! They're buying and selling."

At the stroke of midnight, Noah propped a stool by the piano. Jesse riffled the keys and all the little spots over the bar and tables dimmed to pitch. Rose light bloomed all over Mama. This is new," I whispered to Nick.

Jesse's impish and twinkling improvisations settled, too soon, to stardust and our hopeful, but rapidly aging, hostess blued Deep Purple. The expected standards followed. Jesse's piano, receiving her sometimes nervous, sometimes scolding glances, unrolled mechanically. I caught a glimpse of Hank, aghast in the gloom, and cheerlessly enduring Noah. Fidgeting Nick took to husking and hemming. Body and Soul reared their ugly and inevitable heads. She fought and killed them and, all lost, the lights came up. We all clapped. Mama beamed and bowed and bobbed through the suspiciously delighted crowd. She stopped by our table and we were nice.

"What a surprise!" I chirped.

Nicholas nodded enthusiastically, but he blushed. We soon left.

We laughed in the car and, at home, fell up and down the stairs and all over the echoing hallway in boisterous, mimicking, hiccupping merriment. "Body and soul," roared Nick. "She has little enough of either."

We were locked out. He admitted his fault, "I assumed – "

"Should I transform myself into a mist and pass in through the keyhole?" It was more fun climbing the fire escape and tumbling through the open window.

The next day, he decided to take the cat and me to the mountains.

He speeded and was silent at the wheel. I babbled and bantered and we took the first eighty miles northward in a professional hour. We stopped for dinner at the American Revolution. It was crowded and our knees mixed skittishly under the plank table in the rough-hewn booth. Father Nicholas, in full clerical uniform, hummed over the birch bark menu. I squirmed and sucked a pigtail in my peppermint pink pinafore and plastic purse, maryjanes, brown loafers, narrow suit, and narrower blue four-in-hand. "Maybe I'll just have three appetizers and forget the rest."

"Try the trout."

"I've never had it."

"I recommend it."

We arrived in darkness after a very slow half-hour chasing our crazy headlights up a crooked, pitching tree-choked trail to its summit and down the other side. The night bumped, cold and gusty. I listened to the tossing lake and trees while Nicholas built a reassuring fire on the stone hearth. We were sleepy and shared a slow bottle, wrapped in blankets, on the floor between the blaze and its spirited reflection in glass doors that faced, I supposed, the water.

I asked if we were on church property. "Oh no," he said firmly. "Well," he added, "it belongs to my brother. But he's very generous. We have an understanding." He fed me red wine from his glass. "When he was six and I was nine...Ah! well, yes," he reaffirmed. "It's mine."

I fell asleep. Later, I let him carry me to bed. It was cold and smelled of cedar.

A perverse little daybreak fragment (Nicholas murmured infinite endearments, but I couldn't hear him, and it made me feel sinking and sick) woke me, early but alone, in the brass and redwood bedroom. I wrapped myself in a daisy quilt. The stairs floated on iron rods from the beamed ceiling and halfway down I got my first view of the bottle-green lake riding a strong fist of rock and pine mountains and Nicholas rocking the lake with silvery oars. I tumbled down to the deck, down to the dock, and met him, and we stood, stark raving naked in the echoing outdoors and Coocoo, fishing cross-legged in an old straw hat off the back of the boat, thundered. "It's all mine," the man shouted. The lake and the hills and every tree! Every inch of it!"

I laughed and ran inside because the morning chattered my white teeth.

We idled, breakfasting, while I worried about his conscience, his sense of sin, so surprisingly scattered for the nonce, and wanted to ask him, Please, when righteousness returns, when the time comes, quietly, no defenses, no recriminations, none of that, and, finally, he surprised me asking, "Is something wrong?"

"Enchantment is an uneasy condition," I answered. "Can the distant heir of potted Polish barons and fantastic Irish gleemen cope with all this nature?"

The chill bright fist of the morning opened and expanded, warming the vast bright Saturday. We shared the oars, the three of us, and rowed the enigmatic surface, over and back and, taking it easy, followed the erratic, graceful shoreline. We pulled the boat ashore in a shy and silent cove. The gravel beach crunched our feet, stinging. I demonstrated my very prehensile toes. Behind our backs, as we peered into the forest, a blue and rusty rock rose straight from the slapping water. We turned and bounced our voices off it. Catspin spun from my arms, ran up and down a tree, and headlong, showing off to Nicky's admiring shouts, up another, where he sat on a sunny branch and laughed at scolding birds and squirrels. "What a secret place," I whispered, but it seemed intent, suddenly, upon announcing our arrival.

"We always swim here," said Nicholas.

"You and who else?"

"Me and my brother."

"Shall we explore?" We might have been more sensible and pulled on jeans and sneakers. We abandoned them, rolled up with sandwiches and a thermos in a canvas bag, and wandered, fresh as the flesh and feckless, over carpets of molding leaves and dusty needles, through shadowed woods, with the elusive shrill of mosquitoes teasing our ears, and nestling hillside meadows filled with sun and flowers and the bloomier buzz of golden, fat bumblebees and the surprising heavy, brown-and-orange monarchs. Cat played peek-a-boo with us and the world. "There are lots of deer and – oh, raccoons and porcupine and, oh, but they of course would hide from us."

I knew the evergreens were, vaguely, pines and I could recognize a birch. Daisies and sweet Susans and the purple clover were old friends. But what are all these others? "And what is this moss?" A bright green swarm of pinpoint stars. They really seemed to light the darkness of the forest floor. How brave to be so small in this huge universe. But, of course, the lichens, here and there, were smaller still and quite, quite perfect. "I scarcely know the names of anything," I admitted shamefully.

"Perhaps they have none. I sometimes think naming is just another human failing."

We fell to picking whatever we couldn't find words for and most of what we could and returned, beautifully laden, fairly scratched and bitten, to our sandwiches and coffee. I found a weary pack of cigarettes tucked into my torn sneaker, but I decided not to smoke.

We swam. There was a braided rope – long in the family – and, standing on a hairy great knot, one held on, swooping out loud and, gasping, sprawled just a second on the graspless, brawling air. Then the shocking water splits and splinters all over and you plunge and then burst upward without having reached any bottom. I would scarcely catch my breath and hair out of my eyes and the pool would cannonball again. Roughneck Nick claps a thunderous hand on my head and I'm ducked. Or he pursues my ankles underwater. Or we swing together, bellowing, and tumble hand in hand. We race to the rock and float back squinting at the careless blue sky through glittering lashes. That sky, of course, took no interest in us at all and in a very little while, the birds and squirrels found us noisy, to be sure, but not very important. So we felt very much at home and swam all afternoon. "Your church believes in a bodily resurrection, doesn't it?"

"Well – "

"But what can that mean?" I called back on the rush of air and dropped.

Finally, we noticed we were shivering and hungry and it was time to climb into our fern and flower boat, where Cat had long been napping, and row back to the dock and the deck and a nice fire. "I think it's too bad you didn't get to wrestle a crocodile and rescue me from yawning jaws," I said. "But there is one more thing I really have to do before we go." I climbed a tree. It was rugged getting up and touchy coming down, but I did it. Nicholas razzed and worried and, at last, rewarded me handsomely on my resonant, slaphappy rump. We crawled into denim and flannel and went home.

"Where did this come from?" I had tagged behind him into a little storeroom, gathering wood, and discovered a dusty hula hoop among abandoned lamps and a dressmaker's dummy: "Your mother, I assume." I struggled to extricate the cherry-ripe wheel from its cast-off tangle. "I made a great hit at the senior class picnic with one of these things."

On the deck, while Nicholas chuckled and fussed over the charcoal, I bumped through a series of false starts to a rolling flotilla, the whirling red slash on the violet air riding, like satellites and Saturnalia, my rollicking flip-n-fanny through fifty-seven count-em revolutions and a solar plexus, ribald, spiraling, at last, over my shoulders and upstretched arms to sail free, aiming at Venus. I sank to my knees. "You'll find there's plenty of hot water," purred Nicholas.

After shaving tunefully – "It ain't no sin to take off your skin and dance around in your bones" – I lingered steaming in a careless half-doze. I dressed nicely for dinner in a knobby white sweater, borrowed from Kenneth rather a long time ago, and we ate our barbecued chicken under the stars but took our coffee, with brandy, indoors, cherishing the blaze, reflected, not only on the doors, but everywhere in the room's woodwork, leather, porcelain, and metal. We enjoyed keeping quiet. Later, stretched across the floor, from here all the way over to there, Nick chortled and said, "Your little friend was really funny in that get up."

"You think so?"

"I think he was cute."

Then I worried him with questions and opinions about Saint Augustine. I'm very fond of Bishop Hippo: an infinite sea, and somewhere within it a sponge. The mystery of incarnation and of incarnations, flowings and flowerings, through eons and ironies. "I don't believe it, but I do sense, when we're together, a dim remembrance of other creations."

"It's not a matter of belief," he said. "One gets perspectives."

Four masked faces watched us behind the doors with timid and timeless curiosity. In slow motion, so as not to frighten them away, we gathered scraps to feed them. They eat like orphaned refugees, childlike but awfully serious, keeping always one eye on the generous stranger. We left them with the dishes and climbed the stairs and Nicholas filled me with his lake and hills and trees. I opened to him. All my petals dropped upon the turning current and spread to the widening spindrift edges of old night.

I piped an antic ditty in my wolfish chaps. Someone was rolling a drum on the roof and something very blunt and damp fell onto the bed beside me. It was The New York Times. Cat was with me and Nicholas, dripping in a great black rubber slicker, loomed above us.

The nearest village is less far than one likes to think." I smiled up at him, feeling like dew and the daisies. Then I tried to stretch and yawn. "Oh, Nick," I moaned.

"I feel a bit stiff myself."

"So many muscles. So many painful little places."

"Can you name every one of them?"

"I'd like to."

Then there were the bites. I crept downstairs, however, and stood naked in the pummeling rain until I'd been thoroughly washed and frozen. The sky and the lake and the mountains had merged. Then, chattering and cautious, I climbed back to bed. We had the newspaper with toast and coffee, dozing on and off, to waste the morning. Morning, afternoon, and evening merged.

We rubbed each other with liniment and calamine. I found among the books beside the fireplace Professor Wherry's "Wild Flower Guide: Northeastern and Midland United States (Garden City, 1948)," and tried to identify some members of our gathering. I discovered some entertaining pretties – Bergamots, Skullcap and Bladderwort, Rough Spike and Gayfeather, Jointweed and Candyroot, Catchfly and Butter-and-Eggs. The flora of our lakeside and escape, however, seemed to be unique, for I really couldn't match, to my satisfaction, any of our pixies to Miss Tabea Hoffman's pics. Nicholas, meanwhile, wove wreaths for our ankles and hair. We didn't have much appetite and Cat, perhaps also feeling his age, refused to get up at all. Nick suggested dominos, but I found the Scrabble. I played English. He played Latin. "If the rain falls all night," he suggested, "We'll be mudbound tomorrow."

"We don't really have to go back," I said. But the storm stopped before midnight and, in the morning, we packed up and, after a last good feed, climbed the muddy but passable trail. He studied the rearview and, on top, he braked and said, "Look back. That's the view I'd like you to have had arriving."

"I don't want to," I mumbled, but I did. I looked back, over my crumpled blue suit on the seat, at God-Be-With-You. Then I turned to the lighter and my cigarettes.

I was not to see him again until Thanksgiving. "Do you mind?" he asked. "I love it."

Shortly after midnight, everything was cooking, the stuffing in the bird and the bird in the oven, or standing ready to be cooked. We cleaned up the kitchen and took our drinks into the parlor. I turned the records over and put a fresh candle in the artichoke. I stretched on my back, matching the light play on the ceiling to the playful music in my ears. He sat behind his big knees on a cushion. He's the only man I know who whistles to Mozart. He held the ashtray watchfully while I thoroughly enjoyed a cigarette.

"Have you been to the lake?"

He had not. My brain became for a moment a shock of bright wildflowers and I felt the water cradle me as if we'd been swimming all day. Or perhaps it was too many martinis. I turned onto my stomach and rocked my chin in my hands which smelled of cologne and salami. We were quiet for awhile, living in our noses and ears. Then I offered to refill his glass but he felt he'd had enough.

I made a short trip to the john and brought back, from the kitchen, the camembert and pumpernickel. I chatted about my students, happy goofs – one in particular, a passing ogler of my passing cowpoke. I decided not to tell that story.

He grew anecdotal about his church folk that, having no spirit, never break a rule. "Somehow I don't think that gets them into heaven."

"Are there no exceptions?"

"I can't divulge the secrets of confession."

"Mercy no!" I scrambled to help the diamond out of an old rut. The night flew by, an easy glider.

After some last minute hustling, we sat down to our banquet at 3:33 AM. "Strictly speaking, Thanksgiving has passed," I observed.

He stood behind my chair with his hands on my shoulders. "Time clocks and calendars," he said, "are mere conventions." His fingers tempted my shaggy nape. Then he kissed the top of my head. He poured the wine.

"I've never had goose," I announced.

"Good. Then you can't compare mine to another's." "Oh, my dear – "

And so we had our holiday together. We ate heartily. We toasted and blessed each other with the white wine and the red.

At dawn, we carried bubbling tulips into the bedroom and stretched out in our clothing, side by side, and drifted, slow and easy, out the window and across the rose-washed sky. I dreamed of plain ice.

When I awoke, he was gone of course. The kitchen, I discovered, was spotless. And he had left his little note of explanation.

I have put it down as I remember it.

AMAZING GIF
Kyle Stone

It always began the same way with Tony, that odd tingling in the fingers and toes, the way his right leg trembled ever so slightly. As the words scrolled by on his screen, he leaned forward, tense, expectant. He was waiting to connect, in the only way he could. To reach out and release his own crying need into the electronic sea of desire that was such a big part of the Lambda Gate BBS.

Tony Mantanero had just turned 18. He lived at home, up in the attic, in a room without even a door he could close. It was his space, but it wasn't. His father's old audio tape collection was stacked in one corner. His mother insisted on cleaning and dusting, rearranging his things in spite of frequent requests not to. The only thing that was inviolate was the computer.

Uncle Sal had given him the computer when Tony started college. His parents were in awe of it. They were proud of Tony for knowing how to tame such a technological monster. He showed them how to log onto the library on the modem, check for books without even going out of the house, reserve them. He showed them how easily he could edit term papers for school. He showed them how to draw pictures and print them, how to talk to groups of people who were all separated from each other by hundreds of miles. He never showed them anything about the Lambda Gate.

That was his secret, his door into another world, where he could talk to people like himself, men who were attracted to other men and were not afraid to say so. Afraid? They were proud! They had their own secret language and codes, a whole series of short forms and affectionate phrases. They called each other Boytoy, Bear-Cum and Boner, Jockstrap and Leatherboy and Top man. Every time he saw these names he felt a small shiver of delight, a thrill of recognition that validated his own secret identity. He felt embarrassed by his juvenile handle, but all the same, he didn't want to change it yet. He wasn't quite ready to send a more sophisticated message out onto the glowing boards. The Tigger handle made him feel safe, just a little longer.

He always logged on late at night, after his parents had gone to bed. He told himself he didn't feel guilty about what he was doing, but this was a lie. Every time the screen came up, he felt a strange thrill, made sweeter by the acid tinge of guilt. All those words, gay – lesbian – studs – gifs, loaded words, each one carrying its share of guilt and glitter of temptation, each one a part of another world he yearned to enter, but only dared to come to late at night.

He had discovered a new persona on the boards. Tigger was funny and sexy and playful. He was hunky and hung like a horse. He could talk for hours in the chat lounge, sending private messages loaded with innuendo and public messages of open invitation. He was more than a flirt. He was a downright slut! In the Wildside Game, where players gained points by collecting sexual favors from others, he was almost the board champion. But whenever someone took him seriously and gave out a phone number, he fled, sometimes ending up sitting in front of his computer in tears of frustration, overcome with guilt and remorse at how close he had come to direct contact.

Was there any way he would ever have the nerve to actually meet any of these men he cruised verbally, he wondered. Had the reputation he was fast acquiring for playing head games, spoiled his chances? Secretly he yearned for some man to be so insistent that he would have to respond, would be forced to finally take the chance and show himself in public as a gay man. Shit! It was only recently he had come out to himself, and sometimes, he still denied it.

"Where's the stud who's man enuf to take all nine inches of prime meat?"

"Are we talking salami here?"

And is it kosher, that's what I want to know!"

"It's kosher if it's cut! Is it cut?"

"I'm drooling, guy! I'm on my knees, waiting for your hot pulsing rod! Ram my throat, baby!"

When Tony first started logging on to the BBS, he would hear these voices in his sleep – dark and seductive, light and suggestive; whispers, moans, invitations...

He'd hear the wet slurp of sweaty skin slapping against hot flesh. He'd wake up with a hard-on. Sometimes the sheets were wet and sticky and he got up in the night and rinsed them out in the toilet bowl so as not to have to run the water.

The voices had slowed down, sorted themselves out so that now each belonged to a particular handle with a picture he had made up in his head that corresponded to it.

Then he discovered gifs. He had noticed the word on the main menu when he first logged on, but it was merely one more technical term he didn't understand, and he didn't stop to worry about it. The term began to creep into the public posts, used in questions like, "Where can I get hold of Bare Bear's gif?" or "Is it true the Marky Mark gif showing the great hard-on is a fake?" Then one of the sysops explained that members could take a photo of themselves and scan it, then upload it for others to see. There were hundreds of gifs on the system, hundreds of pictures of hot men of all types, into all sorts of activities, baring it all and reveling in it. Tony was delighted.

And tonight, having discovered how to hide files, he had finally got up the nerve to try to bring one of these pictures into his computer.

It was very late. The old house creaked around him, settling in the night air. Outside his dormer window, shadowed leaves waved gently, black and silver in the faint light from the moon. Tony watched the screen intently, the tingling in his fingers making him feel very alive as he read the labels that tried to capture the impact of the hidden image: "Leather stud unzips for his slave," "This leather man struts his stuff," "Boy next door bares all for the neighbors," "Two bears at play." What did the words actually mean? How real would the image be?

At last he settled on one of the simpler gifs called "Jason alone." There was something wistful about the title that called to him. Jason alone. Tony alone. Put them together...

He adjusted his glasses and keyed in the download sequence. To his delight, everything proceeded smoothly. The numbers clicked over, counting down the time till he could actually look at his new acquisition.

Two minutes later he logged off the BBS and went into his viewer program. After a tense wait, a compact young blond flashed into view, his nearly nude body stretched out lazily in bright sunlight. One arm was flung back, his hand cradling his blond head against the brick wall. His other hand explored under the waist band of his skimpy Speedo. It was obvious there was a lot going on under there.

Tony stared long and hard at the image, so lifelike, so real. Jason's eyes gazed dreamily over his right shoulder. They were deep blue. The blond hair on his arms and legs glistened gold, his long sun-bleached curls almost stirring in the unseen breeze. Tony shivered. His own shorts were clammy and with a furtive look in the direction of the stairs behind him, he pulled them off. When he sat down again, his naked ass squeaked slightly against the wooden chair. He thought about the feel of his buttocks flattened against the wood, the edge pressing into him, marking his skin, leaving its pattern on him, the way fingers would leave their imprint from kneading his ass cheeks in an agony of shared pleasure.

A small moan escaped him. He had never shared anything like that, only one fumbled hurried encounter in the darkness of the gym cupboard at school that showed him clearly what he really wanted from another male. What he had started to look for, at last.

He gazed at the image in front of him, caressing the screen with his eyes; that body, so compact, lithe, muscular without the bulk that he admired but found a little intimidating. He felt his own cock stiffen, hanging out in the naked air, reaching for contact. What did Jason's cock look like under that thin strip of red nylon?

He leaned closer, trying to see the tiny beads of sweat glistening on Jason's smooth chest. He could almost smell the salty tang of the damp blond hair, feel the heavy moist heat of it against the warm neck as he burrowed closer....

He blinked. The tree sighed outside his window and as he turned his head, he heard another sigh almost in his ear. He snapped his eyes back to the screen and at the same time, pushed his chair further away from his desk.

"Jesus," he murmured. He wiped the sweat out of his eyes. Something was wrong. He stood up abruptly and pulled on his shorts, feeling all of a sudden as if he was no longer alone. "Moron," he breathed. He glanced again at the screen and froze. Was he losing his mind? Or was the image different? Jason's right hand had moved, pushing his Speedo lower on his narrow hips, showing more of the dark blond pubic hair curling through the boy's fingers. And his face! Those green/blue eyes were looking right at him, smiling, mocking, tempting.... Tony stared back, mesmerized. It was like looking into water where you can see all the way down through different levels of color.

"This is crazy!" Tony hissed, but he shivered in the closeness of the attic room. His cock stirred again in his shorts.

Back on the screen, Jason winked at him. Maybe this is an electronic thing, Tony thought. He watched closely as Jason pulled out his cut cock and began to pump it slowly, slowly, the slit gleaming with pre-cum, while all the time, those eyes stared right at Tony. It's like my own personal porn flick right on my own computer, he thought. He'd heard of such things, but weren't they called something else? GRASP, or something like that? Not GIFS, were they?

Whatever they were or weren't, Jason didn't seem to care. He had turned over now, presenting his trim ass for Tony's enjoyment.

Tony went over and switched on his bedside table light. Too many shadows, he reasoned. When he turned back to the screen, there was nothing there at all! The screen glowed a blank silver in the darkness. Now what? A power surge? Disk crash? Would it cost a lot to fix? Oh, God! Would he be able to wipe off the evidence of his double life before anyone saw those tell-tale files?

All these thoughts raced through his mind as he stared at the blank monitor. Then he heard a soft ripple of laughter behind him, like the sigh of the breeze outside his window.

He froze. It wasn't outside. Not this time. Was someone playing tricks on him? He took a deep breath, then very slowly, he turned around.

Jason lay stretched out on his bed, one hand behind his head, the other teasingly pushing his cock back out of sight under the drawstring of the red Speedo. He grinned.

"Shit," muttered Tony. "I must be losing it."

Jason shook his blond head. "Finding it, you mean, don't you? And its about time, too."

"What the hell is that supposed to mean?" Tony shot back, stung by the retort.

That low intimate chuckle sounded again, almost as if inside his head.

"Aw come on! You're not exactly a high scorer in this game, are you, sport?"

"I'm not playing games!"

"Sure you are." Jason grinned at him and ground his hips into the bed suggestively. "But you're too chicken to play out your hand."

"You're pretty cocky for a bunch of electronic dots. 'Tony sank onto the desk chair. It was either sit down or fall down at this point, and he didn't want to wake up his mother by crashing onto the floor.

Jason seemed to be considering his words. The impish grin had given way to a thoughtful look as he scratched his bare chest. Tony was seized with the sudden fear that he might disappear. He leaned forward, reaching out impulsively. At the last moment, he pulled back.

"What are you?" he whispered.

Jason shrugged. "The boy next door. Your first date. Whatever. Does it matter?"

"Of course it matters! Shit!"

"Don't be so uptight."

"Yeah, you're a great one to talk, porn star or whoever you are."

"Porn star? Me? Hah! I'm not big enough to do porn." "You look pretty good to me," Tony admitted.

"I'm average, that's all." He shrugged. "You don't have to be hung like a horse to look good."

"Sure sounds that way, the way guys talk."

"Talk. Sure. Anyone can talk. You should know, right, guy?"

Tony flushed uncomfortably.

Suddenly the Speedo was off and Jason's beautiful cut cock sprang into view. Tony stared, all the banter and jokes and leering lines gone from his mind. There was no way he could talk now, no way he wanted to. He watched Jason twirl the swim suit around on one finger, a swirl of blurred color that suddenly went flying across the room and out of sight. Jason got to his feet and moved closer, his perfect compact body glowing with sun and sex and invitation.

Tony groaned. He felt weak behind the knees and his breath came in short soft gasps as he leaned towards the boy, slowly, by imperceptible inches. It was like being pulled by an unseen cord. He was so close he could smell the sweaty hair, clinging in damp curls on Jason's forehead, his neck. Jason ran his tongue over his lips, slowly, looking into Tony's eyes. Tony's cock jumped against the thin cotton of his shorts, leaking precum. Without taking his eyes off the golden dream, Tony yanked his shorts down and kicked out of them.

"Yeah," breathed Jason.

The dark hair on Tony's chest stirred as Jason's hand hovered barely an inch above his skin. Suddenly, tears spilled out of his eyes, making the naked blond vision so close to him sparkle in the dim light. He had wanted this for so long, but his dreams had always been a hot, shifting kaleidoscope of anonymous cocks straining against tight swimsuits, cocks swelling the front of gym shorts, sturdy legs pumping up and down, asscheeks clenching beneath brief track uniforms. There had never been a clear specific picture, one face, one body. Now, all the disjointed images coalesced into one likeness -- Jason, with the golden haze of hair on his arms and legs, the swirl of thick spicy curls clustered around the base of his cock. Tony closed his eyes, trying to cope with the naked desire shivering through him. His body was tense with lust, his cock rock hard, stabbing the air in front of him, hot for contact with Jason's luscious mouth. But he was afraid to move, afraid he might shatter this tenuous reality.

He felt a shift in the close stillness and his eyes sprang open. Jason was gone! A sigh coming up from below made him almost laugh out loud with relief. Jason was on his knees, his bright head poised above Tony's rigid cock. Slowly, his arm shaking with the strain of control, Tony lowered his hand. As his fingers touched the gleaming curls, a sharp tingle went through him, as if a mild electrical current crawled through his nerves, down his spine, jolting his cock into delicious spasms as Jason's hot mouth slid around the swollen tip.

"Ahhhh." The breath poured out of him in a long sigh, the sound hanging in the dense, hot air.

Jason's hands moved up the backs of his legs until the strong fingers molded themselves around the cheeks of his ass, lifting, separating, radiating heat like small suns. Tony was on fire, within, without, even his face dripped, sweat rolling down his sides, down his back. He could almost hear the sizzle as drops of perspiration hit Jason's searing flesh. His cock slid down the kneeling boy's yielding throat like magic. He could feel the caress of the strong muscles, undulating against his swelling shaft, until he began to shake, his whole body vibrating so much he was afraid he was going to lose his balance.

"I'm coming!" he growled between clenched teeth.

Jason pulled away, his face bright red, slicked with sweat, his eyes laughing. He rolled back on the bed, pulling Tony on top of him and put his ankles on Tony's shoulders.

"Fuck me," he whispered, making those two words one long alluring invitation.

Tony was beyond thought. He looked down and saw the boy's brown puckered hole winking at him from between the deep perfect globes of his ass. Steadying himself with one hand on the wall, he guided his aching cock past the tight circle of muscle that opened to him with a soft sucking noise. He gasped as his soul was pulled deep inside the hot velvet center of his dream Fuck. His body shuddered. He bucked against the charged flesh, his tight nuts hammering on Jason's muscled ass as suddenly his need burst out of him with a great crescendo and he shot his load with a strangled animal cry of triumph.

When he looked down again, he saw the strings of pearlized come gleaming on the boy's chest, dripping from the perfect mushroom head of his cock. Tony grinned down at his companion, his chest heaving as he tried to catch his breath.

"Tony? Are you okay?" His mother's voice.

For one terrified instant, Tony froze. Then he scrambled to his feet, crawled around on the floor in a desperate search for his crumpled shorts. "Under the bed," he hissed, not stopping to see if Jason understood his urgency. When he found the shorts, he yanked them on, realizing too late they were back to front.

"Tony? I thought I heard something up here. You okay or what?" His mother's unkempt grey head appeared as she slowly made her way up the attic stairs.

Total helplessness rushed through Tony as he watched her pause at the top and reach for the light switch. He pushed both hands through his hair as if looking presentable were all that was necessary, when the smell of sex was heavy on the air and his lover lay naked, covered in come on the bed behind him.

Finding his voice at last, he stepped forward, trying to ward off this invasion of his privacy. "I'm okay, Mom. Really. You don't need to come up here just because you heard me talking to my computer!"

"You should be in bed at this time of night, not sitting up in front of that thing playing games." She waved at the computer.

"Look, Mom, I don't play games anymore. I'm not a kid. I have a life!"

"A life. Sure. What kind of a life when you're up all hours of the night?" She snapped on the light. "Let me fix your bed. It's all messed up."

"No!"

"What's the matter with you? Heat stroke?"

"Nothing's wrong. You just ... startled me, okay? I'll go to bed now. Honest."

His mother looked at him for a long moment, her dark brown eyes unreadable. Then she shook her head, turned and made her way back down the stairs.

"Jesus," muttered Tony. He looked towards the bed. It was empty. Thank God Jason had made himself scarce. "Okay. You can come out now. She's gone." Nothing. He looked under the bed, but even shining a flashlight under there revealed nothing but dust bunnies and an old sock. "Jason? Where are you?"

Tony stood in the middle of his attic room, looking around. There was no one in the cupboard, no one in the closet, no naked sweating body behind the dresser. He was alone. He turned back to the computer and looked at the softly glowing screen. Then he took a closer look. As he watched, the silver shimmer slowly tightened into a small blue/green eye in the very middle of the screen. Then with a wink, the eye vanished, leaving the screen blank.

THE BIGGEST ONE OF ALL
Leo Cardini

"Tell us a story, Uncle Bill," my nephew Bobby pleaded as he sat squirming on my left leg, just like I was a department store Santa Claus.

"Yeah," said his boyfriend Brendan who was seated to my right on the sofa, admiring the splendid job we'd done of decorating the Christmas tree, "something nice and Christmassy."

And to coax me into the mood, he slowly slid his hand across my thigh, inching towards my crotch.

"Don't you boys think you're a little old for this sort of thing?"

"Nah," said Bobby, giving me a quick peck on the cheek. "We may be almost nineteen," said Brendan, now kneading my crotch, "but we're very young at heart."

"Okay, but only if you promise to be good little boys tonight, and to obey your Uncle Bill, no matter what he might want you to do."

"Don't we always?" asked Bobby, sliding his right arm around my neck and slipping his left hand under my shirt. "Sure we promise," said Brendan.

"Okay, then I'll tell you all about the night I met Elliot." "Elliot?" repeated Bobby, scrunching up his face, making clear his distaste for such a nerdy name.

"Yes, Elliot, the clumsy elf."

"Hmm," said Brendan doubtfully. "This better be good."

It all happened about a month ago. I was sitting here thinking about all the preparations I had to make for the Christmas season. I had everything just about figured out, except for one detail; what to get you two boys for presents. You see, I wanted to come up with something really special and out of the ordinary – gifts you'd never forget.

Well, I finally gave up and decided to think about it again later. I got up from the sofa and headed for the attic, where all the Christmas decorations are stored, dreading the annual untangling, bulb replacing and sorting out of all those seemingly endless strands of Christmas lights. I swear somehow they manage to multiply and knot up during all those months they're stored up in the attic, like they get bored and can think of nothing better to do.

Well, just as I'd reached the top attic step, I heard this thump-thump-crash-tinkle-tinkle off to my left in the vicinity of the Christmas decorations.

I grabbed the flashlight I always keep just at the top of the steps and scanned the area. The cardboard boxes of Christmas decorations I had so neatly stored away last January had fallen all over the place in terrible disarray. And the Christmas lights? It was like someone had ransacked them. All those strands of colored bulbs were spilling out of their boxes, snaking all over the place in the biggest tangle you've ever seen.

Well, I ran my flashlight back and forth and back and forth over this disorganized jumble, thinking over what possibly could have happened.

Then I noticed something strange. In the middle of all this mess there was what looked like a manikin elf from a department store Christmas display that had fallen over onto its side. The reason I say elf is because it was short and slim, it had a boyish face, and its ears were slightly pointed. Not that I've ever actually met an elf. Anyhow, whatever it was, the oddest thing of all was that it looked like someone had tied it up with several strands of my Christmas lights.

I didn't remember coming into possession of any manikin, and I was trying to puzzle this out as I drew nearer.

Then, when I was just about a yard away, it sneezed! Its body suddenly jerked, the jumble of lights shuddered, something rattled, and one box that had been precariously perched on several others fell, hitting it on the head.

"Ouch!" it cried out. Then it played possum again, lying there as still as could be. But I could see its eyes were glued on me, and its face betrayed its anxiety over what I might do.

I scanned it again with my flashlight. An involuntary shiver ran through its body.

"What the hell?" I questioned out loud.

"Sorry," he said, breaking out into the cutest, little-boy smile you ever saw.

Then he giggled, like he was trying to cover up his embarrassment, setting some of the lights a-shivering again. Whoever, or whatever, he was, he was an adorable little bugger, looking like he was just on the verge of puberty. You know, smooth, clear skin and no facial hair.

Open-mouthed, I just stood there and stared at him.

"What are you going to do with me?" he asked, suddenly turning apprehensive again.

"Uh...what do you want me to do with you?"

"Untangle me, and get me somewhere warm. It's freezing up here."

And with that, another shiver ran through his body.

Well, I got down on my knees, set the flashlight by my side, and untangled him.

"How long've you been up here?"

"Oh, about an hour or so, maybe?"

"And what are you doing here in the first place? And how did you ever get so tangled up in my lights?"

"Well I...uh..."

But he was interrupted by an involuntary attack of the giggles. What happened was I was working on the lights around his waist, slightly distracted by the remarkable bulge in his green corduroys. Anyhow, during his captivity, his little white tee-shirt had inched up out of his pants, and he was ticklish to the touch of my fingers against his smooth, taut abdomen. Maybe my fingers lingered around the vicinity of his belly button longer than they actually needed to, but what the hell.

"Sorry," I mumbled, not really meaning it.

"I'll bet you do that to all the boys," he quipped between giggles.

"There," I said as I unwrapped the last coil of lights from around him. "You'd think someone left you up here as a hostage, or something. Come on downstairs and I'll give you something to warm you up."

As we made our way down to the kitchen, I was able to observe him a little more carefully. He must've been about five-foot seven or eight. He was lean, lithe and tight-muscled, like a swimmer. But a little clumsy. Well, not a little. A lot. Just going down to the kitchen he managed to trip twice on the stairs and upset that Chinese vase that used to be on the telephone stand.

He had an unruly shock of dark brown hair on the verge of needing a cut, pale skin, and delicate, regular facial features. And he would've been exceptionally handsome if it wasn't for his smile, which was perhaps just a little too large for his face.

In the kitchen, I made him some hot chocolate while he sat at the table and explained how he'd come to be all tied up in my attic.

145

He was an elf. Yes, an elf. His assignment: Christmas lights. Did you ever wonder how it is that every year when you go up into the attic to pull out the Christmas lights, there always seem to be more than you stored away the previous year? And no matter how carefully you put them away after first replacing any burnt-out bulbs, when you drag them out again the next year, they're always in a tangle and you always have to replace just enough bulbs to have to make at least one unplanned shopping trip to buy some more.

Well, there are elves whose sole responsibility is to go around to attics and create all this trouble. It's an unpopular, entry-level job foisted off on junior elves. If you're really good at it, you get promoted to closet coat hangers. "Out of the attic and into the closet," they say.

Now, why do they bother about such things in the first place? I don't know. Elliot wouldn't tell me. He just stared at me with a puzzled look on his face, like he was amazed that anyone would even raise the question.

Yes, his name was Elliot, and he was on attic assignment. Except that in tangling up my Christmas lights, he'd somehow managed to get himself tied up in them.

"It happens to me all the time," he explained to me sadly. He sighed and sat there, elbows on the table, resting his chin on his hands, looking lost in thoughts of past attic misadventures.

"C'mon," I said, rousing him from his reverie as I set a cup of steamy hot chocolate in front of him. "Let's move into the living room."

"Sure," he said, lifting the cup. "Oops. Do you have a sponge?"

In the living room (I offered – or rather insisted – to carry his hot chocolate in for him) we sat side by side on the sofa.

"Mmm...that's good," he said, sipping, "better than anything we ever get served."

"Uh huh?"

But he ignored my prompt for more detail.

"Yeah, I've been clumsy all my life," he said, switching back to an earlier topic. "Always have been, and always will be, I guess. And the other elves used to laugh about it and make fun of me while I'd be wiping up spills, sweeping up broken dishes, or nursing my bruises. 'Ha ha, clumsy Elliot's done it again!'"

"But the most humiliating thing was whenever they'd choose up teams to play a game. Guess who was always picked last? That is, if they let me join in at all."

"I think," I interrupted, "I've heard of something like this once happening to a reindeer. But why do you talk about it like it happened in the past?"

He took another sip of his hot chocolate, and as he leaned forward to place his mug on the coffee table, he looked up into my face with this broad, mischievous smile. He looked so cute and enticing at that moment that I chose to ignore the steamy splash of liquid onto the table.

Placing his left hand on my right thigh, he replied, You see, it's like this. So Rudolph has this red, shiny nose. What's a red shiny nose compared to what I got?"

"Oh?"

"Yeah."

His smile widened as he slowly nodded, acknowledging my glance down at his crotch and affirming that what I was thinking was indeed correct.

"Even when I was a little kid, though I never really gave it much thought until one night almost year ago, the day after my eighteenth birthday."

"You're eighteen?"

"Yeah, I really am. You see, we don't age as quickly as you humans do. Anyhow, I had just reached puberty. No, we don't get any facial hair to speak of. Or chest hair, except for maybe a few right there..."

He tapped my chest between my pecs.

"...but nothing like that," he added, his voice full of admiration as he reached into my half-unbuttoned shirt and ran his hand across the soft spread of black hair that fans out over my chest.

No, everything happens below our belly buttons. Hair comes in and there's this sudden spurt in our growth, if you know what I mean."

Again, my eyes focused on that intriguing bulge in the crotch of his green corduroys.

"Yeah. That's another way we differ from humans. Even the smallest of us is pretty darn large. But mine started out greater than standard elf size, and then just kept growing and growing. For a while there I thought maybe someone had planted a magic bean down there.

But I was so used to spilling and dropping things, bumping into people, and in general upsetting whatever was going on around me, all I could think of was, 'Great. Now I've got one more part of my body to worry about getting into trouble.' So I used to stuff it into my briefs, nice and snug and out of the way, embarrassed that if the other elves discovered it, they'd just consider it one more thing about me to laugh at."

So here's this poor, unfortunate elf pouring out his soul to me, and all I can do is wonder about his briefs – the size, the brand, the style, and how does the cotton in its crotch cope with the deliciously cruel and unusual demands placed upon it?

"Well anyhow..." he continued, dragging me away from my lewd thoughts...

...on that particular night after dinner, all the other elves had gone upstairs to play before bedtime. I had to stay behind in the kitchen, though, to sweep up a bowl I'd broken.

When I was done, I went upstairs and walked down that long corridor all our bedrooms are off of. There's usually two or three elves to a bedroom, but since no one wanted to share a room with me, I had this tiny one all to myself at the far end of the corridor.

Well, when I passed Elvis and Earl's bedroom, it struck me that it was strangely quiet inside. You see, it was like the central hangout and it was always the noisiest place on the second floor.

I bent over, steadying myself with one hand on the doorknob so I wouldn't fall over or bump my head or something, and put my eye to the keyhole.

All the other elves were there, all right. But one of them must've been sitting on the floor in front of the door, because his head blocked my view somewhat so I could only see their faces mostly.

Whatever they were doing, they were sure busy doing it. The ones facing me, well, their eyes were glazed over in the strangest way and they had the most urgent-looking expressions on their faces.

Suddenly, Elvis, who was on the opposite side of the room from the door, started going "Oh! Oh! Oh!" like he was in a lot of pain, except it didn't seem like he was feeling any pain.

The others turned and looked at him as he got to his feet, still busy doing whatever it was they were all doing.

I was so intrigued by what was happening on the other side of that keyhole I didn't realize my hand was gradually turning the doorknob in an effort to keep me balanced.

Suddenly the door flew open, bumping Eldin away from where he was seated on the floor, and I fell in, breaking my fall just before my chin hit the hard, wooden floor.

I looked up at the shocked, surprised stares of all the other elves. But not one of them was half as shocked and surprised as me, because I could now see that they all had their little green corduroys down to their ankles, except for a few who had them off entirely. And they'd all been stroking their things, which stood out hard and erect in front of them, except they were now clutching them, frozen in mid-stroke, gaping at me.

All except Elvis, that is, who continued to stroke his thing like he'd lost control over his body and couldn't stop. Suddenly, gobs and gobs of this milky-white stuff gushed out of his thing and jetted across the room. And believe me, when we elves shoot, we shoot.

Elvis spurt out huge hot wads of it like he'd been storing it up all season. I know it was hot because a lot of it landed on my face, and some even in my mouth, nice and salty to the taste.

Well, when he was finally done, my face was sticky-wet with the stuff and a tell-tale path of it dribbled all the way across the room from me over to him as he just stood there like he was out of breath.

"Gee, fellas," I said, "sorry about dropping in like this." "Leave it to Elliot to ruin a circle jerk," Earl complained. And everyone else chimed in with "Yeah," and "Wouldn't you know it?" and stuff like that.

"A circle jerk? What's that?" I asked, knowing from the little I'd witnessed that I was definitely interested.

"And how did you get your...umm...thing to do that, Elvis?"

At this, all the other elves laughed, and I knew I'd said something stupid. You see, up to then I'd never had an orgasm. I mean, sometimes I'd get stiff as a wooden soldier and it would feel real good when I'd try to wrap my fist around it – I say try because I could never get it all the way around – but I hadn't figured out exactly what to do. When you're a clumsy little elf you don't share in these experiences with the other elves. All I knew at that moment was somehow Elvis and the others had discovered a way of handling their things that I hadn't quite figured out yet.

When the laughter died down, Elvis, who was always the ringleader, said, "Sure, we'll show you, Elliot, won't we guys?"

The others said, "Yeah," and "Sure," and looked at Elvis to see what sort of a prank he had up his sleeve.

"But first you gotta take off all your clothes," Elvis ordered.

"Then you gotta get down on your knees," said Earl, stroking his thing and sharing an inside joke with the other elves.

"No," said Elvis, taking control again. "You have to turn around and bend over," he said, to the amusement of all the other elves. And they all broke out in laughter.

"Gee, I don't know about this."

You see, I was beginning to have second thoughts, especially since seeing the rest of them with their things exposed I realized how much bigger mine was. I was feeling kinda freakish and I was afraid they'd laugh at me when they saw it.

"Don't you want to join in our little game?" Elvis coaxed in this real seductive tone. "I guarantee you'll like it. Honest. Elf's honor."

With that, he approached me and started to remove my T-shirt. His hands brushed against my nipples, and I could feel myself growing bigger. Then he started on my corduroys, unbuttoning my fly and getting so close to my...you know... that it just continued to grow like it just couldn't wait to greet him. Finally, with one expert tug, he got my pants to drop to my ankles.

I looked down. I was definitely hard, no mistaking it. It pressed out against my briefs, leaning over to one side with the tip of it sticking out beyond the elastic waistband like it was curious to see what was going on in the outside world.

"Gosh!" exclaimed Elvis.

"Ahh!" gasped Earl as he inhaled a sudden, surprised breath.

And the rest of them stared, bug-eyed and open-mouthed. And as they stared I could see that their things, most of which had softened somewhat after I had dropped in on them, had begun to stiffen again as they unconsciously resumed stroking them.

"Why, Elliot," said Elvis. "You little devil, you. You never told us about this little secret of yours."

He pulled the elastic waistband of my briefs as far away from my abdomen as it would stretch and looked inside. There it was, jumping up to full attention under Elvis's astonished gaze. I could feel myself blushing.

"Gee," Earl said drawing closer, stroking his own thing, "would you just look at that!"

With that he reached in with his free hand and wrapped his fingers around it, making me feel good in a way I've never felt good before. My skin got all tingly and my nipples tightened like something cold had just brushed against them, except they felt much better than anything could had ever made them feel.

Earl hefted it out of my briefs and into full view as he pulled my shorts down to my knees, exposing me to everyone's astonishment. They all just oohed and aahed and began stroking themselves with greater enthusiasm than before.

"Elliot," Elvis said admiringly, "who'd ever have thought you'd have such an enormous cock!"

"Cock?" I questioned. So that's what you call it!

"Yeah, cock," he said.

"Or prick," said Earl.

Or dick," offered Eldin.

Soon they were all gleefully chiming in with their own favorite names.

As Elvis continued to hold me, he slipped his free hand behind me across my ass. My "cock" felt so good the feeling was almost overpowering. All I knew at that moment was something was beginning to be unleashed inside me, something uncontrollable.

"Well," said Elvis, you just interrupted us playing the one game that I'm sure even you couldn't screw up. Isn't that right, guys?"

Everyone assented in an eager, disorganized chorus.

"But Earl just said a few minutes ago that I'd ruined your game."

"What does Earl know? In fact, I think you're going to be our star player."

"Gee!" I said, impressed by this sudden honor.

"Yeah. You see, this is how its works. First, we start off with a circle jerk, as you've already discovered."

A circle jerk. So that's what I'd interrupted. Now, if only I knew what exactly a circle jerk was and how it worked.

"The first one to shoot his load is king of the circle, and the others have to do whatever he says until they've all come. And I'm king of the circle."

"Yeah, you're always king of the circle," Earl complained.

"That's right," chimed in Eldin, rubbing his rear end with his free hand, "and I always end up with a sore hole."

"That's because you've got the sweetest ass in all of elfdom...and the most eager disposition."

At this all the others laughed.

But seriously," continued Earl. "Eldin's right. It seems like all you ever want to do is to watch us play with our cocks until you're hard again, and then fuck Eldin with the rest of us looking on, you big show-off. Well, I'm getting tired of it."

And soon the rest of them were yelling things like "Yeah," and "Me, too!"

"Hey. Hold on, guys!" Elvis protested. "We do other things, too...sometimes."

No one said anything, but their faces expressed one unified chorus of "Yeah! Sure!"

"No," Elvis continued, "This time I have something else planned."

"Oh really?" asked Eldin suspiciously.

"Really," assured Elvis.

"Well, as long as it doesn't give me a sore ass again."

"No, this won't give you a sore ass again. This is a different game. Someone hand me a ruler."

Well, Earl opened his bureau drawer, pulled out a ruler and, handed it to Eldin.

"What we do is first I measure Elliot."

Now we elves may not be that tall, but a ruler?

"Don't you think a yardstick would be better?" I suggested. Everyone laughed.

"No. Even you don't need a yardstick," Elvis answered, wrapping his fingers around my cock and giving it a tug to make his point.

Then it dawned on me what he was talking about. "Oh!"

"Yeah. 'Oh!' Elvis said with this dirty-joke smirk. And everyone laughed all the louder.

"And then," Elvis continued when the laughter had died down, "I measure each one of us. Whoever comes closest to Elliot in size gets to give him a blowjob while the rest of us jack off all over them."

I'd never heard of a blowjob before, but I could figure it out somewhat, though it seemed to me that having someone huff and puff on your thing 'til they were blue in the face would be more frustrating than anything else.

"Well," said Eldin, rubbing his ass. "Maybe I won't win this one either, but at least I won't end up with a sore behind again,"

"Here," said Elvis to me as the others crowded around with interest, "let me see that."

He grabbed my cock again, kneading it with his fingers like it was such a habit with him he was unaware of what he was doing. In response, my cock started twitching madly, like it was trying to squirm out of his hand.

"Look at that," said Elvis, with an unfamiliar tone of admiration in his voice. "I can't even wrap my fingers around it. And it's jerking around like a fish yanked out of water."

"Sorry," I said.

"Oh, that's okay," Elvis replied, surprisingly tolerant.

Then he started running his fist slowly up and down my cock, to make it as hard as it gets, he explained. Boy, he sure seemed to take his time at it.

Finally he put the ruler in place. Everyone leaned forward with their faces close to my cock, like I was some sort of museum display, and Elvis measured my length between twitches.

Then everyone said things like "Wow!" and "Jeez!" and Elvis let out a long whistle of admiration and amazement.

"Okay guys..." he said, pulling over a chair and seating himself next to me so his face was level with my thing, facing it in profile.

And staring at it, he continued, a bit preoccupied, "Well, ...now time to measure everyone else."

But no one seemed to care. Everyone just continued staring at my cock.

Finally, Eldin reached out to touch it. In response, Elvis knocked everyone out of their trance by barking, "Stop that, Eldin. C'mon guys, let's get on with the game. Eldin you're first."

Then he had each elf, one at a time, stand facing me and stroke his cock until it was hard as it could get and he measured it.

Well, among the many things I learned that night was that there are no small elves. I don't mean height, I mean...you know. You see, since then I've seen lots of pictures of naked men in magazines – you're not the only one who stores old dirty magazines in his attic – and in comparison we tend to be longer and thicker, and with bigger balls that nestle snugly at the base of our cocks.

Anyhow, while all this measuring was going on, the elves were gradually unbuttoning, unzipping and pulling off their clothes. It was like they weren't even aware they were doing it. It just happened unconsciously as I stood there stroking my cock, which Elvis had ordered me to do so it would stay hard and everyone could eyeball the difference in size between me and whichever elf was standing in front of me at the moment.

Finally, Elvis had measured everyone but himself.

"My turn," he said, grinning as he stood up an stroked his cock to full size.

"Go ahead Elliot, you measure it," he said, passing me the ruler, which of course I dropped. And when I bent down to pick it up, my lips almost landed on the tip of his cock and everyone laughed.

I stood up again and measured it. That was the first time I ever handled someone else's. What a wonderful feeling! So warm, so big and fat, so hard and soft at the same time, like ripe fruit, and so...well, I don't know how to express it, except to say just touching it made my own cock twitch with this real sweet feeling that ran all the way down deep under my balls.

Well, Elvis won the contest, which apparently didn't surprise anyone, but like one of the elves said afterwards, "Sometimes you don't play the game to win, but just because it's so much fun to play the game."

Anyhow, by then everyone was completely naked.

Elvis got down on his knees in front of me as the rest of the elves crowded around to watch, stroking their cocks and breathing heavily.

151

And that's when I discovered what a blowjob was.

But first, though, Elvis just stared at my cock like a hungry kid looking into a pastry shop window. Then he stretched his mouth wide open, leaned foreword and wrapped his lips around my cockhead. It felt so unexpectedly good I felt like I was going weak at the legs.

He ran the tip of his tongue along the underside of my cockhead and then toyed with my piss slit like he was trying to gain entry. The sensations this produced networked throughout me, sending my entire body a-tingling.

Then Elvis took his right hand (his left hand was stroking his own cock) and wrapped his fingers around my balls. By now I was feeling so good I couldn't help letting out a long, slow moan, which I was afraid to do at first, because I thought the other elves might laugh at me. But they didn't. Some smiled, some took on that same hungry, urgent expression Elvis had on his face before he had taken me in his mouth, and some even moaned a little themselves. But whatever they did individually, they were each and every one of them hard as a rock and busy stroking their cocks.

Elvis leaned further foreword onto my cock and gradually slid his lips along it. His eyes were closed and I had never seen him look so serene and blissful – almost angelic, if you could believe such a thing about Elvis.

Well, he moved down on my cock. Then he came to a stop. He pushed forward again, but he didn't make any progress. Then I heard him gag and I wondered what mistake had I made to cause him do that. You see, I was so used to being clumsy I automatically thought it was my fault he was having trouble with my cock.

It wasn't until afterwards, when I was a little more experienced in these matters, that I realized he'd gagged because my cockhead was so enormous.

But he managed to relax his gagging muscles and soon he was moving forward again until there was simply no way he could take any more of me inside him. A muffled moan escape from him and then he slowly reversed direction until his mouth was fully off my cock, which jumped up and down in front of his face like it was throwing a tantrum to make him play with it some more.

"Ohh," he moaned, open-mouthed and opened-eyed again, staring at my cock as he continued to grasp my balls, holding me in place in front of his eyes.

Eldin reached out to touch my cock and Earl did the same. I looked around and saw that some of the other elves were touching each other all over with their free hands as they continued to stroke their cocks.

Then Elvis brushed away their hands and mounted my cock again. In no time he was rapidly slipping his tight lips up and down along its length.

All the other elves looked on. It seemed like the faster Elvis worked on me, the faster he and the rest of them stroked their own cocks.

Soon we'd reached such a pitch of excitement that the air in the room seemed thick and charged with electricity. And I felt this strange, sweet feeling under my balls growing, spreading throughout my body, making my skin feel real sensitive, especially my nipples, which had hardened into tight little points.

I looked down at Elvis. I swear he could sense what was happening to me, the way he started sliding his mouth up and down cock all the tighter and faster, like he was trying to suck the sensations right out of me, accelerating his own cock strokes at the same time.

By now the feeling was so overwhelming I was open-eyed and twitchy with passion. With one quick glance around the room I could see all the other elves were working furiously on their cocks, their muscles strained and their faces contorted by the same sensations coursing throughout their own bodies.

Suddenly I was so overcome with pleasure it was like I became a slave to it. I thrust my cock violently forward, accidentally forcing Elvis's mouth off me and pushing him backwards. He landed with his ass on his heels, breaking his fall with the palms of his hands flat on the floor behind him. And then spurt after spurt of milky-white fluid shot into the air, landing all over his head, shoulders and chest. In fact, there was so much of it, some even shot behind him, landing on several other elves.

Way back in my mind there was this tiny, split-second thought that I'd been clumsy again, knocking Elvis off my cock that way and making such a sticky wet mess. But I really didn't care that much though, because the next thing I knew Elvis was spewing his own gusher all over the floor between my legs, and all the elves were doing the same, sending their stuff flying through the air all over the place, but mostly on me and Elvis.

And what a racket! Everyone was moaning, or aahing, or just breathing heavily like someone had held them under water for too long.

And for the first time in my life I felt like I wasn't an outsider, isolated from the other elves by my clumsiness. No, for once I was participating as an equal among them, sharing in their enjoyment.

Well, eventually that wonderful feeling went away, leaving me feeling absolutely exhausted and thoroughly satisfied. And before long all the elves had drained themselves of their juices, the noise died down and our cocks gradually lowered to their previous states of heavy-hanging softness.

Elvis was the first to speak. He wiped the cum away from his mouth with the back of his hand and said, "Gee, Elliot, who'd ever have thought you'd be the biggest one among us."

"Or shoot the farthest," Eldin chimed in with admiration.

"Well, we don't know that for a fact," Elvis cautioned, rising to his feet again. "Maybe the next time we play a game it'll be a contest of distance."

He clapped his still-sticky left hand on my shoulder and said, "Though I think already know the winner of that one, too. Three cheers for Elliot, our star player! Hip hip...

"Hooray!"

"Hip hip..."

"Hooray!"

"Hip hip..."

"Horray-y-yy!"

Well, since then I've always been invited to join in their games. And though I'm just as clumsy as ever, especially when it comes to reaching orgasm and losing control over my body, no one really seems to mind.

Even Elvis is nice to me – extra-extra nice. He treats me like his best friend and he's always putting his arm around my shoulders, or patting me on the ass, and whispering silly things in my ear like, "You may be a clumsy little elf, but with a cock like that, Elliot, you'll go down in history!"

By now, Elliot was sitting so close to me his left leg was pressing close against my right. His hand idly explored my inner thigh, occasionally straying up to the bulging territory of my crotch.

"The only thing is, all the other elves ever want to do is suck my cock, or have me fuck them. I get to suck their cocks too, now and then, when I really insist on it and threaten not to play with them if they won't let me, but when it comes to getting fucked, well..." He blushed, then went on: "I'm a virgin."

Well, Bobby and Brendan, let me tell you, its not every day you meet a virgin elf!

"I could take care of that for you," I offered, being the nice guy you boys know that I am.

"You could? I mean, of course you could, I'm sure," he quickly added, sliding his hand up to my crotch and checking out its ever-growing contents, "and you'd really be doing me a big favor, which I absolutely promise to repay, anytime in any way you like. You just name it."

I couldn't believe my good fortune.

"Let's go upstairs to my bedroom," I eagerly suggested. "Oh boy!"

So we got up off the sofa, looking really ridiculous the way our stiff cocks pressed out against our pants, and I motioned for him to lead the way upstairs.

"If you held onto the banister you wouldn't fall like that," I laughingly instructed as he tripped forward on the stairs. It happened so quickly I didn't have time to stop, so my crotch bumped into his rear end and I had the fleeting temptation to take right then and there on the staircase.

Anyhow, when we made it into the bedroom, he reached up to me, stretching his slim, elfin body, and draped his arms around my neck. He pulled down and forward until he could kiss me, sticking his eager little tongue into my mouth to spar with mine like they were two long-lost buddies eager to renew their acquaintance.

The next thing I knew, his arms retreated from my neck and his hands were busy undoing my pants, pulling them down along my hips until they fell to my ankles. Then he busied himself fondling my crotch through my briefs before moving up to my shirt, deftly unbuttoning it down the front.

With my right hand, I reached around and ran it along the firm contour of his cute, finely-molded little butt. With my left I unbuttoned and unzipped his corduroys and reached in, running my hand down across the soft texture of his bulging cotton briefs. Snugly nestled within its pouch was a thick, rubbery monster that fully fulfilled the expectations his story had led me to have of it. Through the thin material I could feel its warmth as it slowly and steadily rebelled against the cotton that pressed so tautly against it, growing larger and larger and larger.

By now he'd finished unbuttoning my shirt. He reached in and slowly ran his hands across my chest.

I shucked off my shirt as he began fingering my hardened nipples, causing my own cock to press more insistently against my briefs.

I lifted off his tee shirt, reluctantly separating his busy thumbs and forefingers from my nipples. His skin was white as alabaster and his chest was virtually hairless.

I pulled his briefs down several inches, examining with interest the fine line of hair that trickled down below his navel across the hard, flat terrain of his lower abdomen. I pulled his briefs down farther and uncovered his pubic bush. It was surprisingly full and thick, like it was making up for the scarcity of hair above.

I got down on my haunches, lowering his briefs all the way down to his ankles. His now fully-hard cock plopped out in front of my face, huge and heavy, twitching like it was waging a losing battle against gravity to hold its weighty self straight up at attention.

It had to be a good ten inches. But since he was an elf, and not as tall as a human, it looked even larger. His cockshaft was almost as pale as the rest of his body —

though slightly flushed – and a few fine blue veins traveled along it. He was cut, which I don't think I expected in an elf, and he had this huge, pink cockhead that bobbed up and down in front of my eyes like a self-centered little boy eagerly trying to capture my attention. As if it needed to try! And below, this hairless, reddish, furrowed ballsac, looking big as a baseball as it rested there encasing his two huge nuts.

When I had finished my appreciative inspection of his huge organ and balls I looked up into his eyes.

"Yeah, I know," he said. Everyone's amazed at its size."

I stuck out the tip of my tongue and ran it along the underside of his cockhead, just below his piss slit. His cock sprung up in front of me like a miniature gymnast.

"Ohh!" from above as his hands fell lightly onto my shoulders.

So how else could I respond than to do it again? And again and again, setting his huge cock helplessly bobbing up and down in front of my greedy eyes until I finally surprised him by capturing mid-bob in my mouth. I slowly descended his over-sized cock until I had to suppress the urge to gag as his cockhead slid down my welcoming throat.

His fingers on my shoulders had stiffened like they were absorbing the excess of pleasure that was running through his body.

"But you said you'd fuck me!" he interrupted in a low, urgent voice, pulling the two of us away from giving into the pleasure of the moment.

I dismounted his cock and stood up.

"Yeah. You're right."

"Besides, let me see yours," he said, placing his hands on either side of my briefs. "I've never seen a human's before – except in pictures."

So we reversed positions as he got down on his knees and lowered my briefs. To be honest, I was apprehensive of what he'd think when he saw I only had about nine inches (you don't believe me, measure it for yourself sometime), but he didn't seem to mind at all.

"Gee," he said staring in open-eyed amazement. And then wrapping on fist around it, he added, "I've never seen one that was brownish before. And your balls!"

He cupped them in his hand.

"There's hair on them!"

"Sorry."

"Sorry! Boy, what we elves are missing!"

And with this he stuck out his tongue and began lapping my balls with long, slurping licks, as happy as a kid with an ice cream cone. One hand automatically went down to his cock, slowly working its way up and down its log-like shaft.

He sucked one ball into his mouth. Then the other, coaxing it in with his tongue. With his cheeks bulging and his mouth full, he accelerated his jack-off strokes as he playfully tugged at my ballsac.

With his free hand, he reached up and grabbed my cock, causing me to groan deeply as I settled into the pleasure of his attentions.

When he'd had his fill he released my ballsac and pulled away to stare at my cock; sizing it up, as it were. Then he opened his mouth again and moved forward, clearly preparing to mount my rod. But just before he did, he stopped himself, saying, "If I begin working on it, I'll never stop, and then I'll never get fucked!"

"Go ahead," I coaxed. "I'll pull you off in time. Promise." "Gee, thanks!" he said, like I'd just done him the biggest favor in the world.

With that, he began sucking me off, losing himself in a frenzy of vigorous, enthusiastic activity. And believe me, he was really good at it. So good, I had to push him off me in no time at all, and not without the passing temptation to renege on my word.

"Sorry," I said, bending over and holding him away at his shoulders. "If you do that to the other elves, you must be very popular."

"Yeah, but they always pull me off sooner than I'd like, also. They just can't seem to tear themselves away from my cock for very long."

He stood up. As he did so, his stiff, at-attention cock got stuck between my legs, pressing insistently upwards against my spit-damp ballsac as he wrapped his arms around my waist and hugged me close to him.

"Ready to fuck me?"

"Ummm."

He released me, sat down at the foot of my bed and fell back onto it. He reached up, stretching his lithe body under my appreciative gaze, and grabbed one of the pillows. He bent it in half and used it to prop up his head so he could watch while I fucked him. Then he pulled his legs up with his hands under the back of his thighs until his knees were nearly touching his shoulders.

I got down on my knees and inspected his butt. The tight little pucker of his baby skin, rosy pink asshole and the area surrounding it were absolutely hairless.

I examined his butt hole with my right hand.

"Oh! No one's ever touched me there before! Just me. You know, exploring myself, imagining what it would be like to actually have someone's cock up my ass. Go ahead."

I played with his hole some more, watching the way he'd clench it in reaction to my touch, like he was trying to lure me inside. With my free hand, I reached under the bed for the container of lotion I always keep there. I squeezed some out onto my fingers and lightly rubbed it onto the rim of his enticing hole.

I gradually worked my lubricated fingers inside him. I could hear his soft, whispered oohs and aahs in response to my probings, seducing me into further investigations.

I swear I've never known anyone so eager to have his asshole explored! The deeper I went into him, the more he seemed to like it. Two fingers got him tossing his head from side to side, and three fingers got him clenching the pillow with both hands in an unsuccessful attempt to exercise some control over his writhing body. And I just kept on, wriggling my fingers inside him, eager to drive him crazy with pleasure.

Finally, when I could slip four fingers in and out of him with ease, he said in a hoarse, almost desperate voice, "I think I'm ready for you to fuck me!"

I withdrew my fingers, stood up and went to the bureau, pulling a condom out of the top drawer.

Standing between his legs I unwrapped it.

Elliot sat up to watch.

"Here, let me do that," he offered.

I handed him the condom and he carefully put it on me. He had a little difficulty, though. You see, every time he touched my cock, it would jerk upwards. Not that he helped the situation any, the way he was deliberately handling it more than necessary.

Well, he finally got the condom on, squirted a thin line of lotion down the topside of my shaft and spread it all over my condom-covered cock much more thoroughly than necessary.

Then he lay back again, raising his legs, pulling his ass right off the bed in his eagerness.

I spread my legs, bent my knees against the bed and pressed the tip of my cock against his asshole.

"Ohh!"

With absolutely no difficulty whatsoever, I slipped my cockhead inside him. Another, more prolonged "Ohhhhhh!"

To make it easier to fuck him I placed my hands behind his knees in the crook of his legs while he removed his own and rested them behind his head.

We looked into each other's eyes. He was heavy-lidded and smiling, like he was half-drugged with pleasure.

Then, without breaking eye contact, I ever so slowly pushed the length of my cockshaft all the way into his asshole. Eventually, I could go no further. I paused, luxuriating in the silky feeling of being inside him.

He giggled.

"It tickles."

"What tickles?"

Your pubic hair – brushing against my asshole."

"You can feel that?"

"I'm very sensitive. Especially down there. Now go ahead and fuck me."

I slowly withdrew from him until only my cockhead remained inside. Then I pushed in again.

"Ohh!"

"Sorry."

"No, that's wonderful!"

I moved in and out of him, gradually accelerating with every thrust. Soon I had established a mutually-satisfying rhythm. All this time our eyes were locked onto each other, silently communicating our pleasure.

He grabbed his hard cock that had been bouncing on his belly like it was a trampoline and began stroking it. His big balls rose and fell just above his asshole, looking like two pieces of exotic ripe fruit ready for the plucking.

I accelerated some more. My breath got low and quick. Elliot stroked on his cock all the faster, his own thinner flow of breath picking up my pace.

As the sheer physical pleasure of the moment wrapped itself around us, binding us together, I felt like I was falling deep into his eyes, down into the core of his being, as if we had merged, becoming one in this absolute ecstasy.

Soon I could feel the cum churning in my balls and my entire body becoming super-sensitive with the onrush of an approaching orgasm.

I moaned. Elliot joined in. Our tenor-and-baritone wail rose as we fused together in shared, mutual pleasure, man and elf uniting, until I finally felt a flood of cum exploding out of my cock, the overwhelming feeling of orgasm taking possession of my body.

And as I fell slave to this ecstatic draining process, as forceful and tenacious as an outgoing tide, I watched Elliot beneath me, violently stroking his cock like he had no control over his actions. He was so vigorous in his efforts the bed began to shake. The headboard slammed against the wall and one side of the bed banged against my night table, knocking my alarm clock and several odds and ends onto the floor. And then, as his moans drowned out my own, huge gushes of cum began spurting out of his cock, landing all over his chest, shoulders and face, and even further onto the sheets and pillow, the headboard and, yes, the wall behind it.

Who'd ever had imagined that so much cum could have been stored up in so compact a being, or that he could ever have shot it so far, creating such a tell-tale mess?

When we had depleted ourselves, we gradually relaxed our bodies, breathing heavily as we slowly recovered from this welcomed ordeal.

Then, as I carefully withdrew from him, he unclenched his cock and cupped his balls, pulling them and his cock up and over to one side, out of the way so he could have a better view of my retreat.

When the final few inches of my almost soft-again cock plopped out of him, Elliot said, "Here, let me help you with that."

He pushed his hands against the bed to rise. I dismounted him and he sat up and carefully removed the condom from my cock, holding it up in front of his face and observing it. Then he got up, and walked out of the room. Several seconds later I heard the upstairs toilet flush.

He came back in and restored the fallen objects to my night table.

"See what I mean? No matter what I do, I make a mess of things."

"Believe me, it was worth it."

You want me to clean off the wall and headboard?"

Of course not. C'mon, lie down next to me."

The two of us settled down next to each other on the bed, resting on our sides. His back was towards me and I draped my free arm over him, and hugged him close against me as I idly fingered his nipples. We bent our knees, fitting together like we were made to rest in such union.

And I won't forget I owe you a favor."

"I was thinking about that. In fact..."

I whispered my proposal in his ear. A wide, enthusiastic smile came over his face.

"Oh, yes!" he said, twisting his head towards me to seal the agreement with a kiss on the lips.

"So what did you ask him for?" Bobby wanted to know. "Yeah," Brendan added.

Just then there was this calamitous noise coming from the attic.

The three of us sat silently, straining our ears.

We heard the attic door open, the outer knob smashing against the upstairs corridor wall. I winced, thinking of the dent in the plaster I'd someday have to fix.

Then a pair of footsteps sounded on the stairs. A second set of footsteps joined them. And finally a third.

Elliot appeared at the bottom of the staircase.

"Hi, guys!" he said as he regained his balance from misjudging the number of steps below his feet.

Brendan and Bobby jumped up in open-mouthed amazement, just in time to watch as two other elves descended behind him.

"You boys must be Bobby and Brendan. I'm Elliot, this is Elvis, and this is Earl."

Bobby and Brendan managed to stammer out hellos as Elvis and Earl approached with wide smiles on their boyish faces, each looking a little shy and a lot eager.

I stepped over to Elliot, gave him a quick kiss, and directed him back up the stairs.

"C'mon Elliot," I said, slipping my hand in between his irresistible asscheeks once he was two steps ahead of me. "Let's leave the four of them alone – to get better acquainted."

"Yeah."

Twisting his head around towards Elvis and Earl before continuing up the stairs, he winked and said, "See, I told you. Someone likes me for more than just my cock!"

And as we ascended the staircase I turned to say, "Oh, and by the way, boys – Merry Christmas."

HOME FOR THE HOLIDAYS
L. Amore

*"So many plans, so much to be prepared
And then the day itself is gone so soon;
I think of this whenever I recall...
Our sex in the barn on a Christmas afternoon."*

I had barely hung up the phone with mother back home in Australia before it was ringing again, giving me no time to feel sorry for myself that my folks just couldn't afford to bring me home for the Christmas holidays. Claire Cunningham was on the line, inviting me to spend Christmas in Iowa. I went from down in the dumps to cloud nine in seconds.

I had spent three months at the Cunninghams when I was an exchange student, before I came here to Princeton, and it was one of the happiest times of my life. The only thing wrong with it was that the Cunninghams son, Christopher, was away at college that spring and I never got to meet him. Now Claire was telling me, "And Christopher will be here too. You'll finally get to meet him."

"Great!" was all I could say. Just how great I could never have imagined. I had slept in his bed, sat at his place at the table, even wore his jeans a couple of times, and ever after I fantasized about what he was like in the flesh. Well, the Chris of my fantasy – my wildest fantasy – couldn't hold a candle to the real thing. My problem was, how could I tell him?

I had arrived two days ahead of Chris and was helping Claire with some last-minute decorating when he came through the front door in his bomber jacket. I nearly dropped the string of little white twinkling lights I was hanging in the pine branches on the mantle. At first I was dazzled by his big, toothy smile and how his emerald green eyes glittered in the glow of the fire.

"Hi," he said, pulling off his leather gloves. You must be Thayer."

"Yes," I said.

"I've heard a lot about you," he said, sliding out of his parka. He was over six feet tall and even bigger, bulkier than in the photographs I had remembered. Obviously he found more time to spend working out at the gym than I ever did. By the look of him, it was amazing he found time to attend any classes at all.

"I'm glad to finally meet you," I said, reaching down from my perch on the little ladder to take his extended hand.

His handshake was firm as he looked up into my eyes and grinned. "Same here."

As I held his gaze for a moment, I could have sworn we connected, as if we were each saying, "Let's go upstairs right now and – "

But he turned and was off to the kitchen to greet his mother. I could hear them catching up on things, laughing and happy and, not wanting to disturb them, I went upstairs to Chris' bedroom where I was told I was to sleep. Chris, his mother said, would be "perfectly happy" on the couch in the living room. Making me "perfectly happy" obviously never entered her mind. Still, Chris would have to use his bedroom to change clothes and we would have to share a bathroom. My mind was racing with those possibilities as I was trying to concentrate on my reading assignments.

Suddenly Chris came barging into the bedroom. "Boy, I need a hot shower," he said, dropping down into the chair across from where I was lying on the bed on my stomach. "It's been a long day."

He tugged off his tennis shoes and tossed them in the corner, then slipped his socks from his feet. As he stood up and jerked his T-shirt off over his head like an impatient boy and slung it to the floor, he began asking questions: about Australia, how I liked Princeton, and, finally, how I liked Iowa. As he stood before me in the briefest briefs I'd ever seen, the sheen of the hair growing down his torso in the shape of a tree trunk brighter than the streaked blond hair on his head, I managed to say, "Oh, I like Iowa just fine."

I fear he could see my eyes were riveted on the huge bulge of his crotch because he chuckled and said, "Yeah, I can see that." He snapped the elastic of the briefs and quickly disappeared into the privacy of the bathroom, gently closing the door behind him. I shut my book and as I was picturing him in the shower, soaping that magnificent torso, Claire called from downstairs: "Father's here!"

Father Cunningham, as everyone called him because he took his job as a lay reader at the church so seriously, was a gentleman farmer. He hired people to tend the place while he saw to the business of the hardware store in town which Claire had inherited from her father. In fact, it seemed that between the business and the church, he was seldom at home. Even when he was there, he was largely absent, tending to paperwork or reading the Bible in this study. Chris, I saw, inherited his easy, outgoing manner, and his good looks, from his mother.

Chris came down for dinner wrapped in a terry robe and a Santa hat on his head. He was, as was his custom, going out on the night before Christmas Eve, to play Santa at a party for children the church held every year. "It pleases the old man," he said with a shrug. My eyes keeping his, I said, "I can relate to that."

After dinner, at the door as he was leaving, now in full costume, he asked, "You sure you don't want to come along?"

"No, thanks, I want to help Claire with the sugar cookies. I've been told my job is to ice them."

He grinned. No, your job is not to eat 'em all. Save some for me."

Watching him rush through the snow to his red Camaro, all liquid movement, I thought, 'Hey, stud, I'm saving it all for you!'

Around eleven, Claire and I had finished the cookies and, since Father Cunningham had already gone to bed, she asked me to get some more logs for the fireplace. I donned my parka and bravely faced the harsh winds and swirling snow as I made my way to the barn, pushing the wheelbarrow ahead of me. If it had not been for the wind, it would have been a perfect winter's night. The moon was full and the snow glistened as it crunched under my footfalls.

I put down the wheelbarrow and slowly opened the door, which creaked on its rusted hinges. I peered into the dark. I was surprised to see Chris' car parked directly ahead of me. "Chris?" I called out.

There was no response. I flung the door all the way open and pushed the wheelbarrow in. Closing the door, I raked my fingers across the wall looking for the light switch. Finally finding it and flicking on the lights, I heard a deep voice say, "Hey, turn that out."

I promptly did as I was told. Quickly my eyes adjusted to the darkness and I stepped deeper into the barn, moving in the direction of the voice. I slowly ran my hand along the warm, long hood of the Camaro, as if I was caressing a vital part of him.

Climbing up to the hayloft, I was almost to the top when I saw him, in the moonlight, with his Santa cap cocked at a rakish angle. He began chuckling as I climbed higher and saw he was sitting on a hay bale. And he was nude, with one leg coyly raised to cover his genitals.

"What are you doing?" I asked.

"Well, it's kind of hard to take care of things in the house, sleeping in the living room."

"Take care of things?"

"Yeah, and I was hoping you'd be the one to take care of getting the wood tonight."

"Oh?"

Now he lowered his leg, revealing all of his glorious stiffness to me. "Yeah," he smiled, "and maybe you could take care of this while you were at it – "

A smile broke my face as I saw his cock bobbing in the dim light.

"You... want me to... take care of that?"

"Did I stutter?" he asked, one eyebrow cocked as he watched me struggle not to drop to my knees immediately. "Of course, if you don't want to," he said and raised his leg to block my view of his amazing appendage.

In a choked voice I managed, "Oh, I think I can take care of anything you want."

"Good, now that we understand one another, why don't you slide over here."

It was less of a slide and more of a jump. But as soon as I had his penis in my mouth, all nine incredible inches of it, all of my ultimate fantasies about what his cock would be like were realized. In fact, everything about him was sweet. Even in the cold barn, his body was warm as I settled in between his muscular thighs for a nice, long suck. My hands ran the length of his flanks, feeling the soft blond down that covered them. I gripped his torso tightly as he held my hand over his crotch and slammed it into me. My mouth had never been happier. The musky scent of his pubic hair came and went with the rhythm of his strokes. He was all blazing boy-next-door fucking my face, leaning back against the hay and moaning with pleasure, letting me know I was doing what he wanted.

"Santa only gets his chance once a year," he said, letting me catch my breath.

"Once a year my ass," I retorted.

"Okay, your ass is later," he said with a wink, then slammed it in again and I continued trying to choke myself. Oddly enough, I didn't. I was so turned-on, I took all of it with little effort.

After a few minutes, he was letting me go again and a strand of spit and precum stretched the distance between my mouth and his dick.

"The cocksuckers' tear," he said, smiling as he wiped the droplet from under my eyelash. I grasped the base of his penis and gazed at the magnificent stretch of it. It was throbbing and appeared as if it were about to burst.

You can't stop now," he groaned.

"Can't I?" I said teasingly.

"No! Shut up and suck."

I took it deep.

"Yeah," he said, be a good little elf and help Santa bust a nut." With that Santa grasped my head and shoved it all the way in. It was even sweeter now. I thought, 'I could suck this stud's cock for a lifetime and never tire of it.'

He released my neck and reached down to grasp my raging hard-on. His moans and cries of, "Yes...yes," let me know that he was as near to ecstasy as I was.

Having his hand gripping my cock tightly made me come almost immediately. Expertly he milked me; he had done this before. I shot what seemed like buckets, as if I had been saving it all for months just to give it to him for Christmas. I soaked his ass, his parted thighs and balls, not to mention the hay bale. He was next and not a drop was wasted. I ground my lips to the base of his cock, firmly and securely wedging it down my throat. It burned; boy did it burn, but it was an exquisite sensation. He brought his hands back to my head again and alternately pushed and pulled but couldn't quite move it. I was tenacious. I didn't want to give it up but, slowly, the intensity subsiding, I pulled away and the spent cock slipped out of my mouth. But still I would not let it free. I grasped the cock and licked the last of his cum from the head. He shuddered with the sensation.

"Waste not, want not," I said smiling, tears rolling down my cheeks.

He leaned down, grabbed my head and kissed me full on the lips. As our lips parted, he murmured, "God, Thayer, you're fucking incredible."

"Likewise I'm sure," I chuckled. I laid my head on his thigh, savoring the moment. "Oh shit," I said, finally remembering the time. "We'd better get back. Your mother will becoming out here soon wondering what the hell happened to me."

And just as we had gotten our clothes on and the wheelbarrow full, Claire did come through the door of the barn. "I was worried you sprained something getting the wood," she said. "Thought you might be lying here unconscious or something."

"Oh, no, I'm fine. Chris came home just as I got out here and we were – " I looked at Chris. He smiled.

"Yeah, I offered to help him out," he said, picking up the wheelbarrow.

"Well, come on boys, it's late and we have a big day tomorrow."

"I've come to find every day's a big day around here," I said, winking at Chris as I held the door open for him.

Chris and I brought the wood into the house and he had a fire started in no time. I had no idea how to start a fire, but he was more than proficient.

Claire came into the living room, "Oh that's splendid, Christopher. Why don't you make a fire for Thayer up in your room?"

"Would you like me to start a fire for you, Thayer?" he asked with a sarcastic tinge to his voice that was lost on Mrs. Cunningham.

"I would most definitely, that is if you wouldn't mind," I replied, with the same sarcasm.

"No problem at all, just let me get my temporary bed ready."

Chris took all the pillows and cushions off the fold-out couch, then reached for the fabric handle to pull it out. But it didn't pull out. As he kept tugging, I couldn't help myself but look at the bulging muscles straining his forearms as he struggled. "Mom, when was the last time this was used?" he asked.

"I'm really not sure. I think it was when your Aunt Esther stayed for the weekend. My, that was over a year ago now."

"Well it's not working now. Father'll have to have a look at it."

"Oh, my. I don't know what to do – unless you two boys wouldn't mind sharing the bed upstairs." She turned to me, going into shock at the prospect. "Would you mind that Thayer?"

"No, not at all." I replied a little too quickly.

———"Well," Chris said, winking at me, "let's get that fire started so we can get to bed."

"I'm following you. Goodnight, Claire."

"Goodnight boys," she said after us.

Once upstairs, while I undressed and got into bed, Chris grabbed some wood from a pile on the right of the fireplace, opened the screen and started to form a rough triangle after putting down a base of three logs. "Well, that ought to work," he said finally as he was rolling up some old newspapers. He had the fire roaring in no time.

"I hope you don't mind this," he said, stripping off his clothes.

"Mind? You've got to be kidding."

He chuckled as he dropped down next to me on the bed. "Yeah, it would have been a waste sabotaging that old fold-out bed if you felt differently." He slid under the covers.

"You didn't?"

His hand went to my thigh and slid upward. As he stroked my erection, he said, "And by the feel of things, you seem to be kinda glad I did."

Most definitely." I leaned into him and ran my tongue along his lips. I sucked his clean-shaven chin and rubbed my cheek against his. He kissed me and held me in his arms. I responded like a drowning man thrown a life line. As he fell back onto the mattress, I went about getting to know every inch of that perfect body intimately. I didn't rush but I didn't exactly take my time either.

The covers were like a cozy tent closing out the world and intensifying the moment. There was no sight, just scent and feeling. His body was still emanating that incredible warmth and there was no other way to describe the light musky odor that worked on me: He smelled like a young stud in heat.

As I moved down his body, my hard-on firmly wedged to his hard thigh, I ran my tongue along the underside of his pecs, feeling the hard definition. I swooned and ground my wanting even harder into him. He pressed persistently between my legs to let me know that my own needs were not forgotten, but to get back to the business of his tits. The rock hard mounds that I was sucking were free of hair except the few that grew between them. As I licked, they gathered spit from my mouth and made a sandpaper like noise as my tongue went over them again and again.

I went for his nipples next and he grabbed my hips and firmly mounted me over him. We were matched flank for flank and his cock criss-crossed mine, his hard pillar biting into the base of my own shaft. I was almost doubled over as his fingers dug into the flesh of my ass.

"God what a nice ass. I told you that it was later and I meant it," he growled.

"I never doubted that for a second," I murmured, feeling his fingers wrap around each cheek and finding the bud of my anus.

With sure, skilled movements his index finger found its mark, while the fingers of his other hand successfully spread my cheeks wide apart. He shifted my body, positioning me so that I felt the heat of his erect penis against my wanting hole. I leaned over to kiss his lips and the smell of his warm breath only increased my desire. I started to writhe, pressing my ass to his cock with a rhythm as old as time itself. I reached behind me to grasp it so that his cock rested straight up and nestled in the crack of my ass.

He stretched to his right and grabbed some lube from his bag that was lying by the bed. He first slicked my cock, his hand masterful as I shuddered with the sensation. He lifted my hips and placed me right over him. As he pressed the head of his dick into me, I loosened the muscles of my ass.

"Look at me," he whispered hoarsely, "I want to see your face as I finally enter you."

Silently, I did as I was told. I made only a slight moan as he slowly lowered me, inch by fantastic inch, onto his cock. Incredibly, there was no pain. Chris was an expert, taking his time, letting me get comfortable with the hugeness of it. I wanted so badly to rush it, to feel it all in me, but the muscles on his arms strained and kept me from making my descent. The look in his eyes said, "We're going to do this my way or else," so I was patient, letting him control me.

Chris' hands gripped my waist even tighter when his cock was all the way in. My head snapped back as I became overwrought with his strokes, both smooth and fast. He would slide it all the way out and then push up to the hilt, giving my prostate splendid abuse. Finally he was in so deep as to make me catch my breath and giving me the slight feeling of nausea that comes when pleasure is too fine. But my only reaction was a whimper. My eyes were caught by his, just barely visible in the darkness. His breathing was harsh, my hands on his magnificent chest felt every intake and exhale. My fingers worked on his erect nipples as expertly as I could manage.

Without even a helping hand laid to my cock, I was nearing orgasm. His stokes increased and then came my inevitable plea of, "Oh, fuck me, fuck me harder." No more could his arms keep me from grinding on his rigid pole.

"Oh my God," he said loudly and if I wasn't taking my own pleasure I would have been worried that the Cunninghams might overhear us, but nothing else mattered at that point. Rope after rope of semen flew from my cockhead leaving rivulets running down the barrel of his chest after the heat of his body made the stuff more viscous. He kept plowing as his own climax hit him. The fingers that gripped my ass tightened, hurting and digging, as his hot load flooded my innards. I bent down to cover his lips with my own to stifle the moans that came forth, so as not to be caught, but it seemed to just make them louder. His fingers grabbed my head, tangled in my hair and he kissed me full on the mouth.

"Good God," he whispered as I fell onto him, the cum on his body gluing us together. I was too exhausted to say another word. I fell asleep that night on top of him, his arms tightly around me, and the fire slowly dying in the fireplace.

The next morning I awoke to the smell of coffee brewing and cinnamon buns baking in the oven. As I threw back the blankets and started to get up to shower, I glanced back at the slumbering Chris. His morning hard-on was poking out from where the comforter had been turned down. I had to use all my self-restraint not to hop right back into bed and service that piece of meat that seemed to be beckoning me. Even in sleep, hair all tousled and a tiny bit of drool in the corner of his mouth, he was flawless. I decided my morning shower might just have to be a cold one.

The "share and share alike, all for one and one for all" mind-set in the Cunningham family which brought me to the farm in the first place extended to distant kin. Christmas was traditionally the time when all assembled at the farm for a turkey dinner on Christmas Eve, then early to bed because, Christmas morning, Father read the lesson at church. Claire had expected family from all around, even some from as far away as Idaho, but a fierce blizzard that no one had predicted came blowing in from Canada and the relatives were stranded, dampening everyone's mood. But the Cunninghams went about preparations as always, trying to make the best of it. After a call from my Mom in Australia, with Christmas Eve in Iowa being their Christmas

Day, I felt a bit homesick and, after dinner, I felt like being alone. As I went out onto the porch, the snow, whipped by a vicious wind, swirled around me. It was beautiful though, I thought, the snow shimmering like diamond dust in the different colored lights that shone from the various rooms of the house.

Suddenly, a soft, seductive voice said, "What are you doing out here?"

I jumped; I had been so lost in thought I hadn't heard him. "You scared the shit out of me."

"Sorry." He ran a hand up under my coat and squeezed my butt cheek.

"Quite all right," I said with a smile. I couldn't be mad at him if I wanted to. I wrapped the collar of my coat tighter around my neck. "It's so beautiful out here," I said, feeling his warmth next to me, his hot breath against my ear.

"Yeah," he said as he grabbed my arm, "but I'm still playing Santa so just go into the living room and be quiet or else ya ain't gonna get nothin'."

"Oh, what am I gonna get?"

"Something you'd never expect in a million years."

I smiled and let him lead me, as if I was a child, back into the warmth of the house. He took my coat and hung it up with his in the hall closet. He swatted my ass, propelling me forward. I couldn't help but laugh as he kept pushing me in the direction of the living room. Claire and Father Cunningham were already sitting cozily on the couch. Chris put on his Santa hat and began handing out the presents that were stacked under the tree.

The Cunninghams gave me a pair of jeans and a rugby shirt. There was nothing from Chris. But he winked at me and lifted his eyes towards the staircase. I understood. My present was waiting upstairs.

Claire disappeared into the kitchen and came out with a steaming crockery pitcher. The spicy scent of the fresh brew filled the room, and, mixing with the aromas of the pine tree and the burning candles, I became nearly intoxicated before she even poured my first mug. I found Father Cunningham's traditional holiday concoction smooth in the mouth, smooth down the throat, and lethal. The effect crept up on me. Claire warned me not to have a second helping but I had to. "We have nothing like this Down Under," I said.

Chris laughed. "One more and you'll be down under all right." But since I was having another, so did he and instead of sitting where he had been, safely across the room, he plopped down next to me on the couch.

Then, just as Claire said it was time for them to go to bed Chris brought his knee against mine. "Don't you boys stay up too late now. It's an early day tomorrow. Father's reading the lesson."

Chris shook his head wearily. "He always reads the lesson," he mumbled. "Someone oughta read him one." He threw an "OK" at her over his shoulder while looking at me with twinkle in his eye. Suddenly he jumped up and turned off the lights. The embers were dying in the fireplace and once he settled back down next to me and put his arm around me, the holiday glow was complete. All I needed was my present. But what was he going to give me he hadn't already?

In a few moments, I was to find out because he kissed me and said, "I'm going to get your present ready. You come up in a few minutes."

I threw him the same "OK" he threw his mother.

I waited a good five minutes, managing to sober up a bit, finding the alcohol had not in any way lessened my desire for sex with Chris, a want that had kept my cock hard most of the day. But there never seemed to be a moment that Chris wasn't busy

166

doing something with either his father or mother. Luckily, no one had time to fix the fold-out bed.

As I entered the bedroom, I could see Chris had made a small fire and was lying face down on the bed, his arms under a pillow, his legs spread in a V pointing to the bottom bed posts. He was naked. As I stripped, my eyes feasted on the sight of the perfect globes of his muscular ass. After I climbed on the bed, I brought my face close to the crack of it. The smell drove me wild. I ran my tongue over the soft hair that guarded what I now understood to be my present. He was going to let me fuck him. He was right, I had never imagined he would be versatile. My tongue slowly dug deep, until I pressing the little pink bud. Relaxing it, giving pleasure to it. Chris gently moaned, a moan that came from his throat, barely audible. He ground his groin to the mattress and I instinctively thought of reaching under him and grasping it, but my hands were too busy spreading his luscious cheeks. His ass was, I thought, as sweet as his cock and I savored it for several minutes before he called me to move up. As I went to him, I licked along the indentation of his lower back, loving with my tongue the muscles that started to form the valley in the center of his back that ran all the way up to the nape of his neck. My tongue was a fierce explorer as it made its way to his shoulder. On top of him fully now, I was overcome with the desire to take a bite of him for my very own.

"Ouch," he said, laughing lowly.

"Sorry," I said, nuzzling against his ear, then sticking my tongue in it.

He moaned again and ground his hips to the bed. My erection, wedged in the crack of his ass, took the small ride with him. The urge to be inside him, to be buried in him as far as I could go, overwhelmed me. The thought must have been on his mind too, because when I looked up at him he was smiling and had the lube in his hand. "You'll need this."

"So cute and so smart. I am lucky," I said as I playfully slapped his ass. "What a Christmas gift!"

"I thought you'd like it."

I wasted no time slicking us both up, just the thought of fucking him enough to start me coming. But still I entered him slowly. My bulging cockhead went in easily but he was so tight and making so much noise, groaning with every move, that I began to wonder if he was a virgin or not. I quickly threw this thought aside. If anyone was not a virgin, in any respect it was Christopher Cunningham. But when I was in him completely, his ass gripped me like a hot vise. I pulled the head of my cock out. I was half expecting it to make a loud pop, but it didn't.

His handsome face crushed against the pillow, he moaned and whispered, "Please, I can take it."

I brought my cockhead back to the opening and slowly, steadily I pushed forward. His moans became a little louder. I didn't know if it was because of pain or of wanting but I didn't care. I wanted to feel the end. The end of what he had to offer me. I wanted to feel his warm anal lips clenched around the base of what I had to offer him. And finally I did. As I pressed the last inch into him, he cried out. I knew he was in pain, but he was also grinding into the bed, so I assumed he was enjoying what I was doing. I withdrew a bit and, placing my hands on his massive shoulders, I began my stokes. Each time I pulled almost all the way out I felt as though my world was taken away from me. I wanted to be inside him completely, to be a part of him. I slammed into him again till my pubic hair grated against the smooth inner part of his asscheeks. He wasn't grinding now. He had no room to. His hand went to reach underneath him but couldn't because of my weight. Feeling generous to my Santa, I let up so that he could do what he wanted.

Now each stroke was ecstasy, pulling out till the slimy hole beckoned me again, the hot sheath engulfing me. I pushed hard, hitting the webbing of his ass deep inside of him. He moaned and pushed further away from me as if telling me I had pushed too far. But then he swung his ass up to regain the position again, urging me to fill him to the hilt once more. I forced into him as far I could. So far that the base of my cock hurt from pulling the skin and grinding my body hard against his butt. Finally, I could take no more. I grabbed each of his shoulders again and slammed him back against my groin.

To my surprise, he came. I took one hand from his right shoulder and grasped his pulsing cock underneath him. The hot jism flooding my palm then dripping onto the bed sheets. Having his throbbing cock in my hand pushed me over the edge. I took his ass in my hands and began slamming into him, looking down at my penis, a great piston rod working a shaft, and soon my semen flooding out from the entrance to his ass. I collapsed onto him, my full weight pushing him flat to the mattress. My hands caressed his sides of his arms and I kissed the back of his head.

"If I'd known it was gonna be that good," he whispered, "I wouldn't have waited so long."

"You're kidding?"

No, you deflowered a virgin."

"Rosemary Rogers couldn't have said it better."

"My Christmas present."

I was still incredulous. I rolled him over. "You seemed to know what you were doing."

"After a certain point instinct takes over."

"I'm glad you waited. I've never had such a nice Christmas present."

He hugged me to him. "Yeah, I think this was the best Christmas I've ever had."

"Me, too," I said. And, snuggling against him, I realized the fire had gone out in the fireplace and we were lying there without any blankets over us, but still I was incredibly warm. No, I wasn't in Australia, but I felt I had truly come home for the holidays.

A LITTLE LOVE MEDICINE
John Patrick

I seldom went home at any time, much less at Christmas. My memories of Christmases past were awful ones, what should have been joyous holidays ruined by my father and his drunkenness. But this year my mother called to say my father was failing, that this might be the last time. I suspected it was a ruse to get me there but I really missed my mother and let her get away with it.

When I arrived at their home on the bay, I saw my father sitting outside on the boat dock. He had given up fishing off that dock years before. No boat was tied to it anymore. "Hello, Paddy," was about as much as he could muster, accompanied by a perfunctory handshake. He was Daddy, I was Paddy; at one time, I was even Pretty Little Paddy. He was fond of nicknames. In private, I am sure I was Cocksucker.

He had wizened and toughened since I had seen him last. He wore a stained, crumpled cap that seemed so much a part of his head, not even Mother thought of asking him to remove it. Over the next few minutes, he'd talk about one thing, then another, with no rhyme or reason. He shook his head, remembering dates but with no events, events with no dates. Names without faces, things that happened out of place and time. Perhaps his loss of memory was protection from the past, absolving him of whatever had happened. He had lived hard in his time and lived calmly now. I left him there counting something under his breath. The clouds perhaps, or the boats, or the fish jumping in the sun-dappled water. Or the number of times he thought I had disappointed him.

Supper time was soon upon us. In a crowd, at a party, Mother was always hushing him up, talking loudly so no one would hear him. If I was present, she knew I would become upset over his blurted secrets from the past.

But tonight it was only us at the table and when Mother went to the kitchen I was defenseless against his attack.

"Robby, that was the one," Father said, chewing his prime rib. "Randy Robby, I called him. You had the nerve to bring that one here, remember?"

I nodded, looked away, made a disgusted face.

"I remember the name because I liked it, but the kid, he was a little snot. What do you see in those boys?"

"Now Tom, leave the boy alone," Mother said, rushing back into the room, pointing at him with her chin.

Father fell silent. I had to wonder, as I always did, how much they really knew. I finished my glass of wine, then told my mother, "I'll be back later on. I've got to go see a friend."

"Don't you be bringin' 'em back here," Father barked after me.

"Oh, for heaven sake, Tom," Mother said.

But I was no longer paying him any mind. Father's mention of Robby aroused my curiosity. I hadn't thought of the boy in years. Blond, blue-eyed, big dick. And randy indeed; insatiable was more like it. If he was still alive, I knew where I'd find him.

I had to close my eyes after a while. The mix of beer and wine and cigarette smoke made my head whirl. The lights, pulsing and fading, made the floor rock under me. I waved away the bottle when the stranger next to me bought me another.

His voice was slurred and dreamy. Like me, he was amused by both the bad and the good. He was managing to keep a slim hold on the conversation. His voice was serious all of a sudden, and it scared me. I decided to leave. He followed me.

Outside the Round-Up, we stumbled straight into an ambush. A young black man was pushing a youth's face into the gravel. His arms were whirling. He struggled powerfully but the black was stronger. I grabbed a beer bottle from the gutter and hit the black on the back of the neck. The bottle bounced out of my fist. The black pushed the boy lower and he gurgled. I grabbed the black's shoulders. I expected the stranger was behind me. The black hardly noticed my weight, pushing on the boy. Now I pushed the attacker, very hard. He reeled backward, bucking me off, and cocked his hands in boxer's fists. I turned around and realized I was alone. The stranger had disappeared. Sober now, I was afraid for the first time.

You goddamn motherfucker!" the black yelled, his eyes widening. "Why don't you mind your own motherfuckin' business?"

He grabbed my arm and tossed me against the wall of the bar.

As I slumped down, a look of confusion swept over his face and he rushed past me. I looked to the street and saw a squad car had pulled up. The officers flashed a light, then took off after the attacker.

The stranger now appeared, helping me up. "I thought I should call the police," he said.

"I'm so glad you did." The pain blazed in my back. "Oh, God," I muttered.

"Here, let me help."

"No. Somebody should help the kid."

The kid, who introduced himself as Gerry, didn't need help. It was I who needed it after all. I couldn't get up from the pavement without his help. The stranger suggested we go to his place, just a couple of minutes away. All I wanted to do was lie down. The old building was quiet. Gerry held me as we followed the stranger up the narrow staircase to a small apartment. Inside, the air smelled stale, as if the door had not been opened for years.

The stranger let Gerry use the bathroom. He showed him where the everything was. He said he could take care of himself.

The stranger showed me to the spare bedroom, made me comfortable. He tugged my shirt off and began making slow, wide circles with his hands, stopping the pain. I closed my eyes. I expected to see blackness. Peace. But instead all I could see was the black attacking Gerry. Ugly. Threatening.

"I have to go," I said finally. "Let me go." But he held me down.

"Don't go. I've just begun."

I lifted up so that he could undo my belt buckle and lower my pants. After neatly folding my pants on a chair, he continued rubbing. I was weakening. My thoughts were whirling pitifully. The pain had kept me strong, and as it left me I began to forget the fight.

"I don't recall your name," I said.

"You never asked it."

"I'm sorry."

"Happens to me all the time. I'm Paul."

"I'm John."

"We're all apostles here," he chuckled.

"Speaking of apostles, I wonder how Gerry is."

"Sounds as if he's in the shower. I'm sure he'll be fine." "Awful thing."

John Patrick

"That man didn't get any money. Maybe he just wanted to beat up a gay man. Gerry said he'd never seen him before."

I heard the rustle of clothes. Gerry stepped into the room. He was naked and smooth. I went helpless at the sight of him. Paul stopped massaging me to stare at the sight of Gerry. He walked over, as if in a dream.

It was his eyes. They were bold, gleaming blackberry eyes. He held out his hand, raked it over my arm. "Thanks, man." "It was nothing."

I felt his eyes resting upon me and I couldn't look up at him. I didn't want him, but I wanted him. If only we were somewhere else, if only I didn't ache all over. But as he drew nearer I knew what his intent was and the thought of this boy joining me in bed, this stranger's bed, caused the strain to go out of me. I finally looked him in the eyes again, eyes that were black, sly, snapping with sparks.

Paul stood up suddenly, muttering he had to fetch something, and left us alone.

In that quiet moment something about the boy struck me as somehow dangerous. But my uneasiness gave way to the sweet apprehension he was about to touch me again. I felt my heart knock urgently as he touched me through my briefs. His hands roamed my body; his massage was better than the stranger's had been. My eyes shut. I was helpless now. His mouth fell on my shoulder and kept traveling. Passion overtook him. I hung on to the pillow as he tugged my briefs down my legs, stripped them off. He took my asscheeks in his hands and spit between the crack. His tongue followed. He massaged my ass, my torso as his tongue invaded me.

The boards creaked as the stranger came back into the room. I felt his weight on the bed. He sat still watching us. He moaned along with me as Gerry's erection slid into me with little effort.

I rolled with Gerry's urgent current like the sand in the gulf. He fell on me like a wave, but unlike a wave that washes away, leaving no sign that it was there, he soon was leaving his seed on my backside. Paul jerked himself off and then went to the bathroom. Gerry rolled away and his breathing became deep and soon we were both asleep.

When I woke up, I was alone in the bed. I heard the clanging of metal, pots tumbling somewhere. My back still ached but I managed to slip into my briefs and make my way to the kitchen after a stop in the bathroom. I walked in, letting the door whine softly shut behind me.

"Hello."

Paul looked up from the stove. He was small and sprightly, his face craggy, deeply tanned. His eyes were sherry-colored and timid. He was dressed in a fluffy white terry robe and slippers. "Hungry?" he asked, stirring something in a pot.

"No, not really," I said.

"I'll bet you are," he said, a purposeful excitement in his eyes. He poured me a cup of coffee and as I sipped it, the stranger apologized for the cold. He said he liked the window halfway open although the mornings were "a bit chilly" now in Florida.

"At least there's no snow," I said. "It's snowing in Cleveland, I just know it is."

"It's nice you have parents to visit who live in the sunshine."

"Don't go to any fuss," I said, sitting at the little table. "I really have to be getting home. They're going to wonder – " "No fuss. Just a little oatmeal and we just got fresh strawberries in at the grocery where I work."

Suddenly, Gerry appeared in the doorway, holding a bulging brown bag in his hand. He was even more beautiful than I had remembered from the night before.

"Thank you, Gerry," the stranger said, taking the bag of groceries from him. "I needed more milk. You need lots of milk on oatmeal."

Gerry stood there in his tight black T-shirt, smoothing his black hair behind his ears. There was a delicacy about the way he did this. He moved backward until his ass hit the edge of the sink and he parked himself there, looking at me. His eyes were wild and wary as a cat's. So many of the things he did reminded me of the many beautiful models I had photographed, standing naked before a mirror, how they touch themselves, lovingly, conscious of their attractions. He nodded encouragingly.

"Hi," I said.

The boy's black eyes fairly swallowed me up in their short glance. The contrast between his light coloring and his deep black eyes made him so startling to look at.

"Hi." He looked at me like I was a sad case. "How do you feel?"

"Okay."

"I'll never forget what you did – "

"I'll never forget it either," I chuckled. "And I'll never forget what you did last night."

He shrugged. "Least I could do."

Our host opened the carton of milk and poured some in a pitcher. He put the pitcher and a bowl of fresh strawberries on the table, then got bowls and spoons. He served us giant portions of oatmeal, then left the room.

Gerry used his fingers prettily. His littlest fingers curled like a woman's at tea. He disarmed me. When he had finished his cereal, he fished a soft pack of Marlboros from his jeans. I watched his hand as he struck the match and his eyes narrowed. They were so black the iris seemed to show within like blue flames. He smoked exotically, rolling smoke off his tongue.

He said he was an Indian but lighter than most. He said his parents had always called themselves French or Black Irish and considered those who thought of themselves as Indians quite backward. "But I'm proud to be an Indian," he said. Before I had sensed the boy was everywhere in his life and yet nowhere, but now he fit less easily into my fantasy of how he lived.

"You should be," I said. "All that money in bingo."

He laughed. "You'll have to come out and play sometime." "I'd like that."

His face lit up for a moment. He tossed his napkin down. "Yeah, let's play."

I nodded. He pushed away from the table and left the kitchen.

I sipped the last of my coffee gratefully.

Paul came back into the kitchen and stood over me with the coffee pot in his hand. "More?"

"No, thanks. Where did Gerry go?"

"I bet I can guess – "

I found Gerry in bed, naked, smoking another cigarette. A beam of light suddenly broke through the curtained window and flooded down directly on his body. I sighed. "You are beautiful. Those muscles are something else. Especially the one between your legs."

He smiled and flexed his arm. The wings of a bird were carefully tattooed on certain muscles so that the bird almost seemed to hover in a dive or swoop. He made me ache in hidden, surprising places. I had the urge to lick the smoothness, slickness of his cock. He let me do this for several minutes until he was fully erect. Then I guided him forward into me with my hands. I wanted to be on my back for this one, to watch him over me, his muscles rippling. It did not matter that his fucking was rough, less than perfect. He was so enthusiastic in his enjoyment of it, I was excited as well and jacked off as he slammed into me.

I had left the door half-opened and Paul came in and sat down on the bed. He watched for a few moments, then took his cock out and began masturbating. He was more forward now, reaching over and taking my penis from my hand.

"Please, let me," he said, his eyes riveted on the sight of Gerry's cock as it slid in and out of me. I concentrated on the stranger's rhythm rather than Gerry's and as I came, the stranger put his head down on my belly so that the jism splashed in his face. Seeing me come spirited Gerry on. He pulled out of me and jacked off. Paul put his head over my groin so that he could catch the Indian's cum as well.

"Oh, yeah, yeah . . . " Gerry cried as he let go. It was a wild orgasm, his body shaking, his head back, his eyes closed.

Paul wiped the cum from his face and applied it to his own cock and soon was coming himself. After he silently went to the bathroom, Gerry held me in his arms, catching his breath. I rolled over and closed my eyes. Before long, he was massaging my skin again. He alternated between light and heavy kneading of my muscles. "How does that feel?" he asked.

"Wonderful," I groaned.

"I use a feather when I'm at home. You must come home with me."

"Yes, I must." I had an erection again.

His fingers fluttered over my body and when he was finished, I was ready to go to sleep again. All the pain was gone. He said he'd given me some love medicine. "It's something of a Chippewa specialty," he said. "No other tribe has it down so well. We try to cast a spell, you know. It's like magic."

"It's magic all right," I said, as he lifted my ass from the bed and began applying his tongue to where his cock had just been. And I knew it wouldn't be long before he'd be entering me again, giving me another sample of one of his specialties, giving me yet another reason to stay in Florida, or at least to visit more frequently.

Paul took us to the parking lot at the bar and to our cars. Gerry sat with me in my car for a long time, his hand in mine, stroking me. We agreed to meet later that night. "I have to feel the feather. I just have to," I said, kissing the tips of his fingers before letting him go.

Arriving back at my parents, I found my father on the dock. "Where have you been?" he asked, putting down his newspaper.

'Taking my medicine."

"What?"

"I met some friends -

He shook his head, looked out to the bay. "Yeah, I know what kind of friends."

Tears shot up behind my eyelids and yet it was nothing. I could feel Gerry's hands, so strong, squeezing mine. I smiled. "No, it's true feeling, not magic."

"What?" my father asked, his eyes slits.

"Magic. It was magical."

"Oh." He looked off, lost in thought again, perhaps of some magic in his own life, over time, over distance. Yes, for a instant I silently hoped he had experienced just one such moment. But just one.

YOU DON'T HAVE TO BE AFRAID
John Patrick

When I was a little boy, I worshipped my stepbrother Bo. I wished my ugly brown curls would grow straight and blond, like his, I wished my brown eyes would turn blue, and I wanted my body to look just like his when I got big.

When I was six, Bo was sixteen. We slept in the same bed in the same cramped little room, so I'd see him naked nearly every day. I used to watch him out of the corner of my eye when we were getting dressed in the morning. We had to get up pretty early to do chores before breakfast, so we'd both be moving in sleepy slow motion. In the winter, my stepbrother had a frayed white terry-cloth bathrobe that he put on first thing. He used to ask me how many colors I could see in it that day, and I'd say some ridiculous number like 97 or 468. His old robe hung on a nail by the window and every morning I'd stop in the middle of pulling off my old pajamas or dragging on my socks and watch Bo glide across the room and pass through the slash of pale morning sunlight to reach for his robe. I used to think the sunshine came through the window just so it could land on his perfect body.

The thing I liked most about his body was his pubic hair. It was a tiny little triangle of golden blonde curls, just a few shades darker than his hair. It seemed perfectly proportioned to me. I'd seen other, older guys naked a time or two, but their pubic hair seemed too dark and thick and bushy to me. Bo's cock was also fascinating. It too was in perfect proportion. I'd seen my stepfather's cock and it was ugly, way too big to my mind.

When I was eight, Bo shot himself with Ben McKenna's antique Colt 45. No one ever figured out how he got a hold of it, although everyone in town knew Ben kept it in a Maxwell

House coffee can on top of his refrigerator.

At first, some people were saying Bo was "queer" (a word I didn't figure out until many years later) because Bo never went on a single date, despite the fact that every girl within 50 square miles had a terrible crush on him. Every Valentine's Day, our mailbox would be choked with frilly red hearts and crudely printed love poems. Bo, though, would just stare through them like they weren't even there.

I asked myself a million times, like everyone else in town, I guess, what Bo was doing in Ben McKenna's kitchen. Then I remembered one day in the middle of a dust storm Bo didn't come home from school and everybody was worried. Then he called from Ben's, saying he had stopped there on his way home waiting for the storm to let up. He ended up staying for dinner and spent all night there. Nobody seemed to care. Then.

My brother always seemed to know some secret that no one else was privy to. He was so beautiful and so quiet that I think some people in town were a little afraid of him. I guess that's why no one raised a fuss over anything he did.

Despite what doctors might say, I don't hate 13o, though plenty of people in town do, deep down. Old Ben McKenna, for instance, although I've never asked him. I never speak to him. I am careful never to mention Bo's name to anyone. It seemed like people pretended Bo never existed. No, I don't hate my stepbrother. In fact, I get scared sometimes thinking about how much I still love him, how clear I can hear his voice and how I've never forgotten the least little thing I ever knew about him. Every chance I get, I stand out on the dirt road in back of the house and stare out at the mountains and watch the sky, knowing it was his favorite view. Each time I look, the mountains are still the same and the sky is still changing.

And Ben McKenna still lives across town, near the high school, and when I pass his house he always smiles. I smile back but hurry on my way. Except yesterday. He was out in front pruning the bushes and when he saw me he smiled like always, but then he did a funny thing: he put down his clippers and walked over to his fence. I stopped, clutching my books to my chest, watching him come toward me. He was a small, wiry man with dark brown hair and deep-set brown eyes. He almost looked Mexican, not a good thing in this town, but he was very handsome, I thought, for a man in his forties.

"It's the anniversary today, you know," he said.

"Of what?"

"Ten years ago today it was. I thought we should talk about it, now that you're older."

Ten years ago. Bo. The gun. Ben McKenna. "Oh."

"Come on in, have some lemonade."

It was an unusually warm day for May and I was thirsty. "Okay," I said, following him into the house.

We sat in the living room. He served lemonade and put a plate of cookies in front of me.

"You know what a homosexual is, don't you?" he asked after a little bit of small talk.

"Yeah," I said, sipping my big glass of lemonade. It was fresh-made and was about the best I'd ever tasted.

"Your brother was one. Did you that?"

"No."

He took a cookie from the plate and was bringing it to his mouth when he said, "And I'm one."

"Oh." I set my glass on the table and picked up a cookie. It was oatmeal chocolate chip with nuts and raisins.

"I'm telling you that because I know it will remain a secret with you. You are very much like your brother – "

"I am?" I was crunching the cookie. It was about the best cookie I'd ever eaten.

"But you're even better-looking. And I hear you're smart as a whip."

"I study a lot."

"You are homosexual, too, aren't you?" He picked up his glass of lemonade and took a long swallow.

The gulped. "I guess I am." He had shared his secret with me, I felt safe telling him mine.

He nodded. "You've just made the step Bo would never make. He would never admit it. Ten years ago, it was about the worst thing in the world to be. But times have changed. The fact that you can say that, even though you hesitated a bit, kinda qualified it, proves it. You don't act like one, don't look like one, but I can always tell."

"You can?"

"The way you smiled at me every time you saw me."

"I wanted to talk to you – about it."

"At first, I thought you hated me. That you thought I might have even pulled the trigger."

175

"No. I never thought that. And I never hated you. I felt sorry for you, having it happen in your kitchen."

"I know. Because after awhile you did smile at me, sort of. A half-smile that told me you maybe you understood. That was the worst time of my life. I couldn't explain it to anybody. I thought of moving away but I had a business here then, my mother lived here, God rest her soul. Nobody knew my secret, though. I never did a thing here. I would always go to Los Angeles or some place and do my thing. I still do. Bo was the only one. Do you believe me?"

"Yes. But why Bo?"

"I guess he was just about the most beautiful boy I had ever seen."

"He was."

"And he wanted it so badly. I knew what he wanted. I wanted to give it to him, but I was afraid. I kept him at a distance as long as I could but then the day of the big dust storm – "

"I remember."

He stayed overnight."

"I remember."

"It was the most perfect night of my life. We did everything that night that two men could do to each other. I say men because he was a man, in every way, except emotionally. He was still a baby. He couldn't admit what he wanted. He thought he should be dating all those girls that sent him Valentines. To date those girls, have sex with them, it was something that he felt he had to do. But he didn't want it. The thought of it made him sick. He was so confused. He wasn't a bright boy like you are, you knew that?"

"No."

"Well, it's true. He was not a bright boy. A smarter boy could have figured it out. I tried to help but he went crazy with it. He'd stay away, try to avoid me, but he'd always come back. He knew what he wanted and where to find it."

"I know what I want, too, but I don't know how." "How?"

"I'm afraid."

He got up out of his chair and began walking toward me, very slowly. "You don't have to be afraid," he said, extending his hand.

Somehow I knew it was going to happen; the minute I entered his house I got the feeling I was never going to want to leave. And I didn't for about two hours that afternoon.

I poured me another tall lemonade and we took the plate of cookies with us to the bedroom upstairs. He was very gentle with me, undressing me slowly, caressing my skin the same way I always wanted to touch Bo's. He said he was going to do what he had done to Bo and then he would stop. There were many other things we could do, he said, but we had plenty of time to do them. When he slipped my briefs down and my erection popped out into his face, he said, "You know what I'm going to do next, don't you?"

"Yes."

As my cock entered his mouth and he took it down to the pubic hairs, then kept going back and forth like that, I stared at him. I wanted to ask him if it was at least as good as Bo's, but he answered it before I could ask. He slipped it out of his mouth and, stroking it, slick with his saliva, he said, "You're smarter 'n Bo and your dick is bigger. You'll go far in this world."

I knew I was bigger. I took after my father, but I didn't know till then that was other men wanted, as big a dick as they could find. Bigger, to men like Ben, was better.

What Ben did over the course of the next ten minutes was get me so hot I would be close to coming, then pull it out and play with my balls, run his hands over my body, twist my nipples, then put my cock back in his mouth again. Finally he let me come and, as he did, he brought his hands to the cheeks of my ass and pushed, sending my jism deep down his throat. As he pulled it out, he said I even tasted better than Bo.

I begged him to let me spend the night but he said it was best if I went home to dinner, like everything was still normal. There would be plenty more afternoons like this, he said. I said I hoped so.

I got dressed and went downstairs. As I passed through the kitchen to set my empty glass and the plate on the counter, I saw the Maxwell House coffee can on top of the refrigerator. I went over to it, took it down, and opened the lid. It was empty.

THE HANDY MAN
John Patrick

It was still dark when I woke up, but the rain had stopped and the power had returned to our cottage on Bear Lake, which my parents had rented for the sixth straight summer. I could see the light was burning in the hallway outside my room so I got up to turn it off. Then I went about the cottage, turning out the lights no one else knew were on; I felt very responsible for my age; I was conserving energy. I went to the bathroom and took a piss, then, as I passed my parents' room, I noticed the door was slightly ajar. I put my hand on the knob and began to draw it shut but, why I don't know, I opened it instead.

There was my mother, spooned up against my father's back, as she always was, and the handy man spooned up against her, his muscular, tanned arm over the covers, his other hand resting on the top of her head.

I stood and stared and then backed out of the bedroom. They hadn't moved, the three of them breathing deeply, almost in unison.

I went back to my bedroom and sat on my bed. What had I seen? I wanted to go back and take another look, to see them again, to make the scene I had witnessed somehow disappear, or perhaps to watch them carefully, as long as it took to understand.

It was a new handy man that season. Johnny was his name. He had been hired by the aged and ailing owner to maintain the cluster of cottages on the lake called Bear Lake Lodge. He kept the boats afloat, painted, fixed. What made this handy man different from the last one, a grizzly old drunk who had passed away that winter, was that Johnny was barely out of his teens and extremely good looking. I lusted for him immediately.

Now I could see I wasn't the only one.

My father would come out to Bear Lake on the weekends, arriving late Friday night and going home to Saginaw on Sunday night. But some weekends he wouldn't come at all. He was an accountant and he had a glorious reputation for constructing tax shelters for his clients. He made a lot of money but it also often kept him very busy in town. This left my mother and I to do as we always did, manage somehow. She was not my real mother; she died when I was five. Emma was my father's third wife, the first having divorced him and the second was my mother. Emma was much younger than Father and beautiful. If I had not lusted after men I probably would have lusted after Emma. So it never surprised me when men would flirt with her wherever we went. I had even supposed that Emma did more than flirt with some of the men she met but I never had any evidence of it. Sometimes she would go into town and be gone all day and seem very happy when she returned but I never thought much about it.

In years past, there were always other kids my age at the lake. A couple of them, Dick Dietz and Kenny Henderson, became very special because we would often go out on the lake and jack each other off.

But this year, both Dick and Kenny's families had taken cottages at a new resort on Traverse Bay and although I would visit them, usually for a weekend, I was bored with them. It seemed that they had somehow discovered girls and that's all they could talk about. They didn't even want to jack-off together anymore.

I was perfectly content to be by myself all summer if necessary, but Johnny was always getting in the way of my contentment. Just the sight of him sent shivers through me. Besides being handsome, he had a swimmer's body with extremely well-developed pectorals and tightly- muscled arms.

It seemed Emma was always finding something for Johnny to fix. I think she liked looking at him as much as I did. He would lie on his back, with his head under the sink, fixing the leaking pipes and I would just stare at the mound at his crotch. There was never an outline of anything, just a big mound. I figured maybe he had it all coiled up in there or something.

Father got along with Johnny too. When Father was at the cottage, Johnny would be the one he would take fishing. Johnny had the weekends off and could do as he wanted so it seemed as if he was honoring my father with his presence. Besides, my father always did most of the talking and he said Johnny was a very good listener.

What else Johnny was very good at was now becoming evident. I had never thought much about Emma and father having sex and the thought of them having sex with Johnny – separately or together – was beyond the realm of possibility. Yet there they were, all snuggled up, with Emma in the middle.

I knew they had been playing cards and drinking when I went to bed and then the storm came and the lights went out and I remember overhearing Dad say to light some candles. That was the last thing I remember.

I took my time getting dressed and by the time I got to the kitchen for breakfast, Emma and Dad were there but there was no sign of Johnny. As Emma busied herself making the French toast, she was humming. I had never heard her hum at breakfast. Sometimes while she was making dinner, after she'd returned from one of her shopping expeditions in town, she would hum, but never at breakfast. My father seemed in an especially jovial mood himself; he began talking to me about all the things I should be doing at the lake but all I ever seemed to do was read and go for walks and occasionally take a swim.

"Aren't there any children your age here this year?" he asked finally.

"I'm not a child."

"No, I guess you're not. You're nearly as tall as me now. But you'll always be my child, even when you're forty. I'm sorry Dickie and Kenny aren't here this year but there's nothing stopping you from making new friends."

"I'm fine."

"I'm sorry I can't take some time off. I've got this big contract for some people at the phone company and it's very complicated – "

"I said, I'm fine." How my father could go on.

"Well, today I have to go back early. I have to get ready for a big meeting tomorrow. But I asked Johnny to come here on his day off and take you waterskiing. You'd like that, wouldn't you?"

"Johnny's coming here on a Sunday?" I gasped.

"Just for you."

"Just for me?" I tried to restrain my joy.

'That's what I said. What's wrong with that?"

"Nothing. It's just that I thought Johnny would have a lot to do on his days off, he's so busy here during the week." "Well, he is, but he said he'd be glad to baby-sit."

"Baby-sit?"

"Yes. You see, your mother is going back with me. And we didn't want to leave you here by your lonesome."

I was in shock. I couldn't believe it. Johnny was staying at Bear Lake on a Sunday, taking me waterskiing and even sleeping in our cottage overnight? What had I done to deserve this? Or, perhaps, what had they done?

"Besides, I think you'll be seeing a lot of Johnny and you two should get better acquainted."

A lot of Johnny? This was getting better every second. By noon Emma and Father had everything packed into his blue Imperial and we were all sitting in the living room waiting for Johnny.

Father was reading over some papers and Emma was straightening up the room. When she was nervous, she straightened things up. I just sat in the corner watching television but only looking at it; my mind was doing somersaults planning my unexpected "night with Johnny."

When Johnny appeared at the door, Emma rushed up to him, began fussing at him, telling where everything was in the cottage. Father handed him a roll of bills, "in case anything comes up," and he winked at him. It seemed they had their own private jokes. They ignored me until just before they left, Emma kissing me on the top of the head and Father waving to me from the front door. I didn't bother to get up to watch them drive away, but Johnny stood at the door for the longest time. Finally, he came over to me. "Well, kid, you ready?"

"I guess." I didn't want to appear the least bit excited; it was difficult but I managed to make him believe I was bored silly.

"We don't have to go waterskiing, you know," he said, moving towards the back door, out to the water. "That was only your Dad's idea. You can do whatever you want. But I'm going to race that boat whether you go or not."

"I'm coming," I said, running after him.

I figured he'd had enough of my father's talking so I didn't say a word. I let him put the life jacket on me, show me how to put the skis on, strap them onto my feet, and demonstrate how I was to move as he roared from the shore. I couldn't get the hang of it; I kept letting go of the lines.

"Let's just go for a ride," I said.

"Okay."

It was a sunny, warm day and the spray of the water against my face seemed like caresses as I sat in the stern of the boat next to Johnny. We must have made circles in the lake a hundred times. My stomach was growling by the time we came in and he tied the boat up to the dock.

I said I would start fixing dinner.

"I'm supposed to do that," he said. "I'm the babysitter." "I don't need a babysitter."

"You need a babysitter more than you think you do." "I don't," I said, stepping away from him.

"Oh, yes you do!"

He snapped his beach towel at my ass. It hurt. "Stop!" I protested, but he kept on snapping me. I grabbed the towel and jerked it away from him. As I ran to the cottage, he said "You're gonna get it now."

He chased me into the house, to my bedroom. I slammed the door behind me but it had no lock so Johnny followed me in. I lay on the bed panting. He stood over me, his hands on his hips.

"You still like me, after what's happened?"

"After what's happened?"

"Between your folks and me?"

I stared at him blankly.

"I saw you come into the bedroom this morning. Or, rather, I saw you leave." He sat down on the bed. "Has this happened before with your folks?"

"Well, I don't know exactly. Probably. I've never been sure." He leaned toward me. My eyes were fixed on his crotch. "You're old enough to understand," he said. "As some guys get older, well, they have trouble satisfying their wives."

I got the picture, sort of. My father could no longer get a hard-on, or maybe just too busy to screw Emma very much.

And your mother is a very pretty woman."

"Yes, she is."

He stroked my chin. "And you are a very pretty boy." "She's not my real mother, you know."

"But she could be. You have the same hair, the same eyes." He ran his hand up my leg. "Same soft skin."

With Johnny sitting on my bed, touching me, I couldn't help it: I got a boner. Johnny looked down at it and smiled. "But that's something your mother doesn't have."

"What?" I said, raising up on my elbows.

"That," Johnny said, flicking my dick with his finger. "Looks like our little discussion has excited you."

"A little."

"A little? Looks pretty big to me."

"It gets bigger."

"That's hard to believe."

What was hard to believe was that he was actually staying there, on the bed, leading me on. I wondered what game he was playing; how could a guy go to bed with a woman, with her husband looking on, and be interested in their son's dick? Still, I was game to find out. I lifted up and slid my swim trunks from my waist, down my hips and off. Lying back down, I said, "There, see." I made my cock jump for him just for good measure.

"Yeah. Shit, you're almost as big as me."

"Really?" Now I had him. He had to prove it to me. "I can't believe that."

He stood up and slowly lowered his denim cut-offs. He wore a jockstrap that bunched everything together, but now his cock was straining the fabric. The head of it was peaking out at me. He stepped out of the cut-offs and put both hands on the elastic at his waist. He wanted to torture me a bit, making me wait to see it. First the head slid into view, big and bulbous, then one or two inches of the shaft. Then the flesh began to harden. By the time he had his balls exposed, the eight-incher was sticking straight out at me. I felt puny in comparison but still I said,

"Yeah, mine is bigger."

He laughed and stepped out of his jockstrap. He tossed it off to the side and took his cock in his hand. "It gets even bigger when some broad's suckin' it."

"Like Emma?"

"No, like your father," he chuckled.

"Yeah, sure."

"Hey, I've turned on some husbands. But I never tell what goes on in a bedroom. Nobody ever knows but us."

"Is that the same for boys, too?" „Boys?„

"Yeah, like me. Would it be a secret, what goes on here?" "Of course. Do you think I'm crazy?"

That was all I needed to hear. Lying on my chest, I flung my arms around his hips and brought Johnny's cock to my mouth. Dickie Dietz' cock was the only one I'd ever touched with my mouth, and then only for a moment. He said I hurt him; that I bit him with my teeth. I was careful not to bite Johnny. In fact, I took such care that he was soon demanding that I practically chew on that beautiful slab of skin. "'Eat that dick!" he cried. I felt like telling him I would gladly eat it for breakfast, lunch and dinner if that's what he wanted.

What he really wanted was to suck my dick. Quickly, we were in my bed, lying on our sides, sucking each other. The thrill of having anyone – let alone Johnny – making me feel so good was indescribable. It seemed he knew something was deep inside of me and he just had to get it out. It didn't take long for him to draw out what had been bottled up inside of me probably for years. I came once, my cock never leaving his mouth, but he kept right on sucking. Soon I felt his cock vibrate, then he groaned, "Oh, yeah, yeah," and I knew. I pulled it out of my mouth and held it. It was fascinating to watch him close-up spurt gobs of cum onto the bed sheet. When I thought he was finished, I put it back in my mouth and he came a little more and it tasted strange, unlike anything else, and made me hungry.

While we ate the stew Emma had left, Johnny talked and I listened. He said he liked Elvis Presley's music, fast cars, speedboats, boys and older women, not necessarily in that order. He said he was lucky to have the handy man's job because he'd gotten in trouble the year before when he was a camp counselor in Indiana. It seemed he had trusted a boy who later turned him in. He was put on probation and got permission to move to back to Michigan where his parents lived provided he not have any contact with children.

"You've kept your pledge," I said. "I'm no child."

"That's for sure," he laughed. "No one with a dick like that could be called a child."

"Yours is bigger. At least two inches."

"Yours'll grow."

"It seems like it's grown two inches just today."

He grinned. "Took the right mouth to suck on it."

My parents felt safe leaving me in Johnny's care. As the weeks passed, while I knew Emma would send me off in the boat in the afternoon so she could entertain Johnny in the bedroom for an hour or so, he would always leave Bear Lake at sunset. But I knew he would be back after dinner to keep our rendezvous. After I went to bed, I would climb out the window and make my way to the far end of the property where the owner had provided a little cabin for the handy man. I would rap on the door twice and wait. Johnny would unlock the door and let me in.

To the accompaniment of "Love Me Tender," Johnny made love to my body the way no one ever had, before or since. Our sixty-pining gave way, eventually, to his fucking me. Emma was completely different, Johnny said, because a cunt is different from an ass. Actually, he said, he preferred an ass, but it didn't matter to him what sex the person was. "A fuck's a fuck," he said.

Years later, after my father passed away, I was visiting Emma and we reminisced about that last summer at Bear Lake. She told me that she loved both Johnny and my father, and that they all loved each other, each differently, each special, each deserving of that love and appreciation. "People don't think it can be that way but it can."

"Oh, I know," I said, smiling but unable to look her in the eyes. "I really do."

THE STEAMY SIDE OF LIFE
Thom Nickels

I had my first bathhouse experience when I was 19. I was on Amtrak headed for the New York City gay pride march when a Philadelphia activist noticed my Gay Liberation Now! button and introduced himself. Fred proved to be good company, and so his offer to show me the Village hot spots proved irresistible: Of course I would team up with him for the weekend.

On the evening of the march, Fred introduced me to the Continental Baths, which he said was the most famous bath house in America at that time. The Continental (ten times as big as other baths and decorated like the Ritz) was equipped with steam rooms, saunas, pools, gyms, snack bars, lounges and floors and floors of unparalleled fun in the form of hundreds of half naked men. To me, it seemed the Continental was straight out of Coleridge's "Kubla Khan" or a (gay) Arabian Nights. Where else could you see a 250-pound "daddy bear" reading Simone de Beauvoir while stroking the back of a blond out-of-work actor?

Happily dazed, I ambled through the corridors eyeing the small rooms containing naked men on cots in all manner of repose. In the various dark orgy rooms, I couldn't see but had to feel my way through a maze of bodies. Smelling of sweat, freshly showered bodies, poppers and marijuana, they would prove to be some of the handsomest men I'd ever seen.

During that first evening, I noticed a huge cluster of men near a makeshift amphitheater by the pool. The woman on stage had a funny voice; she was not sexy or pretty but smallish with a big mouth (and nose), but the men were going crazy.

Bette Midler at this time was still a "nobody," so there were no straight society buffs (in gowns and tails) in the audience, just hundreds of semi-naked guys applauding furiously.

Standing on the fringes of this mob, I tiptoed to get a glimpse of the future superstar's face, annoyed that show biz antics had temporarily shelved the pursuit of sex. Fred, it appeared, had been swallowed up; after he marched off in pursuit of his room, I never saw him again.

A few months later, I returned to the Continental and once again witnessed the rush of exhilaration accompanying Bette Midler's act. Still, I was not amused. Actually, I was worried be-cause it seemed to be hard for me to meet men in New York. For one thing, the pandemonium and confusion of Manhattan's streets seemed to rule bathhouse pedestrian traffic and, as an out of towner, this further activated my shy and awkward cruising style. Still, I remember thinking that if straight America could only get a glimpse of the goings-on here they'd be beside themselves with wonder – or outrage. Outrage that so many good looking men were not going to be dating their daughters.

I met only one man in a New York bath. This was during Midler's act, when I was wandering the deserted corridors. He was a muscle-bound god.

He led me on a merry chase and finally I caught him, or he caught me, depending on your view, in the shower stall. He had one of those lanky, muscular bodies with soft skin and not much hair. His nipples were the size of half dollars and made me think of suns on an Inca breastplate: the shock of that chest was something to remember: it was practically immoral the way the sculpted pecs jutted out at such sharp, delicious angles a perfect ridge for a curious tongue. He had a Mediterranean-look and a short haircut which made his face to appear to square, as if it had been "engineered." His prominent nose hinted at the power of his penis, which cocked to the left, a bent marvel that kept getting caught between my thighs as it swung pendulum-style every time he moved.

I don't remember his name; I think it began with a "J." His fingers were long and thick and he was big on running them over my lips as he whispered something in his native tongue. I don't know what that language was; perhaps Greek. I do remember I did almost everything he wanted, though the space was tight; we kept colliding against the soap dish and bumping our heads on the shower head. Yet these collisions were nothing compared to the sensation of him pressing into me from behind, his marvel wedged between my crack and sliding gracefully in its own juices.

He came twice, the first sending a warm spray over my back, the second when he turned me around and held my head to his abdomen. He wanted me to rim the universe of circles inside his navel, a little oval suck that sent him into a major tailspin.

Finally, he gave me the full golden slope of his back and naked butt, so that my own spray became like a splattering of hot shower soap.

The fuck was well worth the wait, even though it was over too quickly. Like Peggy Lee, I had to mumble, "Is that all there is to a Continental connection?"

Although, in retrospect, I'm probably alive today because I didn't score that often at the baths in New York, at the time I couldn't help but feel that the fates were against my meeting people in the Continental as well as other baths I visited, including the seamy St. Mark's, the Tom Waits-style bath house where it was rumored that W.H. Auden rambled around in his bedroom slippers.

In Boston the baths were more malleable, if a little incestuous. By this I mean you couldn't turn a corner or lie on an orgy cot without meeting an activist friend from the MIT Gay Liberation Front or coming across somebody whose face you'd seen in Harvard Yard. And I found that, unlike New York, there was a lot of talk in Boston bath houses. Consciousness-raising sessions took place in the orgy rooms as circles of people gathered to discuss Stonewall. I recall one overweight white guy with a huge Afro drawing cute young things to him because of his powerful rhetoric. Boston was like that. Other things besides the sculpted slope of somebody's butt inspired feelings of lust and attraction.

In those days, the baths were the classic rite of passage for most urban gay men. Not everybody participated, of course. There were plenty of gay men who objected to the slutty behavior bath houses encouraged. But baths were legendary, and so for the adventurous they had to be experienced. After all, if people like W.H. Auden, Edward Albee, Paul Goodman, Ned Rorem and Tennessee Williams could amble about in towels and then write poems or diary entries about "the baths," there must be something to it.

Most baths were open 24 hours a day. For a meager $7 or less you got a clean cubicle with a cot (clean white sheets and a pillow) with a night stand, towels, soap and a key to lock your valuables in a footlocker. Things like wallets or jewelry were held in the front in manila envelopes with your name on it. Only the clerks knew how many wedding rings were in these envelopes, but rumors circulated (especially in the Philadelphia baths) that Thursday nights was married man's night because of the huge numbers of rings said to be in the envelopes.

The time limit was seven or eight hours, during which you could sleep, shower, sauna, eat, watch movies or television, meet the person of your dreams or go on a literal erotic rampage, fulfilling a dozen sexual fantasies with different types of men.

A frequent complaint of the younger men in the baths was that old men followed them around and then, given a moment's opportunity, pounced on them like wolves. Still, there were enough young men willing to experiment outside their immediate age group, since this was a very democratic table and people hooked on specific types tended to hide in their cubicles anyway.

In a dark orgy room, for instance, the unwritten rule was: never, under any circumstances, keep your hands to yourself (this was the baths, not a church). A guy might protest a come on, but often a "compromise touch" was okay (a 70-year-old man stroking a young dude's foot as that kid made it with somebody more his type was not an uncommon sight). Egalitarian to the max, as they say.

With a bath membership card you could go to any chain in any city (Denver, Salt Lake, Honolulu, Camden, etc.) and stay the night for a few dollars and get clean sheets, a shower and a steam bath. If you wanted (platonic) privacy, you could lock your cubicle door and nobody would bother you. Like the Holiday Inn, you could even arrange to have the clerks wake you at a certain hour.

For me, going to the baths was like taking a vacation from reality. They had the ability to project one out of a (seemingly) humdrum life, and they had all the healing power of a quick trip to Thailand or the South Pacific. I can remember standing with a towel around my waist after a wonderful sauna and back rub from an agreeable stranger and looking out the bath house windows at the poor slobs walking on 13th Street and thinking how boring and predictable life would be if there weren't baths to escape to.

At times, conversation came easy in the baths, because erotic tension was usually worked through. When one fulfilled a sexual fantasy regarding an ideal type, there was nowhere else to "go" but to a calm and relaxed state of mind: After all, once you've seen the lights of Paris, why worry? What we call "attitude" was very rare.

For some people, the baths became a home away from home. "Regulars" populated center stage like Dick Clark's American Bandstand dancers of that era. Same people spent weekends there, and it is said that novelist Sloan Wilson holed up in a cubicle with his typewriter and wrote a novel, going out only when he had to eat, shower and find a lover.

In the '70s, the Philadelphia baths were sometimes raided by the police. I remember the overhead lights going on and a buzzer going off at odd times. This meant to put your towel on and walk around as if you were strolling through Longwood Gardens. I never saw any uniformed officers march through, but rumors flew about hunky undercover cops reclining on wooden benches like Alexander of Macedonia, their hairy legs (and more) extended for caressing.

New baths cropped up daily. One, Man's County in New York City, had a real tractor trailer truck in one of its rooms to simulate "the trucks," an outdoor cruising place near the Hudson with dozens of parked tractor trailers with their back doors open. For me, the baths were a kind of exorcism. In high school and college, I rarely had sex and was so shy about being gay I let many opportunities pass, whereas my heterosexual friends were getting laid every week.

Do I miss the baths today? No, because I've learned that having sex with lots of people only appears to be satisfying. Actually, it just whets the appetite for more sexual variety. Ann Landers wasn't kidding when she said that sex without emotion or a deep connection leaves one feeling empty. But empty or not, I will never regret – nor forget – my experiences on the steamy side of life.

MY BROTHER, MY LOVE
Bud O'Donnell

In our household, there was no dating until we attained the age of sixteen, but I know for a fact that my older brothers lost their cherries before that time. I used to catch bits and pieces of their conversation and found out they were screwing girls at times they were supposed to be at a buddy's house studying or something. I guess they figured I was too young to have any idea as to what they were talking about. It seems that some of my brothers even shared the same girls at times. But as for me, by the time I was in high school, my sexual partner was my own right hand. Often, by the time I finished with diving practice, gymnastics lessons and my homework, I was so tired I would fall asleep before I could even finish jacking off.

Although the entire family rooted for me in whatever activity I got involved, the one sibling I was closest to was my next youngest brother, Mike. Mike is the one who had to give up his private room and share it with me when I was moved out of the nursery. Actually it was supposed to have been a "sitting room" off my parents' bedroom, but it became a nursery for the first child and remained that for some 25 years. We had a seven-bedroom house, but one was always a "guest" room; usually used by my grandparents or other out-of-town visitors, which happened quite often. All of us children eventually had to share a bedroom.

If Mike resented my moving in with him when I was less than two years old, he never let me know. In fact, for whatever reason, Mike was always good to me. He was five when I was born and had just started school. He was seven and in second grade when I moved into his room. I remember he used to talk to me a lot. I don't remember what he said, but I liked the time he spent with me. I think he liked the idea of having someone to talk to. I never grew tired of listening to him.

The thing I liked best about Mike though, and I remember this clearly, was when we would be getting ready for bed and he'd run his bath, he would always ask me to join him in the tub. There was a bathroom between our room and that of two older brothers. He continued his talking while he bathed and I splashed. As he got a couple of years older, we would shower together. Those were really favorite times. There was nothing sexual about it, at least on Mike's part, but I sure got my infantile jollies watching his naked male body; a habit I've never quite broken.

When Mike got into his teens, he used to tell me about the girls he was interested in. It was during some of those talks that I'd often notice that his boy-cock was sticking straight up against his belly when he got ready to take his bath or shower. It looked awfully big to me, and by that time he was of an age where we didn't shower at the same time anymore, but often I'd sit on the toilet and watch him through the glass shower doors waiting my turn. He never seemed to be embarrassed over the fact that he had a hard-on, although I didn't know that's what it was called at the time. I did know though, that under my pajamas, I had one too, only then, it didn't stick out a far as his did.

When we were ready for bed, he'd always tuck me in, kiss me on the forehead and say, "G'night Big Guy." Then he'd go off to his own bed. When he was about fourteen, he started sleeping in the nude. I wanted to do the same but the first time I tried it, I nearly froze my ass off. It was much later that I copied Mike's naked habit.

I remember when he started getting hair around his cock. He explained it to me in a way that I knew that before long I would get the same. I asked him if he thought that my penis would ever get as big as his. He ruffled my hair and said, "I think yours is going to be even bigger than mine from the looks of things." It was about that time that I began keeping tabs on how big mine was with a ruler when no one was looking.

There were several times when I was supposed to be asleep, but I'd be lying with my eyes partly shut just watching Mike sleep.

Sometimes, after Mike had been in bed about half an hour or so and he thought I would be asleep, he would slowly pull the covers down and I'd see his cock lying hard against his belly. He'd look over at my bed and I had my eyes closed...almost, and I lay perfectly still. He'd turn his head back and began stroking his cock up and down.

My little dick would get as hard as a stake and I had a lot of trouble keeping my hands off my own, but it was such a thrill to watch him jack off. He kept a box of tissues on his night stand and after a few minutes of stroking his cock, he'd reach over and grab several of them and then start beating his meat faster. I could hear him breathing hard and suddenly he'd groan and cover the end of his prick with the tissues. I knew that something must have come out of the end of his cock although I didn't know what. He spent quite a bit of time wiping himself off afterwards. He'd then get up and go into the bathroom. His dick would still be hard and he sort of played with it as he went in to flush the tissues down the toilet. As soon as I was sure he was asleep, I would try stroking mine the same as he did. I used to get this wonderful feeling. I didn't know I was having a dry orgasm, but I did know that I sure liked the feeling. It would put me to sleep quickly.

I was just eleven the first time I actually shot cum out of my cock. It felt so good, but when I suddenly felt all that wetness inside my pajamas and on my hand, I let out a panic cry. I thought I had pissed my pants. My yell woke Mike up. He flipped on the light and I quickly sat up in bed. He asked me what was wrong and I started to cry. He came over and sat on my bed, put his arm around me, and I told him I peed in bed. He helped me out of bed and into the bathroom, but as I pulled off my pajama pants and he saw the white goo on my belly, he just laughed. He hugged me tight and right then and there explained that I'd had a wet dream. He told me what it was, and that it was okay and that I was now a "man." He thought it had happened when I was asleep and I was just too embarrassed to tell him that I'd been stroking my cock up and down the way I watched him do.

From that point on, I would jack off in the bathroom or when I was taking a shower. I didn't dare keep a box of tissue on my night stand like Mike did because I was afraid he'd know what was going on.

The older Mike got the hotter he got, as far as I was concerned. He started growing hair all over his chest and his dick looked bigger when I had a chance to peek at him jacking off in bed. I guess mine was getting bigger too because once in awhile if I was naked and getting ready to shower or something, he'd comment on how big my "pecker" was getting. Then he'd joke with me by saying again he thought mine was going to be bigger than his. Little did I know he was quite a prophet.

When he started dating, his nights of jacking off got less and less, and I suspected it was because he was laying some of the girls he went out with. He sure had a lot of them after him, but I can't say as I blamed them. Mike was a good looking guy.

I knew that my feelings for Mike were stronger than just his being my brother. But I was awfully happy that he was. He always had time to talk to me, even though I could be a prick once in awhile and get on his nerves. It was always Mike who would apologize after we had an argument, even though I knew it was mostly my fault. I wasn't big enough to admit my own faults at that time.

When Mike graduated from high school and went off to college, I thought I would die from loneliness. I sure missed him. He was only forty miles from home and he'd get home nearly every weekend because that's where his favorite girl lived. I know he fucked her and I was jealous because I couldn't give him what he was getting from her, at least I thought that at that time. What I wanted most and thought about all the time was just being able to crawl into bed with my naked brother and have him hug and kiss me. The most I figured two guys could do was possibly jack off together. I guess my imagination wasn't completely developed at that time.

I was in an accelerated program and I was only fifteen when I was a senior in high school. At that time, I knew that I was a homosexual but I hadn't done anything except fantasize. My fantasies were limited to thinking about hugging and kissing and maybe jacking off with another guy.

Although I didn't date because of my age, I did manage, one time out in the backyard, to feel a girl's tits and cunt. The girl felt me up too, but it never went any farther than that and I wasn't unhappy about it.

I was really involved in my diving by that time and had been offered a scholarship at the same college my brother Mike was attending.

When it was certain that I'd be attending that college the following fall, Mike invited me to spend a long college weekend with him. I was absolutely thrilled. I got permission from my parents and from school to take a Friday and a Monday off and I took a bus to Mike's college campus on Thursday afternoon.

Mike and three other guys rented a four-bedroom apartment off campus. He worked a little for spending money, but my dad paid for his tuition and room and board and I guess gave him some allowance too. Dad told me that I'd get a bigger allowance than the other kids because I was the first one of the nine kids to win a scholarship and so my tuition was taken care of.

When Mike picked me up and we got back to campus, I was overwhelmed by the fact that the other guys, who were jocks, treated me almost like a hero because I'd won the State Diving Championship for our school..

When Mike took me to his room and I saw that he had just one double bed, I blushed. He sensed how the idea of sleeping in the same bed with him embarrassed me and he shrugged it off. "It's only for a coupla nights. We can handle it."

Mike told me that he was taking me along with him for a special seminar on Saturday. But when Saturday afternoon rolled around, he said, "Something's come up and I have to skip the lecture. Will you go and take notes for me?"

"Sure."

Little did I realize what was in store for me in the lecture hall. The speaker was Dr. Rodney Doyle, a physician who went on to become a psychiatrist but was currently working in the area of genetic research. His lecture topic was human sexuality. I could hardly wait. Then Dr. Doyle came onto the stage. He looked about thirty, but given his background, he had to be older. Whatever his age, he was one of the handsomest, sexiest men I'd ever seen: about six feet tall, with curly black hair and a meticulously trimmed beard and mustache. His broad-shouldered body was draped in a beautifully tailored beige suit and my eyes locked on the front of his pants. He was displaying a hefty bulge and I swear I saw a scant outline of the shaft of his cock.

A cordless microphone was clipped to his tie so that he had free range of the stage and he covered a lot of territory on it, speaking almost intimately to every person in the audience. But when he returned to center stage, I felt his warm smile was just for me.

For the next two hours, I literally sat on the edge of my seat, trying to write down every word he said. He talked about "sexual orientations," a term I'd never heard before. When he said his research had convinced him a person's sexual orientation was genetic and not a matter of choice or based of environmental influence, my ears really perked up. When he stated that science was on the very threshold of discovering the gene that determined a person's sexual orientation, there was a round of applause from many members in the audience. It was then that he said religions would have to get their act together or go out of business because people were intelligent enough to know that religious and political leaders can't continue to bury their heads in the sand when facts are proven; their hypocrisy would eventually be exposed.

He compared sexuality with other genetic factors over which we have no choice, such as the color of eyes, hair or skin, tall and short, differing bone structures and genital size. Then smiling, he said, If humans did have a choice as to their sexual make-up, I have learned over the years that the one choice that most males would make would be for an increase in the size of their penises." That brought a loud laugh from the audience. "Why has our society become so convinced that bigger is better when we all know a diamond weighing less than a gram has more value that a million pounds of sand?"

It was only after he left the stage that I realized I was going to have to tell my brother what the lecture was all about. That scared the shit out of me: How could I possibly explain the nature of the lecture without my excitement showing and giving myself away? My head was spinning as I walked down the main street of the little town which was surrounded by the campus. When I saw the Holiday Inn and a sign advertising a steak special, I was suddenly hungry. Mike said he wouldn't be back until late so I was on my own. I decided to blow my allowance.

I had just been served my salad when I heard a familiar voice say, "You're all by your lonesome?"

I blushed as I looked up into the handsome face of Dr. Doyle. I nearly choked on the lettuce. "Yes," I managed to stammer.

He slid into the booth across from me and smiled. "I noticed you in the second row and I thought perhaps I should have asked you to leave."

"Why?"

"You're obviously not eighteen and – "

"No, but I was in an accelerated program in high school. I'm going to be a freshman here next fall. But, actually, the reason I was there was to take notes for my brother, he goes here now."

"And where is he?"

"Something came up – "

He smiled. Well, I'm sure he'll be happy with your notes. I bet you got every word."

"I did. Every single word."

After he ordered, we talked; as we ate, we talked and then after the meal we talked and talked and talked. Every feeling I could ever remember having came bowling out of my mouth. I admitted for the first time in my life to anyone that I knew, that I was a homosexual and that I was scared to death because of what my family might think of me if they ever found out.

He talked about the difficulty I would have in society, but at the same time, assured me that I should never feel ashamed of myself and that I needed to learn how to love me for being me. When I would show nervousness and begin clenching my hands that were on top of the table, he would lay one of his hands on top of mine. As soon as he touched me, I felt a wonderful calming effect.

Before we walked out of the restaurant, he suggested that judging from my bits of conversation it was possible Mike had "set me up" and that maybe he thought I needed to hear his lecture. Then he said, "If that's true, then your brother must love you more than you can imagine." He gave me his card. His research laboratory was not too far from the university. He told me to feel free to call him at anytime, and if he wasn't in, he would definitely return my call.

When I got back to Mike's apartment, no one was there. I was happily exhausted. I took a shower and crawled into bed. It was sometime later that I heard Mike come into the room. Even in the dim light, I could see he was walking unsteadily. "Mike, anything wrong?"

"Just a little too many brews, Big Guy. I'll be fine. You go back to sleep." He stripped off his clothes and fell into bed. "How'd you like the lecture?" he asked as he settled in.

"Great. I took down every word." I scrambled out of bed and went to the desk. I picked up the notebook and brought it over to him. "See."

He didn't take the book, just nodded, rolled over. "Okay. okay. "

I sat down on the edge of the bed. 'Thanks, Mike." "For what?"

"For sending me to the lecture. You knew I needed to hear Dr. Doyle, didn't you?"

"I don't know what you're talking about, but if you think I did you a favor, great. Now we're even."

"I had a great time but I missed you. In fact, I've missed you so much since you've been here at college."

"I know you have. And I've missed you."

"You have?"

"You know I have. I didn't realize how much until now, with you here, us talking." He rolled over again, reached up and put his hands around my neck. He kissed me on the forehead. "I love you, Big Guy. I really love you."

It seemed like a perfectly natural thing to do, for my lips to go to his. At first, I was repelled by the smell of beer on his breath but he settled into a long kiss that had me shivering all over. My cock sprang to attention and, as he left my embrace his hand fell to it. "My, you are a Big Guy now, aren't you?" He playfully squeezed my erection.

"Not as big as you I'll bet."

He tossed off the sheet and said, "No, not quite, but you're still a kid – "

Seeing his hard-on stirred me to action. I seized it with my hand and squeezed it. "Oh, Mike – "

"Hey – " was all he could say as I lowered my head over it. When I took the head of his cock in my mouth, he gently moved his hand down my back and over my ass. I shivered.

"I know you've wanted that for a long time and tonight I really need it. You have to start somewhere, Big Guy, it might as well be here."

I let the big cock pop out of my mouth and I looked up into his eyes. "Mike, I love you so much."

He put his strong hand on top of my head and pushed down. "Okay. Show me just how much."

I was sort of dry humping his leg as I sucked his cock. He ran his fingers through my hair furiously. I pulled up and began working my hand up and down the shaft. I loved his cock. It was about eight inches long and very thick. A large dollop of juice bubbled out of the mouth of it and ran down the shaft, then another. He was really moaning now.

I could wait no longer. I moved my head down and my hand followed the force of his cock so that it was almost lying against his belly button. The thickness of my fingers wrapped around it kept it raised off his belly. I stuck out my tongue and lapped the cum. Mike's body jerked and he sucked in some air. I licked it again, then again, and finally moved my mouth over the top of the glans.

"Ahhh...ahhh...ahhhh...ohhh...ohhh," Mike gurgled and his whole body shook.

I moved my mouth further down, taking in more of his cock. I closed my lips and sucked hard as I drew back up. Mike's body shifted and then I felt his hands on my shoulders. He began to massage them.

I opened my mouth as wide as I could and moved down his dick. I felt the head push against the back of my throat. I gagged and I pulled back, keeping the head of it in my mouth. Just then, he came. I moved my hand off his cock and reached down and cupped his big nuts and gently rolled them in my palm. Mike groaned and squirmed. As I played with his nuts, wet and slippery from his sweat and from my spit drooling from my mouth, I returned my mouth to his cock to suck some more. I found that I could force the head of his cock through the stricture of my throat without gagging. I couldn't keep it there, but every time I squeezed him, his body would tremble. I felt the hard root of his cock underneath his balls and ran my fingers over that. By doing so, my fingers slid into the wet, hairy crack of Mike's ass. He heaved a deep breath, bent his legs at the knees and then heaved his ass up off the bed. When he did that, his cock went deep into my throat, but my fingers slid deeper into the crack of his ass, rubbing over his asshole. It was obvious from his moaning that he liked that so I continued playing with his ass and sucking his cock. The more I rubbed, the loser the ass rim became.

I got real nervy and began pushing one of my long fingers through the opening of his asshole. The noise coming from Mike's throat sounded like he was gargling and he was pushing his ass against my invading finger. As it slipped into his asshole clear to the third knuckle, the end of my finger felt a hard bump inside. It was kind of rounded. I rubbed the end of my finger over the top of it and I thought Mike was going to jump through the ceiling. He was gasping for breath and his cock suddenly ballooned out much thicker, he thrust his ass down hard against my hand and the next thing I knew his cum was shooting off again into my mouth, It took me by surprise.

I opened my mouth even wider and a deluge of hot, thick cream gushed out passed my lips and down my chin. I closed my mouth and began sucking as slug after slug came into my mouth faster than I could swallow it.

I kept his cock in my mouth long after his spasms stopped. He was ruffling my hair and when I finally stopped nursing on his cock, I slithered up along his body, wrapped my arms around him and held him close with my head on his shoulder.

He reached down, took hold of my cock and began stroking it. I looked up his face again and his eyes were shut. It took about a full minute of Mike's hand on my cock before I whispered, "Oh shit, Mike, I'm going to shoot." With his free hand, he reached over on the nightstand and pulled a bunch of tissues from the box. He got the head of my cock covered just as the first jet plowed into and through the soft paper; a big glob on his stomach. He grabbed more tissues and tried to catch my load, but it was shooting out all over me and him.

He started laughing as he threw the wad of tissues on the floor and reached for the entire box. It took a lot of them before he had wiped up the mess I made.

"Goodnight, Big Guy," he said, kissing me on the tip of my nose. He rolled over onto his side and I snuggled against his back. I could feel my semi-hard dick pressed against the crack of his ass. He twisted his upper body and laughed. "Tell that Big Thing to go to sleep. It'll get lots of chances to do some buggering." I pulled my arm up around his chest and held it there. I laughed too, simply because he did, but I didn't have the slightest idea of what he meant about buggering him. We both fell asleep, snuggled up to one another.

The next day, as he was walking me to the bus, Mike put his arm around my shoulder and said, "Remember, if you ever need to talk, you know where to find me."

"Thanks, Mike. Thanks for everything." I managed to suppress the urge to kiss him right there at the bus station.

A few weeks later, Mike was home for a long weekend. The first night, I was in bed when he came into the room. He didn't say anything to me as he undressed and slid under the covers next to me. I rolled into him and dropped my hand over his prick. He gripped it and brought it up to his chest. He put his arms around me and in a near whisper, he said, "Hey, we can't do that again. I felt awful after that night, like I'd taken advantage of you. I was drunk and horny and – "

"No, I took advantage of you."

He chuckled. "Okay, so you did. But I figured if you were going to do that to somebody for the first time it really should be somebody you love. But you weren't fooling me – "

"What?"

"You sure practiced on somebody. That was the best blowjob I've ever had."

"Really?"

"Really."

"But it was the first. Honest."

He laughed. "Well, maybe guys can do it better. I really don't know."

As we went on talking, he confessed that while I was sucking him he had closed his eyes and pretended I was one of his girl friends. He must have seen the hurt in my eyes because he kissed me on the forehead and asked, "Hey, Big Guy, you remember when we all went out for ice cream?"

"Yeah," I answered, trying to smile.

"Well, your favorite was butter pecan and mine was strawberry, right?"

"Yeah."

"Well, sex is like that, okay?"

I suddenly realized that if no other person in the world understood how I felt, I knew Mike did. I snuggled up close to him and said, "Thanks, Mike. I love you." And drifted off into a deep, peaceful sleep in my brother's warm embrace.

MY COUSIN BOBBY
Buddy Wayne

My messing around with Cousin Bobby began during the summer of 1955. Bobby's job was to bring the big loads of hay down the long hill to the valley, to be stored in the barns for winter feeding. He was only fifteen, but was physically and mentally more mature than his years, and farm boys are often operating machinery much younger than their city counterparts. At eleven, it was my chore to hook up and unhook the wagons to the big John Deere Bobby drove. I also opened and closed the gates between the valley and the ridge.

School ended a week before and one day Bobby was still talking about that last day and about Betty, one of our neighbors. She was eighteen and, he said, "a real knockout." She lived on a farm just a holler from our place and had to walk down their lane to our dairy barn, on the main road, to catch the school bus. Betty was a tease and had Bobby hooked.

"Did you see Betty's tits in that halter she wore on the bus?" he asked me, remembering that last day.

"Yeah, I saw 'em. She couldn't have worn that outfit before the last day."

"I had a hard-on all the way home," Bobby went on. "I thought I'd bust before I could get it off."

I'd never seen Bobby's dick but I thought it was probably big because he was big. He wasn't tall but he was stocky and very strong, with a round chest, big arms and legs. He had dark hair and naturally dark complexion; he would tan to dark brown.

Cousin Bobby was my hero. In fact, he was a hero to all the boys around here because of his ability to work on cars and machinery and his knowledge of sexual matters. I wanted to hear about all the sex stuff. I knew something about sex, of course; I had fooled around with my buddies Mike and Ricky in our hideout. Ricky was thirteen and Mike was eleven, just a month older than me. They were also my cousins. Ricky lived on the next farm down river and Mike lived on our farm.

My dad and his two brothers, Bobby's dad and Mike's dad were partners on the farm which was about 900 acres and was in a big valley with the Little Ohio River running through the middle. Each of the three families had their own home with ours being on the other side of the river. Bobby lived in the old Victorian home place where our grandparents had lived and Mike's dad had built a new house up the road from there place. We raised tobacco, hay and grain and had a dairy and beef operation.

Since Mike and I were the same age, we were close, like real brothers, and were almost always together. Every day we watched "The Mickey Mouse Club" and our favorite part was "Spin and Marty." Often, Mike would pretend to be Spin and I was Marty. We were both good-looking: Mike was slim with light brown hair in a flat top and had blue eyes. I had blond hair with a similar flat top and green eyes. I was built a little bigger than Mike, and was to mature physically sooner than Mike. Ricky was bigger than either of us and had red hair, freckles and a tall, lanky body.

We all had ponies and rode a lot during the summer months. Bobby also had a pony and sometimes he rode with us but most of the time he was working on cars or the machinery, helping our fathers.

We had hideouts all over our farm and on Ricky's farm as well. Mostly they were inside clumps of bushes where we could not be seen from the outside. There was a huge grape vine on one of the lower ridges, in the pasture they used for the dairy cows. We could ride into the middle of that grape vine and it would conceal four horses and riders. We used these hideouts to smoke corn silks, grape vines and cigarettes, when we could get them, and to talk about sex. We had also built rooms in the hay lofts using the bales of hay. These rooms had intricate tunnels to enter them, with secret traps and cow bell alarms to warn us of unwanted intruders.

It was in one of these rooms that Ricky, Mike and I had played around, the summer before. We didn't get into anything serious then, we didn't know how. We just got naked and played "bull and cow," riding and humping each other. That's when we made a rule that no one could come into our hideout with clothes on. Later, we would make an exception for Bobby. because he turned out to be a little shy about being naked, but not shy about talking about sex.

Bobby couldn't stop talking about Betty. He told me that sometimes she would sit on his lap on the bus coming home from school, and let him feel her titties under her coat and move around on his lap, rubbing his peter with her butt. "She drives me so crazy," he said. "I would ride a half mile past our stop to get off with her and then walk back home. She wouldn't let me near her when we were off the bus. She told me I was just a kid and she was dating an older guy. I want to do it to her so bad my dick stays hard all the time."

I looked at the bulge in his jeans and saw that was true enough all right.

A couple of minutes later, Bobby said, "I have to take a dump."

He walked over to the bathroom, a new one his father had put in off the kitchen. He started talking to me from the bathroom. I was still sitting at the kitchen table and I couldn't make out what he was saying and told him to speak up.

"I don't wanna yell. You come in here."

I hesitated, thinking of him sitting on the toilet and the stink that would be there, but I went in anyway. There was no stink. Bobby was sitting on the toilet all right, but he was leaning back playing with his dick, his pants around his ankles!

"Close the door," he said.

As I did as I was told, my eyes were glued to the prick he was massaging. It was huge! All hard and red as he slowly stroked it up and down.

I walked over to the tub and sat down on the edge.

He could see where my eyes were fixed because he said, "You like it, Buddy?"

I didn't answer; I just kept on staring.

"Well, do you like my dick?"

"Yeah, I guess," I answered weakly. "But God, it's so big!" "You can touch it if you want to."

"No, that's okay. I'll just watch you."

"It would like you to touch it."

I was dumbfounded. Here was my hero with his huge hard dick out, inviting me to do what I had done so many times before, but only in my mind. I was frozen to the spot.

"C'mon."

I wanted to. I desperately wanted to touch that big dick. "Okay."

As I moved over to where he was sitting, he scooted out on the toilet and leaned back on the tank. He took my hand and guided it to his dick. It fell wet and hot as I slowly moved my hand up and down.

I was leaning over to reach him and he put his arm around my back and pushed gently. "Get on your knees."

I knelt.

195

"Jack it off slow and easy...it's ready to shoot but I want it to last a little longer."

I did to his dick what I so often did to my own and with Ricky and Mike. I had never touched their dicks and they had never touched mine. Their dicks were about the same size as mine but Cousin Bobby's was something else: long, thick, uncut. Just plain incredible.

"That feels great, just keep going, slow and easy, Buddy. You really know how to make it feel good."

He was enjoying it so much, I began to think of ways I could make it even better. Actually there was competition between Mike and me; we were always trying to out-do one another to please Bobby and I wasn't going to let Mike beat me at this, if he'd ever been asked. I moved my hand around as I went up and down, but he winced as I did that and I took my hand away.

Bobby must have realized my feeling because he looked up, and, smiling, he said, "Hey, it's okay, it just needs to be wetter."

He was still smiling as he raised up and drooled onto his fingers. He moved his hand to his dick and spread the spit around the head and shaft with his finger, rather artistically I thought, like spreading icing on a cake. Then he took my hand and moved it back in place as he leaned back on the tank.

It was real slick now and much easier to work on. He wasn't moaning but his breath was coming short and fast. As I continued to work on him, I noticed he had hair around his dick and on his legs. This was another first for me. My cohorts, Mike and Ricky, didn't have any hair down there and neither did I. I also noticed that Bobby didn't seem to have any balls; his dick seemed to just disappear into his body. I knew from the hayloft and exploring my own body that there should have been balls down there.

Being a dumb kid, I blurted out, "Where are your balls? Do they go away when your dick grows so big like this?"

Bobby leaned up and pushed his fingers on the area to the right of his shaft. As I watched, an oval mound started to appear, just to the right and under where he was pushing. "Sometimes, when I jack off it goes up inside. I don't know why, but it still shoots a gusher when I get off," he explained.

I noticed a change in his voice, like he was worried that maybe I wouldn't like him because of his balls. I caressed "the ball" as I jacked him with my other hand.

Soon he was leaning back saying things like "Oh, God, yeah! Good! Yeah....slow down....a little faster. That's it. Oh, yeah!" After a few minutes, he raised up, took his dick out of my hand and, as I stood up, he said, "That was real good, Buddy, but there's something else we can do that'll make it feel even better

"Okay," I said.

He let go of his prick and it throbbed. He unhooked my belt, unbuttoned my jeans and pulled my zipper down.

As he pushed my jeans down to my ankles, I said, "Hey," but I made no move to stop him because my own dick had been hard all along, since he started talking back at the kitchen table, and now it was hurting me stuck in my jeans. He started feeling my little dick through my underwear. He rubbed it up and down and reached under and felt my balls. The feeling was wonderful, taking my breath away. I was about to tip over on Bobby's head but grabbed his shoulders to break my fall. My hero was touching my dick! Bobby stooped and reached for the elastic band of my underwear. I gasped as he shoved my underwear down to my ankles.

"Now I want to try somethin' different, something that will really feel good."

He put his hands on my hips, turned me around, sat down on the toilet again and pulled me down into his lap.

I felt his hard dick against the cheek of my ass, then he moved me around so that his dick was between my legs and pushing up against my balls. I had heard about "cornholing" but I'd really never thought much about it. In the hayloft, we hadn't gotten around to putting our "pee pees" in the other's "tail hole."

Bobby's dick really felt good when he put it between my legs and I knew he would never hurt me. He told me to squeeze my legs together and he started to raise and lower me. I looked down and could see his dick appear and disappear between my legs, a hot red poker contrasting with my white legs. Just the head of his dick seemed bigger than my whole dick and balls.

"Ah, yeah....that's good.... squeeze tighter."

He gripped my little pecker and was jacking me off. I was in heaven!

After a few minutes of this, he said, "This is really good, but there's one thing I think will be even better."

Everything so far had been great. Here I was naked in my hero's lap with his big prick massaging my little balls, his big hairy arms around my middle and his hand was jacking my hard horny little dick. I couldn't imagine anything better than this, but I said, "Okay."

"I want to put it in your butt," Bobby said softly.

All those thoughts of cornholing rushed back and I tensed. "Hey," he said, realizing my fear. "We'll go really slow and easy and if it hurts we can stop, okay?"

I wanted to please Bobby more than anything in the world. "How do we do it?"

"Stand up and take your pants and underwear off," he instructed. He began to undo the strings in his boots. I stood up, and took off my boots, jeans and underwear, he did the same and sat back down on the toilet.

"What if the folks come back?"

'They'll be gone another hour at least. Now look, I'm going to slick it up real good and then you turn around and sit on it and slowly let it slide in your butt hole," he answered. I watched him do the "spit icing" thing again, and, as he sat back down on the toilet, he turned me around. I heard him spit again and I felt his wet fingers on my butt hole, rubbing the icing around just like he'd done to his dick. This felt really good and I was thinking maybe his dick might not hurt after all. Then he pulled me back and down and his dick was rubbing back and froth across my hole. He was guiding it with his hand. Now, ease down on it, real slow." He was whispering. There was nobody within miles and he was whispering. We were being really naughty now. I was so excited I just sat straight down on it. "Ayah....OH....OH....IT HURTS....IT HURTS," I shouted. The pain was searing, stabbing my hole and small tears came to my eyes. I pulled forward and his prick plopped from the opening.

"Okay, its okay. Take it easy, it'll stop hurting in a second," Bobby pleaded as he massaged my butt cheeks.

I staggered around the bathroom, bent over a couple of times and the pain eased. "Wow, that hurt like hell," I said as I tried to wipe the tears away without Bobby seeing.

"Let's try it again, only very slowly. You can't rush it."

"Okay, but I don't think this is going to work," I squeaked.

This time, after the "icing," (it seemed he'd used a gallon of spit by this time) I held his dick in position and started down again. At first there was no pain, just a pleasant pressure on my hole, but as the shaft parted my hole, the pain was there again. I jumped but didn't yell and the tears weren't coming this time. I moved around a little and the pain disappeared, again.

"Was that any better, Buddy?" he asked. "You almost had it in."

"No....yes....not as bad....but pretty bad, but let's try it again before it dries off."

"That's my Buddy."

I guided it to my hole and as I felt the pressure again, I spread my hole as it slid in.

"Stop, stop," I yelled, as I felt the pain start to return. We froze there for a minute or so. Feeling him raising just a little and the pain returning, I moved away and his dick slipped out of my hole.

As beads of sweat formed on my forehead, I moved back down so that he could shove it into me again. This time he went a little deeper than before. The pain was there but it had dulled to the point of being bearable. He started pushing me off, then back on his dick, going in a little deeper each time.

Bobby moaned and groaned as he slowly worked the big dick deeper and deeper into my butt. When I tensed from the pain, he would stop and pull back.

Finally, he was all the way in and we were still for a little bit before he started to move inside me. He held my body still as he worked his dick in and out, slow and easy, sending it very deep. Then he started to move me opposite to his movements and soon he was getting real hot and pumped me very fast; the pain was getting harder to bear. I was about to cry out when he pulled me off him. I turned around and watched as he jacked his dick.

This was the best part so far: he was turning red, his body was jerking wildly and a fountain of jism came pouring out.

Bobby did the "icing" thing again, but it wasn't spit he was spreading this time.

I'd never seen it. None of us had actually made any jism when we jacked off in the hayloft.

Very efficiently, Bobby got up, took a wash cloth and wiped off his dick, rinsed it out and gave it to me and told me to wipe my butt. It stung a little as I wiped. Bobby rinsed the wash cloth again and threw it into the dirty clothes hamper. Then, as if we had just been swimming or something, he said, "Put your clothes on and let's get a Coke."

I liked being that close, being hugged, making Bobby happy and it got easier each time. We did it every time we got the chance. Once I told him he couldn't do it to me unless he let me do it to him. He tried it but didn't like it, but I still let him do it to me as often as he wanted.

Before long, Bobby was joining Ricky and Mike and me in the hayloft and he wasn't shy any more about taking his clothes off. We showed the other guys what we were doing and each of them had to do to me what Bobby did. I would lie on a bale of hay with my legs up and they'd come over a shove it in or I'd stand over the bale and they'd come up behind me and have their fun. A few times Bobby actually came while he had his dick up my butt, but mostly they'd all do it to me and then gather around me and let their jism drop all over my body, mixing with mine when I came. It always seemed that no matter how big we got, Bobby was always bigger and had a bigger load. I still think it had something to do with his having only one nut.

Oral sex or "getting off" while being fucked never entered our minds, not until later. For the other guys, it was just a substitute for the girl they really wanted. They all married and had families. I was best man for Mike and was in Bobby's wedding party. And I still see them when I visit my parents down on the farm. I have never married, of course, but they never ask why; perhaps they know.

Southern boys have learned a lot in the past forty years. For instance, perhaps you noticed, I didn't use the term "cock" in this memoir. For whatever reason, all of us at that time and place used the term "cock" for a girl's pussy. We would say, "I bet she has a tight cock." It was a long time before I found out that southerners had the terms confused, and apparently the confusion is over. I guess it all got straightened out when Southern boys went into the service and learned about "cocksuckers."

SOMETHING FOR THE TEACHER
Jesse G. Monteagudo

I teach American history at a small community college in a Midwestern state. Each semester, I deal with forty nondescript nineteen-year-olds who couldn't care less about American History but who need to take it as a requirement. More often than not, I have to interrupt a lecture in order to stop a student from talking to his girlfriend, filing her nails, playing with his Game Boy, or taking a nap.

Though I have been gay as long as I can remember, I never had a lover, or much of a sex life, for that matter. Looks have nothing to do with it, for I manage to keep myself in shape with regular visits to the gym. It's just that, in this small town, opportunities for sex are hard to find. There was a time when the men's room in the library had a well-earned reputation as a sexual hot spot. However, as a young instructor who was seeking tenure, I did not dare go near the place, for fear of being caught by campus security. In any case, when the present Dean (a devout Mormon) took office, he immediately cracked down on tea room sex to such an extent that nobody uses the men's room any more, not even for ordinary purposes.

You probably want to know if I ever had sex with any of my students. For a long time the answer was no. None of my kids seemed worth the conflict of interest, not to mention the wrath of the administration. My sex life was limited to fifty-mile trips to the nearest gay bar and annual vacations in New York, San Francisco and Chicago. My life, such as it was, consisted of teaching, grading papers, working out at the gym, eating, reading, beating off, and sleeping. This routine would have been mine for life but for the day that Jon Wade walked into my classroom.

Though Jon Wade is an ordinary name, Jon himself is anything but ordinary. He is an Amerasian, the son of Jon Wade, Sr. and a Vietnamese woman he knocked up while on duty in 'Nam during the early '70s. Most of our G.I.s who were in such predicaments simply abandoned their bastards once their tours of duty were over but the senior Wade, a conscientious father if nothing else, sent for his offspring just before the Vietcong chased our troops out of South Vietnam. Young Jon's mother, who had problems of her own, was glad to let her unwanted son go.

Once in the states, Jon lived with his father and his wife Amanda, who put up a front but who obviously disliked this constant reminder of her husband's infidelities. Jon Wade, Jr. grew up to be a brilliant boy and an accomplished athlete, with a shelf load of swimming and martial arts medals to prove it. Like many Amerasians, Jon is a striking beauty, who combines his father's build with his mother's features. When I first met him, he was barely nineteen, at the height of his physical beauty and well aware of the effect his looks had on others.

I was struck by those looks on the first day of class, when Jon sauntered in in the company of an admiring female. He wore a tight white T-shirt and tight white jeans, which only accentuated his shiny black hair, dark, almond-shaped eyes, swimmer's build, tight buns and tasty crotch. Before I knew it Jon grabbed a chair in the front row, right in front of my lectern, and sat in it, his legs spread wide and inviting. I immediately canceled my plans to seat the students by alphabetical order (which would have sent Wade to the back row) and allowed them to stay wherever they were for the remainder of the course.

From that day on, Jon stood out like a sore thumb (though one very becoming). Too clever by far, he went out of his way to show his contempt for American History, try as I did to make it interesting for him. Often it seemed that I was playing to an audience of one student who would, from his front row center seat, alternatively beckon, tease, smirk, reject and ignore my attention. I tried to ignore him as best as I could, not just because I had a job to do but because the scamp was obviously trying to get my goat. Besides, I thought, the guy was obviously straight, since he was always surrounded by one or two admiring females.

What made things worse was the fact that Jon was no dumb jock, more interested in his biceps than in books. Athletic as the boy might be, he was definitely not dumb. There was more to Jon Wade than swimming and martial arts: computers, electronics, dancing, music and poetry, to say nothing of keeping much of the female population (and at lease one male faculty member) enthralled. Jon became my obsession as I began to attend swimming meets and martial arts competitions, just to see the my hero in action. However, try as I would, I could not get Jon interested in American History.

"But Professor, why do we have to learn all this? I mean, what does it have to do with my ability to get a job?" Our golden boy had missed another deadline, and needed more time to finish his paper on the Battle of Gettysburg. But it was a hot day, and Jon was wearing a rather fetching tank top and cut-offs. I couldn't be rough on the kid.

"Because, Mr. Wade, if we don't study the mistakes of the past we are likely to repeat them. Look at the War of Vietnam. We thought we could go in and save another country without asking if they wanted to be saved. And this mistake we keep repeating." The War in Vietnam made Jon possible. Talk about a silver lining. Changing the subject, I asked how his parents were.

"I never see them. Dad is never around, and Amanda keeps getting on my nerves. But I don't have to deal with them much these days, since I moved to the dorms."

"Which means you have more time to study," I added, extending the deadline for a student paper for the first time in my teaching career.

"Thanks, Professor. You won't regret it." With his words on my ears, Jon turned away, giving me a parting shot of his luscious buns and masculine thighs.

This wasn't the first or last time I bent the rules to accommodate young Mr. Wade. The paper on the Battle of Gettysburg was careless and sloppy, but I discovered enough originality and interest in it to give it a passing grade. His book report, ostensibly about David McCullough's biography of Harry S. Truman, had more than a passing resemblance to a review in the local paper, but it had such interesting insights on the Man from Independence that I gave it an OK. However, the "final exam," actually given a week before classes ended, was another matter. Twenty correct answers out of fifty questions do not make a passing grade, no matter how fond the teacher might be of that particular student.

"But Professor, I tried, I really tried. Give me one more chance," pleaded Jon, who was wearing tight bicycle riding shorts for the occasion.

"Mr. Wade, I've been given you 'one more chance' all semester long," I replied, taking in the sights. "But I'll tell you what. You are a product of American history, whether you like it or not. You have until the last class to write me a five-page essay about yourself. Your parents. Where you came from. And so forth. You have an interesting story to tell, so go tell it! Read it in front of the class tomorrow and it might serve in lieu of a final exam."

"I don't know," Jon sputtered, suddenly vulnerable. "I don't need to be reminded where I came from. From Amanda. My half-brothers. My 'friends'. Even my old man." I inadvertently touched a sore spot. Jon knew what it was like to be "different", just as I knew what it was like to be "different".

"But that's what makes you special." And so appealing, I wanted to add. "You have a personal history that is different from anyone in your class. Let them know about it."

"You are a smart young man," I continued. You obviously don't like American History because you think it has nothing to do with you. Here is a part of American History that has a lot to do with you. Tell us about it."

Jon looked at me, smiled, and nodded. "You're right, Professor. I'll do it. I'll see you in class."

The rest, as they say, is history. The next day, Jon gave a report to the class that kept even the most somnolent student awake. He talked about being a byproduct of the Vietnam War, about his distant mother, his enigmatic father, his American family and his introduction to American society. He got a round of applause, a kiss from a girlfriend, and a thumbs up from yours truly. So that was it, I said to myself. I would give him a passing grade, and I would never see him again. The administration would give me grief for giving a student preference, and it would all be for naught.

That afternoon I stayed late in my office to wrap things up for the semester. I was surprised to look up and see Jon standing on my door, asking to come in. I did, not noticing that Jon closed the door behind him as he came in.

"Professor, I came to thank you for what you did for me. Not only did you give me a passing grade when no other teacher would have done it but you gave American History meaning for me. And you got me to do something I was afraid of doing for so long. You got me to be open about who I am and where I came from."

"Well, thank you, Jon. That's what teachers are here for."

"Well, I want to show you my gratitude. I have something for you." Without a word, Jon removed his clothes and came towards me.

I could not believe my eyes. I had seen his bare torso before, his smooth swimmer's body packed with youthful muscle. And I hungered for his firm, masculine thighs, the product of hours of swimming and karate practice. But I was not prepared for what awaited me when he removed his shorts. Nestled in a bed of dark pubic hair was a healthy, neatly-circumcised cock that pointed in my direction. But what really got my juices flowing was the sight of Jon's low-hanging balls, like two ripe plums ready for my picking.

I stood up. We smiled at each other, our unspoken "deal" about to be consummated. He knew what I wanted all along, though he kept it from me until the end, as a tease perhaps and certainly as a bargaining chip. I had kept my end of this unspoken bargain, and it was now his turn. Without a word I reached out, taking his cock with one hand and his balls with the other. He moaned softly as I stroked his perfect genitals, getting him as aroused as I was.

He surrendered himself to my attentions, leaning back against a bookshelf while I removed my clothes. My own cock throbbed in anticipation as I knelt before to worship this young god, who spread his golden thighs apart to allow me his maleness. His cock beckoned at me as I took it deep inside my mouth and down my throat, a hot pillar of flesh that filled my insides with pleasure. My hands continued to massage his inner thighs as I sucked on his dick, closing in towards the center of his maleness. He groaned as I worked on his body, surrendering himself completely to his teacher's experienced mouth and hands.

Having made a mess of the bookcase (not that I cared), I guided my student over to my chair, where I continued my assault on his lower body. Taking some oil from my desk, I gently massaged his cock, driving him wild with unbridled passion. I kept up the stroking with my left hand, while with my right I reach down to grease and stroke my own hard dick. his thighs spread further apart, allowing me greater access to the treasure within. His masculine scent wafted through my nostrils, intoxicating me beyond reason.

Having paid homage to his champion cock, I proceeded to give his full balls the workout that they deserved. Without skipping a beat, I took the young athlete's nuts in my mouth, savoring each low hanging sack. I licked above, below and in between his testicles, all the while keeping his dick hard with my strokes. His gasps of pleasure indicated that he was enjoying the workout on his balls as much I enjoyed giving it to them.

I kept my oral assault on his man eggs for some time, keeping them wet and shiny with my expert tongue and working my way around his scrotum, reaching beneath them to give them the treatment that they deserve. This made Jon lose all control, pushing me closer to his maleness, begging me to go on. It was obvious that I was giving him the workout of his young life. Only a man knows how to work another man's cock and balls and soon his groans of pleasure let me know that he was at the point of no return. I held his cock firm with my left hand and pumped him fiercely, while burrowing deeper beneath his balls with my mouth and tongue. Giving himself up to the pleasure that engulfed him, my student let out a yell and a geyser of jism that spilled over my face, the floor, the chair, the desk and the bookcase. It was more than I could stand. Still holding on to his genitals, I jerked out a full load of my own man milk.

Seconds passed. I stood up to face him, our mutual smiles attesting to our mutual pleasures. Without a word, the student I lusted for a whole semester pulled me over and gave me a deep, passionate kiss, a kiss I was quick to reciprocate.

In a few minutes, we broke the barriers that kept us apart. We were no longer white and Amerasian, student and teacher, nineteen year-old and thirty-something. We were just two hot men, basking in the pleasures we took from each other's bodies.

This might have been the beginning of the end, but in fact it was the beginning of the beginning. As it turned out, he needed an unofficial "counselor"; one whom he could get together with once a week for intimate, one-to-one sessions. Though Jon was not a history major, I readily agreed. And he never missed a single "counseling" session.

The new semester begins this week and Jon discovered that his increased course load requires a larger place for him to live and study than the ever more overcrowded dorms. He's moving in tomorrow.

MY FIRST MAN
Frank Brooks

It was a muggy spring morning on the golf course, rain threatening, and I was on the practice putting green, waiting for an opportunity to tee off. I hadn't reserved a tee time and was waiting for a friendly group to come along that I could join. As usual during my high school years on the golf course, I was dressed scantily, wearing only a pair of tight, threadbare, faded blue jeans – no underwear, no shoes, no shirt – and I was well aware of the effect I had on other golfers, men and women alike, who appreciated boyish looks and a lithe physique. I was always self-consciously aware of how I looked and moved, especially while trying to appear the opposite – nonchalant, natural, innocently unaware of my sexiness and boyish charm – but I doubt I ever fooled anybody.

Suddenly I was aware of eyes on me, trailing down my slender fingers, touching my tightly muscled back, misted with sweat, my rounded pecs, my smooth flanks and tight, boxed buttocks, my sexy bare feet and wide-spread toes. When I glanced up, my admirer looked quickly away and concentrated on his putting stroke. He was a handsome, dark-haired man in his forties, dressed like a touring pro. His tanned forearms were covered with sun-bleached hairs.

Bending over to retrieve my ball from the hole, I gave him a good look at my upturned ass and sensed his eyes all over it. Straightening up, I tossed my blond forelock out of my eyes with a jerk of my head and glanced his way again. He pretended to be looking past me, down the first fairway, then lowered his head for another putt. I smiled at his attempt to hide his interest. My dick stirred in my jeans.

He certainly wasn't the first man who had paid attention to me – I'd started noticing the furtive and not-so-furtive glances of men years ago – he was certainly the best looking, and my heart started pounding at the wild idea of giving myself to him. I'd never given my body to a man before – not that I hadn't had fantasies of doing so. I had just never encountered a man who at the time made me want to make it with him like this man did.

Boys were another story. I'd been making it with other boys for a long time, since boys were what really turned me on. Men I found intriguing, but not a great turn-on. When I did fantasize about making it with a man, I pictured myself in the arms of a real stud, with my slender frame tight against his huge muscles. My only experience with a female was with Olga, a buxom, thirty-year-old I'd met in a park some time ago. She teased me about the way I always watched myself in her mirrored walls while bouncing between her legs. I was more interested in the pretty boy in the mirror, she told me, than in the naked woman beneath me and I couldn't deny it.

A twosome I could have joined teed off, but I was enjoying myself too much on the putting green to ask if I could go with them. My observer was starting to ogle me more openly now, letting his eyes linger a few extra seconds before turning away when I caught him looking. I gave him a show by stretching, thrusting both arms high overhead while contracting the muscles of my torso. Sweat trickled down my flanks from my armpits, which were decorated with only a few sprigs of recently sprouted hair. My body was completely smooth otherwise except for the silky blond tuft at the base of my cock, which at this moment was half-hard in my jeans. As the man resumed putting, he took a quick glance back at the bulge and moistened his lips with his tongue. His putt missed by a mile.

Soon it started to sprinkle and golfers on the clubhouse terrace ran for shelter. The foursome about to tee off fled back to the clubhouse. My observer put an umbrella over his head and moved toward the first tee. I gathered up my clubs and scampered after him.

"Mind if I join you?"

"No," he said, "if you don't mind getting wet."

We shook hands and introduced ourselves. His name was Paul.

We teed off and our balls flew to opposite sides of the fairway. By the time I reached mine, I was thoroughly drenched. The rain felt like warm bath water. My jeans clung like a straightjacket and I wanted to tear them off and golf naked. When I reached the first green Paul laughed at me and said I looked like a drowned rat.

The rain came down so hard that by the time we teed off on the second hole we had the course to ourselves. When we reached the third tee with its gazebo-like shelter, Paul was as drenched as I was.

"Let's sit this out awhile," he said.

We sat side-by-side on a bench in the little shelter watching sheets of rain water slide off the roof. We were on the most-secluded tee on the course, surrounded on three sides by woods, and I felt secure and happy sitting next to Paul, who seemed about twice my size and three times my age, probably as old as my father. I leaned against him, almost resting my head against his shoulder, trying to entice him to put his arm around me. Instead, he jumped up and started doing exercises and jogging in place, as if he was trying to warm up.

'Take your shirt off," I said. "It's that wet shirt makes you shiver. Look at me, I'm not cold."

"At your age you could walk out in a blizzard without your shirt on and not be cold," he said. "It's that all that – " He hesitated, smiled, then went on, "Young blood."

When he took his shirt off, he was more muscular than I'd imagined and the amount of dark hair on his chest and abdomen. That also surprised me and, in a strange way, thrilled me, being such a contrast to the boyish smoothness I was used to. When he noticed me ogling him, his face reddened and he dropped down to do pushups. I had the urge to sit on his lower back and ride him, feeling the muscles of his back as he moved up and down. When he couldn't do another pushup, he stood up and leaned against a corner post, gazing out at the rain. Sweat was running down his back. I wanted to lick it off.

"Forty-five," I said. "Not bad."

"One for every year of my life," he said without looking at me. "Next year I'll do forty-six."

I stepped up onto the bench and started reading the graffiti on the roof beams.. I'd read them so many times before I about knew them by heart. "Listen to what somebody wrote up here – " I said, and started reading them aloud. Some of the entries were dated decades ago. I read him a couple of the dirty ones. He chuckled but didn't turn around. "Hey, here's one from thirty years ago, when you were a teenager like me: 'It rained and rained and we were trapped here for hours and we got bored, so we pulled out our pricks and jacked off in unison. Signed, Billy and Paul."

"Ha," he said after a pause. "You made that up."

"I did not. Come, see for yourself."

He was tall enough that he didn't have to step up on the bench to read. "You just wrote it then."

"I did not, it's always been there. I bet you wrote it thirty years ago. Your name is Paul, isn't it?"

"You've got quite the imagination."

As he started to move away I clasped my hands behind my head, yawning and stretching, and he paused to watch. I posed like a muscleman, showing him my armpits. His nostrils flared when he got a whiff of boy. In the middle of another yawn, I asked, "Well, you wanna do it?"

"Do what?"

"What Billy and Paul did thirty years ago."

His face turned crimson and he looked out onto the fairway.

I opened my jeans and pushed them to my knees. My rigid cock throbbed, a drop of lubricant oozing from the slit in my excitement. The breeze sliced between my legs as I stepped out of my jeans and kicked them off the bench. He turned his head and his eyes followed every twitch and wiggle of my cock as if it were a dancing boy.

"God, that feels better." I ran my fingertips up and down my hard, flat belly.

He was breathing heavily, as if he were running a race, and he shrugged. "Well, remember, you asked for it." His back to me, he removed his trousers, then his boxer shorts. As he turned to face me again, my mouth dropped open at the sight of his hard cock, which looked about as long as my forearm, with a knob as big as my fist.

"Man! It's a fucking monster!" I howled.

He started to laugh, I started to laugh, and suddenly we had our arms around each other – me still standing on the bench, him on the ground – and then I kissed him, giving him some tongue, and that changed everything. Our laughs turned to growls and moans and we started kissing and making out like a pair love-crazy schoolboys.

"Baby," he said, stroking my head. "Sweet baby." He covered my face and throat and pees with kisses. He raised my arms and licked my armpits, sucking at the flesh. He sucked my nipples and nuzzled down my belly. His dripping tongue lapped at my balls and perineum. His lips and mouth slipped over my cock.

"Daddy," I moaned, my toes curling with the sensation, and I sank my cock down his throat. "Oh, suck it, daddy!"

He sucked expertly, rotating his tongue just where I like it best and driving me wild. I hugged his head and fucked his mouth as if it were Olga's cunt or a boy's asshole. Paul's lips smacked as he sucked greedily for my cum. The sensation was fantastic. I wanted it to last forever but I couldn't hold off.

"Coming!" I gasped. Humping like a jackrabbit, I exploded down Paul's gullet, my cock flexing and squirming with each ejaculation, my toes clawing at the bench top. The pleasure was almost more than I could bear.

Paul swallowed every drop and continued sucking after I'd stopped squirting. I whimpered and my eyes nearly popped out. My cock was so sensitive that the sucking was almost painful, but I gritted my teeth until at last the excruciating sensitivity of my cock lessened and I felt my lust mounting again. Paul released my cock.

"You sure fuck a load," he said, kissing me. He let me suck his tongue, coated with boy-spunk, then he lifted me off the bench as if I weighed nothing and set me on the ground. He turned me around and bent me over and I braced my hands on the bench. His cock slid up and down between my asscheeks like a slippery rattlesnake. He was going to fuck me and I knew it would split me in half but I wanted it.

"Oh, daddy, oh, daddy," I said, wiggling my ass.

"Squeeze your legs together."

I did as I was told and he slipped his cock between my thighs. Holding me by the hips, he started to fuck. "Work your thighs together. Make me feel it. Christ you're smooth!"

When I saw his blood-gorged knob popping in and out under my balls, its open pisshole dripping lubricant, I forgot all about my initial reaction, which was disappointment that he wasn't fucking me up the ass. I reached up and played with his sizzling cockhead, catching some of his lubricant on my fingers so I could taste it. I found it stronger and saltier than the sweet, sappy-tasting dick-lube of boys.

"Oh, fuck me, daddy!" I moaned, urging him on. I shimmied my legs together and wiggled my ass. My cock was glued to my belly like a hot bone. "Fuck me, daddy!"

Paul hunched forward over me, his humping quick and rhythmic, his cock torpedoing between my legs. He hugged me around the loins, gnawed the back of my neck, and with a violent shudder began to squirt. A white jet exploded from his pisshole and splashed in my face. I giggled. Paul grunted and fired again, then again and again, shooting sperm into my open mouth and onto the bench top. His last spurts hit my feet and ran down my legs. I scooped up man-spunk and sucked it off my fingers, savoring the thick, slimy feel of it on my tongue. I wiped up a handful of the slippery fluid and slapped it on my cock. When Paul got off me I told him to bend over and spread his ass. He looked at my rigid cock dripping with his cum and, after a few moments of hesitation, shrugged and did as I'd asked. He had a hairy crack and a fat, moist pucker and I leaned over to lick it. He moaned as my tongue slipped up his hole.

"You filthy little animal!" he sighed. "Oh yeah-h-h!"

I could have licked him out all day but my dick was screaming for release and I was afraid I'd pop off against the backs of his legs if I didn't watch it. I pulled my tongue out of him and mounted his ass, shoving my spunk-dripping dick between his asscheeks and pressing hard against his pucker. After several seconds, my dickhead slipped inside him, followed by the rest of my cock. I was getting off on just the sight of my ivory-smooth boy-cock disappearing up his hairy man-ass. The two of us moaned in unison.

I held him by the hips and started fucking, thrilled by his muscular buttocks and the way his asshole gripped my cock. The hairy pucker added extra friction, making it feel as if I were skinning my cock alive with each screwing thrust. I let go and fucked like a barbarian, grunting and growling with each ramming penetration. The intense pleasure brought tears to my eyes.

You filthy little animal!" Paul gasped. "Fuck me!"

His words brought me to a climax. Humping out of control, jerking like a rag doll, I began to ejaculate up his asshole. It was as if I'd plugged my cock into an electric socket. I whimpered like a baby, clutching the man around the loins and bucking against him, pumping hot boy-cream up his ass.

Paul let out a groan and his asshole began to contract. His right arm was jerking and spurts of his cum shot onto the shelter floor. I almost fainted as his asshole sucked my unbearably sensitive cock. It was a relief to finally pull my cock out of him.

We stood in the puddle of his cum, hugging each other and kissing. "You beast," he said. "You've corrupted me." "You've never had a boy fuck you?"

"Not by a long-shot," he said.

The rain had stopped. I was all for continuing our lovemaking, telling him that if he'd never had a boy before he should start making up for lost time right now, but he was nervous about other golfers coming along. We got dressed and continued with our game but neither of us could concentrate on hitting the ball so after nine holes we called it quits.

"I don't have time for the back nine, anyway," he said. "I'm expected at home."

I nodded. The fact that he wore a wedding ring did not go unnoticed. I asked him when we could see each other again and after some hemming and hawing he finally wrote something on his scorecard and started to hand it to me, but before I could take it he tucked it in his back pocket.

"Maybe we ought to just meet out here again sometime."

"When?"

"I can't say – but keep a lookout for me, okay?"

"Okay."

All that spring and summer, I watched for him and, as the weeks passed, my disappointment at not seeing him turned to resignation. I finally told myself that I'd never see him again, that I should just forget him. I was right about never seeing him again, but as for forgetting him, how could I? He was, after all, my first man.

MY FIRST DAY AS A HUSTLER
Michael Cardwell

The man who let me into the room at the Holiday Inn was about forty. He wasn't unattractive, just what Louie had told me to expect, an average-looking businessman in town for a little fun. But what really surprised me was the sudden revelation that there was a second man in the room, sitting in the armchair next to the window. I figured he was only a couple of years older than me and he was gorgeous, with blond, curly hair and blue eyes that magically reflected the smallest hint of light. He was wearing a tank top so I could see he was very well built, especially his arms, which looked like they were carved from ivory.

"I'm Hank," the older man said, then pointing to the young hunk in the chair, "This is Luther, he's travels with me. I should have mentioned on the phone that there were two of us. I suppose there'll be an increase in price."

"Yes," I mumbled, "I guess." The only thing that really mattered to me at that moment was getting my hands on Luther's body. My mouth went dry in eager anticipation.

Hank poured himself a stiff drink, then stood next to the window. 'Well, there's no point in wasting your valuable time. I'm just going to stand here for the moment while Luther takes care of you. I'll be joining you in a bit."

"Sure." I said, my voice cracking. This was not what I had expected, in more ways than one.

Without speaking, Luther stood up and walked over to me. I held my breath, not having the slightest clue of what I was supposed to do next. Luther undid the fly on his jeans and pulled out a cock larger than anything I had ever created in my filthiest fantasies. It had to have been a good eleven inches long and three inches wide, and it wasn't even fully erect; it just sort of hung out of his pants and the veins along the shaft bulged with anticipation. I just stood there staring at that cock. Luther placed his arms on my shoulders and forced me down to my knees until my face was parallel with his huge organ. He grabbed the back of my head and forced my face into his crotch. It smelled of musky sweat; it wasn't an unpleasant scent, on the contrary, it was one the best things I'd ever had the pleasure of ramming my nose into.

"Lick my balls," Luther instructed, in almost a whisper.

I didn't have to be told twice to start licking those balls. I began licking his huge, hairy balls, succumbing to the delicious salty taste that instantly gave me an erection. My tongue danced hungrily against those balls and then up along that thick shaft with magical delight. More than anything I wanted to take that huge cock into my mouth, but just as I was about to, Luther pushed me away. I knelt there, confused by this sudden turn of events and watched as Luther turned around and pulled his pants down far enough to reveal his solid, shaved ass.

He bent over. "Lick it, kid. Lick that ass."

I've got to admit that the thought of it sort of frightened me. I'd never envisioned licking someone's asshole before and I wasn't really that sure that I wanted to do it, but it was, after all, my job.

"Do it!" Luther snapped as he reached back and separated his asscheeks to reveal his dark pink hole.

I leaned forward and gingerly ran my tongue along the crevice. It tasted sort of acidic, but it didn't smell bad.

"Stick your tongue in deep. Yeah, like that. Use your teeth, Now, I don't want you to just lick it, I want you to eat it out. Oh yeah, that's right. Eat it. That's right. Now you're earning your money."

I buried my face between his cheeks and began to do as he asked; he moaned in appreciation. I could feel my own cock pushing desperately against my jeans. It felt like an hour had passed while I ate that hole before, again, Luther surprised me by pulling away. He drew his pants back up until just his dick hung out.

As I wiped my mouth, he stepped closer to me and dangled that huge instrument of his in my face. There was no way that I was going to be denied my one true desire so I lunged forward and took his pulsating cock into my mouth, stretching my lips to their limit as it slid deep into my hungry throat.

Luther grabbed a handful of my hair and began to pilot my head, sliding my mouth up and down his huge shaft. It hurt a bit and I thought I was going to gag a few times when it hit the back of my throat, but I really didn't mind; all I wanted at that moment was for an explosion of cum to fill my throat and give me the experience that I had frequently envisioned during my many hours of self-pleasure.

But once again Luther pushed me away as if I was nothing more than a mechanical device, which I suppose, as a hired hand, I was. "Take off all your clothes," he commanded, beginning to pull on his cock.

This was the part that I was really dreading, terrified they would laugh at my teenaged, undeveloped physique, or at my prick, which was only about six inches long and surrounded by the tiniest amount of black pubic hair. Slowly I pulled off my T-shirt and placed it carefully on the edge of the bed. Then I removed my rotting sneakers and soiled gym socks and set them down against the wall. I hesitated momentarily before undoing my pants and allowing them to drop to the floor around my ankles. Neither of them laughed; in fact, they smiled contentedly. Slowly I lowered my briefs and my erection bobbed up to greet them.

Hank chuckled, "Where does Louie find these cute little boys?"

Luther, all business, barked, "Bend over the bed."

In moments, my eyes closed, I felt Luther's huge cock sliding up and down the crack of my ass, teasing me. I tensed. Then I felt nothing. Then I turned around to see Luther placing a condom on his dick, though it only slid two-thirds of the way down its amazing length. As he approached me, I turned away and held my breath. This is my job, I kept remembering. I felt the tip of his cock poke gently at the entrance of my hole and soon I was thinking, Hey, this isn't so bad. He pushed it in a half of an inch and I gritted my teeth as it was already hurting a bit. I was about to tell him to stop, but with a single breath, he shoved that massive cock deep inside of me. I: screamed out in pain; it felt like I was being torn apart. Luther slapped me in the side of the head which made me stop screaming, and I just stood there, hunched over the bed, in shock. He began to ease out and just when I thought he was going to stop, he rammed himself back into me.

"Come on you little piece of shit. Take that cock deep like a man. Yeah, just like that."

I began choking as he thrust himself into me again and again. Then I opened my eyes to see Hank climbing on the bed in front of me. He was naked and muscular. He edged up until his cock was parallel to my face. He slid his slender, eight-inch long erection into my mouth and began to fuck my face, matching Luther's ferocity stroke for stroke. I felt like I was having a wild dream; the sensations overwhelming me. But before long, Hank pulled his cock from my mouth and let it hang there momentarily; he wasn't even touching it when cum began flooding out and splashing me in the face and in my hair.

Luther also pulled out and, turning my head, I saw him, with one swift motion, yank the condom off of his cock and send a stream of cum flowing down my back and on my sore ass. He then grabbed me by the arm and turned me over on the bed, forcing me onto my back. He produced another condom and fitted it on my cock that now was sticking straight up, begging for attention as it never had before.

I watched in astonishment as he climbed on top of me and, with little effort, sat on my cock. I couldn't help but moan as I felt the heat from his asshole surround my dick. He began bouncing on top of me like a madman. Hank pulled my legs up until my knees were next to Luther's bouncing hips, then stuck his finger up my asshole. I gasped.

Hank fucked me with his fingers for awhile, then produced a dildo that was even bigger than Luther's dick. It looked real, with big purple veins and a convincing slit at the top. Hank disappeared behind Luther and with one determined shove, planted that dildo up my ass. My whole body began to tremble as Hank plowed away at my hole as Luther bounced up and down on my cock. When I felt my own cum preparing to spurt out, I squealed pathetically which made Luther bounce even faster as he began jerking his monster cock, already hard again. I thought I was going to black out when I ejaculated into the condom that was buried deep in Luther's asshole. Luther sprayed another geyser of cum all over my chest and face. I opened my mouth and caught a few drops on my tongue and eagerly swallowed them.

With almost parental gentleness, Hank removed the dildo from my ass and Luther lifted up and let my cock plop from the opening. "Yeah, Louie finds the best, doesn't he, Luther?"

Luther, grunting, fell back on the double bed next to me and rolled over.

A mess of cum and sweat, I asked to use the shower and, as I stood under the warm spray, still trembling with the shock of it all, I decided that even if I wasn't going to be paid double, I was more than compensated. What a way to begin my career as a hustler! And, as it turned out, I forgot to ask for any money at all because when I walked back into the bedroom, Luther was stretched out on the double bed and he had a raging hard-on again. This time, he was smiling and...

MY FOUR SAILORS
Terry Cross

Guys always ask me why I have this lifetime penchant for seafood. I reply it probably stems from having grown up in Norfolk, Virginia – the seafood capital of the world. I've become somewhat of a gourmet in this matter over the years but space permits me to share only four delicacies.

I found one of these four right in Norfolk. When my brother was away at music camp and my parents had driven up to get him, I found myself alone and bored on a Saturday evening. I decided to go to the Ocean View amusement park, a couple of miles away. I wasn't there long before a sailor caught my eye. My mind has lost the details of the pickup, but the next thing I remember we were under a secluded bush and I was giving him a blowjob.

What made him special was that, unlike most men in my experience, after he came he showed no desire to get the hell out of there, so we started talking. Bobby was, like me, just a teenager. Short and muscular, he was an alumnus of an Ohio orphanage and while I had been sexually active with other boys for about seven years, Bobby was to be the first person to spend the night with me. Before long we were in my big double bed (inherited from my grandmother) and I was blowing him again. His cut peter was in perfect proportion to his body and while he loved being blown, was not into cuddling; he was just a sweet piece of trade. Later he fucked me. This was my second time for that, my anal cherry having been copped by another 13-year-old four years earlier (appropriately enough, the "copper" was of Greek extraction).

When we awoke the next morning, I blew Bobby again. Then I fixed breakfast and, just as we were finishing we heard the crunch of tires on the gravel driveway – my folks were home early! As they came in the back door, I hustled Bobby out the front. How I explained two sets of dishes on the table I don't remember. Bobby didn't show up for a subsequent date, a facet of gay life I was to learn over the years to come. My lasting memory of him is his wallet, which he had made from leather with the hair still on it, brown and white.

Another sailor who especially caught my fancy was Rod. I met him when I was 24 and living in Boston, where we were fortunate enough to have a naval presence until "Tricky Dick" Nixon closed the base down. Rod was another short 17-year-old, a farm boy from Wisconsin who was part Dakota Indian. He was in blues and wandering around the Esplanade by the Charles River looking for something to do. I was delighted to take him home. His face was rather plain but he had a beautifully muscular body. His peter was larger than Bobby's and uncut, though the skin wasn't tight and went back nicely. He was basically trade, too – no mugging up. But he sure loved sex and managed six distinct, productive orgasms in about an hour. I was sucking away for number seven but my jaw was getting tired. Besides, I had been fingering his asshole during the previous two blowjobs and he was responding beautifully, so I asked if I could fuck him and he surprised me by saying yes. After I deposited my load about eight inches up inside him, he decided that was about as much as he could take for one night. He dressed and left, still carrying the load.

In 1960, when I was about to board a plane in Portland, Oregon I noticed my third memorable sailor. It was open seating and I was number two in line. As boarding began for the long night flight, I hung back saying my goodbyes so the sailor, in blues, would be seated when I boarded. I fear I was a bit obvious when I stood in the aisle asking him if the seat next to him was taken when every other seat on the plane was empty. Once airborne, we settled in and started playing kneesies. A blanket covered the two of us and as my fingers slipped toward paradise I was surprised to find that the sailor, who introduced himself as Bob, had already unbuttoned the side of the flap on his 13-button blues. Another piece of trade, uncut but loose, and relatively small but hot! And yes, another eager 17-year-old!

While playing around, I noticed the toilet not far in front of us had a useful defect: the "in use" light didn't go on when the door was locked. So I hit on a stratagem. Bob went to the toilet, then came back a moment later and asked me how it worked. I went in with him, locked the door, gave him a blowjob that probably took all of thirty seconds (yes, he was hot), and then returned to my seat while he stayed in the toilet an appropriate interval. Once we were snuggled into our seats again, I gave him a hand job, and yet another one just before we landed in Chicago. Bob stuck a bit more than the others and we corresponded sporadically for about ten years. He was straight and later married and divorced. We did get together once more years later, when we happened to be in Norfolk at the same time. But, sadly, this time the sex wasn't particularly exciting and it signaled the end of our relationship.

In 1964, at 29, I took a cruise on the Homerica, a ship of the Italian Line. My expectations of the crew were high, but nothing developed. After steaming into Nassau, we stayed there for about 24 hours. I discovered that Prince Philip was in town dedicating a stadium and the royal yacht Britannia was in port. We had to anchor out of the harbor and come in by tender. My first adventure after watching Philip's motorcade was sucking off an American in his early 20's in the tearoom of a small department store. He was cute and cut and was the plaything of some rich American who lived in Nassau.

Late that evening, on a corner of the main drag, I spied a sailor who seemed to be looking for action. We struck up a conversation and when he said he had been serving on the royal yacht and was horny, things seemed to be moving in the right direction. I did have a scare when a car drove up and the driver tried to sell us sex with the woman in the back seat. In unison, both of us declined. Certainly I had no interest and the sailor probably couldn't afford it. He was typically British, fair and nice-looking, though no raving beauty. But boy was he willing! Eventually the two of us ended up in the backyard of the Bahamian pottery factory about midnight and I began to blow this young man whose name is now lost to me. After a few minutes of sucking on his medium-size, uncut cock, he told me the only way he could get off was by fucking, so I bent over the tailgate of a pickup truck and received his spit-slicked tool. When I made sounds of pain, he assured me that everything would be all right once he "got past the ring," so clearly he was no stranger to such activity. He was right, and in due course deposited a healthy load up my butt. He then made a subtle dive for my wallet which I was able to deflect gracefully. After we parted, I just made the last tender back to the cruise ship. Fortunately, the tender was big enough to have a head, where I blissfully parted company with another souvenir yet another sailor had left inside of me.

WHAT'S YOUR NAME?
Al Lone

The summer between my freshman and sophomore years, I stayed at college, taking a course in machining as part of my engineering curriculum. I spent my days making nuts and bolts and gears, a pretty easy time for me. There wasn't any homework so while the other brothers in my fraternity drifted toward the chapter house to do their studying, I could indulge in some games with the teenagers in the neighborhood.

One evening, at twilight, a group of younger boys was trying to finish a last game of hide and seek. The shrill voices of their mothers' could be heard calling, more and more stridently, for them to come home before dark.

Our game of touch football was breaking up at the same time and I noticed there was one boy who was lagging behind. I had observed him earlier: he hadn't played in the game of hide-and-seek and sat off to the side and watched our game. I could feel his eyes on me during the entire game, but every time I looked in his direction he quickly looked away. I had been aware of him on other occasions hanging on the fringe of the same group of kids, and noticed the others ignored him except for some teasing that I really hadn't been able to hear fully, except a few taunts that came through such as "suck my" or "don't goose me again" which I remembered from my own childhood.

As he approached on the sidewalk just in front of where I was sitting, relaxing on a grassy knoll before going in to bed, he stopped and looked up at me.

He smiled but didn't say anything.

I smiled back and said, "Hi."

"Hi," he said, looking down at his sneakers. Then he lifted his head and said, "I was watching the game. You were the best player out there!"

"Thanks." There were some good athletes in our house, but none of them were there that summer so maybe I did look good by comparison. "Do you have to get home?"

He smiled shyly. "No."

"Then why don't you come up and sit a spell. It's so nice and cool here under the tree."

As he climbed the incline, his eyes never left mine. Sitting beside me on the grass, I had the opportunity to observe him closely for the first time. He was dark-haired, slim, and, although not conventionally handsome, he was attractive, with high cheek bones. And there was a feline quality about his dark eyes that I noticed when he finally looked me full in the face and said, "You must be tired and sore after playing so long."

I had to admit that my back did ache a little from a couple of touches that had turned into near tackles, sending me sprawling to the ground. I fell back completely on the grass. "Yeah, I'm a little sore. I think I might have pulled a muscle in my back," I said, bringing my hand under my torso and rubbing, "but I'll be all right by morning."

My lifting of my body put my crotch directly in his face and from the way he stared at it, I knew for certain he and I were going to, somehow, make beautiful music together.

He looked up from my crotch long enough to ask, his long silky eyelashes fluttering, "Would you like me to rub your back for you? I do that for my Dad sometimes and he says I do it pretty good."

"I'll bet," I said, rolling over, away from him. All was quiet on the block now. The last of the little hide-and-seekers had been captured by their moms and sent to bath and bed. All of my brothers were inside engrossed in their studies. Night had captured the street and there was only a flicker of the dim incandescent streetlight half a block away.

"Do you want me to rub it?" he asked, hesitant still. "I'd love it, but don't you have to be getting home?"

"No. I'm older than those other guys. I get to stay out until nine if I want to."

Resting my chin on my hands, I stared dreamily at the fireflies making ghostly phosphorescent trails across the lawn as he straddled my legs and began a gentle fingertip motion all over my back that soon left pulsing paths of pleasure so intense I shivered from head to toe.

"Are you cold?"

No. That feels really nice. Your father is right, you are good."

"Show me where it hurts the most?"

I stretched to reach my lower back and his hand touched mine briefly. I murmured and as his hands moved busily at my belt line his fingers slipped in and out of the top of my pants. I sighed and closed my eyes giving myself entirely over to the sensations radiating throughout my entire body.

With the rhythm of the boy's caresses, my mind wandered to the evenings spent with Bud at summer camp when we were around thirteen and very into tactility. Anyone who watches "best buddies" at that age will see a lot of touching – constant assurance that the friend is really there adding to the bond that makes you think of him as the last thought before sleep overtakes you at night and the first thing that comes to your waking mind in the morning. Constantly planning time together – wanting him all to yourself – faint vibrations of future jealousies and insecurities if he isn't there that day with you. No matter that he had to go somewhere with his parents – you still ached to be with him, that little emptiness in your heart growing to a chasm by the next day when you could be together again.

Bud and I were like that. We didn't know what it meant, but we knew we were happy together and miserable apart. As all of the boys lay on their bunks joking and yelling near bedtime at camp, Bud and I would give each other back rubs. I could picture him lying under me in his brilliant white jockey shorts. His supple sun-browned skin smoothly undulating under my fingers as I stroked his back finishing every stroke at his favorite place between the bulges at the top of his firm smooth buttocks rising gracefully from his lower back just below the stark tan line left by his skimpy swim trunks. The almost blazing whiteness of the hidden skin revealed nearly ethereal in its purity. Then it would be my turn and we changed places with Bud now sitting across my upper thighs, me closing my eyes and releasing control to allow my excitement to burgeon where it lay hidden under my prone body.

"Hey! Are you sleeping?" he asked.

"Almost. That was wonderful."

"Want to turn over now?'

He moved aside and I slowly rolled over. I could not see his eyes but I could well imagine they were glued to the now obvious bulge at my crotch. He leaned over me and his soft hands begin the same motions on my chest and stomach, titillating my nipples then on down to my lower belly where my erection strained the fabric of my jeans. As his fingers slid coyly down over my groin, he let me know he knew what was there and that he was glad.

At last I knew I could stand no more. I rolled over again and looked up at him. "'Would you like me to return the favor?"

Without speaking, he nodded his head slightly and lay on the ground beside me, his belly pressed to the grass. He had a T-shirt on and I asked if he would like his massage over or under his shirt. Again without speaking, he pulled his shirt up away from his pants and laid his head back on his hands.

I reached out, tentatively at first. Smooth skin layered over developing muscle structure so tightly they were one, skin and muscle united for those few short years before they seem to go their separate ways as youthful bodies lose their vigor to the dissolution of adult habits of too much sitting – not enough living. The glory of youth is to have such bodies without effort – just by being young, happy and a little bit wild, getting everything out of the day right up to the moment of sleep.

I was luxuriating in the warmth and firmness of his body when he turned over to allow me access to his chest and stomach. His excitement, I could now see, matched my own. I moved my hands from his shoulders to his nipples, then to the concave belly and jutting hip lines below. "Would you like it lower?" I whispered.

He nodded.

Quickly my fingers slipped under his beltline, teasing the tip of his throbbing cock.

Suddenly, a car drove by and I pulled my hands free. I had been lost in my passion for the boy; I was not thinking clearly. "It sure is hot. Wouldn't a swim feel great?"'

He sat up, a glazed look of lust in his eyes, then he brightened with excitement and jumped to his feet. "Yeah, I know a place not far from here."

He led the way down the street towards town and as we crossed the road, a couple of frat boys passed us going the other way. When they turned and they could no longer see us, our hands reached out one to the other, guided without words from either side – just the need to touch. As his fingers closed easily in mine, we both let out sighs of contentment.

He turned off the street and took me down a path to railroad tracks and then to a trestle bridge which carried the tracks over a deep gully. We started across the bridge hand in hand, but suddenly he pulled his hand free of mine. I stared into the gloom and could see a figure coming out of a small shack on the other side of the bridge.

I froze.

He whispered close to my ear, "It's okay, just act like you've known me for years. That's John, a friend of Dad's. He won't give us any trouble."

My heart thudding in my chest I hardly heard him greet John as we continued on past the shack. I didn't begin to relax until I felt his hand slip into mine again. Soon we came to the banks of a canal flowing sleepily by into a roar I could hear ahead. "What's that noise?" I asked.

'Where the water goes over the dam into the creek. Don't worry there won't be anyone around down here at this time of night." He moved closer as if to reassure me further and our shoulders brushed together. When we reached the dam, we began to take off our clothes. Both of us stripped to our under shorts, the excitement we both felt was still blatant.

He turned his back to me and pulled off his briefs, tossed them with his other clothes and stepped into the water. Before doing the same, I looked about, saw no one, not even any city lights. There was a thickly wooded hill on the opposite bank that continued past the dam, mirrored on our side of the water beyond the grass some twenty feet away. I slipped off my shorts and followed in his wake. He was about twenty feet upstream and as I started toward him I could see him shivering, his arms clasped around his slim body in water nipple high. I soon closed the gap and said, "You cold?"

"Yes," he chattered.

I came up behind him and pressed my body to his. I put my arms around him and pulled him into an even closer embrace, bringing my hands together in front of him. I moved my hands lower and took his erection in my hand. Even the cold water had not dampened his ardor. He sighed and rested his head back against my shoulder and neck. "Better? I asked.

"Yes, much," he breathed.

He lay in my embrace for several moments and I stroked his cock. Then he turned and faced me, taking my erection in his hands. Looking up into my eyes, he brought his lips to mine. We kissed lightly on the mouth. By now we were both shivering from the chill of the water and the excitement of our encounter. Hand-in-hand, we walked back to shore and dried each other's backs with our T-shirts. Then embraced again. Our hands went instinctively to each other's erections and we stood there, kissing, jacking each other off. He came first, but I quickly followed. We dropped to the ground and lay together with a comfortableness born of our mutually acknowledged passion for each other. In a few moments, my hand went to his cock again and, finding it hard, I began to stroke it once more. I was leaning over, about to take it into my mouth when, suddenly, a booming voice behind us was saying, "Great night for a swim, huh fellows?"

It was his father's friend from the bridge. He was shining a flashlight down on us. I quickly turned my back to him and shot into the grass holding my breath to keep from groaning. By the time I got myself together and turned around to get dressed, the man had gone off, laughing loudly. I could see he was halfway into his trousers, which, I realized he was trying to put on backwards. It was a sight I would laugh about later but at the time I was too frightened to do anything but jump back in my clothes and head out of there. We were quiet as we headed back up the path, our hands now staying closely by our sides. We ran past the guard shack, but no one came out.

When we reached the sidewalk, he finally said, "I better get on home."

"Yes, I know. Will we be able to see each other again?" But before the words were fully out of my mouth he was crossing the street away from me.

"I don't know," he said, stopping in the middle of the street, turning to look at me one last time. "I'll try, but I think I'm in big trouble." He turned again and, over his shoulder, said, "I've really gotta go. Goodbye." With that he ran on and quickly disappeared into the darkness.

"Hey," I cried out. "What's your name?"

But there was no reply.

PRECIOUS CARGO
Lawrence Benjamin

Reaching through the haze of alcohol and sleep, I grab the phone. "Hello," I breathe thickly, speaking around the cotton in my mouth.

"I have a collect call for Aaron Waters..." An operator's high pitched whine.

"From Erin--"

"Eric," his sweet, sexy voice softly corrects.

Eric! I accept the charges and then he is on the line. I try to focus swollen, red eyes on the bedside clock. 11:25. The sports report has just ended. His mother has gone to bed. He is alone. A little afraid. Thinking of me. I know him so well.

"Hi, sexy," I say.

"Hi, sexy, yourself," he echoes. He is shy, tense on the phone.

"What's up?"

"I have to see you." Then, apropos of nothing, or at least not triggered by any response from me, he adds, "We have to talk." "Okay," I agree, drawing out the word, unsure, and now, also, somehow, a little afraid.

"Can I come down on Friday?"

"Of course. Will you spend the weekend?"

"Yeah."

"Can we do it?"

He laughs. "You are a pervert. Is that all you think about?" "Yes. You know we perverts have one-track minds." Silence. The conversation is littered with awkward silences, sudden advances, voices tumbling over each other, apologizing, retreating.

"Listen," he says at last, "I'm sleepy. I'll see you on Friday."

"Yes, Friday."

Silence.

"Hang up," he says.

You first."

No, you first," he insists. It is an old argument: who will hang up first? He always wins, as he does now. I hang up, loving him. Eric. Sweet, sexy, caring Eric Estevez Echevaria Sanchez. How long had I known him? Almost a decade. And we'd been lovers for most of it.

We'd met at the University of Pennsylvania when I was a sophomore and he a freshman, handsome with dark hair and eyes so black, you couldn't distinguish pupil from iris, and a smoldering street-corner sexiness, too young and skinny for me. Somehow we became friends who took their meals together. We studied together and almost flunked out together. The realization that I was in love with him, hit me as suddenly and subtly as a particularly well-aimed blow delivered to my solar plexus; I found myself breathless, disoriented, somewhat shocked. I confessed the awful truth to him late one night on the second floor of the creakily ancient Fine Arts Library, where we gathered most nights, ostensibly to study, but where we would talk and laugh, our books opened piously before us, but ignored, as we drank greedily from the fountain of friendship, becoming intoxicated on each other's company. He laughed at my confession and kissed me on the mouth. "I'm glad you've finally caught up with me," he said. "I've been in love with you since the first day we met. You had that flaming red hair and you were so obvious – the way you looked at me, I mean, all sexy like, well, it made me horny as hell. I just wanted to be with you. And then, you called me darling...well, that was it. I was hooked."

We made love for the first time the year "Gone With the Wind" made its debut on network television. Our young bodies came together, that first night, awkwardly as we struggled with nascent desire, while Atlanta, ignored, burned, pennants of crimson and gold fluttering against the night sky. As the city collapsed on itself, embers faintly glowing, grey smoke rising, a stairway to heaven, so, too, did we collapse, exhausted, the platinum stickiness of our spent passion ruining the cheap, faded sheets, sinking into the thin mattress. Afterwards, propped on one elbow, he looked at me stretched out beside him, naked. "What happened?" he asked lightly caressing the backs of my legs which were badly discolored.

"Nuthin'," I'd mumbled, twisting away, embarrassment and shame engulfing me like the flames of long ago. The smell of burning flesh seared my nostrils. I felt the pull of strong brown arms, saving.

"Were you in a fire?"

"...lucky to be alive..." The words spinning through the void. Daddy!

"Yes," still trying to twist away. Reaching for the sheet, now, too. Don't look at me! Ugly!

He pressed his hands against my back, holding me still. "Don't ever think that you have to hide from me," he said. "I love you. Your legs are as beautiful to me as the rest of you." Then, bending his head, he kissed each patch of faded ruined skin.

There had been other men, lovers. Not many. Two or three. Just memories now, like old photographs, badly focused and jaundiced with age, curling slightly at the edges. Memories and a depth of feeling were all that remained of them. Yet, it was only with Eric that I was myself. It was only with him that I could walk from bed to bath, naked and unselfconscious. It was only with him that I could cry unashamed when I heard Susan Hayward plead, "I wanna live," for the hundredth time.

Like I said, it was only with him that I could be myself. The rest of the time I was a motley unreasonable compilation of my parents, characters out of F. Scott Fitzgerald novels, deposed monarchs, anyone I'd seen or read of and admired, in unmatched socks and dark glasses.

With his voice echoing softly inside my head, I drift into sleep.

Next morning: Friday. I call the barbershop and schedule a haircut, manicure, a facial. Before leaving, I give special instructions to my housekeeper – a stern, cheerless woman who comes in twice a week for an exorbitant fee, to change the sheets and frown at me. On my way to the barbershop, I stop in Wanamaker's and pick up half a dozen pairs of silk boxers, matching T-shirts and a dozen pairs of cashmere socks.

It is late afternoon when I return home. The housekeeper is gone. Eric has not yet arrived. The house, splendidly turned out by a decorator whose fees were even more outrageous than those of my housekeeper, is immaculate. And, unbearably empty. Dropping my purchases on the pigskin sofa, I head for the wet bar, whose green marble top is a perfect compliment to that flawless, empty room. I pour from a pitcher full of laughter and light. Stab aimlessly at the hard olive that has sunk to the bottom of the wide-mouthed glass. Bored. I take the pitcher and glass into the bathroom. In the shower, I wash carefully, paying special attention to my asshole. I feel it pucker against my intruding finger. Open. Sucking. Greedy. Full of need. Quicksilver seed scatters. Sown on white tile. Fruitless. Sliding down the drain.

In the bedroom, I stumble, dropping the glass, ruining the new carpet. Dusk fills the room with shadows like secrets. Depression stalks. Around the corner. Clinging to the shadows. Following me. Down these mean streets. Alcohol creeps up. Behind me. Slamming me. Into unconsciousness.

White light presses uncomfortably against my closed eyelids, dissolving the inchoate images of my dreams, making colors jitterbug. A hangover crawls around me. I curl into it. A band is playing rather loud rock and roll. Somewhere. Inside my head. Out of reach. A hot familiar hand on the back of my neck, which is cold. I roll over, open my eyes. Eric...

"Shhh...don't say anything."

"Eric...I think I'm going to be sick..."

In the bathroom, I am violently ill, while Eric holds my head low over the toilet. Occasionally, he wipes my forehead with a cool washcloth. Weak, I lean against his chest. His arms close around me. He, too, is tired.

"Are you okay?" His voice rumbles in my ear which is pressed against his chest.

"Yeah. I just drank too much."

"You always drink too much," he accuses lightly.

I shrug at his disguised concern. "I know."

"You need someone to take care of you," he says in his irrelevant way. "Why?"

"You're precious cargo – " "You want the job?"

"You willing to give it to me?" he teases.

"Nah. You're too unreliable," I answer offhandedly, distracted by his proximity.

"You thought I wasn't coming," he indicts. 'That's why you got drunk."

I unbutton his pants. "I get drunk so that I can get through all those days and nights when you are not here." It is an angry admission; I want to make love.

He stands up, shaking my hands off. "We need to talk." "Later," I say, reaching again, for his crotch.

"No," he ejaculates into the silence of that tiny room. "No sex."

"Why not?" I am more disappointed than angry.

"We need to talk," he repeats.

"About what?"

"I can't keep doing this to you."

"What exactly is it that you think you are doing to me?"

"I come in here whenever I feel like it and then leave when I'm ready, leaving you to get by the best way you can," he says, Paul Henreid to my Bette Davis. "It's not fair to you. I'm so self-conscious and embarrassed by our relationship that I won't go out in public with you. I won't meet your friends. I won't even tell anyone about you." He turned to face me as if he'd just remembered that I was there. "Doesn't that bother you?"

I shrugged. "Sometimes. I mean, I'd like to take you home and say, 'Mom, Dad, here's someone special that I want you to meet. This is the man I love'. Or, I'll hear a joke on TV and I wish that you were here so that we could laugh together. Or I'll go to the museum and see a picture that I really like and I'll find myself wishing that you were there so I could show it to you. But, basically, I'm happy with you – when we're together. Just the two of us. Sometimes I pretend that we're the only two people in the world. I can see no such fantasy has occurred to you."

And I was happy with him. I was happy lying in bed with him late at night watching black-and-white movies older than either one of us, or taping "I Love Lucy" reruns, carefully editing out the commercials which he hated, or leaning with him over the kitchen sink eating cold spinach pizza in the morning.

"Then, maybe I'm the one who's unhappy," he says interrupting my thoughts. "I can't stand leaving you. I see that look in your eyes and I know that you'll cry as soon as I leave. I know, because I cry too. I love you, Aaron Waters. But more importantly, you love me. Your love is a precious cargo in my heart that I will cherish always. It's so important to me that you love me. Usually, I feel pretty shitty about myself. I'm poor and I'm a coward, but, you love me and I think you're a terrific person, so I stop and think, 'hey, this terrific guy loves me, so, maybe I'm not bad after all'." He stops talking abruptly. His eyes glisten with unshed tears.

"Let's go to bed," I say getting up off the cold tile floor. I stand nearly a head taller than he. I lean down and kiss his mouth. He frowns at the stale taste of bile.

"I'll sleep on the sofa," he says.

I am too tired to argue.

He settles on the sofa with his pain, while in the bedroom, I slip between pale satin sheets. I have a bottle of Absolut for company. Eventually, the expensive booze silences my body's screaming need for him. I plunge headlong into sleep, while he cries helplessly into the soft suede of the sofa.

Next morning: I am awake. Too awake. Raw. The shaking starts deep inside me, working its way out. I want a drink. He comes up behind me. He discovers me, as I discover the decanter is empty. We are both bitterly disappointed.

"What do you want for breakfast?"

"Nothing."

You need to eat."

"I need a drink."

"No."

A sudden movement punctures the air. A cartwheel of light. An explosion of expensive crystal. A crystal shard, fragile, pitted, full of spite, licks his ear, a lover's tongue, drawing blood.

"You little bitch," he flings, advancing through a hailstorm of Baccarat, pinning my arms, tumbling me over backward. His mouth tastes of honey. It always does. Even in the morning when he wakes, last night's dreams clouding his eyes. I can taste it now, through the bitterness and bile of my hatred. His body, a Bosco-colored emulsion flows around me, comforting. He stops moving, slipping out of me. What's wrong? Am I hurting you?

Confused. No. Reaching for him, feeling him fill me again. He touches my face. Hot, wet tears. Why...?

"I need you, Eric. I love you." My open mouth swallows the words, as he fills me again with his gentle movement.

When he comes downstairs, fully dressed, a black knapsack over his shoulder, I am leaning against the stove, a glass of lukewarm Absolut in my hand like water; we both accept the pretense.

"Are you leaving?"

"Yes."

I nod without speaking. Except for that tiny, almost imperceptible movement, I am motionless. He looks at my feet and smiles. I look down and see what he sees: Black sneakers, brown laces like twin spiders perched on my instep. Is this how he will remember me?

"Julio?"

Why does he call me that? He has always called me that. We face each other across the silence. We are both unhappy, victims of his cowardice. "I'm sorry, Julio."

"For what?"

"I never wanted you to be my dirty little secret – " "But, I am. Aren't I?"

"Julio," he pleads.

"It doesn't matter. Don't you see? I would be anything for you. Do you want me to get down on my knees and beg you not to go?" Kneeling now, I am despising him for his lack of courage, hating myself for needing him.

He steps forward. Holds my head between his thighs. A pulse beats against my temple. The masculine scent of him fills my nostrils. My open mouth. Welcoming. The triumvirate of his manhood.

"I would die for you, Aaron Waters."

"I live for you," I answer, my mouth still full of the taste of him.

"I have to go."

"I know...Will I see you again?"

"Probably, but not for awhile."

"What will you do?"

"Try to get on with my life. I think I'd like to get married."

Married! My head snaps up. He rushes on, his words crowding against each other. "You should too. Get on with your life, I mean. I've kept you in this state of suspended animation long enough."

Funny, I thought, he had said he wanted to come down to talk to me and yet, it is only now that he is about to leave that we are actually talking.

"You'll be fine, you know. You're indestructible – like the elements."

"That's what my mother told me, when she named me." AIR AND WATER. YOU'LL EXIST FOREVER. My mother's words. Had I ever told him what she had said?

"There'll be someone else for you, you know," he consoles falsely. "You'll fall in love with him and forget about me and what we meant to each other."

FORGET? HIM? Impossible. He's unforgettable.

A coiled rattlesnake, I strike. My aim is accurate and deadly. "I know." The words wrap around him, a viper's tongue, poisoning.

He watches me with belladonna eyes full of pain. Regretting the lie, unable to watch him die, I turn. Beyond the window, the white morning stretches; silent, eternal, inescapable as a tomb.

A FARMER'S BOY
Peter Rice

To plough and sow,
And reap and mow,
For to be a farmer's boy.
For to be a farmer's boy.
– Old English Song

Pete had the sun in his eyes and, in the late morning glare, the heat rose from the ground in a shimmering haze. It had been an unusual summer, that first year of World War II. Harvest was early, the rich golden wheat cut, threshed and stored, and it was still August.

He glanced back over his shoulder, appreciating the evenness of the furrows he had ploughed across the stubble so far this day. The old tractor coughed and he coaxed it lovingly with the throttle. As he ploughed, he was one with the machine. This morning his mother had brought a letter down to the field. He felt in the breast pocket of his shirt. Yes, it was there. The envelope containing his call-up papers. He was eighteen now and he had known they would come. As if to reinforce the necessity he heard the distant chatter of machine-gun fire. Distant, above.

He stopped the tractor and looked up. Vapor trails betrayed the location of sparring planes. In his mind's eye he saw those young men in the teeth of a life and death struggle as he sat engaged in an occupation as old as civilization and of such quality of peace on a day like this as to refute the horror of war. But the reality fought in the blue sky above him. He took out the papers and looked at them again. His heart lurched. Not fear exactly, though he knew that if he were in the situation of the fighter pilots he would feel fear. He desperately hoped that he would show some courage if or when such a time came. Once again he folded the papers and put them back in the envelope and into his pocket.

How would it be in the forces for a man like him? He wondered that for at least the hundredth time. No one would guess the way he was. He wasn't a pansy. But he liked boys, not girls. That is, when he masturbated he thought about boys, beautiful boys, like himself. Not that he didn't like girls' company. He did. He enjoyed flirting with them, enjoyed the way they admired his good looks, how they enjoyed holding his firm young body. He knew many of them could have been his for the asking. He never asked. He wanted to be possessed by another such as himself but apart from less than gratifying moments in the toilets in the market square on market day he had never had the male contact he craved for. Few of his partners on those occasions had been even remotely desirable. They had provided him with a moment's essential gratification, nothing more.

There was someone over by the hedges. He shaded his eyes from the sun. He gasped – or was it a sigh? Perhaps it was both. It was a boy, the boy from his dreams. As he stepped from the shade of the hedgerow the sun gleamed from golden hair. It shone on the bronzed skin of his body – all of his body. The boy was naked. And yet his nakedness was not undress. Clothes on this body would have been a sacrilege, Pete thought. The boy waved.

Pete waved back, at first tentatively, glancing behind him in case there should be another person for whom the gesture was intended. There was no one else. He waved back again more confidently. Jumping down he ran towards the boy, stumbling a little in his haste over the uneven ground. He stopped ten yards from him. Perhaps a bit older than himself, the boy was so handsome, his physique so perfect that for a moment he could only gaze with the awe ordinary folk reserve for confrontation with the ultimate in works of art. But this was no canvas representation.

"You called me?" the boy asked, smiling, blue eyes twinkling under the tousled blond hair.

"Me? I didn't." Pete paused, uncomprehending. "I couldn't have. I don't know you; how could I have?"

"Oh, if I made a mistake, I'm sorry."

The boy was still smiling, a mischievous look in those intense eyes. He looked down at his naked body, at the large erection standing above the sac weighed down by the two equally impressive balls. He looked up again, those two eyes meeting and holding Pete's in a look so warm that Pete knew that he had at last met another boy, not only whose desires matched his own, but whose very soul was the mate of his soul.

"If I was wrong, I'm sorry," said the boy. He turned as if to go.

"No," Pete cried, running forward and catching him by the shoulder. "No, please don't go!"

"But if I was wrong," the boy responded, looking at him again, "you can't want me here."

Pete put his hands on the boy's upper arms. "I don't know you, but I want you to stay."

"You do know me. You have always known me, but I could not come until you called. Now you need me enough I am here."

Pete's mouth opened as though to ask for an explanation but the boy gently placed a forefinger on his lips.

"You will see it all soon, Pete. I am here. That's all that matters for the moment."

"But who are you? What's your name? How do you know me? And what do you mean, 'I've always known you?' I'd know if I had, stands to sense."

The boy laughed. "My name's Sylvan. That's enough for now. You want me to stay with you, I will. You see I have waited for you to need me for a long time. I'll just say that when you have closed your eyes you have seen me many times. You knew my face as soon as you saw it"

That was true, Pete considered. So the boy he had always dreamed about was really a boy he had seen somewhere before. Funny he didn't remember where. And he hadn't called him, that was certain. How could he when he only remembered him as an image in his mind? Sylvan, too – he had never even heard the name before, let alone known anyone with such a name.

Sylvan looked at him and put his arms around Pete's waist. The longing in the lad's eyes was equal to his own. Pete felt him press his hardness against his own, at the same time leaning his torso backwards. They ground their sex together and Pete began to play with the other boy's nipples rousing them to rigidity and greater responsiveness.

"Take these off," said Sylvan, indicating Pets's clothes. "I want to see you. Really see all of you," he acted, as though explanation were needed.

It took only seconds for Pete to be as naked as his new – old – friend. They held each other close and Pete knew that this was what he had desired and needed for so long a time. All questions faded from his mind and he gave himself to Sylvan, with all his being.

"I want you," Sylvan sighed, lowering himself to Pete's engorged cock. He let his tongue trace its form, lingering at the taut foreskin which was peeling back, exposing the moist slit. He gently, tantalizingly, inserted the end of his tongue and teased its tender inner walls. Pete moaned with the pleasure of it. Sylvan's hands caressed Pete's lightly haired legs, sending shivers of delight through his body. He played his tongue about the inside of the protective skin, teasing it back until it slipped behind the rim of the glans leaving the cock's most sensitive and vulnerable areas quite exposed. With no further preparation he opened his mouth wide and plunged his head forward, engorging its full length to the back of his throat and down until he was impaled on it.

Pete had never felt such sensations before. Without even realizing what he did, he put his hands behind Sylvan's head and began to control its movement. Sylvan's eyes were closed and in time with Pete's prick delving into the depths of his throat his right hand massaged himself pulling his ample foreskin back and forth, repeatedly exposing and hiding the swollen head. With his left hand he reached up and played with Pete's nipples again. Pete sighed in wonder. Sylvan was waking him to a sensual world beyond his wildest imaginings.

Suspended in time; detached from the sun-drenched world about them the two boys made their own reality. Their rhythmic movements, mesmerizing in their concentration, gradually increased in pace. Each boy was lost in the being of the other yet focused on one essential part of himself. The moment drew near and then Pete's cock throbbed, violently ejecting its creamy seed down Sylvan's throat. His body spasmed in unison with the gusts of pleasure from his groin. Almost together with Pete, Sylvan urged himself to a gushing climax, the thick white cum spattering the brown earth.

Momentarily exhausted from their experience they tumbled together to the ground, lying there without speaking for some time, content in their new oneness of being. Gently each caressed the other, exploring the contours of the smooth-skinned muscles and delighting in the physical sensation of their naked proximity.

Sylvan spoke first. "I must go now, and you have plenty of work to do."

Pete was aghast. "Go? Where do you live? Please Sylvan, I must see you again."

You will," Sylvan reassured him. "I will be here again to-morrow. Now, you go and get on with your plowing. Tonight we will meet in our dreams and in the morning I will see you again."

"You really will come, won't you?" Pete was almost begging him.

"I will be here when you look for me. It won't be long before we can be together always." Sylvan got to his feet, his cock already hard again. Pete took it in his right hand and squeezed it and was aware that his own long dick was in the same state. 'So soon,' he thought with some surprise.

"I need you now – and I need...this," and he got to his knees and kissed the tip of Sylvan's prick where a crystal drop of precum had emerged like dew on a leaf. He began to lick the glans but Sylvan gently pulled away, running his hands through Pete's dark brown hair.

"Tomorrow," he said, smiling his enigmatic smile.

Pete kissed Sylvan's feet. 'There is nothing I wouldn't do for you," he whispered.

"And I for you," said Sylvan, reaching out and drawing him to his feet.

Again they kissed and again Pete had the strange feeling that they were one substance.

"I must leave now," said Sylvan again. Don't worry, I won't let you down."

Taking him firmly by the shoulders he turned Pete around to face the abandoned tractor and gave him a little push towards it.

"Work." he commanded, a light-hearted laugh coloring his voice.

"I'd better put my clothes on first," chuckled Pete. "I don't think I'd look right driving the tractor in the buff."

Sylvan laughed aloud this time as he slapped his friend across his bum cheeks.

"Oh, I don't know about that," he rejoined. "I think you would look very fine, particularly sporting this."

He reached round Pete's hips, resting his big cock between the two downy globes of his arse cheeks, and sliding his hand up and down Pete's cock, making it jerk uncontrollably. Kissing Pete's right shoulder, suddenly he had gone. Pete didn't turn round for a few moments. When he did he found himself alone. A sob escaped his throat. The power of this meeting and of his new friend's presence overwhelmed him and Sylvan's departure had left him desolate in spite of his promises. Simply being parted from Sylvan was a bereavement.

And then, as he picked up his shirt and put it on, he felt again the envelope containing his call-up papers in the pocket. If he could not bear so brief a parting how would it be to be parted for months, perhaps years?

The sky was at peace, the battling fighter planes gone. Their confrontation was resolved. Somehow. The only sounds were the occasional chirrup of a grasshopper and the ascending song of a skylark. Pete looked up into the blue but his eyes were full of tears and he could see nothing of that tiny spirit of the fields.

The hot late summer weather was hanging on and the next day was going to be the same as the last. Pete was in great haste to get down to the field to see if Sylvan were there. He did not recall his dreams of the night before but their nature was born out by the fact that he had woken twice during the night after wet dreams. He was not embarrassed about the state of his sheets. His mother had told him years before that it was quite a normal thing for growing boys and men and so he just stripped them from the bed and bundled them into the big washing basket standing by the door of the lumber room. When he got down to the big farmhouse kitchen he did not want anything to eat and his worried mother thought he might be sickening for something.

"I'm all right, Ma," he told her. "I'm just not very hungry."

She had packed up his sandwiches, a slice of fruit cake and a big flask of hot tea, straining off the tea leaves so that the drink would not become stewed and unpleasant.

"Well, at least be sure that you get this down you before you come back in this evening," she ordered, not convinced at all by his words.

True, he didn't look at all ill, she considered, just a bit flushed and excited. She would have sworn he was in love except that he had not been around with any particular girl, and none at all recently, he had so much work to do on the farm.

Shouldering the rucksack containing his dinner he hurried out to the barn, quickly started the tractor, and swung out of the farmyard on to the quiet country lane. Normally he would have reveled in the early morning air but this time he could only think of the ten-acre field. He wanted to believe that Sylvan would come today. His stomach knotted into a hard ball at the possibility that he might not, that it had all been just words. In his heart, though, he knew that was not true. If anyone in this world were honest than Sylvan was. He had no doubt of that.

Yet anxiety plagued him all of the mile down to the field and as he drove the tractor in through the gate he looked about him to see if Sylvan were already there. There was no one. It was not very warm yet, and a wisp of mist still lay in the dip at the bottom of the field. Despite that, he stripped off his red plaid shirt and enjoyed the sensuous feeling of the cool air on his bare torso. He shivered, raising a rash of goose bumps but he ignored them. Driving around the field, to the point at which he had finished the night before, he stopped, walked around to the plough and lowered it, taking care to set it at the right depth.

Now that he was in the field, some of his nerves were dissipated but he still looked for him, in the hope that in the next moment he would see his beloved. The word brought his thoughts up with a jolt. Yes, he had to admit to himself that the word was the right one; he truly thought of Sylvan in those terms.

Although the sun had not yet lifted the clouds, a ruddy glow suffused the air. All the time he drove the tractor, still taking care over the quality of his work, he continued to look about. It was becoming warmer and the mist was lifting in the dell. Then with theatrical suddenness a shaft of sunlight stabbed across the field and there, over by the far hedge was Sylvan. It was as though he had been conjured by amazing trickery. His friend's beauty was beyond his words to describe and he felt an intoxicating elation as he laughed for sheer joy and called across to him.

"Sylvan! Sylvan! So you did come. I'm coming over, wait there!"

He stopped the tractor and jumped down, immediately running as fast as he could; nor did Sylvan wait, he ran towards him. As Pete ran a crazy thought entered his mind that, to anyone watching, the scene must resemble one in a mushy romantic film between two lovers. The thought made his laughter the more delirious. As they fell into each other's arms Sylvan was laughing as well.

Sylvan was clothed this time, wearing dark green corduroy trousers and a light green shirt. The thought flitted across Pete's mind how the colors suited him, only to be driven away the next moment by the sensation almost of electricity when he touched him. It was like the feeling of static he sometimes felt when he touched the door handle of the old Morris saloon after a long run. But that was unpleasant; this was stimulating.

Sylvan's hands seemed to be everywhere at once, stroking Pete's back, massaging the pectoral muscles and rosy nipples, cupping his balls and cock trapped within old grey trousers, kneading his buttocks. It was frenzied and yet controlled at the same time. Their lips pressed hard together, bruising, and their tongues invaded each others mouths fencing for dominance, for possession of the other's oral cavity.

Feverish hands were tearing at the buttons of Sylvan's shirt, pulling it forward over his head. Then Pete took Sylvan's waist in his hands, sliding them up and down the strong muscles, up beneath the arms and back again, marveling in the silky texture of the skin. They continued to kiss, as each boy took his friend's body into his ownership as with a freely given gift.

"I want you," murmured Pete. "I want that beautiful arse, my big dick deep inside you. I want my thick cream shooting into your guts.

Sylvan responded to the crude words by beginning to kiss Pete's neck, his shoulders, his chest and abdomen, licking the cords of muscle, nibbling his tits and then biting harder, building up a mountain of passion, a mountain which grew ever more precariously balanced.

Both boys began to fumble with belt buckles, haste making a simple task difficult; then fly buttons, boots and socks. Bare feet, now, on the stubbled ground. Sylvan turned his back to Pete, reached behind and pulled his friend to him. After a long embrace Pete crouched down and started to lick Sylvan's arse cheeks, tasting the essence of him, loving every inch of him. No part of Sylvan was taboo. He found himself wanting to do something for Sylvan which, because of its very nature, was for Pete the utmost in abasement, the ultimate worship and reverence. He parted Sylvan's succulent mounds and allowed his probing tongue to approach nearer and nearer to his friend's sphincter. When he reached it he lingered there, teasing it with fluttering touches. When he heard Sylvan's groan of pleasure at the wonderful sensations being lavished on him Pete pressed his tongue hard in the center of the little rose and felt the muscle give way, allowing him entrance.

His tongue acquired an independence removed from his active mind which received and feasted on its discoveries, the soft inner walls of the rectum, the musky taste, which was in no way distasteful to him now. It was all new and a special knowledge between Sylvan and himself.

"Pete, fuck me now, please, I can't stand any more," Sylvan moaned.

Realizing that he was nearing a climax already without touching himself, Pete slicked his rigid prick with a lavish supply of saliva and eased it into the prepared entrance to Sylvan's eager passage. The twitching muscle after a moment's hesitation opened wide to admit the large presence. In a smooth unhurried movement the whole of the shaft took up residence in the hot, hugging tube.

"Aaaaagh; oh yes, Pete. Oh yes. That's just what I want. I want you inside me. I want you to massage inside my arse with your splendid cock. Please give it to me hard."

Sylvan was enraptured and he thrust himself forcefully onto the searching probe. As Pete leaned back to withdraw Sylvan eased forward and as Pete pushed home he pressed back to meet him. As they quickened, Pete's firm belly slapped against Sylvan's shapely rear. More and more violently their united efforts worked for Pete's release until his manhood pulsated massively and erupted a flood of cum into Sylvan's abused interior. Time after time Pete ejaculated, the deliberate contractions of Sylvan's arse muscles milking every last drop of white jism from his friend's balls. Each of the final spasms racked Pete with almost insufferable pleasure.

As the tension receded from his prick Pete drew back to withdraw but Sylvan was reluctant to lose it and with a sudden tightening of his anal muscles abraded its acutely sensitized surface as he did so.

"Oooh, you bugger," giggled Pete. "It's like raw meat at the moment."

"Not for long, I'm sure," said Sylvan, turning and putting his arms round Pete. They relaxed, embracing, and lay on the ground uncaring of the discomfort, their thoughts totally occupied with each other. Pete was again aware of the feeling of yesterday, that time had stood still; was standing still. Then he suddenly thought of where they were. In the middle of an open field.

"Oh, my God!" he exclaimed.

"Yes?" answered Sylvan, laughing.

"Not the time for ancient jokes," said Pete. "Do you realize that we've done this in the middle of the field, right by the lane? Anyone might have seen us. They might see us now and we haven't got a stitch on.

"Mmmm," mused Sylvan. "Then they will have seen something rather special, I reckon."

"Special enough to fetch the Constable for, you mean." half shouted Pete.

"Oh, quit worrying. There's nobody about." That smile again. "Anyway, don't you think it makes it even more fun to take a risk?"

At that thought the exhibitionist in Pete, previously almost completely suppressed, came to the fore and his dick began to lengthen again. He pulled Sylvan close to him.

"Yes it does, doesn't it?"

Sylvan had left after they had lain together just a little longer, with the promise of being there again the next day. Ten-acre was almost done and the neighboring four-acre was the last. He would be able to finish before he had to report for duty. Some Land Girls were coming to help his mother then, for the duration. He had not told Sylvan about his call-up. It would have spoilt everything, but he would have to do it next time.

The third day dawned fine and promised to be as hot as before, but Pete was heavy-hearted as he drove down the lane. He wondered how he could tell Sylvan that in a few days he would have to leave and that he might never come back. That made him wonder why Sylvan had not been called up himself. He felt almost sure that his friend was older than he was. At least a year, he estimated. He would ask him.

It wasn't until early afternoon that Sylvan arrived. Pete had eaten his dinner and started on four-acre. He was just passing the open gateway connecting the fields when a naked Sylvan, howling like an ancient warrior in battle cry, leaped up onto the moving tractor and started to smother him with kisses. He slammed on the brake stalling the engine.

You crazy boy, you might have killed yourself!" he attempted to say when his lips were not being appropriated. But, in spite of the anger caused by the shock, he was laughing as so often Sylvan made him laugh.

"Oh, god, Sylvan, but I love you, you mad bastard," he sighed.

And I love you, Pete. And now we have found our love we shall never be apart again."

Now Pete would have to tell him. It could not be put off any longer.

"Sylvan," he said softly, "we will soon be parted. I've got to go in the army. I've been called up."

Sylvan looked at him, his blue eyes steady. "Believe me, we will never be separated."

Pete was looking into Sylvan's eyes, down into the depths of them where he felt himself falling and then as though suspended in mid-fall he heard Sylvan's voice.

"I am going to make love to you, Pete, and we don't want any clothes between us when I do. Take them off."

Sylvan's voice was remote, yet warm, as full of love and lust as always. Pete ripped his clothes from his body and was naked in Sylvan's arms. He looked down and saw that both of their cocks were straining upwards, seeming larger than ever before. "Turn round and lean over the steering wheel."

Pete did as he was told, spreading his legs apart as much as was possible there. He wanted this, wanted so much to have Sylvan's huge prick in his arse. He had not long to wait. A moment or two of positioning as Pete felt the hot glans at his puckered opening and then with one swift lunge Sylvan was right inside him, striking his prostate gland with shocking force. The wave of pleasure pain engulfed him, blotting out the sun and the world. The world was himself and Sylvan, united; one soul. The battering of his passage was inducing an ecstatic state. Sylvan's hands gripping his hips used him as a means for his own pleasure. Yet the fact that at the same time he gave pleasure to Pete and that he knew how to make it the maximum was only the other side of the same coin. He rode Pete as though he were a horse being broken, roughly but with a concern for him. Many times hence, roles would be reversed, but this time he was in the saddle. Pete was his now, quite completely, just as he was Pete's.

The sun was going down and the sky became a carefully blended wash of color. A small group of men surrounded the tractor. An ambulance stood across the field in the lane. An ambulance man was leading away a woman who was crying inconsolably.

The local Police Constable surveyed the scene, black notebook in hand.

"Terrible thing," said an old man.

"Aye," responded the Constable. "Dirty work here and no mistake, the lad's clothes scattered about. He was naked when he died. Can't rightly see how it could have happened, though."

"I've never seen anything like it in all my life," said another. There were rumbles of agreement from the rest.

"I mean," said the Constable, "how could the lad fall off the tractor and under the plough without something getting in the way?"

"That's true," said another. And what stalled the tractor, that's what I'd like to know? Tractor engines don't stop dead just because you fall off 'em. That lad's right under the plough. It's sliced right through him and then stopped."

It's up to the Coroner now, anyway."

The Constable in that statement washed his hands of all responsibility for the matter although C.I.D. would look into it. Some more policemen were coming across the field, carrying screens.

"It's appalling," another man, previously silent, added superfluously.

"Awful waste," agreed his companion. "Such a fine, handsome lad, too."

The ambulance man supported Pete's mother over the newly ploughed field. She wept for her wonderful son. She would always grieve for him. But at least, she thought, he would not have to go and fight in that terrible war.

Later, just as the last remnants of red tinted the dark sky, she was looking from her bedroom window out across the fields when she thought she saw two figures in the shadowy garden below. It was probably only a trick of the dwindling light on the glass. The impression was of two young men hand in hand, beautiful young men, and quite, quite naked. One, dark haired, raised his hand to her in a wave of greeting. He looked just like Pete.

JACK LEAVES HOME... FOREVER
Dirk Hannam

Seated at the kitchen table, Jack's head was down. He was crying. Not delicate little sniffles but great gulping sobs that shook his whole frame. He was a poor lad who lived with his mother in a tiny cottage way out in the boondocks. His father had long ago died leaving Jack the sole man of the house. All of this was long ago in a far country and in those days there was no government-supported welfare or social security – not even widow's pensions. And things had been getting worse and worse for months.

At last, in desperation, Jack's mother had sent the boy off with their last asset, the family cow, to sell wherever he could get the best price.

Everybody knows the result. Jack was just a country youth and not too bright. He went to the village and in a high-level commercial transaction he traded the cow to the first stranger he met in exchange for six beans. He started for home rejoicing because as a practical matter six beans that you could cook and eat were better than one cow that you could not. After all, the cow was part of the family and you can't eat a relative!

When Jack arrived home, however, and proudly showed his mother the six beans, she ranted and raved and tore her hair and shrieked that he was a stupid dolt, even stupider than his father. The woman was so beside herself with fury she grabbed the beans from jack's hand and threw them out the window. Not only that, she boxed his ears and stormed out of the house, screaming and crying all the way through the yard and over the hill.

So the poor lad was sobbing great sobs. His ears hurt and he didn't know what he had done wrong. This went on for some time but eventually, of course, he began to calm down. Just then he noticed movement on the stairs that come down from the attic of the cottage. His mind focused and he began to watch.

What he saw was a mouse coming down the stairs. It would creep silently, silently across a step to its very edge, wait a moment and then jump lightly to the next step down, creep across that and then repeat the jump. In its own quiet way it was advancing lower and lower down the stairs.

Jack was intrigued and then curious. He turned around so he could see better and stared at the little gray creature.

When the mouse discovered the boy staring from across the room it stopped, sat back on its haunches and stared back.

"Why are you looking at me like that?" said the mouse, "Haven't you ever seen a mouse before?"

"Well, yes" said Jack, "but I've never seen one coming down the stairs like that. Where are you going?"

"I don't know. I just know I have to get out of this house today. My mother is impossible, always on my case. Night and day, she never lets up on me. I'm going to seek my fortune elsewhere."

"It's the same with me," said Jack, swallowing the last of his sobs and smearing his tears across his cheeks, "My mother is always on my case. I want to run away too."

"Well then," said the mouse, "we have a lot in common. Maybe we should take off together. With my brains and your brawn we should make a good team."

"What do you mean: 'your brains'? I've got brains too."

"Of course, dear man, but I'm managing to get away without having to have my ears boxed first. Anyway, never mind that. Get a bag, gather up what you need and let's get out of here. Don't forget a comb, your hair is a mite tousled. And perhaps a handkerchief would come in handy."

There was little if anything in the cottage that Jack wanted to take. He tucked a comb in his back pocket and stuffed a handkerchief in the cuff of his sleeve and started for the outside door.

"Hey! Wait a minute!" piped the mouse from the bottom step, "You're going too fast. I can't keep up with your enormous strides. Why don't you pick me up and carry me?"

Jack went over, picked up the mouse and started off again with the furry creature in his hand. Before they got to the doorway the mouse was squirming in his hot and sweaty embrace. He spoke to the lad:

"Say, boy, what's your name?"

"Jack. I'm called Jack."

"Well, listen, Jack, it's too uncomfortable here in our hand. Why don't you put me in your shirt pocket? I'll be able to breathe better and perhaps look out on the passing scene."

That suited Jack so he slipped the mouse into his shirt pocket and again proceeded to the door. At the very threshold he stopped and asked the mouse:

"Do you think I should leave a note for mother telling her I'm leaving home forever?"

"Don't be a damn fool, Jack. Use your head, kid. Who knows how things will turn out? You may want to come back some day. Burnt bridges are never rebuilt. Forget the note and let's get to hell on our way."

So out of doors they went and into the sunny yard.

At once they were confronted by six giant plants that sent their stalks higher and higher into the sky, their tops disappearing into the clouds.

'Wow! Where did those come from? They weren't here yesterday!"

"They're bean plants," said the mouse. They were magic beans you brought home. When your mother threw them out of the window they immediately took root and shot up into the sky."

"I wonder what it's like at the top?" said Jack. "It must be bright and airy up there."

"Why don't we climb up and see?" said the mouse.

"Oh, we couldn't do that. Who ever heard of two guys running away from home up a beanstalk?"

"Jack, let's get something straight. We're never going to have adventures and win our fortunes with that stick-in-the-mud attitude. If nobody else has ever run away climbing up to the clouds, then we'll be the first. We'll be pioneers! We'll get to be famous! Every corporation in the country will beat a path to our door offering gold like you wouldn't believe for us to endorse their products. I wouldn't be surprised if a publisher didn't offer us a king's ransom just for the rights to the book we're going to write of our experiences. So get with it, lad, let's start climbing." "If you say so," mumbled jack as he pulled the two of them up by the first leaf-branch.

Jack climbed and climbed. Every once in a while he looked back to judge how far they'd come. The house and yard looked smaller and smaller, first like a doll's house then like a mere chip. At one point, while he was resting, catching his breath, he asked the mouse:

"Say, mouse, what's your name?"

"Well my full name is Mus Musculus but you can call me Joe for short."

"Well, Joe, it's nice to know you."

"The pleasure is reciprocal, jack. However, we better be moving on. We can't spend time chit-chatting, exchanging reminiscences, when we are only halfway up this bean stalk.

So jack returned to climbing and found in time that they were getting close to the clouds. At last they reached them and, still climbing, found themselves surrounded by a glowing white fog.

"How much further do you suppose this bean stalk goes?" asked jack.

"I wouldn't hazard a guess. I hope we're climbing to somewhere. It will be a damned nuisance if we have to go all the way back down again because there's nothing above. Especially as I think I saw your mother at the foot of the bean stalk shaking her fist up at us."

Just then the fog cleared and they broke through to the top of the cloud. They were climbing up out of the bottom of a well and all around the well wall was another country spreading far and wide.

"Well, I'll be damned," said Joe, "will you look at that. And all this way up in the sky, too."

Jack said nothing but climbed from the bean stalk over the wall and onto solid ground.

"Which way are you going to go now?" asked Joe.

"I don't know. You said we should be pioneers and get famous so we can endorse products and get scads of gold --maybe write a book. So I'm just going to march forward and see what happens"

"OK, Jack, but let's not be foolhardy. Watch what we're doing."

The new country was much like the old but brighter and more colorful, being closer to the sun. As they walked along Joe commented on the scene. He was the one who noticed the mouth of a cave tucked away at the foot of a hill. He pointed it out and Jack turned his steps in that direction.

They reached the cave and walked in. It was quite commodious, well lit and with an entrance hallway that led back into the hill. As they proceeded it looked more and more as if someone lived there.

"I'm not sure I like this," said Joe. "It doesn't smell right."

"I don't smell nothing," said jack. "Come on, don't chicken out on me now, Joe."

Just then there was a mighty sound from up front and a voice roared:

"BY THE PRICKING OF MY THUMBS SOMETHING EVIL THIS WAY COMES!"

Jack and Joe were terrified.

Then they heard another voice, that of a woman but loud: "Giant, dear, that should be 'wicked', not 'evil'. Anyway that's not the correct apothegm. You're supposed to roar 'Fee, Fi, Fo, Fum...'"

"Oh, all right. I'm tired of that old chestnut, but okay: "FEE, FI, FO, FUM
I SMELL THE BLOOD OF AN ENGLISHMAN
BE HE LIVE OR BE HE DEAD
I'LL SMASH HIS BONES TO MAKE MY BREAD."

Jack had been inching forward and inching forward and at last turned a corner and confronted a strange scene.

At the far end of the cavern, seated before a fireplace with a blazing fire were two very large people, a man and a woman. He it was who was roaring. There were tables and chairs around and a meal on the center table. It seemed to consist of a large roasted leg of something surrounded by assorted vegetables. Glasses filled with glowing red wine accompanied the meal.

When Jack appeared the man arose. He was truly a big man, half again as tall as Jack. He had huge arms and legs, a hogshead, rather than a barrel, chest. His face was strikingly ugly, his hair unkempt and scraggly. Actually, his head looked like a hubbard squash under a wig.

"Ah-hah," bellowed the man, "come forward, boy, and be recognized. What's that poking its head out of your pocket? Is that a mouse? Mice make fine tidbits in this house. Now then, step up here."

"For god's sake, do as he says," whispered Joe from the shirt pocket.

So Jack stepped forward, too frightened to say a word. "'TAKE OFF YOUR SHIRT," roared the giant.

Jack carefully took Joe out of his pocket, spread his handkerchief on the floor by a table leg and set the mouse down on it. Then he slowly unbuttoned his shirt, pulled it over his head and laid it on a chair.

"Nice chest you've got there, boy. Well muscled arms, too. You're going to be a welcome particularity around here. Now drop your pants."

Jack didn't comprehend and just stood there, gawking. "I SAID, 'DROP YOUR PANTS.'

"Dammit, do as he says," yelled the mouse from the handkerchief.

The woman spoke up: "That's right, sonny, spread your legs a little, disengage your belt, shuck off your braces, unbutton the front and just let your shorts drop to the floor."

With so much advice coming to him from all directions, Jack complied. Like all the peasant boys of that time and country, he was wearing lederhosen, knee-length pants made of soft goatskin that had become stiff and grimy through use. He unfastened the buckle of his broad belt, pushed his braces off his shoulders, and slowly, button by button opened the front. When the shorts dropped by their own weight around his ankles he was exposed, totally naked to the view – except for his boots, of course – because the refinement of underwear wouldn't reach his country for centuries.

"WELL!" said the giant, "I thought you were a mere boy. I see that instead you are a full grown man, although still young. Full grown and very generously gifted for your size. Now turn around and bend over.

"I SAID TURN AROUND AND BEND OVER.'"

Jack was too embarrassed to comply. By this time he was blushing from head to toe. He was also both frightened and angry at being put to this indignity.

"Giant, dear," said the woman, "haven't you discomfited the young man enough? See how he is drawing up one leg and trying to hide his manhood with his hands? He doesn't want to expose himself in my company."

"Be quiet, wife" the giant commanded, "Go to the kitchen for awhile. I'm not finished with this ripe young morsel."

The woman rose and left the cavern. On her way, she patted Jack on the shoulder:

"Be of good cheer, youngster, the end is quick and not at all painful and you will afford us such a rare treat."

As he comprehended the thrust of the woman's remarks Jack became terrified.

"KICK THOSE PANTS OUT OF THE WAY," roared the giant.

He slowly, with a faint smile on his lips unbuttoned and set aside his own shirt, sat down and took off his heavy boots, then, standing before the fireplace, he dropped his own britches to the floor. Underwear hadn't reached the wardrobes of giants yet, either.

The sight that greeted Jack's stricken eyes was appalling. Used to his own generous sexual equipment and that of the other farm boys in the neighborhood, he was horrified by the girth and length of the giant's flaccid member. As he watched in fright it started to fill and stiffen, becoming in minutes a shockingly enormous ram thrusting straight out from the dense black forest of the giant's crotch. The shaft was half a yard long and thicker than Jack's brawny arm. The head was the size of Jack's two fists held together.

"I said 'turn around,- ordered the giant, "I always explore the inside as well as the outside of the creatures I intend to roast before I roast them. TURN AROUND AND BEND OVER, LITTLE MAN."

Jack had only two thoughts: to avoid having his nether region torn asunder in the process of being deflowered by that outrageous prong now, and to escape being slaughtered and roasted for dinner later. The former was the greater concern to in the light of the immediate danger presented by the giant's aroused condition. He was not blessed with an overabundance of wit but he had a powerful desire to protect his own skin.

With no thought but to escape, he lunged forward, shoulder lowered. He struck the giant with his head, square on the solar plexus. The giant was knocked backward, caught his foot on the fireplace fender and landed butt-first in the middle of the fire. At once the smell of burning hide pervaded the cavern and roars rising to shrieks tore the air. The fearsome cock shriveled and went limp as the giant struggled to extricate himself.

Jack didn't stop to observe. He stooped, scooped up the mouse in this handkerchief and fled back to the entrance of the cave, shirtless, pantless but, happily, scatheless.

He and the mouse dashed out of the evil place and didn't stop running until night at last fell. When it became too dark to see any more they dropped exhausted under the low, swept-down branches of a sheltering deodar tree. They were starving for something to eat but too overjoyed to be free of the double threats of debauchment and anthropophagi to moan about it.

It was cool in the evening but not unpleasant and Jack and Joe slept under the tree until morning.

By then both were really hungry. jack, in only his boots, felt very naked – which, of course, he was – and afraid to venture out from under the sheltering branches of the tree. Moreover he found that he was covered with leaves and grass from lying on the ground all night. He had long hair on his head and copious thickets elsewhere and they were snarled beyond easy repair.

"I can't go walking around like, Joe. I'll scare the horses."

"Never mind the horses. Anyway I haven't seen a horse anywhere in the neighborhood. Of course we can solve your problem if I can wander around and find a nudist colony somewhere. Maybe you could slip in unnoticed and stay until we can steal some pants for you."

"Joe, stop being ridiculous. There are no nudist colonies during this era. Think of something practical."

"Well, for a start I see a man in the distance leading a donkey. He's coming this way. Maybe we can sweet-talk him out of his breeches."

"You try sweet-talking. I'll stay behind the tree."

In due time the man and the donkey arrived at the tree. He was a very young man, just about Jack's age. The donkey was just a donkey. Joe initiated the discussion: "Say, hold up a minute, I've got a conundrum for you."

The travelers stopped: "Yes?"

"If you were given a choice, which would you rather do without, your shirt or your pants?"

"That's a dumb question. My shirt, of course. I can't go around without pants."

"Well, there's some folks who do," observed the mouse. He turned and yelled: "Hey, Jack, stop being modest and come out from behind that tree. I want you to meet an agreeable young fellow and his donkey"

Joe turned back. "By the way, fellow, what's your name?" "Hans-in-luck!"

"Well, that's a fortunate name. Hans, meet Jack-lack-pants." (Jack having come out from behind the tree.)

Hans was an impressive young man. He saw the handsome face of Jack, his brawny arms and well-muscled torso. He observed his hardy thighs. Jack came out with his hands hiding his manhood but in offering a hand to Hans for shaking, he uncovered himself in all his magnificence. Hans gulped twice and shook hands.

Jack was understandably shy and left Joe to do the talking. "Hans, " said the mouse, "you see it was this way . . . "

and he related all their adventures up to this point.

"So now Jack needs some clothes – especially breeches -

and we both need food."

"I think I can be of help there," said Hans, "Here are some sandwiches that I have left over. After you've eaten those, what do you say we go for a swim? We can go for the pants afterwards. There's a grand deep pool in a creek near here. Then I'll take you to my home."

"I'll go along but I'm not much of a swimmer," said Joe.

So Jack, Joe, Hans and the donkey made their way to the creek.

Jack, of course, had only to remove his boots. Joe had nothing at all to remove. Hans sat on the bank and took off his boots, then, with something of a swagger, took off his shirt, then his lederhosen. Incredibly he was almost a twin of Jack both in build and in endowment – a sparkling specimen of young manhood, more than generously hung, great, handsome penis, heavy, low-hanging testicles and all.

The mouse watched the two of them dive into the pool then made off into the underbrush, having decided it was a time to be discreet.

He was right, of course. The two youths splashed and played around in the water, naked thigh to naked thigh. After the first high exuberance had exhausted itself the two virile young males paused in their play. They stopped. They looked. They all at once tingled with a growing awareness of each other's physical person- in particular each other's manly attributes. Each could feel a sea-change taking place at the pit of his belly.

Jack put out his hand. Hans grasped it and pulled Jack toward himself. In a moment they were bound together by arms of steel, lips finding lips, tongue wrestling tongue, belly pressing belly and cock swelling and rising to cock in a paroxysm of passion.

Hans led Jack to a grassy bower hidden among the bushes and under the trees alongside the creek. Here, driven by an insatiable appetite, and in the heat of lust, they hugged and kissed, caressed and stroked, sucked and fucked in a whirlwind of carnal frenzy. In time Jack discovered himself spasming inside Hans and later sensed Hans convulsing within him. They both became slick with sweat and each other's sex juices. Here they came to know each other as only true soul mates can.

Eventually, after they had exhausted themselves in the toils of love, they lay back on the grass and exchanged confidences. Jack recounted the tale of his marketing venture. Hans had an almost identical experience.

"I worked for seven years as an apprentice," he told Jack, "When I left my master to return home he was so pleased with my work he gave me a lump of gold as big as my head."

"I was walking along with the lump of gold in a bag over my shoulder. Well, you know how it is, the gold was heavy and getting heavier all the time and it was hot. I met a man who had a lively horse. How wonderful, I thought, to have a horse to ride and no heavy dead weight to carry. The man very kindly agreed to give me the horse if I gave him my gold so I did. I was riding merrily along, free of care, when all at once the horse started to buck. It threw me to the ground. I was flat on my back and furious. Fortunately there was a man nearby with a cow. I thought a cow wouldn't be so damned rough and also it would provide me with milk and cream, butter and cheese so I persuaded the man to give me the cow in exchange for the horse. But, you know, that cow was old, she walked so slowly it tired me out. Not only that but when I tried to milk her, her teats were dry and I got no milk. However I soon found a man with a donkey who exchanged my cow for his ass. And now here I am.

"Just the same, this little old donkey can get mighty stubborn at times. I wouldn't mind working out some kind of a trade for him."

They lay in the grass, stark naked and clasped in each other's arms for some time. Eventually Joe came wandering back accompanied by a very cute young male mouse.

"Hey, men, break it up," said Joe, "I want you to know a friend of mine. Meet Micromys Minutus. You can call him Jerry for short."

"Pleased to meet you, Jerry," Jack and Hans said together. But Jerry was a harvest mouse, unaccustomed to strangers so he stood silent, with his head down and his tail tightly wound against his private parts.

"Listen, men, Jerry and I have become real intimate buddies – just like you two guys. He wants to join us in our travels. Is that okay?"

"'Sure, let him come along," said Jack.

"Of course," observed Joe, "we can't travel far with Jack, running around au natural like he is; he has nowhere to carry us."

"I can fix that," said Hans. "My house is not far from here. I'll dash over and get a shirt and pants of my own. Jack can wear those."

"While you're dashing," remarked Joe, "dash back with some more food. Jack and I are still famished."

"Sure thing," said Hans. He jumped up and started off toward home.

"Hey, man," yelled the mouse, "aren't you going to get dressed? Your mother will be real astonished if you come running in bare-assed and balls-bare-to-the-breeze like that."

"Oh yes, of course." Hans exclaimed. He stopped, pulled on his lederhosen and shirt and then set off.

In a remarkably short time he was back with an extra pair of leather pants, shirt, a huge loaf of bread, a hunk of cheese, and a kid-skin bottle full of orange juice.

Jack and Joe grabbed the food and started wolfing it down. Hans and Jerry joined them.

After everything was eaten up and Jack had put on his borrowed clothes, the crew rounded up the donkey and set forth on their way. Joe was back in Jack's shirt pocket with head out, eyes bright, and whiskers quivering. Jerry was in Hans' shirt pocket, a little less assertive.

"There's a little village not far from here," said Hans, "Why don't we head for that?"

It seemed like a good idea so the two youths, the two mice and the ass followed Hans' directions to the village. The name of the place doesn't matter; it was just a village.

However, it happened that there was a fun fair and a flea market going on when they arrived. They saw all sort of interesting things for sale as they passed along toward the clowns and the carousel.

Over in one corner was a wrinkled old man with the dark skin of a gypsy.

"Whither away, young men," he called, "Come over and see my lamp. It's the last one of my stock. Here it is," (holding up a tarnished old brass lamp) "Buy my last lamp so I can go home and I'll make you a good deal."

"Hey!" said Hans, "a lamp is a useful thing. It's light enough to carry. It doesn't eat. It's not stubborn. I'm going to trade."

In short order he had handed over his donkey and acquired the lamp.

"I'm not sure you got a bargain there," commented Joe, "Perhaps when the lamp gets cleaned up, when you've cleared the tarnish off it, it may look better."

"Well, tonight I'm going to really rub all that tarnish off. I kind of like to clean brass." said Hans.

The four of them frittered away the rest of the day wandering around the fair and market. The food stalls sent out delicious aromas but, of course, neither one nor other had any money so they had to go hungry. At nightfall they bunked down in an abandoned chicken house on the outskirts of the village.

"Man, I could eat that whole giant back there, cock, balls and all," said Jack.

"Don't think about it," said Joe, "maybe something will turn up."

"Well, I've got nothing better to do. I'm going to clean my lamp," said Hans.

With the tail of his shirt, some sand and some water he found in an old saucepan he started to rub away the tarnish. As soon as he got down to shiny brass a strange glow filled the chicken house, a puff of smoke ejected from the lamp and a strange ghostly shape materialized out of the spout. It spoke in tones like those of a great organ:

"What is your wish, Master?"

Hans threw the lamp away from himself in fright. It landed in a heap of straw but the apparition still hovered over it. "Who the fuck are you?" demanded Joe.

"I am the Genie of the Lamp and I don't bandy words with mere rodents."

"Pray with whom do you bandy words, then?" asked Joe sarcastically.

"With my Master, the man who rubs the lamp."

For the first time Jerry spoke. "Hans, do you think that Genie could find us some food? I'm dying of hunger. It's a hell of a long time since lunch."

'That's a good idea," said Hans." Genie, could you round us up some bread and cheese or something? If you need a wish, that is our wish."

"I hear and obey."

There was a brilliant flash of light and magically a carpet appeared on top of the chicken shit. It was covered with urns and baskets and dishes and goblets and ewers and salvers of gold, each one piled high with luscious food or filled with the most delicious nectar. Hot and cold dishes, steaming cous-cous, mounds of savory roast lamb, compotes of icy sherbet, baskets of tempting fruit. All perfuming the air with seductive aromas.

Jack and Hans, Joe and Jerry, set to with a will and feasted like the starved creatures they were. 13y the end of two hours, tremendous inroads had been made and they were replete.

Hans rubbed the lamp and the Genie reappeared.

"Genie, can you clear away these dishes and things?"

Joe spoke. "While you're at it, Hans, ask him if he could find us some beds to sleep in. I'm tired of being around all this dry chicken shit. It's smelly and irritating."

"Yes," said Hans, "Can you find us some beds?"

"I hear and obey."

In a flash all the food and the dishes of gold disappeared and only the carpet remained. Out of the depths of the lamp the Genie spoke: 'Sit down on the carpet."

"That's not what I would call a bed," said Joe, "but it's better than lying on chicken droppings."

They all moved over and sat on the carpet. Slowly it rose and hovered in the air. The roof of the chicken house suddenly flew off and the carpet sped up and out – and away into the night. The four friends sat terrified and rigid as the carpet rushed across the heavens. It was black night so they couldn't see how high they were flying but any height at all was frightening.

In less time than it takes to tell, the carpet swept down and landed in the courtyard of a palace. The shaken quartet rose and hesitantly peered into the window of the palace. A major-domo appeared, bowed, and requested they enter. They followed the man to four spacious rooms lavishly furnished and each with an emperor-size canopied bed.

"We don't need four bedrooms," explained Jack to the factotum. Hans and I will be sleeping in the same bed."

"And Jerry and I will be sleeping at the foot of it," asserted Joe.

Nightclothes were available in a carved armoire but naturally these were redundant. Both Jack and Hans preferred to sleep nude in the great bed – Joe and Jerry likewise. Each pair found comfort in close embrace, warm skin next to warm skin.

They got into bed, but not to sleep. Jack and Hans conducted erotic anatomy explorations under the covers with great delight. Joe and Jerry, no less amorously inclined, conducted their affairs at the foot of the bed secure in the knowledge that the two lads were too interested in their own discoveries to spy on their revels.

After a night of such carnal delights as are beyond description the party woke up to early morning sunshine streaming through the palace windows.

Again the major-domo appeared, showed them where to wash up – here was a novelty; peasant youths seldom did.

Then he escorted them to a sumptuous breakfast.

During this morning feast Jack and Hans discussed their next move.

239

"I'd like the Genie to take us to Araby and the vales of gay Kashmir," said Hans.

"I'd like him to take us to the gay baths in all the great cities of the world," said Jack, "Not to bathe, you understand, but just to let us feast our eyes on the beautiful naked men."

"Jesus, you boys have your heads screwed on backwards," expostulated Joe, "Forget all that foreign travel crap. Let's get down to basics. What we need is hard cash and lots of it. Hans, tell that Genie to take us to where money grows on trees and the streets are paved with gold. Go ahead, call him up and tell him."

Hans rubbed the lamp. It puffed smoke and the Genie appeared.

"We want to be rich. Can you take us to where money grows on trees and the streets are paved with gold?"

"I can, but may I suggest an alternative? You will get rich quicker. Far away from here, hidden in an unexplored region of Arabia, Felix is the Valley of Diamonds. There you can gather jewels unlimited. You can scoop up diamonds, rubies and emeralds in untold amounts. When you return to your homes you will be rich beyond your wildest fantasies."

"OK," said Joe, "take us there."

"I've told you once before. I don't take orders from persons who are not my Master and in particular from members of the genus Mus!"

"Genie, let's not start a feud with our mouse," interposed Hans. "You and we are all together in this. We should be one happy family."

"As you order, but that damned mouse creature really annoys me. He's as irritating as a bug up one's ass."

"Forget it," said Hans. "Take us to that Valley of Diamonds!"

"I hear and obey. Step outside and onto the carpet. It will whisk you away in a trice."

Everybody headed for the door.

"W-a-a-a-i-i-i-t one fucking minute," cautioned Joe. "Before you rush out to sit on that carpet, what are you going to use to carry the diamonds back in? You won't get rich with a mere handful or even a pocket full of precious gems. We need baskets and bags and boxes. I suggest we gather them before we leave."

Following Joe's advice the party scurried around the palace gathering up containers. When the carpet was piled high with hardly room left for the travelers, Hans gave the command to the Genie and they were off.

Faster than the wind the carpet flew through the skies. Before its passengers had time to become rigid with fear it arrived at the fabled valley. Again it swooped down and landed with the four on the floor of the valley.

There is little point in trying to pinpoint the location of this hidden valley, to describe the mountains surrounding it, or the scenery on the valley floor; no one is going to go there again for a thousand years. However, there were diamonds. Drifts and heaps of diamonds. And rivulets of rubies and emeralds. With outcroppings of sapphires here and there. The sun shining down into this sea of gems set such a coruscating dazzle as almost blinded the eyes.

Jack and Hans, to say nothing of Joe and Jerry, were overwhelmed. They all hopped off the carpet and started running their hands through the jewels, picking out the largest specimens, discarding those in favor of even larger ones, gloating over the scene and hugging themselves for their good luck.

Joe cast a blanket of reality on their dreams: "Look, you guys, stop mooning over who has the biggest gem. Get back here, grab a basket, start shoveling the stuff in with might and main. Big or little, who cares? It's all riches. Let's gather it in by the bushel. Who knows when the Genie is going to pull the carpet back out of here? Get the booty first, then waste time picking and choosing."

Jack and Hans each grabbed a basket and each with the help of his mouse friend started shoveling in diamonds by the handful. Cute little Jerry-mouse discovered a prize ruby of purest pigeon's-blood red. He popped it in his mouth as his only way of carrying it. However, a little later, in the heat of his gathering endeavor he forgot it was there and swallowed it.

In due course all the containers were full to overflowing and all set back on the carpet. By this time such a superfluity of gem stones had caused the four to become blasé. They were ready, even eager, to leave the flashing valley and head for home.

Hans rubbed the lamp.

"Genie, after we've all got back on the carpet we want to fly to our home country again. Give us a minute to get organized and then take off."

"I hear and obey."

After considerable shifting and moving about caused by having to reorganize the load to provide better sitting room, Jack, Hans, and the two mice were ready. The carpet shook and struggled and slowly rose.

It was obvious it found the load extremely heavy. Nevertheless it managed to clear the mountains surrounding the valley and set off at a speed considerably slower than the wind.

They were flying high over the ocean when the carpet shuddered, slowed and began to lose altitude.

"What's the matter?" asked Joe, This thing isn't doing so good. Better call up the Genie, Hans. Get him to give the carpet a kick in the ass. I don't like the look of that ocean down there. We wouldn't want to come down in it."

Hans turned to rub the lamp. It wasn't where it should have been.

"Say, men, look around among the baskets. I seem to have misplaced my lamp."

Everybody started looking. No lamp.

Hans and Jack shifted the boxes and baskets around, searching. Still no lamp.

"Where the hell could it have got to?" asked Hans. "I put it right there when we were packing in the valley."

"Well, I dragged it to the side," piped up Jerry-mouse. "It was in the way at the time."

"You mean you put it down off the carpet?" demanded Jack. "Yes. It was in the way."

"Oh my god!" exclaimed Joe. "We've left it behind in the valley. Tell the Genie to turn the carpet around, Hans. We have to go back."

Hans yelled: "Hey, Genie, change course and return us to the Valley of Diamonds."

There was no response; the Genie must be napping. "Hey, Genie, wake up! Steer the carpet back."

Still no Genie to say "I hear and obey."

Slowly the horror was born in on their minds. There could be no Genie. Without the lamp there could be no Genie. "Damn it to hell."

"Of all the fucking luck!"

"Mama Mia! Christ a'mighty!"

"Jeez, I'm sorry."

Jack peered over the edge. The carpet was still going down toward the ocean. And there were icebergs floating down there! "We're falling! What are we going to do?" he exclaimed.

"I suggest we jettison some of this load," said Joe. "We're too heavy."

Jack shook his head. "We can't do that. These are diamonds."

"We'd be throwing treasure away," added Hans.

"Those facts to the contrary notwithstanding," said the mouse. "We're going to be mighty wet millionaires if we don't do something pretty damned quick. Those icebergs are getting bigger and bigger."

With heavy hearts Jack and Hans each took a basket and tipped it out over the edge. The gems made a cascade of brilliance as they fell down through the sky.

But it did make a difference. The fall slowed and the forward speed increased.

However, it was of short duration. Not long after, another two baskets had to be dumped overboard. Then another two and another two. Finally there was only one small basket of diamonds left on the carpet.

"We're not going to dump that," asserted jack. "We need something to take back or we'll be as poor as when we started."

"I agree," said Hans.

"Let me put it to you this way," said Joe. 'Which is better – to save some diamonds or to save our lives? We are now down to about one hundred feet and still losing height. Throw the damned things over the edge into the sea. It's our last hope of clearing the waves."

They did so and indeed it made a difference. They could feel the carpet rising and speeding up in its flight. Soon, far ahead they sighted land and, in time, their own home country. The carpet came to earth by the side of their old swimming hole and the bower under the trees. They all stepped off, breathing sighs of relief. Swift as the wind the carpet took off and sailed away into the sky.

"Well, I assume you men had sense enough to fill your pockets with diamonds before we dumped that last basket," remarked Joe. "We won't be entirely broke."

"Oh lord," said Hans. "I forgot. We were so busy I forgot to grab any. Maybe Jack will share his with us."

"I haven't a single jewel on me. I forgot too! Dammit, Joe, why didn't you remind us?

"I was too busy peering over the side and trying to figure out when we were going to splash into the water."

"Well, at least I've got something," said Jerry-mouse, "a priceless pigeon's-blood ruby."

"Where is it? Let's see it!" the others cried in unison. "Unfortunately I swallowed it."

"That's a dumb thing to do."

"That's no help to us."

"It was in the way, I assume?"

"It's not digestible," said Jerry. "It's on its way back now. No doubt in the near future it will reappear. We will just have to wait for it to materialize."

Which they did and it did.

GYPSY BOY
James Medley

You know me as a gypsy. The Romany. The wandering peddler, fortune teller, musician, sharpener of cutlery, a tinker and seller of baubles, buckles and pins, brightly colored bits of cloth, ribbons and scarves and spices from afar, pots and pans and kitchen ware.

And you may also know me as The Thief. Cunning. Secretive and sly. Pilfering from the villages, rumored to have stolen children. Seductive, raven-haired gypsy girls, having you off while lifting your purse. You've coined the word gyp, from my name. Though actually, it is a corruption of Egyptian. My lineage, the same. I've heard them all and I know the vicious tales.

My name is Marel and I am a gypsy boy. The only thing I will steal from you is your heart.

A man with whom I coupled in the closeness of my tinker's wagon, somewhere in the south of France, I cannot remember where, had left this note for me, upon his departure in the morn. I quote it here so you may know something of me and judge the effect my presence had on him.

"Sweet Marel. I must leave for business in the north. The dewy hollows of your body are fresh upon my tongue, and would that I could tarry long, and drink of your honeyed youth again. I smell your heady aroma now. I watch you naked as you sleep, one coltish leg partway drawn to your smooth and hairless chest, perfect little arse cleaved deeply, and your firm, youthful man-spheres, now taut and relaxed, dimpled as you shift slightly in your slumbers. Your elastic belly moves fretfully. Airy shadows sculpt your nipples and frame your slender loins.

"I've loved your cock and I've loved your bunghole. I see your smooth hard muscle now, nestled in the cradle of your silken thighs, stretching long the length of your trim leg, your downy bush of hair, moist and glistening in this early morning light. An erection of youth. Your balls are slumped like plover's eggs within their sac of velvet flesh. Your hair so black it is bluish like the raven's, thick, and curling about your pretty face. Your black eyes are closed but I remember them. Remember the wildness of their animal need, snapping fire as you spat your sweet young seed on me. I taste again your firm and yielding lips as I frigged my milk in you.

"And your heart I will miss and covet and hope to meet again. I love you, Marel. Farewell."

Perhaps he was a bit too poetic and wrote with a touch of superfluous flourish, but you will take his meaning right enough. Though I asked him not for it, he left a gold doubloon for me.

I was, shortly before the time of this writing, journeying with my father's caravan through Bavaria, making our way eastward toward our native Hungary. Winter would shortly be upon us and the rugged mountain passes would freeze over with bitter cold along our route. We had encamped this very night in a baron's game preserve.

Just before an early twilight, the dusk swiftly descending on the primeval forest, we had circled our wagons around a great clearing, mine closest to the dense and heavy wood. Our horses were tethered and fed. A bonfire had been lighted and my companions, huge family and all manner of relatives, were disporting in the light of the dancing flame. Pipes played and a hurdy gurdy wailed, drums pounded a frantic tattoo, wild dancing among the young. I had not joined in, feeling low and dispirited among the raucous folk. I sulked in my wagon.

My nature is such that I lie not with the dark, sultry girls of my clan. In truth, I yearned for the touch of a man.

One year hence, when I had but attained my majority, I had met a fellow in the smoke-filled tavern of a rustic village. He was a Saxon Earl. A giant of a man to my diminutive size, and shaggy as the golden bears which roam our lands. Lemon bearded and mustachioed, his mouth was wet and rosy, with even white teeth and the brightest blue eyes I had seen. His tunic was red satin and open at the throat, it being very hot that summer. The mountains of his muscles were heavily furred and grew most thickly in the deep valley of his chest. His name was Jason and he sat across the single table from me and smiled. Have you seen any unicorns in your travels?" he asked in a teasing way.

"You will be having me on," I said earnestly. "There are no such creatures."

He laughed and said, "Perhaps." Then he bought me more ale, and still more as he regaled me with thrilling tales of his adventures on the road, so much more splendid than mine.

Being somewhat smitten with the heady mead, I had grown aroused with his later bawdy conversation. As best I can recall, he had led off with asking did I have a wench. Then told to me how hard it was to find one who could fit his need.

But a boy, now. Ah – there it is," he said.

I am certain that I blushed. Then beneath the table, his knee brushed mine. Returned and stayed, pressing against my leg. I felt my cock swelling inside the loose cotton trousers I wore. I returned the pressure and his face lit up like the sun.

"Early evening, boy," Jason said. "We have time to catch the unicorn."

My companions were in their cups and I slipped out with him. He pulled me up behind him onto a great black stallion. "Hold on tight," he said as we cantered off.

I caught up his middle and it was all I could do to get my arms around his chest. He pushed them to his waist. My hands were at his groin, afire to touch him there. He reached behind us and pulled my arse closer to his rump. My cock was still painfully hard and I rubbed it against his warm backside. He turned to me and wickedly grinned, pulled me tighter to him. The friction from the jolting horse nearly brought me off.

Emboldened, I felt his cock.

Yes, it was an awesome sword. He was as hard as the spine I so eagerly clutched to my thin torso. He took my hand and pushed it down the cinch of his leather drawers. He was naked beneath and I felt the heat from his erection and the swollen mass of his balls. Thick hair and yielding flesh, a mushroom crown so immense, my palm could not contain it. Jason's pee hole leaked with manly juices and wet my hands as I fondled him. His cock flesh was thick and slid slippery on the bone as I stroked him.

Jason rode like the wind to a crude hunter's cabin. He tethered his steed to a sapling tree. It was now quite dark in the little wood. With his hand on my shoulder, he pushed through the door and lit a single lantern which cast a warm yellow light over the barren walls and rough dirt floor. Along one side were two crude pallets of straw. He stood me before him and looked me up and down. "My pretty gypsy boy," he said. "You are all that I would dream."

And then he touched my face, and took my cheeks between his palms and drew my mouth onto his fully open lips. It was as though his tongue shot the length of my body, inflaming my throat like a lightening bolt which burst all the way to my groin. I trembled in his arms and he held me fast to him. He was on hard and hunched his loins against mine. He caressed and kneaded my buttocks, drawing me ever tighter to his embrace. His muscled flanks framed my slender pelvis and I rutted and ground against him, deep-tonguing all the while.

And then slowly, gently, Jason undressed me. With nimble fingers, he unlaced the thongs of my jerkin, slipping his heated hands across my chest and teased my hardening nipples till they were thick and red. Gliding the folds across my shoulders, he bent and suckled on my chest. His hand caressed my groin. My cock had never felt so hard, swollen and throbbing beneath his tender touch.

Ever so slowly, he pushed my trousers down. He knelt before me and held my engorged cock aloft, kissing along the underside, over and around, up and down with his tongue distended to its fullest. Then Jason suckled at my balls and licked between my legs till I was wet and juicy from his spittle. I could hardly stand still. I trembled and quivered like a frightened colt. His hands worried frenziedly all over my naked body. I twisted my fingers through the coiled mass of his golden hair as he sucked my cock into his mouth.

I hunched out my hips and frigged my prong down his throat. His neck bulged and his lips pouted out, swept in as he set up a rhythm on my burgeoning cock. My knees buckled from the pleasure. His mouth was hot and he washed the head of my root in swirling ripples which caused my cream to almost shoot.

Then Jason stood and began undressing. And then all the glory of this beautiful man stood revealed. His legs were as stolid as logs, his body a hard mass of muscle above them, a cathedral of strength and maleness from the apex of his groin. His belly was broad, flat and concave to his barrel chest. His cock a battering ram and his arse a fortress of hard solid flesh. In the warm light of the lantern, Jason shone like the golden fleece of his namesake.

"Come here, Marel," he said in a mellow voice. "Feel me."

By all the gods of my forefathers, I had never touched a man like that. But wondrously I encircled his mammoth cock with both hands and bent to lick on it as the cattle do salt. From out my two hands clasped round combined, his awesome crown protruded. His prick was as hard and white as alabaster. He tasted of sweat, mellow juices and a pungent scent which was feverishly pleasant assaulted my senses.

"Suck on the knob," Jason moaned gutturally. "I need that." He held my head to him as I sought to engulf the prodigious, plum-like mound of his warm wet cock. By stretching my lips and pushing my head forward, I managed to engulf the thing to the rigid circle where it met the veined shaft. Sweet sticky liquid flowed into my mouth and I thought at first he had expended his cream. But it was the gooey mass of his lubricating fluid which drooled onto my tongue, tasting sweet to my palate.

Then Jason pulled me off like a suckling calf and lifted me in his arms. He propelled me backward onto the pallet and stretched full length atop me. The hardness of his body was all which existed for me at that moment. Until he lifted my legs to his shoulders and dove his woolly head between my legs. He ate at my bunghole.

I write that now and shivers grow heavily upon me. But he sheathed his wet tongue inside my arse and fed hungrily of my funk. It seemed an intoxicant to him, feeding feverishly inside me, ravishing my hole with more and more urgency, wanton and rampant craving to devour my very essence. I nearly spit my seed.

I can hardly describe the impaling. Jason did things to my body which seared my soul and awakened a craven lust to be filled by him. A hundred tongues and a thousand hands birthed that latent spirit to consign my life to him. When he penetrated me, I thought I would die.

"Easy, sweet baby," he crooned in my ear as his cock head slid inside my puckered opening. "I will not hurt you, sweet little boy. Relax, take me easy."

Oh, but by the gods, he did hurt me. At first. I bit my lips to keep from crying out. He kissed them raw. He held his cock fast just inside the fiery ring, until I became used to his girth. Then eased in more, more, another inch, another, still more. I gasped. I panted and heaved. I sighed. I moaned. I grunted like a pig. He fucked into me. He fucked me and he fucked me and he fucked me.

And the spiraling pain crested, broke over into a swelling tide of anguish before it was replaced by the most intense pleasure I'd ever experienced. I gritted my teeth. I could not breathe. I flailed my head from side to side. I thrashed and moaned ecstatically. I wanted to die on this man's cock.

"Marel! Marel! Marel!" he gasped over and over, driving into me with more deep and frantic strokes. He flogged my jerking cock till I thought it would burst and split like a ripe gourd. It felt as though my body was overflowing with youthful milk. And I wanted him to fuck it out of me.

Jason's swift rhythm became more urgent. His breathing grew ragged and gasping. He pounded and pumped my jerking cock. I was close. Near torturous spasms of exquisitely erupting sensations washed from my soles to my scalp, most intense between my widely splayed legs. I clutched his fiercely driving flanks and pulled him fully into me. There he held fast, tense and still. He shuddered.

And the sudden gush of his milk shot me full.

A long strangled cry, "Aaaahhhggg, YES!" And he pumped his juice to me.

I exploded like a pent-up river. Arching streams of bursting honey, blew out of my piss hole and slathered in silver rivulets across my heaving belly, my bursting chest, to my face and into my hair. I had been fucked by a man.

And then Jason grew playful, laughing and tussling with me on the straw. At one point, he placed his arm beneath my spine at the small of my back and lifted my arse in the air, my rekindled prick now jutting to the ceiling. Assuming some odd configurations of his arms and hands, he bade me to look at the shadow on the whitewashed wall.

You see him now, Marel?" he whispered in my ear. "My little unicorn."

In truth, the shadow from the lantern, reflected that very image on the wall, my cock the horn of his horse, our unicorn. So we rubbed the bacon and made the two backed beast again.

But, as I said, that had been so long ago. And now I lay there in my chock-a-block full but forlornly empty wagon, my cock hard with remembrance, listening to my frolicking clan, morose and lonely, unconsoled by the clutter of pots and pans about me.

The night was chill, and the moon was full. A light fog roiled about the pastoral scene. I was naked and swaddled in my blankets. Preparing to pleasure myself, and wishing to see my cream erupt, I parted the canvas flaps at the rear of the cart, away from the gamboling folk, with a vista on the wood. And saw there in the dappled light, and through the smudges of darkness, a golden vision.

Just beyond the ring of leaping shadows, a snow white horse stood still. A young man astride. Through the light mist I could see his eyes were fervently watching my compatriots at their play. Like a solitary sentinel, he spied on them. His hair was lustrous and copperish in the light from the flickering flames. He was wearing a blue velvet cape, white leggings and the crest of the baron was upon his saddle. For surely this was no common man, marked as he and the steed were with signs of royalty. A feathered plume of crimson adorned his horse.

In my excitement, I bolted to my knees. Like a startled deer, his head swiveled at the sudden movement. He saw my nakedness. His eyes narrowed and he peered through the gloom at me. I held my breath. Such wanton exposure had not heretofore been my inclination. Though the night chill tingled upon my skin, and the fog-sheened my body like a cold sweat, I bravely bore it.

And as the stranger leered ever more luridly at my nudity, I grew further aroused and took my hard cock in my hand and stroked it for his view. A wicked smile creased his youthful features and he winked both eyes at me, first one, then the other.

He put a finger to his lips as he slipped from his mount and tied him to a tree. Then he crept stealthily toward my wagon. Surely the Druid gods were having their capricious way with me and I was dreaming this. Or so I thought until he slipped to the parted canvas.

With four soft fingers, he touched my body. Assured of each others' reality, he grew bolder and stroked my heated form. I trembled at his touch. His hot hands salved the cool air and left a trail of warmth through the mist across my chest.

May I come in?" he needlessly asked. For I was literally dragging him up the three stairs and into the dim interior. Once inside, he sat on the floor, his legs folded beneath him and his cape draped across his calves. He was uncommonly beautiful. I had never seen a boy with such bright red hair. And his eyes appeared green with flecks of gold in them. He had the smooth and clear complexion of late adolescence upon his finely hewn features, that mark of wealth and cast. A boyish glow on his pale freckled cheeks.

I scurried to fasten the canvas and made sure the front was secure. Then I lit a candle and sat on the floor in front of him, crossing my legs in the same fashion. I was supremely conscious of my previous audacity at exhibiting my nudity so brazenly to him, so I dragged a blanket across my loins. For but a second, he surveyed the hanging wares of my trade. Then his eyes rested upon my open groin. My cock jutted boldly past my navel, straining upward as if to smite my chest. The bulge of the head was clearly outlined at the top of the tent in my lap.

By the gods, but you are a vision," he said, echoing my sentiments precisely. "How are you called?"

I told him my name was Marel. He said his was Giles. "This is my father's wood. He is Baron Rachelaud."

"I am but a gypsy."

"What matters that with such as we?" he asked softly. I think I fell in love with him then. If not at that moment, certainly on the instant he bent forward to kiss me fully upon the lips. And then in less time than it takes me to set down the words, we were grappling with one another.

I felt him hard, hot and fleshy beneath the silken material of his cloak. We were soon entangled in the coarse fabric of my blankets. His cape and robes and surplice and boots and leggings and all manner of straps and fastenings, metal hitchings and odd accouterments of apparel, were soon enough shed and we lay naked together beneath my comforter. And, oh God, but his body was bliss.

With my hungry, yearning mouth, I explored all the tufted hollows and warm moist curves of Giles' youth. I licked between his silken thighs and he did the same to me. Inverted and inflaming one another, we fed upon our cocks. Delirious and mad with lust, I felt each pulse of his root in my mouth and gave him back the same. A silent language, a pause, his cock hard and fast upon my tongue, the telling twitch, an answer to my own. Then deep down our throats, crushed together and joined, pressing in hard against one another. His balls smashed against my chin and me hunching ever deeper into the hot cavern of his feeding mouth.

Rapture. Ecstasy. Sublime and exquisite passion. All insufficient to describe our union. Sucking. Gulping. Gasping. Grunting. Sighing. Moaning. We spent inside each other.

Giles' juice gushed forth and washed my mouth with a bittersweet saltiness. I swallowed greedily and felt my own fountain spewing forth and into his stroking lips. Bursting all out, again and again, I shot the fluid from my groin. Deep, deeper, deepest he took me in. And held my cock fast and exploding down his throat like a warm velvet vise, milking, milking, milking.

It was over in an instant. But like the minor players who strut a small tableaux, before the master's work's performed, the central play began.

Holding, feeling, whimpering and murmuring to one another, we waded into a warm ocean of sex. Soon all was flesh and coupling again. We resembled the ancient symbol of Yin and Yang, eating each others' bungholes. Then sucking cocks and teats and lips and tongues and gnawing inside our armpits. I wanted to fuck this boy like no other in my life.

"Please go up me easy, Marel," he panted as I straddled his arse with his legs slung across my back. "I have not been fucked before."

And just as Jason had broken me to his hellish weapon, I drooled a strand of saliva to my palm, greased up and eased my cock into Giles.

"Oh! – God! – Yes!" Giles gasped. "Now! Take me now!"

Nothing can be as supremely perfect as a man inside a man. Hot and wet, Giles was open for my penetration. I sheathed my cock into his arse all the way to my balls and those I crushed against his ditch and ground hard into him. My senses rode a river of raw stinging nerves as I held my knob fast to his melting channel. His flesh was tender, soft and yielding inside. I pushed into the warmth of his body and he held me tightly about the shoulders, nibbling on the hollow of my neck.

Can you fuck your brains out? I thought that might happen then. Because Giles contrived to pull my cock all the way inside him, then lewdly rode his buttocks into my groin, both legs astride my middle. Then I sat back on my haunches and held him onto my lap, my legs folded beneath. From there, I held his slender flanks and fucked him up and down, hard and faster onto my root.

"I want to ride you, Marel," he panted, his voice sounding reedy and thin, a boyish whisper. I maneuvered him atop me and he saddled up on my loins, never losing a thrust which I drove into him. Then he became a wild little animal on my cock. Squatting and fucking himself with a demented fury.

Eyes closed and head thrown back, tossing his long red hair from side to side, he bucked on me like an unbroken yearling. I thrust up my pelvis and he slammed down, a furious rhythm of boundless lust. I jerked on his sex. His cock hammered his belly in a rapid tattoo. I wanted him to do it on me.

I wanted to see his cream shoot out. I wanted to fuck it out of him. Afire with need, I matched his strokes, each more vigorous than the last. Heaving and thrashing, he milked my cock. It felt as if the very core and essence of myself was racing to my groin, my body shuddering and quaking beneath his pounding loins. Never had I met a boy who fucked like that.

"Up! Up! Up!" he gasped, pulling up my thighs with his grasping hands. I arched my spine into the air and he bore his full weight upon me, impaled as deeply as he had been all along, and there he wailed and quivered. "Oh! Oh! Oh!"

"Ugh! Ugh! Ugh!" I matched his stifled groans. For it was upon us now. As surely as if we were one, I felt his seed begin to spew even as my own flushed from my boiling balls. My cream spurted deep into his arse and I savagely pumped it to him. So great in quantity, the milk ran frothy from his hole.

Giles' upper torso slumped back along my bent and lifted legs, his cock most prominently erect. I grasped the meaty muscle and felt the spasms of eruption begin. His body was as tense as a startled hare, hard like metal and rigid. And then his cock shot off like a musket.

In the rapturous throes of my tumultuous discharge, I chanced to catch a glimpse of our shadow upon the wall. And there was the unicorn. Its single horn was Giles' great cock, spurting fountains of milk all over the both of us. Our writhing bodies the mighty head of the mythical beast. And I was in heaven at last.

Shuddering down now, easing off, gently relaxing, our breathing paced and measured, we lay still together, holding. I tenderly caressed the wet youth.

Giles kissed me. Outside, the sounds of merriment had equally drifted down, soft night stirrings surrounded our place of concealment. No moment in the past had been so perfect for me. We slept entwined like that.

Would that I could write that I stayed there on the baron's estate with Giles, that we lived happily ever after.

But alas, as I have said, I am a gypsy boy. And from you I only would steal your heart.

THE HANSEN TWINS
Peter Z. Pan

"Bewitched, bothered and bewildered, am I."
– Lorenz Hart

The boy's hands rested on his naked knees. The man could see this out of the corner of his eye. They were just lying there, his left forefinger circling, perhaps tickling the tender skin beneath. Fair, silky skin that ran down his plump legs into his red-striped tube socks. The boy was simply divine, from the shaggy mop of blond hair he wore in a surfer-cut to a figure so well-defined and graceful that beauteous archangels would have been envious. He had his head reclined back against the seat with his eyes closed. Clearly lost in sleep, dreaming, with a mischievous, little boy smile.

Oh, but what naughty images must be dancing in his mind, the man wondered. For the boy's legs were wide open, as if proudly showing off to the world the bulge in his tight, red shorts. And if your eyes could possibly leave such a luscious sight and run up his slender torso to his heaving chest, yes, they would notice hard nipples pressing against the satiny material of his t-shirt. The man was breathless. And the growing bulge in his own pants made him feel guilty. Guilty as sin.

The old Honda Civic sedan was alone on this dark country road now. A gloomy, almost brooding, road that made his skin crawl and brought back silly childhood fears of things that go bump in the night. Like the damn road in "Close Encounters," the man thought. But it wasn't Halloween or Friday the Thirteenth or any of those horrid, pagan eves. On the contrary, it was prom night in the town they had just left. A good, happy night. So get all the stupid thoughts of ghosts and witches and goblins out of your mind right now!

But the road was foreboding.

Oh, they were so lost it was ridiculous. They had stopped to get a late dinner at Denny's and crash in a motel before continuing their long road trip in the morning. The waitress had told him of a cheap motel – ten bucks cheaper than the Days Inn adjacent the Denny's – just a mile down this road. But he must have taken a wrong turn or something because he was sure he'd driven at least two miles and there was nothing out there. Absolutely nothing but loud crickets with their creepy songs, the telltale aroma of skunk, and big ominous oak trees with thick, swaying branches that looked like they were going to reach out into the road any minute and grab hold of the Honda like a Hot Wheels car. And all this for ten lousy bucks, cheapskate!

He would have turned back long ago if he hadn't been distracted by the boy.

Moaning.

The man's eyes were on the boy once more. His small head jerked back and forth, his entire body contracted, and as he moaned with a final shiver, the man noticed the large stain in his shorts. Is he old enough to come?! the man wondered, overcome by both desire and guilt.

The boy opened his eyes and screamed. The man looked out the windshield, his foot slamming down on the brakes when he saw what the boy saw. The car scarcely came to a complete stop within an inch of the two figures. Their safety-belts held them securely in their seats as the car jolted. The man's senses overwhelmed him: the screeching noise, the stench of burned rubber, the taste of the blood where he bit his tongue, the warmth of his urine as it filled his pants, and, oh yes, the strange vision his eyes beheld.

Two young girls in prom dresses!

The man stormed out of the car, driven by anger as well as fear.

"What the hell are you kids doing?!" he screamed at them. "Do you wanna get yourselves killed or something!"

The girls just stared at him as though what he had just said hadn't registered. There was a kind of melancholy on their young faces. And they were twins, weren't they? Identical twins who looked almost catatonic, yet sensual somehow. For some reason, the ghastly image of the twin little girls in 'The Shining" came to him. But why? These girls were far from ghastly, and they were older and much prettier. Very pretty as a matter of fact, with shiny manes of long black hair, porcelain faces, incandescent eyes in a lovely shade of violet, and exquisite young bodies wrapped in white gowns. And, oh yes, they were sensual. But there was something about their Adam's apples. Too big. Out of place.

The man was about to scold them again, when one of the twins spoke: "We just came from the prom," she stated matter-of-factly with a delicate southern twang.

"Yes, the prom," her sister repeated with the same accent. "We didn't have a very good time," said the first girl. "We never have a good time," added her sister somberly. The man was taken aback by their calm manner. Hell, he'd just almost run them over and they were making small talk. "What the hell are you doing out here in the middle of nowhere?!" he demanded.

"Why, we're on our way home," the first twin answered. She looked up and then back at the man. "But it looks like it might rain."

Thunder in the distance.

"It always rains," added her sister sadly.

"Could you possibly give us a ride home?" the other girl requested. "We just live down the road."

And then the rain came before he could say no. Heavy rain that arrived from nowhere, for the sky had been clear just moments before. He wanted to say no with every fiber of his being. There was something so odd about these girls, so macabre almost. He couldn't quite put his finger on what it was, but it bothered the hell out of him.

(Those damn Adam's apples...Too big...Out of place!)

The man's anger had gone, chased away by wonderment and more guilt. How could he say no? He had just almost killed them for God's sake. He owed them at least that much. Besides, they looked so pathetic in the pouring rain: their once-immaculate hair was now drenched, their lovely make-up was running down their delicate faces like crayons in a box melting after a good hit of LSD, and they were shaking from the cold water that enveloped them.

Lighting suddenly struck one of the oaks with a blinding fury, making the tree split in two. The top portion fell directly on the road behind the car, just barely missing it and blocking the path back to town.

The man was trembling, and not from the cold rain pounding his body.

"Get in!" he shouted at the girls as he ran back in the car.

The twins quickly got in the back seat, slamming the door behind them. The man then put the car in gear and they took off with a screech.

He was still shaking when he looked in the rearview mirror. Both girls were just staring straight ahead with that melancholy look again. They smelled of gardenias,

252

the scent quickly permeating the car's interior. He looked over at the boy and found him looking over his shoulder, just gaping at the girls with his big blue eyes.

"Bobert, it's not polite to stare at people," the man reprimanded the boy.

"Sorry," said Bobert quite embarrassed as he turned his head forward.

The man looked in the rearview mirror again. "My name's Rob Thomas," he said to the girls with a nervous smile, "and this is my son, Robert. You know, Robert and Bob combined: Bobert."

"My name is Chris Hansen," said the first of the two sisters who had spoken to him outside. "This is my identical twin, Pat."

"Charmed," said Pat, who sounded like a pubescent Scarlet O'Hara.

"Nice to meet you both," Rob said with another nervous smile. "Where is your house?

"Just down the road, Mr. Thomas," Chris assured him, "just down the road."

Rob decided to give up on the small talk and instead concentrate on the road. He just wanted to unload these two strange girls, find a motel, and get into a nice, warm bed with his son. Probably the last time they would share a bed in a long time. This made him sad. It also made him feel relieved in a way. Relieved he wouldn't be tempted anymore to – He had to get those disgusting thoughts out of his mind! Besides, that wasn't the reason why he was taking the boy to live with his aunt. Bobert had lived with his mother in Miami – just twenty minutes from Rob's apartment in Ft. Lauderdale – ever since Rob divorced her when the boy was five. After she died in a car accident, Rob honestly thought he could take care of his son. Well, he was wrong. Bobert had lived with him June and most of July and it just wasn't working out. He never realized how demanding it would be to be a single parent. Worse, a single gay parent having to stay in the closet for his son's sake. He had to be a good role model after all. Rob hadn't been with a guy in almost seven weeks and it was beginning to get to him. Imagine, having feelings for your own son! How sickening!

Bobert wanted to continue living with his dad, however Rob was convinced he couldn't give the boy a proper upbringing. A first year nurse only makes so much money and sometimes he had trouble just feeding his own mouth. Worst of all, after being only a Sunday Father to Bobert ever since the boy was five, Rob found he and his son had become strangers to each other, sadly enough. So against all of Bobert's wishes, he was driving him to live with his Aunt Laura in New Orleans. It was for the boy's own good.

"Dad, I'm sleepy," Bobert yawned. "When are we gonna get to the motel?"

"Just as soon as I can find it, son," Rob told him. He then looked in the rearview mirror. "Do you girls know where the Happy Traveler Lodge is by any chance?"

"Why they won't finish building that place for months," said Chris. "Who ever recommended it to you?"

"Some damn waitress at Denny's with a sick sense of humor!" Rob said.

"Denny's?" A puzzled Pat looked at her sister who was equally as puzzled. "What ever is a Denny's?"

Rob chuckled. "Surely you girls have heard of – " Utter shock kicked him in the stomach, making him almost lose his Grand Slam Ham-Dinger combo meal. They were dry! They'd been soaking wet just moments ago – as he still was – but now they were dry. And their make-up was perfect too!

"We're here," said Chris without even looking outside.

Rob hit the brakes, then looked out his window. They were there. Unfortunately there didn't look very inviting. If somebody had asked him to imagine the house where these two odd, sullen girls in the back seat lived, he would have pictured this house. A dour old antebellum mansion in front of a lake, with white fluted columns on the front. Two monstrous oaks stood to both sides of the aged gate and the iron lace railings – which were much festooned with the pretty vines of pink bougainvillea, purple wisteria, and yellow Virginia Creeper – were made in what appeared to be a pentacle pattern of all things. A pentacle!

"Mr. Thomas," spoke Chris (or was it Pat?), "you won't find a hotel around for miles and the roads are so treacherous what with the storm and all..."

Rob knew where she was going with this and he didn't like it at all. As a matter of fact, just the thought of entering that spooky old house scared the hell out of him. He was forming the word "no" with his lips.

"And our home is so big," Chris continued. "That my sister and I would be honored if you and your adorable son would be our guests for the night."

This actually brought smiles to the twins' faces.

"We would just love the company," her sister said. "It can get so lonely all alone out here."

"No, thank you. That's very kind of you," Rob said as nicely as he possibly could. There was no need to be rude, "but Bobert and I really have to be on our way."

"I wouldn't mind staying the night, Dad," Bobert interjected, blatantly ogling the girls.

If Rob would have been a violent man he would have smacked his son upside the head right at that moment.

That's when the back, right tire went flat with a loud blast as if someone had just shot at it.

"Shit!" Rob clamored in disbelief. How very 'convenient,' he thought.

"That settles it then," said Chris, again smiling.

Rob had no choice. He wasn't about to change a tire in this tempest. The house was scary, but so was the night. And he didn't want to risk his son's life driving on that perilous road just because he was spooked by his stupid, puerile fears. They were just innocent, young girls for God's sake! So he pulled over to the side of the road and parked in front of the ominous house. (Danger...Get the fuck out of there!)

They hurriedly ran to the mansion and, as the girls opened the immense front door, Rob was slapped by the strongest foreboding he had ever felt. And for some reason he remembered the Jim Morrison biography on his bookshelf, No One Here Gets out Alive. As they entered the house, Rob immediately welcomed the comforting warmth produced by the flames dancing inside the fireplace in the parlor to his left. It illuminated the entire room and the adjoining hall where they stood, the flickering, radiant yellow making everything and everyone look hideously surreal.

Are you sure your parents won't mind?" Rob asked the Hansen Twins.

"Daddy left us many years ago," Chris answered. And Mamma fell asleep waiting for us."

She always falls asleep waiting for us," Pat said dismally.

The twins led Rob and Bobert upstairs, turning on gas lamps as they went along. Apparently the house had never been wired for electricity. How odd, Rob thought. Indeed, everything appeared untouched by time. As if time had simply stood still decades ago for this house. The antique furniture, the great oil paintings that hung on the walls, the lush carpet with intricate patterns of long ago. It all belonged in another time. A more innocent time.

The twins showed father and son to their room. It was as spacious as the rest of the house, with its own fireplace which was, curiously enough, ablaze.

A nervous laugh escaped Rob. "Were you expecting us or something?" he asked jokingly.

"Why, yes, we were, Mr. Thomas," Chris smiled.

"It's not often that we entertain gentlemen callers," said her sister giggling, as she flirtatiously gazed at young Bobert and winked.

The boy winked back, then began to blush when he saw his father looking on.

"Down boy," Rob said to Bobert with a smirk. He had never seen his son flirt with a girl before and, frankly, he found the whole thing unsettling. And the fact that it bothered him troubled Rob even more. His son was heterosexual and he wanted him to stay heterosexual. The world was full of too much bigotry for him to want his son to grow up gay.

"We bid you good night for now, Rob and Bobert Thomas," said Chris. She took hold of her sister's hand.

"Rest in peace," Pat said with a knowing, almost creepy grin as lightning struck outside.

This sent chills down Rob's spine.

And the Hansen Twins left the bedroom hand in hand, the door slamming shut behind them.

"Nice babes," Bobert blurted out with a lusty sigh.

"Yeah, if you like the Morticia Addams look," Rob said. He walked over to the mahogany four-poster and began to undress. All his clothes were drenched. This he found as a stroke of luck for no one could tell he'd peed his pants like a nine-year-old kid his first time on a roller coaster. He needed a shower badly.

Rob then looked up and noticed a peculiar sight: a large, yellow pentacle was embroidered on the canopy over the antique bed. Were these girls witches?

Bobert followed his father to the bed. "Why don't you like them, Daddy? They sure as hell like you. Especially that Chris babe." Bobert playfully elbowed his father in the stomach. "She was feeling you up with her eyes. And I caught you looking at her ass a couple of times too." He chuckled, then began to disrobe.

Rob was stopped dead in his tracks. He was simply aghast. He couldn't believe this was coming out of his son's young mouth. They had never talked about sex before. He always managed to change the subject every time Bobert brought it up – which was all too often – for fear his sexual preference would inadvertently come up. Now the boy was goading him about sex. And the worst part was that his son was right, he was staring at the twins' asses. This from a man who hadn't been turned on by a woman since the boy's tomboyish mother seduced him years ago when he was eighteen and confused. He didn't know why he was perversely attracted to the twins, he just knew that he was. There was just something about them that was so dangerously enticing.

"Have you been watching the Playboy Channel again?" Rob asked, trying to bring levity to this father-son chat from hell and hopefully change the subject. He had now stripped down to his Fruit of the Looms.

Bobert cocked an eyebrow. An impish smile then took over his young face. "No, I don't much care for that soft core crap," he said. "But I have popped a few of those videos you have hidden in your underwear drawer into the of VCR."

Rob couldn't move, he was paralyzed. If his bladder had not been empty, he would have wet himself again.

Bobert continued: "Some of them imported all the way from Amsterdam. 'Naked Schoolboys in Bondage,' 'Naked Schoolboys and Their Pets,' and let's see, oh yes, my personal favorite, 'Naked Schoolboys in Drag.' I kinda sense a theme here. You like that chicken, don't 'cha dad?"

Savage rage blinded Rob. When he came out of it, he realized he had slapped his son so hard, he'd knocked him on the bed. The violence had surprised the boy, who was now crying. This brought tears to Rob's eyes as well. He had never struck his son and he knew at that moment that he could never ever strike him again. It was too painful.

"I'm sorry, son," he whispered. He then walked into the adjacent bathroom. As he was closing the door behind him, he heard his son whisper:

"Dad, why don't you let me in?"

Tears were now running down Rob's face. He muttered into the empty bathroom, "Because I love you, son."

The hot water spraying down his naked, brawny form felt sinfully good as it cleansed him of his liquid waste. He wished it could have also cleansed him of his sins. The jig was up. The little snoopy bastard was on to him. And instead of sitting down and talking to him like a human being, he smacks the fucking kid like his old man used to smack him when he was a wise ass. He had turned into his father and he hated himself for it.

A loud creak derailed Rob's train of thought. He suddenly felt a presence in the room and smelled gardenias. Through the shower curtain he could see the light from the bedroom. Someone had opened the door. He also beheld a figure rushing towards him with a raised hand. (Shades of Janet Leigh...Norman Bates...Courtesy of Hitchcock!) The curtain was torn from its hooks with a fury at the exact moment Rob's heart skipped a beat and a scream escaped him.

"Hello, Mr. Thomas," whispered the figure, quite seductively, like a sultry phone whore on one of those 900 commercials late night TV is plagued with. It was one of the Hansen Twins and she was all decked out in black: a sexy, short teddy; silk panties with pretty laces; and fishnet stockings with six inch pumps. The works.

Rob didn't even bother to cover himself. He was too stunned, too dazed. He convinced himself he was having some sort of weird acid flashback. A wicked, exceedingly realistic motherfucker of a flashback. And throughout the years he had learned not to fight them. Just to give in to them and they would eventually pass. Sometimes he even enjoyed the side effects of his college flirtations with chemicals. Not this time though. He genuinely feared for his life and that of his son's.

"Don't be frightened, Mr. Thomas," said the girl in her bewitching southern drawl. "It's just me, Chris. And I'm not going to hurt you. On the contrary, I'm going to show you some good old fashioned southern hospitality." With that, Chris got into the shower with Rob and wrapped her epicene arms around his strong, hairy body.

"What the fuck are you doing?" Rob managed to get out with a lump in his throat and a growing lump below the equator. "I'm not into this scene!"

"Why, I do declare, Mr. Thomas," she stated, grinding her crotch against his, "something is telling me you're a liar, sir."

She was right. Rob's fat ten-incher was prodding the girl's stomach.

"Look, you're a beautiful girl and all, but you're just not my type."

She chortled wickedly. "You'd be surprised just how much 'your type' I really am."

Rob was more stupefied by his erection than by anything else. Chris then began to tongue his nipples, ever so lightly gnawing at them with her teeth. As usual this torrid act propelled him into complete, unadulterated ecstasy. He dropped his manly arms, purely out of reflex, around the girl's slender, young figure. His spidery hands weaved their way down her silken back, into her naughty tight panties, to rest upon her round, shapely buttocks. They felt so soft and virginal in his hands, like the ass of a vestal young boy. Yes, he was well under her spell.

By the time Rob realized he had lost control, Chris was on her knees with his sex in her youthful mouth. She wrapped her full lips around his burning cock, taking all of it in, until he felt his balls slapping against her chin. Rob then grabbed hold of her hair and commenced to fuck her mouth, to fuck her mouth hard while the water bounced off their ardent bodies, not quenching their fervor by a long shot.

Chris' lingerie was now drenched as was her hair, yet she looked more heavenly than ever. A splendid, delicate creature that would have aroused man, woman, or child. She was absolutely tantalizing. And to think he had been afraid of her.

Rob's libido took over making him more daring. He lifted the girl to her feet, kissing her hard on the mouth. Her serpentine tongue slithered into his ravenous, receptive mouth. As the tongue was slipping and sliding and gliding its way on in, Rob thought the taste of her was intoxicating, like a sweet daiquiri to an alcoholic who's been on the wagon for months. He was mad with passion as he worked his insatiable hands under her teddy to caress her fleecy chest. She was flat like an unfledged boy of sixteen and that sexed him up even more. Rob then fell to his knees and ripped off her panties with a feral tug. That's when his mouth dropped open in complete shock.

At first it had looked like a normal vagina, though Rob Thomas was a poor judge of what the female reproductive system looked like up close. But then Chris ever so slightly parted her legs, releasing the growing cock that she (he!) had hidden tucked between the thighs.

"My God, you've got a dick!" Rob clamored in disbelief. "Well, nobody's perfect," said Chris with a wicked smile. "You're a boy!" he continued. "You're a fucking boy!" "Really, sir," Chris scolded with his hands on his hips,

"must you use such foul language? It's so ungentlemanly." Rob got out of the shower and grabbed a towel posthaste.

"Frankly my dear, I don't give a damn!" he said, wrapping the towel around his waist.

"Where are you going?" Chris asked dejectedly.

"Look, I'm as kinky as the next guy, but this is all too weird for me." Rob shook the water out of his short, auburn hair. "I'm taking my kid and we're getting the fuck out of here, storm or no storm!" He headed for the bathroom door.

Chris went after him. "No, you can't go!" he pleaded with urgency in his voice.

Rob stopped to look back at him. "Listen kid, thanks for your hospitality...and for your interest in me. It's flattering, really it is. However, don't tell me what I can or cannot – " Rob's face lost all of its color. The boy was dry! He had just gotten out of the shower and he was bone-dry. "How do you do that?" he asked with a wry face. "What, do you have a blow-dryer up your ass or something?!"

Chris jumped into Rob's arms, wrapping his left arm around Rob's neck. "Take me, Robert!" Chris exclaimed. "My loins are burning for you!" He then grabbed

257

Rob's head and planted a wet kiss on his lips, thrusting his tongue deep into the man's mouth again.

Rob managed to break his lips free from Chris'. "Please, my son is in the next room!"

"Well, I'm sure he could teach you a few things," Chris said with a smirk.

Rob didn't like the sound of that. He dropped Chris to the floor and rushed into the bedroom. Just when he thought nothing could shock him anymore, this did.

His sweet, innocent son was in bed with Pat – who was dressed in the same outfit as his brother and had a dick to match. Bobert was lying on his stomach, buck-naked, going down on him. He smiled when he saw his father, taking the dick out of his mouth just long enough to say:

"Dad, you're wet."

Chris, who had followed Rob in, ripped the towel from his waist, revealing a whopping hard-on just oozing precum. "I do declare, you're right Bobert, he is." Chris dipped a forefinger in the jism seeping from Rob's cockhead and brought it to his mouth, tasting it the way a wine connoisseur savors a fine nectar. "Oom, delicious!"

"Robert, what the hell do you think you're doing?!" Rob demanded.

"I'm sucking dick, Dad." Bobert's callow face assumed that mischievous little-boy-smile once more. "Something that you should do more often. Then maybe you wouldn't be so cranky all the time." He continued sucking Pat's small but splendid peter.

"Come on, sir," said Chris taking his own six inch hard-on in his hand, "surrender yourself to torrid, unconditional ecstasy." He dropped to his knees and took Rob's erection in his tender mouth anew.

How could he possibly refuse? How could any gay man with a pulse possibly refuse? The transvestite twins, though mysterious, were absolutely enchanting. Chris straddled Rob's pelvis, then commenced riding him like a wild stallion.

Rob was watching a movie now. It was one of his favorite classics, wasn't it? An adolescent Liz Taylor sat astride a sweaty beast named Velvet as it galloped through a field of celluloid. But Liz was bare-assed naked. And Liz had a dick!

"Yippee-kay-yay, motherfucker!" exclaimed a gleeful, young voice. "Ride 'em, cowboy!" Rob looked over at his son, vaguely realizing it had come from him! Bobert was now kneeling on the bed, thrusting his boyhood into Pat's delicate mouth. Rob was taken by the size of the boy's penis. He had never seen his son naked before and never imagined that a beardless youth could sport a cock that was at least eight-inches long and growing, with plump low-hanging balls. Yet it looked so out of place with no pubic hair around it. just a slight fuzz.

"Like father, like son," said a bouncing Chris, who had somehow read his mind. "Big candy canes must run in your family, sir."

"Caught ya lookin', Dad," said Bobert. "Come on, I know you want it."

Rob wanted to feel embarrassment and guilt, however long it could take. He had almost dropped a load right then and there. Before he realized it, Rob was thrusting his pelvis into Chris' face, fucking the boy's mouth again with his pulsing cock. A cock that seemed to have developed a mind of its own and was dragging the rest of him down into the gutter with it. But the gutter felt damn good. He was drowning in a filthy cesspool of sins of the flesh, yet he didn't want to come up for air. He wanted to submerge himself into the depths of the warm, soothing filth and swim with his beautiful son and the ethereal twins. He yearned to be consumed by this sea of decadence for the rest of eternity. But would Bobert be able to swim back to shore, or would he be washed away forever, deluged by the twins' seductive charm?

(Help me, Dad!...I'm drowning!)

For the second time that night, Rob felt as if he were tripping. As if he had dropped some acid and the world around him was becoming nothing but a warped yet pleasurable hallucination. It wasn't so much a flashback; it was more like being dazed in a sexual stupor. Was the potent fragrance of gardenias that emanated from these beings literally intoxicating somehow? But that was crazy.

Rob scarcely noticed when Chris stood and took him by the hand, leading him over to the queen-size bed where his son's face was still buried in Pat's crotch. Rob lay next to Bobert. The feelings he was having as the boy's feverish skin was rubbing his could get a man put in jail. Rob just stared at his pretty son, wishing he had the courage to touch him.

"Don't fight it, Rob," Chris told him, this time without even opening his mouth. "Just surrender to your incestuous lust."

"Dad, try to get into it a little bit more," Bobert bantered. "You're just lying there like you're dead."

"I knew there was something about him that I liked," Chris said like a Borscht-Belt comic expecting a rim shot. He dismounted Rob, then lay on his tummy with his face at the man's groin. "Join me, Patrick. This sweet candy cane is much too big for my little of mouth alone."

Pat removed Bobert's cock from his mouth, giving it a good-bye kiss. "Coming, Christopher. I'd be honored." He quickly joined Chris at Rob's mammoth cock.

Rob was lost in rapture. The Hansen Twins were working his cock like old pros. One held it while the other went down on it and vice versa. Then they both went down on it at the same time: tongues lapping, teeth gnawing, noses tickling, mouths slurping. It was incredible!

"That's fresh, dad," Bobert jested. "It's like an X-rated version of 'The Patty Duke Show.'"

It was all too much for Rob; the room had begun to spin. He closed his eyes and took in a deep breath, hoping that he wouldn't throw up. Unfortunately it was like being drunk, closing his eyes made it even worse. Soon he felt a different sensation on his cock: one mouth. One solitary mouth had begun to deep throat him. It felt equally as good and familiar somehow. As if this was the same mouth that had sucked him dry in all those realistic dreams he'd been having ever since Bobert moved in. Many a morning, he would wake up expecting to find his underpants soiled from a wet dream, yet they were always dry. And now that mouth was on his cock.

Rob experienced a revelation of sorts. He opened his eyes, not really surprised by what he saw. The mouth belonged to his son. The mouth had always belonged to his son.

Without missing a beat, Bobert looked up and smiled at his father with a full mouth. Rob couldn't help but smile back, for the boy looked like a five-year-old sucking on a big lollipop.

The twins pitched in to help Bobert with his blow job. They worked on Rob's balls, each concentrating on one testicle, whilst Bobert continued his fellatio. The kid was a natural too; he was taking all ten inches down his throat. A chip off the of block, Rob thought.

The twins began to kiss their way up Rob's tanned body, stopping at his nipples just long enough to nibble at them, then moving up to his lips. They voraciously tongue-kissed him, tasting everything his manly mouth had to offer. Chris and Pat tasted pretty good themselves, like a sweet liqueur Rob once had in New Orleans during Mardi Gras.

Suddenly, Rob's head started to clear and he was hit by an abrupt burst of energy, followed by sheer animal passion. It consumed him completely and he suddenly couldn't take it anymore, he had to act upon his sordid desires. Throwing caution to the wind, not to mention morality, Rob sat up and grabbed Bobert by the hair. He forced the boy down on his stomach, then climbed on top of him.

"Do you really want it, son?" Rob asked, not really caring about the boy's answer. That little ass was his!

"Fuck me, Dad," Bobert said. "Fuck me hard!"

"Do it, Rob! Do it!" the twins chanted as if in a trance. "Do it, Rob! Do it! Do it, Rob! Do it!"

This grew to a frenzy. Rob was caught up in this temporary madness. The wild, rabid chanting was music to his delirious ears. He spat into Bobert's boy-pussy and then mounted him, thrusting his throbbing cock deep inside his son's cherry ass.

The boy screamed in pain as droplets of virgin blood soon began trickling down his firm, rounded cheeks. At the sight of this, the twins licked their lips, then poked their heads between Rob's thighs to lap up the blood from Bobert's ass.

Rob was too far gone to allow a little vampirism to break his stride. The vile act actually made him more rigid as he continued to plunge his cock in and out of his son's tight love hole. He was reminded of a beautiful boy he'd met when he was thirteen, who had sworn to him he was a vampire of all things, going so far as trying to bite his neck. A frightened Rob had punched him in the face and then run away, never to see the strange boy again. What had been that exotic lad's name?

"His given name was Julian," an offended Chris told him non-verbally. "And Patrick and I are far from vampires, sir!"

The twins rose to kiss Rob on the lips. Instead of being revolted by it, Rob found the taste of Bobert's cherry quite palatable as it dribbled from the twins' tongues onto his. It was then when he realized that he had lost all decorum; he and his son had been corrupted by these two fiends like a couple of young, silver screen lovers named Brad and Janet. But this wasn't a late-night, double feature, picture show. This was real life! And the twins looked much better in drag than Tim Curry.

Chris and Pat broke away from Rob then, falling beside him on the bed. They lay side by side, locked in a tight, passionate embrace as they commenced to rub crotches and kiss. In their tawdry lingerie, they resembled the comely, twin lesbians in the straight stag film Rob had been forced to watch at his bachelor party.

Rob fell atop Bobert, humping him the way an adult Doberman pinscher would rape his own male pup. He noticed the boy looking over his shoulder at him with puckered lips, clearly yearning to feel his father's hot tongue probing his sweet mouth. Rob didn't even think twice about planting a wet, ardent kiss on the boy's lips, sucking every inch of his succulent orifice. After secretly dreaming about it for months, he was now feasting upon his son like a hungry bear consuming honey after a long hibernation. It was absolutely delicious!

Before the night was over, Rob Thomas had planted his seed in all the barren, yet fruitful, fields about him. Bobert had also done his share of sowing; his budding plow penetrating the moist soil of twin furrows. Approximately three hours and eleven loads between them later, father and son finally collapsed from exhaustion.

Morning. A fatigued Rob awoke in an empty bed. He heard jovial, young voices coming from outside so he staggered over to the open window. It was a beautiful Alabama day complete with a shining sun and singing birds. The voices belonged to the lovely Hansen Twins and his own lovely son. They were frolicking naked in the lake, skinny-dipping the way naughty, little boys do. This brought a broad smile to Rob's face.

He wanted to run downstairs and join the boys, but he was concerned about what the twins' mother would say if she awakened to find a grown man swimming naked with her kids. He frankly didn't understand how in the world the woman could have slept through the orgasmic groans that blared out of that room the night before. She must have been dead to the world, he thought.

Rob quickly dressed, then went to work changing his flat tire. He was on his knees tightening the last bolt when an old man rode by on a bike. He stopped to talk to Rob.

Are you all right, young fellow?" the old man asked in a friendly southern tone.

"Yeah, I am," Rob replied, flashing an appreciative smile. 'Thanks. I'm just about finished."

"This is a fine place to break down," said the old man. "Gives me the heebie-jeebies."

Rob looked puzzled. "What do you mean?"

"You're not from around here, are ya?" The old man continued: "Have you heard the legend of the Hansen Twins?"

As the old man recited the folk tale, Rob got goose pimples and he didn't know why. He stood up to face the old man. "What the hell are you talking about?"

"Some call it folklore, but I've seen them with my own eyes! The twins were crazy and so was their mother. Everyone in town knew that. They were faggots, you know, and took to practicin' witchcraft, of all things. That's why their father ran out on them. It was fifty years ago last night that they showed up at their prom wearin' dresses. Well, all the kids just laughed at them of course, and they ran home in tears. That's when Billy Brandis and some of the other boys on the football team decided to teach 'em a lesson for being queer. They all piled into Billy's car and followed them down the road, just wantin' to put the fear of God into them. But it was raining somethin' awful that night and Billy lost control of his car. He accidentally ran over the twins 'bout a quarter mile down the road. It was a bloody mess too. I know 'cause...I was in the car. You shoulda seen them, they were just lying there like fresh roa dkil l .

"The mother fell asleep waitin' for the twins to come home, but of course they never did. When dawn came and she finally found out what happened, the crazy of crone burned the house down with herself in it. They say every prom night you can see the twins walking home still in their beautiful, white gowns. But no one around here is foolish enough to pick 'em up."

Rob was now furious. "Did you take too much Geritol this morning?" Rob barked. The Hansen Twins were nice enough to put me and my son up last night in this house behind me that you claim burned to the ground fifty years ago!"

The old man looked perplexed. "What house?" he asked, looking over Rob's shoulder.

Rob slowly turned around. When he saw the empty, wooded lot still scarred from that long ago fire, he had to hold on to the car.

Shaking his head with dismay, the old man got on his bike and rode off.

Just then, Rob swore he heard a scream: "Help me, Dad!...I'm drowning!"

"Bobert!" Hysterical now, Rob ran to the lake, knowing deep in his heart that his greatest fear had come true.

It was a picturesque summer's day: a light breeze was blowing; the morning sun shined down on the crystal clear water, making it come to life with a rolling brilliance; the country critters were harmonizing an impromptu song of sorts. Everything seemed pleasantly serene, the way a country lake should be. But there was something wrong with this picture. There was something dreadfully wrong. There was a dead boy floating face down in the water. And the treacherous tempters who enticed him with their cunning guile were long gone, as if they had never existed.

Rob dove in the water and brought Bobert's naked body ashore. With a great heave, he rolled his son over and pumped a good quart of lake water out of his lugs. Then he lifted the boy, pushing himself under him and flopping him again on his back. Rob then slid his left hand under Bobert's neck, clamped his right fingers on his nose, and breathed into his son's mouth.

He switched to the boy's chest, pressing down as hard as he could on the breastbone, then releasing the pressure, over and over for fifteen beats.

The scent of gardenias all of a sudden.

"Don't bother, Mr. Thomas." It was Chris' voice.

Rob looked up to find Chris and Pat standing over him. Between them was Bobert's spirit. All three of them were nude and appeared transparent now.

"No!" Rob's sorrowful scream filled the air.

Chris continued. "Bobert will now stay with Pat and me forever and ever and ever."

" Chris and I get so lonely without a masculine boy around to fuck us," Pat added. "Now Bobert will keep us company, not to mention satisfied, for all of eternity."

"It's all for the best, Dad," said Bobert's spirit. "I love you, but I know you don't want me around."

Rob began to weep. "I do want you around, son! I love you! And I just realized that I can't bear to let you go. I'm sorry for wanting to make you live with your Aunt Laura. I want you to stay with me, son. Please, come back to me!"

"I'm afraid it's too late for that, Mr. Thomas," said Chris. "He's ours!"

"No!" Rob screamed. "Breathe, dammit! Breathe!" he shouted at the inanimate body beneath him. "I'm not giving you up this easily! I'm going to fight for you, Goddammit!"

Rob went back to the mouth-to-mouth. Nothing! He then pressed down again on the boy's breastbone. Then as he made to lift Bobert's head again, his eyes snapped open, and his face suddenly fired with life. His son's chest gave a heave against him; he felt the breath surge out of him, warm against his face. Rob was crying again. He took the boy in his arms and hugged him tightly, never wanting to let go. Looking up, he saw his son's spirit had vanished from between the twins.

"I love you, Dad," Bobert said coughing.

"I love you, too, son." Rob kissed him on the cheek like a father, then on the lips like a lover.

"Damn you!" cursed the twins. They were also crying. "Now we'll be alone forever."

"You don't have to be," Rob said, remembering a book on the supernatural he had read for extra credit in college. "You're dead, you're free, you're not of this world anymore. Why remain earthbound when you can enter the next plane?"

The twins had become more limpid, as if vaporizing into tiny particles. Then the strong wind came from what seemed a nonexistent place.

"Please spare us with your paranormal psychoanalysis, Dr. Freud!" Chris stated bitterly. "And consider yourselves lucky that as the minutes tick away we grow weaker. Or else, both you and your son would have become our beaus for all of eternity whether you liked it or not!"

"And here's a bit of advice," Pat stated with a menacing face. "If we were you, we wouldn't be caught dead within a ten-mile radius of this spot come next year's prom night. You might not be as fortunate next time."

The twins completely vanished, swept away by the tornado-force winds that now battered Rob and Bobert.

"Let's get the fuck out of here!" Rob said. He took his naked son in his arms and ran to the car as the wrathful gust threw branches in his path. They reached the car safely and sped away, not looking back until they were on the interstate bound back home to Miami. Rob held his son tightly, caressing his hair and periodically kissing his forehead during the drive.

Maybe the Hansen Twins had been a blessing in disguise, Rob reflected. After all, they had brought him and his estranged son together. Whatever they may have been, he knew the Hansen Twins were unforgettable.

THE BITING TONGUE
John Patrick

In the little family of the King's players the most powerful and influential individual was a certain eunuch named David, known for his "biting tongue." And the other eunuchs became jealous of his profound influence on the harem and they willingly compromised their own secret trysts with the harem by reporting the eunuch to the King.

"I shall investigate," the King told them. "I must see for myself." The King was privy to all and all would be in his service.

David was summoned to the King's chambers. The King was lying on the monumental bed and the eunuch trembled with delight, stretching his limbs before he approached the King. Seldom had the King showed himself completely nude to anyone, but David undressed him saying, "I want to see you, master, to admire you." David had the eyes of an artist, his eyes were ever hungry for beauty, and he always searched for the beauty in all things. When David saw the King nude he clapped his hands in childish joy, because, although the King was a man some might have thought obese, he was blessed with a beautiful prick, remarkably long, fat, and magnificently shaped.

Flustered, a bit angry, the King snorted, "What is wrong?" "Nothing, master. You are so beautiful."

"Ha!" cried the King. "Don't be foolish. Come to bed."

"Human beauty is meant to be enjoyed in all of its majesty," David told the King. "Nothing should be hidden, nothing should be despised."

"Then you undress as well," the King ordered.

David willingly obeyed, slipping his lavender cloak from his body. The King was stunned. David, he realized, had the loveliest male body in all of the Kingdom. It had the grace and beauty of a woman's form and the strength of a man's. And, freed from the cloak, the body shone with the whiteness of pearl.

"Turn around," the King ordered.

The perfection that greeted his eyes intoxicated the King. David, he thought, possessed the most graceful, most perfect buttocks in all of the known world.

He tried to restrain his hands because he feared hurting the eunuch but he could not help himself. He gently pulled at the boy's arms, drawing him on top of him.

"Wait," David said.

No, I cannot wait. I shall not wait. I must have you."

David knew well enough he should not disobey the King and he turned the sensuous curves of his ivory back to the King and slid between his thick thighs. Soon the King was hastily probing his anus with his magnificent rod. David lay still, cradled in his master's thick, hairy arms, knowing that even when the King had finished taking his pleasure there, he had not even begun to enjoy the full measure of the power David had to offer.

He admired himself in the great mirror of the King's bed chamber, dazzled by the beauty of the throbbing cock as it slid into him from behind. As David lost himself in self-consciousness, the King came, but still he did not lose his erection. He continued on, rolling the eunuch over and mounting him. In the mirror, David watched the mighty King astride him, having his way with him, and he was moved to tears because the King was so easily pleased.

Finally, the King was satiated and lay still on the bed. David smiled because he knew the best was yet to come. He started to leave the bedchamber but the King motioned to him to sleep nearby.

On the divan across the room, the eunuch slept, abandoned, tender and soft. During the night, the King crept from his bed, aroused with desire. He lifted the blanket that covered the boy and pushed open his thighs. As he began to caress them, David stirred and rolled over. The King took his penis fully in his own strong hand and stroked it until he was released from his torment, his cum splattering the boy's asscheeks. He then returned to his bed, satisfied.

The next night, David pleaded with the King to simply lie on the bed and let him service him. Although he was still savoring the memory of the tightness of the boy's anus, the King reluctantly agreed.

While many fellatrices and cunnilingists in the Kingdom restricted themselves to merely kissing and licking the cock or the clit, others knew the way to their master's heart was to suck, and to suck so ardently that the master would be close to coming before they stopped, then start again, extending the pleasure beyond all endurance. But David went beyond what any others had practiced. He invaded the private areas of his masters with his tongue, a tongue so powerful it was said to actually bite, causing his masters to have an unprecedented number of multiple orgasms while in his company. These were techniques that David had perfected early on. How he came to learn them he would never say, but he had mastered them as no other eunuch in the Kingdom. The women of the harem came to drawing lots to determine which of them David would service first. Knowing how insatiable the King was, how ever eager he was to discover new masters of sexual technique, they feared David's reputation might some day become known to the King and now their worst premonitions were realized.

The King was soon convulsed in pleasure as David worked him over. David began by holding the King's substantial prick with his hand, then placing it between his lips. Soon he was pressing the sides of it with his lips, using his teeth as well. Then we would stop. The King would beg him to continue. At intervals, the eunuch would also express his desire to stop, not to continue this ritual, but always the master would beg him to continue. David would kiss the cock as if he were drawing it out, pressing the insides until the master begs he can take no more. David stopped, but then the master begged him to continue, whereupon David would touch it with his tongue everywhere, passing his tongue over the end, then back again, on the balls, then the anus. His mouth returned to the prick and, getting the King's consent to progress, David would swallow up the entire shaft, his tongue seeming to bite all about the base of it, then withdraw, only to continue over and over until the King was close to eruption. The King would beg him to continue and David would until the King was royally satisfied.

So smitten with David was the King that, during the day, he would have the eunuch stay in a room adjacent to the great hall. Several times during the day, weary with affairs of state, the King would enter the little room and David would apply his tongue to the King's skin as only he could. Refreshed, the King would go back to his business with a gigantic smile on his face.

Each night, the King would send for David and he would come and satisfy the King, often sleeping on the divan until dawn, so that he might be there to service the King again before breakfast.

But David had to be careful; he had fallen in love. As fate would have it, his favorite was the Prince. A mere lad, the Prince had discovered David merely by chance.

He had overheard one of the women talking to another and, although barely out of puberty, the Prince knew what he liked. He was insatiable in his desire for the biting tongue of the eunuch. David, never having lain with anyone younger than himself, and finding that the King's son had inherited his father's admirable prick, was instantly besotted.

But I visit your father at night. This is wrong."

"No, no. I know about you. You are at his side all day as well. I do not like it, but what can I do? He is my father." "But I love only you."

That is why we shall continue our own rendezvoused. Always." And the Prince kissed David on the lips and watched in awe as the eunuch's mouth returned to his crotch and began again to make him a slave to pleasure.

One day, when the King returned from a carnival, he took a different path and came upon the Prince and the eunuch in the garden. They were behaving lasciviously. The eunuch was kissing the Prince's cock, fondling it between his legs, finally taking it the way he had taken the King. The Prince seemed driven into a frenzy of lust for the eunuch. Seeing their unbridled sensuality, the King became distraught, insanely jealous that he was sharing the same carnal pleasures with his son. He interrupted them and ordered the guards to take the eunuch away in chains.

No, Father," the Prince cried in desperation.

"Yes. He has violated my trust."

But I love him," protested the Prince.

And so do I. But it is finished. Over!"

As the long days of David's imprisonment passed, illusion mingled with nostalgia and the King thought of acquiescing but soon came floating back to reality. Then at night he would awaken with an erection and, unable to satisfy himself, a profound sense of loss would come over him again. A vague premonition came to him that made him uneasy, but he knew, to keep his pride, he had to put the eunuch to death.

Day after day, the lonely Prince begged his father to spare David's life. And finally, the King saw the desperation of his handsome son and he devised a compromise. He agreed to banish all of the eunuchs from the court and all of those of the harem who had laid with them, sparing David's life.

With all of the givers of pleasure removed from the palace, the King began to consort with harlots. None could satisfy him the way David had and yet he kept trying. Before long, he became diseased and was steadily going mad. In all corners of the palace, it seemed plotting never ceased.

On the outskirts of the Kingdom, the harem became again, as it always had, a coven of witches, and the eunuchs became, as they always had, warriors. And leading the warriors was David. The harem girls bewitched the palace guards and, before long, David was leading a march through the unsecured gates. The King, fearful he would be taken alive, drank poison; David found him slumped on his throne. As the eunuchs began to storm through the many rooms of the palace, David told them not to enter one of the chambers, the one nearest the great reflecting pool. There, he knew, would be the Prince, and he wanted him all to himself.

The Prince hid under the bed, fearing for his life. When he saw it was David who entered his chambers, and David alone, he came out from hiding and fell to David's feet, kissing them, begging for mercy. David held the blade of his sword over the Prince's fair head and proclaimed him his master.

"Rise," David ordered. "It is I that should kneel to you. We have made you the King."

The Prince grabbed David about the legs and brought him to the ground and there, in the ornate golden splendor of the young prince's bedchamber, the two of them hugged and kissed each other and made love all through the night.

And it was said that, over the many years of his reign, while the young King had many wives and fathered many children, never far from his side was David and his splendid biting tongue.

ABOUT THE EDITOR

JOHN PATRICK was a prolific, prize-winning author of fiction and non-fiction. One of his short stories, "The Well," was honored by PEN American Center as one of the best of 1987. His novels and anthologies, as well as his non-fiction works, including Legends and The Best of the Superstars series, continue to gain him new fans every day. One of his most famous short stories appears in the Badboy collection Southern Comfort and another appears in the collection The Mammoth Book of Gay Short Stories.

A divorced father of two, the author was a longtime member of the American Booksellers Association, the Publishing Triangle, the Florida Publishers' Association, American Civil Liberties Union, and the Adult Video Association. He lived in Florida, where he passed away on October 31, 2001.

TAKE A **LOOK...**

STUDIO.V
Male Model Photo Studio

Vlad Fedotov was born in Lviv, Ukraine, but made Edmonton, Canada his home. As a photographer for **STUDIO.V**, he focuses on depicting sensual aspects of the male physique, emphasizing the connection between the body beautiful and body sensual. His photos have appeared on covers of books published by STARBooks Press and his latest work is exhibited at the Seattle Erotic Art Festival in Seattle, WA.

STUDIO.V caters to the needs of a variety of markets that seek artistic material for their advertising. The studio is also open to private bookings and event photography.

FOR BOOKINGS AND OTHER INFORMATION:
www.studiovmodels.com
studiovmodels@aol.com

Vlad Fedotov